D1136510

Alan Gibbons

Alan Gibbons is a full-time writer and a visiting speaker
and lecturer at schools, colleges and literary events
nationwide, including the major book festivals. He lives
in Liverpool with his wife and four children.

Alan Gibbons has twice been shortlisted for the Carnegie
Medal, with *The Edge* and *Shadow of the Minotaur*,
which also won the Blue Peter Book Award in
the 'Book I Couldn't Put Down' category.

JULIE
and ME

and
Michael Owen
makes Three

Alan Gibbons

Northumberland County Council	
3 0132 02104619 3	
Askews & Holts	Mar-2012
JF	£7.99

Julie and Me . . . and Michael Owen Makes Three was originally
published in Great Britain by Orion Children's Books in 2001

Julie and Me: Treble Trouble was originally published in
Great Britain by Orion Children's Books in 2002

This new edition first published in Great Britain in 2010
by Orion Children's Books
a division of the Orion Publishing Group Ltd
Orion House
5 Upper St Martin's Lane
London WC2H 9EA
An Hachette UK Company

1 3 5 7 9 10 8 6 4 2

Text © Alan Gibbons 2001, 2002, 2010

The right of Alan Gibbons to be identified as author of this work has been asserted.
All rights reserved. No part of this publication may be reproduced,
stored in a retrieval system, or transmitted, in any form or by any
means, electronic, mechanical, photocopying, recording or otherwise,
without the prior permission of Orion Children's Books.

A catalogue record for this book is available from the British Library

ISBN 978 1 4440 0086 3

Printed in Great Britain by Clays Ltd, St Ives plc

www.orionbooks.co.uk

To those who perished in the
Munich disaster and at Hillsborough.

May you have peace.

Prologue

Ten years.

Can it really be that long? I stare at the invitation:

Friends Reunited
Knowsley Manor High School
Prescot
Merseyside.
Monday, 18th January 2010

Yes, that's how long it is since I fell in love with Julie Carter, ten years. I knot my tie in front of the mirror and the time melts away. We were fifteen when I fell for her – suddenly, hopelessly, completely. Two things stood in our way. The first was her adoration of Michael Owen and Liverpool Football Club. The second was a Grade A creep by the name of John Fitzpatrick.

I slip on my jacket and examine my reflection. Looking good. I haven't put on much weight and my hair's darkened a bit. I'm less of a Ginger Ninja than I was in my teens. Suited and booted, I slip the invitation in the breast pocket of my suit. I go out to the car and head for the M62.

Ten years. Where does it go? Just look at the world of football. For starters, Michael Owen's signed for us. Imagine that, Michael Owen, Anfield legend, playing at the Theatre of Dreams. That's not all, United have equalled Liverpool's record of eighteen league titles. That makes this year the big one. We could overhaul them. We've both won a Champions League final in the last decade. Liverpool came back from 3–0 down to 3–3 on a crazy night in Istanbul and won on penalties.

We took advantage of a John Terry slip on a rainy night in Moscow and won…on penalties! I mean, football, you couldn't make it up. Just to complicate things , some megabucks Sheikh has bought Man City and they're trying to break into the top four. Like I said, football!

I leave the M57 at the Knowsley Safari Park turn off and my heart starts pounding. I'm back on Merseyside for the first time in two years. There it is, Knowsley Manor High. I pull into the car park, lock the car and wander into the hall. The first face I see is my mate Bobby Quinn.

'Bobby,' I say, 'Good to see you.'

'You too,' he says. 'Have you changed your mobile?'

'Yes, I did. Didn't I send you my new number?'

'No, you numpty,' he says with a grin. 'What is it?'

I reel it off and he taps it into his address book. 'Did you get that job?' I ask.

'Stanlow, you mean? Yes, I'm in.' Bobby's a scaffolder. 'Have you still got that flat near the Lowry?'

'Yes,' I say. 'Five minutes from Old Trafford. Couldn't have turned out better.' I look round the room. 'Is she here?'

'Nothing's changed then,' Bobby says. 'You're still pining for the lovely Julie.' He shakes his head. 'You're an idiot, you know that?'

I sigh. 'Yes, I know.'

Bobby looks around. 'Ten years, eh?'

'Yeah, Michael Owen at United.' I sigh. 'A bit ironic, don't you think? Do you remember what a crush she had on him?'

'Sure do,' Bobby says. 'They're weird, all the comings and goings. Who'd have imagined Phil Neville and Louis Saha ending up at Everton?'

'Bobby Robson passed away,' I say.

'Yes, great man,' Bobby says. 'We deserved to win the World Cup at least once under him.' He shakes his head. 'Ten years.' Then he punches me on the arm. 'How could you let her get away?'

My eyes stray to the door. 'Do you think she'll come?' I wonder out loud.

'You don't deserve her,' Bobby says.

'I phoned her,' I say, trying to redeem myself.

'When?'

'Last week,' I tell him. 'I heard she was back from Barcelona.'

Bobby looks interested. That's the great thing about him. He always wanted Julie and me to work out. 'And?'

'She got a bit of a surprise when she heard my voice on the line,' I tell him. 'But it wasn't long before we were chatting away the way we used to. She sounds great.'

'Please tell me you made your move,' Bobby says.

'Kind of,' I mumble. 'It turns out she's got a choice. She can go back to Spain or she can take a job at Manchester University.'

'I don't believe you,' Bobby says. 'You make every mistake in the book and you still end up falling on your feet. So, what's she going to do?'

'I don't know.'

Bobby waits for an explanation.

'Honest,' I say, 'I don't. I begged her to stay. I told her I was an idiot, a moron, a miserable excuse for a human being. I said I wasn't worth the dirt on her shoe.'

Bobby laughs. 'You really know how to sell yourself, don't you? So, is she staying?'

'I don't know,' I say.

'You didn't get a decision from her?'

'No,' I say, 'but I sent her a text.'

At that, Bobby gives his forehead a Homer-Simpson-slap. 'You've got to be kidding, the most important words you'll ever say and you put them in *a text*!'

I nod miserably. 'It does sound a bit daft when you put it like that.'

Bobby cocks his head. 'So what does it say, this text of yours?'

I hand him my phone and watch him read it:

Please stay. We had something wonderful and I blew it. It's always been you, Julie. Marry me. Stay with me in Salford. It's only 40 mins to Anfield...

Bobby's staring at me.

'What?' I ask.

'That's it?' he says. 'You're asking her to spend the rest of her life with you because she'll be able to get to Liverpool home games?'

'Do you think I should have missed that bit out?' I ask.

'Well, duh!' He carries on reading:

Come to the reunion tonight. If you stay away I'll know it's over.
Please don't let it be over.
Terry.

And we both stare at the door … and remember … ten years …

Part One

Mad About the Girl
Or
Phil Neville's Lunge

1

'Who's that?'

What's that might have been a better way of putting it. What I'm looking at is not so much a girl as a creature from another world. It's as though I've just been born again and suddenly I know what life is for.

'Who *is* that?'

My question is directed at my best mate, Bobby Quinn. The way I say it makes his head snap round. I've gone all gaspy and urgent and breathless and he wants to know why. Probably thinks I've plugged myself into the electric mains or something. He joins me staring through the little oblong window in the sports hall door.

'Which one?'

What does he mean, which one? That one. The one with the hair and the shape and the grace.

The one.

'Over there, in blue.'

'Oh her. That's Julie Carter. She's new. She's in my maths set.'

That does it, I've got to work harder in maths! I'm in the second set. Bobby's in top... with Julie.

'Where's she from?'

Spirited from Wonderland ... wafted here from Paradise ... newly materialised from the planet Wow?

'Huyton. Just moved up from Page Moss.'

'You seem to know a lot about her,' I say, my eyes narrowing with suspicion. I don't believe it, I only saw her for the first time a minute ago and I'm jealous already.

'I talk to people,' says Bobby with a shrug. '*I'm* sociable.'

'*I* can be sociable,' I protest.

No, scrub that. I can't. I've never been more than a couple of steps above the hard core nerds. I'm often awkward talking to the other guys in my year, but with girls I'm completely tongue-tied and hopeless. I heard somewhere that the average tongue weighs seventy grams – from Bobby probably. He's a mine of useless information. So if your average tongue weighs in at around seventy grams, how come mine swells to a mouth-clogging, word-dumbing, heavyweight two hundred and fifty? It's like talking with a boa constrictor in your mouth.

'Fancy her, do you?' Bobby asks.

Fancy her?

Fancy her!

That's not the word for what I'm feeling. It doesn't even come close. My skin has gone hot and prickly. My heart is break-dancing in my ribcage. My mouth is as dry as sandpaper. I'm Mount Vesuvius and molten lava is surging up my oesophagus. What's more, for the first time in my life I actually understand what people mean when they say they've got butterflies in their tummy. Butterflies! What I've got is a swarm of enraged hornets.

'Why don't you ask her out?'

I stare at Bobby. Doesn't he understand what he's saying? Ask her out! This vision in blue. It takes me all my time to ask a girl to pass the salt in the canteen. So how exactly do I go about asking somebody as amazing as Julie to go out with me? She isn't just *a* girl. Suddenly, she's *all* girls.

'I couldn't.'

'Course you could. She's only a girl.'

Only!

It's all right for Bobby. He must have kissed the Blarney stone when he was little. No, he swallowed the thing whole. He could charm a fish out of the sea, could Bobby. He's popular with everybody; the teachers, the other boys, even the girls. He asked Caitlin Brady out at the end of last term. I watched him do it. He just marched up to her and popped the question. She's good-looking too. Not one of your needy, desperate girls. She agreed right away. They've been going steady ever since. He doesn't seem to have any problem chatting up girls. He calls it the Nike technique. Just do it. And if they say no –

13

what the heck – there are plenty more fish in the sea. Their loss, that's Bobby's philosophy. He's got self-confidence to burn.

'She wouldn't give me a second glance,' I stammer. 'I mean, just look at her.'

Bobby looks. 'Yeah, she's nice.'

Nice!

She's gorgeous.

For starters, she's tall. Oh my God, she's probably taller than I am, and what girl wants to be seen out with a midget? I can actually feel myself shrinking as I stand here. She's not skinny, though. No way, she's curvy. Sturdy-looking. Do you say that about girls, sturdy? Listen to me, will you, when it comes to the dating game I don't even know the vocabulary. She's – what's the right word? – sleek. Yes, that's spot on. Julie Carter is sleek. Tall, curvy, athletic and *sleek*. Then there's her hair. It's long and black and glossy. She's got it in one long braid down her back and it skips and jumps as she runs down the crash mat. Look at her, you can see every muscle moving in her legs. She's amazing.

'You have got it bad, haven't you?'

Bobby's right there. I've never felt anything like this. Except maybe that May night in Barcelona when Peter Schmeichel lifted the Champions League trophy and sealed the treble. That was the same sort of thrill. The feeling that makes you clench your fists and yell: Yiss!

But this is different. That was about Man U fans everywhere. I was sharing something magical with millions of others across the world. But this surge of electricity, it's all about me. Me and Julie C. I watch her in her royal blue leotard and matching shorts and it's like she's there in a spotlight going through her routine just for me. Then this nagging thought comes knocking on my brain door. What about her personality? What if I pluck up the courage to talk to her and I don't like her. Think of it, she could be Miss Universe on the outside and the Wicked Witch of the East on the inside! A bit like the women on *Jerry Springer*. Oh no, don't tell me she's a bimbo. What if Julie's trailer trash?

'What's she like to talk to?'

Let her be nice, let her be nice, let her be nice.

'I like her.'

Yes!

'She's really friendly. She's dead popular already. I've never seen a new kid make friends so quickly.'

I press my nose against the window, my breath clouding the glass and almost obscuring my view of her doing a handstand, then gliding effortlessly into a perfect forward roll. Bobby brings me back to earth with a playful thump on the arm.

'Terry, I know you're head over heels in love and all that, but can we get to English? Spotty doesn't like you being late.'

He's right. Mr Spottiswood is the strictest teacher on the staff. Reluctantly, I start to detach myself from the window. That's when it happens. Julie pads to her Reebok sports bag and pulls out, of all things, a Liverpool shirt. I go through agonies as she slips it over her head. How can this be happening to me? Here I am watching the girl of my dreams and she's wearing the colours of our arch-enemies, the evil empire at the opposite end of the East Lancashire Road, Liverpool FC.

'Something wrong?' asks Bobby.

'Uh huh,' I tell him. 'Everything. She's only a Liverpool fan.'

Bobby shrugs.

'Never stopped me. I've been out with two Liverpudlians and I'm an Evertonian. I've even been out with one girl who didn't like football.'

We move along the corridor.

'Hurry up,' says Bobby. 'Your mind's still in the gym.'

He's right, it's up there hanging on the wall bars, transfixed by Julie Carter. Luckily, we beat Spotty to class. Just. That's when Bobby comes out with one of his famous useless facts:

'Do you know where the word gymnasium comes from?'

'No.'

'It's Greek. A place where you exercise naked.'

My mind falls off the wall bars. Bobby gives me a funny look.

'Terry, are you sweating?'

Sweating? It's a wonder I haven't had a heart attack!

Tuesday, 20th June
3.10 p.m.

The build-up starts here. No homework tonight, I've cleared the decks so that I can watch every second of studio discussion, every instant of the live match action.

England v Romania.

The last group match of Euro 2000. Win or draw and we're through to the quarter-finals to play Italy. Lose and it's just the latest in the line of Great English Disasters.

'That's all we've got to do,' I remind Bobby, as if he needs reminding. 'Avoid defeat and we're through.'

'Piece of cake,' says Bobby. 'Though the Azurri will be tougher.'

'I'm not so sure Romania will be that easy,' I say. 'They beat us in the World Cup, remember.'

'Only because of that plank, Le Saux,' says Bobby. 'Petrescu did him for pace and strength. Can't trust a Southerner to get anything right.'

I smile. He's right. Whoever heard of a footballer from the Channel Islands? Phil Neville's a good Northern lad. He'll show him how it's done.

'Want to come round to ours to watch it?' I ask. 'You can have your tea first if you like.'

'Don't mind if I do,' says Bobby. 'I'll just phone Mum and let her know.'

So there's Bobby on his mobile and me waiting for him by the school gates when Julie walks past with Kelly Magee. Bobby says she's really fit, but I think he's exaggerating. If you ask me, even in her best clothes and fully made up she doesn't register above seven on the cuteness scale. Bobby probably fancies her. Let's face it, he fancies just about anything in a skirt. Now Julie, she's a definite ten. She even looks good in her school uniform. I ask you, green blazer and tie, blue jumper and skirt and she still looks good.

I find myself staring at her sports bag. The Liverpool shirt is hanging out of the top. It's like a red rag to this particular bull. I mean, football is the lens through which I see the world.

'What're you staring at?' asks Kelly.

'N-nothing,' I stammer, caught in the act.

I look all round me, as if my eyes alighted on Julie for just one nanosecond, purely by chance.

'He was staring at you, Julie.'

There's no conning Kelly. She's been out with more boys than I've had bacon toasties and she knows all the tricks. She flounces by, her eyes raking me with invisible fire. Julie doesn't even give me a second look. She must be used to boys staring.

'Weirdo,' observes Kelly. 'Freak-a-zoid.'

Julie doesn't say a word.

'Made the first move already, have you?' says Bobby as he slips his mobile away. 'You dirty dog. Quick off the blocks this time, eh?'

'Let's go,' I say, ignoring him.

'Put your tongue back in,' says Bobby before coming out with one of his famous useless facts: 'Did you know that by the age of twelve months you've dribbled one hundred and forty five litres of saliva?'

He looks at Julie. 'Mind you, anybody would find Julie Carter mouth-watering.'

I look away. I know I've gone bright red, the colour of that stinking Liverpool shirt.

Tuesday 20th June
7.30 p.m.

Something's up. There's definitely an atmosphere. Bobby's noticed it too. While we were having our tea, Dad said something under his breath to Mum about having a house meeting soon.

House meeting?

What's that about? We're not Guardian readers. We don't have house meetings. Who does he think we are, characters in some divvy sit-com? Ever since he mentioned the house meeting Mum has been stamping round slamming cupboards and plonking down cups. For a while I thought it was this new cabbage diet she's been on, but it's more than that. She isn't a happy bunny.

'Should I go?' Bobby asks just before kick-off.

Even somebody as thick-skinned as our Mr Bubbly is feeling uncomfortable.

'Don't be daft,' I tell him. 'It'll blow over. It always does. Besides, you'd miss the action.'

'So who's going to be the match-winner?' asks Dad, flopping into his armchair with a bottle of Stella. He's wearing the United away strip for the game so it's obvious what he expects to hear.

'Beckham,' says Bobby, 'Everything comes from his crosses.'

'Scholes,' I say. 'Watch his runs from deep.'

But it isn't either of the United players who catch the eye early on. Or even an Englishman. The Romanians are playing a fluent game of pass and move and within two minutes Ilie cracks a free kick round the wall. Nigel Martyn does well to stop Moldovan's shot. Bobby, Dad and I exchange worried looks. It isn't going according to plan. Twenty-two minutes into the match things are going from bad to worse. Chivu tries a chipped cross and it clears Martyn and bounces in off the upright.

We're 1–0 down.

'Not again,' groans Dad. 'They're going to throw it away as usual.'

Bobby gives me a meaningful look.

'Why are dads always so negative?' he whispers.

'It's genetic,' I whisper back. 'They've got a whinging gene.'

'We'll get back into it, Mr Payne,' says Bobby.

He's right. Five minutes before the interval Paul Ince is brought down in the box.

'Ex-Man U,' I point out proudly. I conveniently forget that he's also ex-Liverpool.

Shearer sends the keeper the wrong way and me and Bobby are skidding across the wooden floor on our knees, arms raised in celebration. Then, in first-half injury time, a touch from Ince followed by the deftest of flicks from Paul Scholes puts Michael Owen through.

He uses his pace to get clear of the advancing keeper and slots the ball into the net. It doesn't get any better than this.

'Told you Scholes would do it,' I yell, bouncing up and down on the couch.

'Owen was the one who scored, you know,' Bobby points out.

'The hard work was already done by then,' says Dad.

He never was one to give a Liverpool player credit if he could help it. I wonder what Julie would make of the scene.

During the half-time break we're eating Kit-Kats. Mum's sadly munching an apple. She's sworn off chocolate. Something to do with the size of her love handles. We keep reading the scoreline. We can hardly believe our luck.

'Romania have played us off the park,' says Dad, 'And we're 2–1 up.'

'Just got to hold on to it now,' says Bobby. 'We were two up against Portugal and we still lost.'

'Not this time,' says Dad. 'You're going to see the old bulldog spirit come through.'

But there isn't much bulldog spirit on show after the break. The game has hardly restarted when Martyn punches the ball out to Munteanu. The Romanian chests it down and volleys it into the net. It's 2–2 and we're gutted. It doesn't get any worse than this.

'See how Martyn flapped at that?" says Bobby.

'Typical Leeds player,' snorts Dad, a bit unfairly I reckon.

'How much longer's this on?' moans Amy, my little sister, as she puts in an appearance in her Disney nightie, the one she got in Florida.

'Ages,' I tell her, waving her out of the way of the screen.

For the rest of the match we're on the edge of our seats. Romania are pressing forward all the time. Their passing is neater and crisper than ours. But if we can only hold on...

'We're defending too deep,' says Dad. 'We're asking for it.'

And we get it.

'Two minutes left,' says Dad. 'Just two minutes. Come on, lads. Dig in.'

'Come on,' I say.

'Come on,' Bobby echoes desperately.

Somehow we all know what's coming. It's like destiny. A locomotive called defeat. But with the seconds ticking away we start to hope.

'Blow, ref,' pleads Dad.

Then the sky caves in. Moldovan drives into the penalty box. Phil Neville is challenging him all the way. Then the ex-Coventry man is past Phil on the outside.

'Stick to him,' I yell.

'But don't bring him...'

Phil lunges and flattens Moldovan.

'...down,' groans Bobby.

'He dived,' I cry, jumping to my feet in outrage as the ref points to the spot. 'Blatant dive. That Moldovan was the same when he played in the Premiership. Phil got a definite touch on the ball.'

Dad shakes his head. 'Not this time, Terry. The ref's got it right. It's a penalty.'

I remember Euro 96. Not penalties again. Not this.

Bobby covers his face with a cushion.

'I can't look,' he says.

I look and I wish I hadn't. Ganea converts from the spot. Agonising moments later it's full time. England 2, Romania 3.

I'm hollow, like somebody's shoved a pipe down my throat and hoovered out my insides. 'It's David Beckham all over again,' says Dad. 'The Man U-haters will be lining up to have a go.'

I remember the way Beckham kicked out in the World Cup game against Argentina and wince. Opposition fans booed Beckham for two years because of his red card. United were hated even more than usual. I took a lot of stick for Becks' rush of blood.

'Phil Neville's going to pay for that blunder.'

I think of all the anti-United feeling at school and Julie in her Liverpool shirt. Phil Neville isn't the only one who's going to suffer.

Tuesday 20th June
10.20 p.m.

Bobby's gone home and Amy's tucked up in bed, so it's just me, Mum and Dad. We've been raking over the ashes of defeat for half an hour now, getting more and more down in the dumps. Even Mum, who doesn't have much of an interest in the beautiful game, is affected by it. The post-mortem is even more painful than usual after an England failure. Dad's ranting about Kevin Keegan like it's personal, and he's taking Phil Neville's mistake really badly, going on about how he's never going to be able to hold his head up at work.

'All those Scousers just waiting to take a rise out of me.'

After a while I start to wonder whether all this hot air really is about football. It's as if football's just the excuse, something to hang his rage on. Something's scratching away at the back of my mind, something about ... yes, a house meeting.

'What's this house meeting anyway?' I ask, never dreaming I'm opening up a can of giant worms.

'Not now, eh, Geoff?' says Mum, a pleading look in her eyes. 'Surely it can wait until you're in a better mood.'

'Better mood,' snaps Dad. 'That's a good one.'

I'm starting to get worried. They've never been much for arguments, my parents. They usually show all the passion of a deep-frozen cod. But tonight I can almost touch the suppressed rage crackling between them.

'May as well know now as later,' grunts Dad. 'The lad's fifteen. It's not like anything's going to change. We'd just be putting it off.'

He's got this wild look in his eyes as though he wants to hurt everybody, especially himself. All of a sudden I'm not just worried, I'm scared.

'Geoff,' said Mum, panicky and anxious, 'don't say something you'll regret.'

But the wildness has got hold of Dad. He's in full flow.

'England throw it away again ... lousy job ... dead end life ... all I do is work and what do I get for it? No thanks ... feel like chucking it.'

'Dad, what are you on about?'

'Shall I tell him what I'm on about, Sharon?' he demands, eyes wilder than ever.

That seals it. This isn't about England. Even thirty years of hurt couldn't get him in this state. No, it's something else. I can feel the earth slipping away from under my feet.

'I'm moving out, Terry, that's what I'm on about. I'm getting my own place.'

That can of worms, the creatures are all the size of anacondas with teeth like vampires.

'Geoff!' cries Mum. 'Not like this.'

The giant worms are chewing through my heart, ventricle by shredded ventricle.

'We've talked about how we'd tell the children.'

I can just imagine it. I've read about it in Mum's magazines when I was hunting for the naughty bits on the agony aunt pages: *It's your partner you're splitting up from, not your children.*

Well, wrong. I know exactly who Dad's splitting up from. All of us. I've read the little guides. *How to explain it to the kids. Letting them down gently.*

Well, believe me, there's nothing gentle about the way Dad's let me down. I feel like I've been run over by a lorry. This has come right out of the blue. Where were the quarrels, the raised voices, the thrown crockery, the slammed doors? Dad, where were the warnings?

'We've been drifting apart for a while,' says Mum, trying to salvage something after the explosion. 'It's not your fault, Terry.'

Not my fault. Well, duh! I *know* it's not my fault. It's yours, you pair of lousy fakes, pretending to be a couple when all the while you were planning to chuck your marriage in the bin.

'How long have you known?' I ask. 'How long have you had this planned?'

'A couple of weeks,' says Dad. 'Well, a month or two actually.'

The bombshell explodes in my head. This has been going on since Easter at least.

'A month or two!'

All the things we've done in that time flash through my mind. Parents' evening, they were both at that. Mr and Mrs Supportive. The day out at Alton Towers. Swimming at Heatwaves. Amy's birthday party. I see it all in freeze-frame. Me and Amy grinning our stupid heads off and all the time our family was a big, fat, lousy lie. Happy families, happy rotten families.

'I'm going to bed,' I say, making for the door.

I don't even want to look at them.

'No, Terry, not like this,' says Mum. 'Sit down for a couple of minutes.'

'Why?' I ask. 'Is Dad going to change his mind?'

Dad shakes his head. He's got this weird look on his face, like the guy who's let the evil genie out of the bottle and can't find the cork.

'Then I'm going to bed.'

Tuesday 20th June
11.30 p.m.

Today's a day I won't forget in a hurry.

When I saw Julie in the gym it was like conquering Everest. The feeling I had, it was like I just couldn't get any higher. But there's something they don't tell you about getting to the top of the mountain. From then on, the only way is down.

And boy, did I choose the quickest way to descend! The key moments flash through my mind as I fall.

Nigel Martyn flapping that cross...

...punching the ball to Munteanu...

...Phil Neville bringing down Moldovan...

...Alan Shearer crying.

The air is rushing more quickly. More moments:

...Dad ranting and raving at the TV...

...Mum with her pleading eyes...

...Dad saying it's over.

20th June 2000: the best of days, the worst of days.

2

To understand how I'm feeling as I trudge towards the school gates, you'll need to know something about Knowsley Manor High. The school is in Prescot on the eastern edge of Liverpool. The town is at the top of a long hill. At the bottom of the hill is Huyton where most of the kids come from. So what does that mean? I'll tell you what it means. Man U fans are outnumbered about ten to one by Liverpudlians and Evertonians. We get more stick than a dog in the park. I missed Bobby this morning so into the valley of death trudged the one.

Here's what I hear as I reach the gates:

'I hear some plank of a Man U player's sunk England again.'

The voice belongs to Fitz. That's John Fitzpatrick, my captain in the Year 10 football team. He's cock of the school. Bright, sporty, good with the girls. He seems to have been out with most of them. I've spent the last four years here trying to be just like him.

'What is it with you Mancs? First Beckham sabotages the World Cup for us, now Neville loses us Euro 2000.'

I'm trying to shrug it off. Dad was gone when I got up this morning and I'm in no mood for this. I'm all hot and red and my skin's prickling all over. Fitz knows he's getting to me.

'It wasn't Phil Neville's fault,' I retort.

'So whose was it?' asks Fitz with a mocking laugh. 'How did Romania get that penalty then, an act of God?'

I'm really starting to dislike Fitz. He's gone from role model to arch-enemy in ninety seconds.

What was I doing copying this Dingus Malingus?

'Martyn was to blame for the first two goals,' I say. 'And Paul Scholes set up Owen's goal, remember.'

I'm taking it too seriously. Why can't I just ignore him, let it roll over me the way Bobby does? I'll tell you why, Julie has put in an appearance and she's watching our argument with interest.

'Hey, Kelly, Julie,' says Fitz, 'Have you heard this one? He says it wasn't Neville's fault last night.'

'So whose fault was it?' asks Kelly Magee.

All these Scousers seem to be reading from a prepared script. I look into her bright blue eyes and want to tell her where to get off. But she's Julie's new best mate so I keep my lip buttoned.

'He was unlucky,' I tell her.

'Unlucky! Is that what you call it?'

The three of them are laughing. At me. I can't stand to look at them, especially Julie. Why does she have to join in? But why shouldn't she? They're in the top maths set together and they all support Liverpool. I'm the odd one out here.

'Look at the state of him,' says John. 'I think he's going to cry.'

'Don't be stupid,' I retort. 'I didn't see any of your wonderful Liverpool players doing much either.'

'In case you didn't notice,' Julie says. 'Michael Owen scored.'

She says it matter-of-factly. There's no venom in her words.

'He took it brilliantly.'

'And he's gorgeous,' adds Kelly, sticking her unwanted oar in.

'Yes,' says Julie, acting all swoony. 'Definitely gorgeous.'

I look at her for the first time and suddenly I'm melting in those dark brown eyes. I like her and she likes Michael Owen. The eternal triangle.

'Yes,' I admit grudgingly. 'He took the goal well.'

'Now that's a first,' says Kelly. 'A Manc who admits he's wrong.'

'Bit like a Scouser who keeps her opinions to herself,' I snap back.

Me and my big mouth. I see Julie's heart-stopping eyes narrowing. Congratulations, Terry, you've just forced her even closer to the dreaded Fitz. Make a mental note: the girl you're mad about is a Scouser too. Now she's in a nark with you. What have I done? Quick, backtrack.

'I didn't mean all Scousers,' I stammer. 'I meant...'

'You don't know what you mean,' says Fitz, twisting the knife. 'Typical Manc. Anyway, I've got something for you.'

He's rummaging in his bag.

'It's here somewhere. I cut it out specially for you. Yes, here it is.' With a flourish, he produces a cutting from the *Mirror*. The headline pierces my heart. It consists of just one word: ROMANIAC!

'Wonder what United have got planned for the next World Cup,' Fitz muses. 'A Gary Neville own goal? You know, keep disaster in the family.'

With that they turn their backs and walk away. Not that I care about Fitz and Kelly. But the third back belongs to Julie and that hurts.

Wednesday 21st June
10.00 a.m.

Over halfway through double French and still no sign of Bobby. I decide to send him a text: *Bobby, where R U? Terry*. The messages comes back a couple of minutes later:

Wot do you mean, where am I? Where R U?

Which sets off a hi-tech, low-sense exchange:

Me: *School, where do U think?*

Bobby: *School! Wot time is it?*

Me: *10am, u dope.*

Bobby: *10am! OMG. Mum didn't get me up.*

Me: *UR lucky.*

Bobby: *Come again?*

Me: *Mum and Dad just split up.*

Bobby: *In a rush. There soon. Gory details then.*

Get your skates on, Bobby. I think of Fitz and all the other Liverpudlians dying to take a pop at me. Something tells me I'll need all the friends I've got for morning break.

Wednesday 21st June
10.30 a.m.

'Robert Quinn,' says Mrs Massie as he bursts through the door. 'What time do you call this?'

'Dix heures et demie,' Bobby answers in his best schoolboy French.

Mrs Massie doesn't see the joke.

'Have you been to the office to tell them you're in?'

'Yes.'

'And what cock and bull story did you give them?'

I can see Bobby biting his tongue. I know exactly what he'd say if he didn't stop himself: *Same cock and bull story I'm giving you.*

That's one of Bobby's problems. He always has to have the last word. Even if it's the wrong word. I've lost track of the times he's opened his mouth and put his size nine right in it.

'My asthma was bad, Miss. Did you know that by the age of twenty-one I will have breathed in enough air to inflate three-and-a-half million balloons?'

'Mm,' says Mrs Massie drily. 'And by the end of this lesson you will have breathed out enough hot air to fill the Goodyear airship.'

Our appreciative ripple of laughter is interrupted only by the bell for mid-morning break. As we elbow our way down the corridor Bobby gives me a sideways look.

'So what's with the Payne family this fine and sunny day?'

'Dad's gone.'

'Gone where exactly?'

'Dunno.'

'How come?'

I open my mouth to answer. Mum's got it into her head that it's because she's put on a bit of weight. If she could only squeeze into a size 12 she'd still have a marriage. Somehow, I don't think that's it. But that's when I realise, *I don't know*. I don't know why he's gone, or even where he's gone.

'He's just gone.'

'I didn't know your folks were having problems.'

'That's just it, Bobby, neither did I.'

We spill out of the side door and make for the far side of the yard overlooking the sports hall. I think briefly of Julie in a blue leotard, permit myself a dreamy smile, then glance at Bobby.

'He came out with it after the match. I think the Romania fiasco set him off.'

'First time I've heard of a footy divorce,' says Bobby.

I do my best to sound off-hand about it, but I don't think Bobby's fooled. He can see how cut up I am.

'No, I mean it's been building up and the match was the last straw. He said all sorts of weird stuff.'

'Like what?'

'I dunno. Like he hates his job.'

'Double-glazing fitter. Don't think I'd fancy it either. They're always knocking on our front door. Nobody wants.'

'Plenty of people have got it. Come to think of it, you have.'

I realise we've got off the subject. Any time now Bobby will furnish me with the number of depressed double-glazing fitters in the greater Merseyside region.

'It isn't right, Bobby. It came right out of the blue.'

'Sounds like my first divorce,' says Bobby.

Of course, I'd clean forgotten. His mum has been married twice, first to the baldy chap from St Helens – Bobby's dad – then to the man with the squint and the budgie from West Kirby. Funny taste in men, Bobby's mum. At the moment she's going out with this bloke from round the corner. Big guy with a cocker spaniel. Long furry ears and a shiny nose. The spaniel, not the boyfriend.

'You didn't expect it, then?'

'No way, I was gutted. That wasn't the worst thing though.'

Right now, I can't imagine anything worse than the split.

'So what was?'

Bobby taps his nose knowingly.

'Access days, Terry. Access days.'

'Go on.'

'Your dad comes round to take you out. You must have seen them in McDonalds, miserable-looking men with their sprogs shovelling chips and chicken nuggets. At weekends they take up half the tables. I call it Access Alley.'

I've got the picture firmly fixed in my mind. Access Alley: lose hope all ye who enter here.

'Oh.'

'Oh is right, Terry mate. I mean, your bedroom can only take so many beanie babies and plastic Disney characters. They take you everywhere at first, Camelot, Blue Planet Aquarium, Chester Zoo, the cinema. It's the guilt, you see, quickest route to their pockets. Then they get their first post-separation bank statement. After a while it's take-away pizza and a walk in Taylor Park. But that's not the worst of it either.'

'No?'

'Oh no. On the rainy days it's back to Dad's one-bed flat to watch a film and eat take-away.'

He looks around furtively. He's enjoying this, initiating me into the terrors of marital meltdown.

'But you've still not hit rock bottom. You know what comes next?'

I hardly dare ask.

'No.'

'One day, one dreadful day, your dad will turn round and ask: *So what do you want to do today?* He's all out of ideas. Either that, or he's just stopped caring. That's when you know your relationship has gone critical.'

'Oh, behave, Bobby,' I say.

'I'm not kidding,' he says. 'You know all that father-son bonding stuff? Forget it. I hardly see my old man now. Better that way, I suppose.'

I can tell by the look on his face he doesn't really mean it. There's a space in his heart that will forever be occupied by a baldy guy from St Helens.

'I know my dad, Bobby. He took me to the Champions League Final in Barcelona, remember. You don't do that if you don't care. It was the greatest day of my life. And we shared it. Me and my dad.'

The greatest day of my life. Rivalled only by the sight of Julie Carter in the sports hall.

'We go to Old Trafford together for every home game. It's the highlight of my week. None of that Access Alley stuff is ever going to happen to us.'

I can see the future stretching out before me, one long Sir Matt

Busby Way, straight and true. The only difference is, Mum and Dad are on opposite pavements.

Bobby shakes his head slowly.

'You can't rely on anything once your parents separate. Things are going to change, Terry. They're going to change a lot.'

I can see Dad and myself walking down the Ramblas singing *Championes* and reliving Sheringham and Solskjaer's goals all the way back home to Prescot. Us end up as two saddos eating greasy take-away in a one-bed?

Never.

Wednesday 21st June
1.15 p.m.

We're getting changed for football when Bobby drops his bombshell.

'You've got a rival for the lovely Julie's affections,' he tells me.

'Who?'

'Fitz.'

I look across at John Fitzpatrick. I thought he'd been hanging round her a lot.

'You know I was wondering how Julie got so popular in such a short space of time?' says Bobby.

'Uh huh.'

It's hard to reply properly with a lump in your throat.

'Well, it turns out she knew loads of the kids here even before she came to Knowsley Manor. They met at the gym club at the leisure centre.'

'Who did?'

'Julie, Kelly, Pepsey Cooper, Fitz...'

'Hang on a minute. Fitz does gymnastics?'

'No, you dope. His little sister does. It turns out old Fitzy's known Julie for the last six months, ever since his Hayley joined the gym club at the leisure centre. If you're going to make a move, you'd better do it sharpish. You know Fitz's reputation.'

Do I? Fitz has had loads of girlfriends. I mean, we're talking two figures. That's why they call him Frisky Fitzy. Some say he's got a bit of a look of Michael Owen, which helps. Oh great, it'll really help with Julie. She's *mad* about Michael Owen. That love triangle's turned into a love quadrilateral. Bobby's about to go when something occurs to me.

'What *did* happen to you this morning?'

'You're not going to believe this,' says Bobby.

'Try me.'

'Mum thought I was staying at yours last night. She didn't see me come in. Too busy with lover boy.'

(That's the one with the spaniel.)

'So when she went out to work this morning she locked the house up. Only locked me inside, didn't she?'

Bobby's front door is a double-glazed unit with seven mortice locks. My dad fitted it cheap.

'So what did you do?'

'I couldn't find my keys. I only had to climb out of my bedroom window and shin down the drainpipe. Got some really funny looks from the neighbours.'

'Bobby,' I say, 'It could only happen to you.'

He shrugs in that *stuff happens* way of his.

'Anyway,' says Bobby, 'I've got to pee. See you out there.'

I watch Fitz lacing up his boots and suddenly I'm wondering where you can buy voodoo dolls with Michael Owen haircuts.

'Something the matter?' he asks, catching my eye.

'No, why?'

'Dunno, just thought you might want to apologise for Chopper Neville's act of madness.'

'Oh, give it a rest.'

Fitz starts to clatter across the tiled floor on his new studs. I admire the boots but not the boy in them.

'What, and let a Manc off the hook? Never.'

I'm last out of the changing rooms. As I go to pull on my shirt I catch my reflection in the mirror. Milk-bottle skin, freckles, bony shoulders, untidy ginger hair and legs like matchsticks.

'Hey, ginger,' shouts Fitz. 'We're waiting for you.'

I bite my lip. Julie and Fitz. No, no that. Anything but that.

Fitz is laughing at me. He's done me twice for pace and his team is 2–0 up already. I've got a great football brain. It's the body that's the problem.

This was my last chance to impress Mr Shooter and get myself into the side for the Knowsley Boys' Cup Final. We're playing Blackridge on Monday after school. It's me or Chris Lawlor for the last midfield place.

'You'd better buck your ideas up,' says Bobby. 'Six Guns has got Chris pencilled in for Monday.'

Mr Shooter is making notes on the touch-line.

'I know. Fitz is doing this on purpose.'

'Then don't let him. Get tighter on him.'

Six Guns walks purposefully to the centre and gestures to the teams.

'Second half, lads. Ready?'

Fitz is doing hamstring stretches on the edge of the centre circle. Suddenly I'm seeing him in a new light. He isn't just into girls any more. He's into *my* girl. He really loves himself. I reckon guys like him must come in flat-packs. Construct-a-Creep.

'Psst,' hisses Bobby. 'Seen who's watching? They must have a free period.'

It's Kelly and Julie. That settles it. I'll get tight on Fitz all right. He isn't going to make a monkey out of me a third time. Jamie Sneddon picks up the ball and looks for Fitz. He's coming my way with his right arm raised.

I decide to close him down and get to the ball first, putting it into touch.

'More like it,' says Bobby.

I permit myself a smile. I hope Julie was watching. Ten minutes later Gary Tudor turns provider. Again I get in before Fitz, clearing the ball downfield. Paul Scully gets on to the end of it and pulls one back for us. 2–1 down. Now we can make a game of it. I can see Six Guns making notes. I'm not doing myself any harm at all. I wonder what Julie thinks. No, don't let your mind wander. Just stay focused, Terry.

No Phil Nevilles.

Five minutes from the end Paul gets on the wrong side of his defender and scores with a glancing header. We've pulled level, 2–2.

'No silly mistakes,' says Bobby, clapping his hands. 'Keep it tight, lads.'

It's easier said than done. Fitz's team are pressing us back. I glance at my watch. Two minutes left. Just like last night. Keep your concentration, Terry.

No Phil Nevilles.

Then I hear Bobby screaming at me. Gary Tudor has played a long ball over the top and put Fitz clear. I scamper across to intercept the ball. He's in the penalty box. God, he's fast. Just like Michael Owen, low centre of gravity and lots of pace. He's weaving and doing step-overs as I go to meet him, then he pushes it ahead of him, trying to turn me. I'm dying to get a foot in. My every instinct is screaming, *Flatten him. Demolish the Knowsley Manor Casanova.*

But no, I can't do it.

No Phil Nevilles.

We're shoulder to shoulder. I'm determined to force him wide. That's when he taps the ball through my legs. The lousy rat's nutmegged me!

I try to get out of his way, but his pace takes him into me. We go down in a tangle of legs and arms. Fitz is up first, arms raised. I scramble up after him waving mine.

'No pen,' I cry. 'Accidental. He ran into me.'

But Six Guns is having none of it. He points straight to the spot. Penalty. Fitz walks up and strokes the ball in. I look over to the touchline. Kelly and Julie are clapping wildly. The next ninety seconds fly past. It's too late to equalise again. I look from Julie on the touchline to Six Guns making his notes. No way am I in the team.

I'm out of luck with both of them.

3

Six Guns finishes the register. He's our form teacher as well as head of PE. He's got these laser beam eyes that instantly lock on to trouble. He spends most of his time wandering round school in his tracksuit looking hard.

'There are still a few of you who haven't given me their preferences for work experience week. May I remind you that it starts in just over a fortnight. Michael Gavin?'

Michael approaches the desk and hands in his slip.

'What's this, lad?'

'It's what I want to do.'

'Poodle clipping?'

Loud guffaws from the scallies at the back.

'I like dogs.'

Six Guns rolls his eyes.

'Are you taking the Mickey, Mickey?'

'No, I really do like dogs.'

'Takes all sorts, I suppose.'

He inspects the crumpled slip.

'Where's this been?'

'My dog got it.'

Six Guns looks like he's about to self-destruct.

'Poodle?'

'Labrador.'

With a look of distaste Six Guns put the slip in a folder.

'John Fitzpatrick?'

I watch as Fitz hands in his slip.

'Pony sanctuary?' exclaims Six Guns. 'First dogs, now horses. What

34

do you lot think this is, the RSPCA? I didn't take you for an animal lover, Fitzpatrick.'

Bobby frowns. It's one of those long, purposeful frowns, the sort that usually signals heap big doo-doo hitting the fan.

'What did you put down?' I ask Bobby.

'Electrical engineering. It's what I want to do when I leave school. You?'

'Promise you won't laugh.'

'Sure, I promise.'

'Fitness industry.'

'You're kidding!'

'My cousin was taken on for a week at one of the big fitness clubs on the Wirral. It was a doss. All he had to do was polish a few machines and sort some paperwork. He spent all his time on the treadmill or in the jacuzzi.'

'You sure there isn't a hidden agenda in there somewhere?'

'Meaning?'

Bobby gives a knowing wink.

'Spend a week working out. Come back from work experience tanned and conditioned. Wow the lovely Julie with your pecs.'

I can just see us. Julie in her blue leotard. Me in my black swimming gear flexing my biceps.

'Don't be soft. I'd only be there a week.'

'So it hadn't crossed your mind?'

'Wouldn't say that,' I confess. 'I wouldn't mind a bit more muscle. The way I am at the moment I can't even fill my T-shirts.'

'That's because you're an ectomorph,' says Bobby.

'You're a flipping ectomorph!' I retort.

'No, it's your body shape, stupid, the physique you're born with. You're an ectomorph – lean and skinny.'

'Oh, what are you?'

'Endomorph – big and brawny.'

Make that little and brawny. I'm at least four inches taller than Bobby.

'Wish I was an endormorph,' I mutter, imagining myself in front of the mirror.

'Don't,' says Bobby. 'You can eat anything you like and still be thin.

If I even look at a cream cake it's hello fatty.'

I glance at Fitz, my rival in love.

'What's he then?'

'You don't want to know.'

'Bad news, is it?'

'The worst. John Fitzpatrick's got the look. He's a mesomorph – broad shoulders, thin waist and natural strength.'

'Lousy mesomorph,' I growl in my best Homer Simpson voice.

Bobby splutters out a laugh.

'Care to let us in on the joke, Mr Quinn?' drawls Six Guns.

'Sorry, Mr Shooter.'

Six Guns shoves back his chair. 'Off to classes, people.'

Friday 23rd June
12 noon

Bobby plonks his tray on the table and sits down opposite me.

'Pizza?' I say. 'Is that the right food for an endomorph?'

'No.'

'So why'd you get it?'

Bobby takes a huge bite.

'I like pizza.'

He wipes tomato gunge off his mouth.

'You're not going to like this,' he says.

My stomach lurches. I remember the way he frowned in class.

'Is this about Julie?'

Bobby nods.

'I've found out why Fitz is so keen on the pony sanctuary.'

'Go on.'

'Julie already has her placement, see. Guess where?'

'The pony sanctuary?'

'Got it in one. So the moment Frisky Fitzy gets wind of it, he puts in his own horsey little request. With his track record, I don't think he's developed an interest in animal welfare, if you get my drift. Listen to me, Terry, you're going to blow this. Ask the girl out before he does.'

'I can't.'

'Why ever not?'

'She might turn me down.'

'So she turns you down,' says Bobby. 'You haven't lost anything, have you?'

I look over to the door where Julie has just walked in with Kelly.

'Course I would. I'd have lost Julie.'

Just then, we spot Bobby's girlfriend looking round the canteen for him.

'Caitlin,' shouts Bobby. 'Over here.'

Caitlin slides in next to him and whispers something in his ear. He laughs. Great, I'm playing gooseberry again. I had to stand for ten minutes at the top of an alleyway last week while they were snogging away.

'Caitlin,' says Bobby. 'You're a girl.'

'Hey, you noticed.'

'Terry here needs some advice.'

I give him a pleading look. Oh, come on, Bobby, don't make a show of me.

'He's mad about Julie Carter. Think he's got a chance?'

'Dunno. Maybe. She's not going with anybody as far as I know.'

'What about Fitz?'

Caitlin wrinkles her nose. Suddenly I like her a whole lot more than I ever have before.

'I went out with him for a while. He was all right at first, then he showed his true colours. He's a creep. His rotten paws were all over me. It's like dating an octopus.'

Bobby leaps to his feet, brandishing what's left of his pizza like a sword.

'The bounder! I'll run him through with my rapier.'

'Sit down,' says Caitlin, smiling indulgently. 'Your rapier's gone limp.'

'Don't be so personal,' says Bobby. 'So you reckon Terry's got a chance?'

'You could give it a go,' says Caitlin, nonchalantly sipping her Diet Coke.

Only a cute girl who's already got a boyfriend could be so casual.

'My sentiments exactly,' says Bobby. 'There you have it, Terry.

Straight from the horse's mouth.'

'Watch who you're calling a horse,' chuckles Caitlin.

'Anyway, got to scoot,' says Bobby. 'We've got double maths.'

I nod. He and Caitlin, Julie and Fitz are all in the top set. I really have got to work harder on my maths. I'm taking my tray back when I see Fitz make a beeline for Julie and Kelly. He's leaning over them, laughing like a hyena. Julie's laughing too. Caitlin's right. Fitz is a creep. I look at him with his wide shoulders, his thin waist and his Michael Owen haircut.

Lousy mesomorph!

Friday 23rd June
3.10 p.m.

I walk as far as the Fusilier with Bobby and Caitlin. They'll be turning left towards St Helens Road. I'll be going straight on.

'Well,' says Bobby as we pause outside the pub. 'Did you?'

'Did I what?'

'Ask her out?'

I shake my head.

So does Bobby.

'What's he like? Listen to your Uncle Bobby. Either you ask the girl or you lose the girl. You've got to be Nike-ad man, like I said. Just do it.'

Easier just said than just done.

'I didn't get a chance.'

'Didn't get a chance? You've been in the same school as her all day, for pete's sake!'

'Kelly's always with her.'

'I don't notice Fitz letting that stop him. He just steams right in there.'

'That's different. He's...'

'What?'

'Confident, mouthy ... mesomorphic.'

'Then get confident,' says Bobby. 'You'll kick yourself if you don't.'

Bobby and Caitlin set off up the road holding hands. He stops by the petrol station.

'Hey, are you coming down to the community centre tonight? The band are practising for the big gig.'

The band is *The Sons of Moe Szyslak* and Bobby's big gig is a fifteen-minute slot at the end of year school disco.

'Yes, I'll be there.'

Anything to take my mind off Julie Carter and Frisky Fitzy.

Friday 23rd June
3.45 p.m.

I hear the key in the door, then Mum and Amy's voices.

'Are you in yet, Terry?'

'I'm in my room.'

'Would you come down a minute?'

I find her in the kitchen, making Amy a sandwich. She looks harassed.

'Listen, love, I've got a favour to ask.'

'Go on.'

'It's Amy. I wonder whether you could start picking her up from school. Karen's asked me if I'd like to work through until five-thirty instead of knocking off at three.'

Karen is Mum's boss at the hairdressers where she works.

'It's another seventy pounds a week. We could do with the money, what with your dad leaving. Well?'

'It'll be a bit of a rush.'

'No it won't. You get out at ten past and Amy doesn't get out until half past. A fit young lad like you can walk the distance in less than ten minutes. You've got plenty of time.'

'Do I have to?'

'Terry, things aren't easy just now. I thought you'd want to help. All I...'

OK, OK, enough with the emotional blackmail.

'I'll do it.'

'Sure?'

'I said I'll do it.'

'Good lad.'

She calls up to Amy.

'Amy, your sandwich is ready.'

Amy is already in her boots and riding hat. Friday night is horse-riding night. A mad rush to the stables just outside Kirkby.

'I've got some news for you,' says Mum. 'From now on Terry will be picking you up from school.'

Amy pouts. 'Why can't you do it?'

'I've got to work late.'

'Why?'

'I just have, that's all.'

'It's because of Dad, isn't it?'

'Well partly, yes. Oh, that's the other thing I've got to tell you. Your dad will be taking you out tomorrow.'

An electric shock fizzes through me. It's just like Bobby said.

'Is this an Access Day?' I ask.

'I never thought of it like that,' says Mum. 'But yes, in a way it is. I know you don't like the idea of Geoff moving out. He may have finished with me but he's still your dad. I'm sure he'll take you somewhere nice. McDonald's maybe.'

A vision of Access Alley flashes through my mind and I shudder.

'Something up, Terry?' asks Mum.

'No,' I tell her, images of Camelot (the local theme park) and the Blue Planet Aquarium and seedy one-bed flats flashing through my brain. 'Somebody stood on my grave.'

Friday 23rd June
7.00 p.m.

I lean over to Caitlin and shout over the noise of the band.

'They're not bad at all.'

'I beg your pardon?'

I'm battling with Bobby's lead guitar.

'The band, they're not half bad.'

'No.'

Caitlin's no conversationalist. Bobby likes it that way. He does the talking for both of them. I move away again and listen to *The Sons of*

Moe Szyslak racing through 'Heatwave'. Bobby likes all that eighties mod-revival stuff. The Jam, Elvis Costello, the Specials. He explained it to me. The Who, the Small Faces, first generation mod. The Jam, second generation mod. *The Sons of Moe Szyslak*, third generation mod. The frenetic pace appeals to him. That's the way he wants to live his life. He says his dad, the baldy chap from St Helens, was a rude boy when he was young. Do they have rude boys in St Helens, I ask myself?

Anyway, the St Helens rude boy gave Bobby two guitars, an acoustic and an electric lead guitar, just before he cleared off. The electric one is signed by Paul Weller, whoever he is.

'The next song,' says Bobby, 'is 'Alison' by Elvis Costello. It's for my best friend Terry. I just hope he gets his Alison.'

He winks at me. Even though there are only the four members of the band, Caitlin, me and the caretaker in the building, I blush right to the tips of my ears. Bobby can be a real wuss sometimes. When they finish their set I collar him.

'Knock it off, will you?'

'What?'

'Stop broadcasting to the world that I fancy Julie Carter.'

'You do, don't you?'

'You know I do.'

'Then stop whingeing. I'm only trying to help.'

'I don't need your help.'

'You need somebody's.'

'Meaning?'

'Meaning there's no point moping around making cow eyes. You've got to go up to her and ask her out.'

By the time he's finished he's almost shouting.

'I'll get round to it in my own good time,' I tell him.

'Then heaven help you,' Bobby replies.

'What's what supposed to mean?'

'In a fortnight we start work experience. Now I'm thinking Frisky Fitzy has got a pretty good chance of getting in at the pony sanctuary. I'm thinking barns, rolls in the hay, get my drift?'

I do. All of a sudden I wish Bobby didn't paint quite such a vivid picture.

'So you're going to ask her out?'
'Yes.'
'When?'
'Monday.'
'Definitely?'
'Definitely.'
Well, maybe definitely.

4

It's Camelot.

As we queue up to pay for our tickets Amy squeals with joy. It's her favourite theme park, except for Disney of course, but she knows that holiday eighteen months ago was a once in a lifetime thing. I watch a cloud shaped like Fitz float overhead and remember Bobby's prophecy. Welcome to Access Alley.

'What do we go on first?' asks Dad.

He's never been before. It always used to be Mum who took us to theme parks. He takes me to Old Trafford. Everything else he seems to wriggle out of. Mum's always been the Family Entertainments Officer, parks, swimming baths, amusement parks, that sort of stuff.

'Log flume,' shouts Amy. 'Log flume, log flume, log flume.'

'Just so long as I don't get wet,' says Dad. 'This shirt's brand new.'

'Oh, we won't get wet, will we, Terry?' says Amy, thinking it's a great joke.

I shake my head indifferently. As we walk away from the log flume I note with satisfaction that Dad is soaked through right down to his designer boxers. Serves him right for busting up the family.

'What's next?' asks Dad. 'Just remember my stomach. I'll go on anything just so long as it doesn't go upside down.'

'Then it's got to be Excalibur,' I say, winking at Amy.

As we walk away from Excalibur I grin triumphantly. The sight of Dad suspended upside down high above the Lancashire countryside with a stricken look in his eyes gives me a special pleasure. Take that, home-wrecker!

'Come on, kids,' says Dad. 'Joke over. No more upside-downers, OK?'

43

'No more upside-downers,' giggles Amy.

We exchange glances.

'Tower of Terror,' we shout with one voice.

As we walk away from the Tower of Terror Dad is definitely green round the gills.

'What did you have for breakfast?' I ask him.

Before he has a chance to answer I add: 'Don't worry. I'll be finding out soon enough.'

'Very funny.'

I have absolutely no sympathy. He's the one who dragged us down Access Alley, so he's the one who's got to pay the price. We all have something different for dinner. Pizza for Amy, fish and chips for me, cheese and tomato roll for Dad. It's three lots of queuing, but what the heck, it's his treat.

'Having a good time, kids?' asks Dad.

'Yeah,' says Amy.

'Whatever,' I answer offhandedly.

He can't really think I'm going to be bought off with a day out at Camelot.

You owe us for what you've done, Dad.

You owe us big time.

Saturday 24th June
3.30 p.m.

I'm starting to go easy on Dad. He's tried his best all day. He's even been on the Tower of Terror three times without barfing. Besides, I've just noticed the time. In six or seven weeks about this time I'll be watching Ryan Giggs unlocking Newcastle United's defence. I glance at Dad. This is the man who takes me to the Theatre of Dreams week in, week out. And no matter what he's done since, we'll always have Barcelona.

'A couple more rides,' says Dad, 'Then we'll have to be making tracks. What'll it be, Amy?'

'Tower of...'

'Whoa there, I think I'm all terrored out. Isn't there a little ride you can go on by yourself? I want a chat with Terry. Boys' stuff.'

'I haven't been on the umbrellas yet.'

'Right, umbrellas it is.'

Dad watches Amy climbing skywards then turns to me.

'I know you must think I'm the bad guy in all this, Terry.'

I shrug.

'Your mum and I were childhood sweethearts,' he explains. 'She was my first girlfriend. It was great at first. I loved the bones of her. Still do in a way.'

He waves to Amy.

'But something's gone. I don't get the butterflies any more.'

I remember Julie in the blue leotard and I kind of know what he means about butterflies. I've got a non-stop fluttering inside.

'When you've been with the same person for twenty years you start asking yourself: is this all there is? I suppose I want to chat people up again. I want the thrill of the chase.'

'Da-ad.'

He's definitely sharing too much.

'Sorry, son, but that's the way I feel. Life became so ... samey. Same old routine, day in, day out. I want a bit of excitement.'

'And you can't have that with Mum?'

He shakes his head.

'She thinks you've left because she's put on weight,' I tell him. 'That's why you don't fancy her any more.'

'I wish it was that simple,' Dad replies. 'I just got bored, that's all. We started turning into each other. I got this feeling that, if I didn't get out from under, we'd wind up walking round Asda in matching pullovers.'

Somehow I didn't think that sounded so bad. I'd walk round Asda with Julie any day.

'What about us?' I ask, my mind still full of me and Julie in our matching pullovers.

'You know I'll always be around,' says Dad. 'My feelings for you and Amy will never change, you've got my word on that.'

I wonder about the promises he's made to Mum. All the *forevers* and *happy-ever-afterwards* that must have dropped from his lips over the years. Suddenly, nothing seems certain any more.

'We'll do this every weekend.'

'It's going to be a busy weekend,' I say.

'I beg your pardon?'

'The match, Dad. The match.'

Dad's been a season ticket holder since the seventies. He started taking me to Old Trafford in the 1992–3 season. I was only seven but I can remember every twist and turn. Our six defeats still hurt, but not enough to eclipse the twenty-four victories, including a 2–1 away win against Liverpool. What a first season that was. That was the year we signed Eric Cantona. It was also the year we won the League Championship, our first in twenty-six years.

'I've been meaning to talk to you about that, son.'

My heart lurches, but before I can ask him what he means Amy's ride finishes. By the look on Dad's face he's eternally grateful to the umbrella ride.

'Only one more, Amy love,' says Dad, glancing nervously at me, 'A quickie.'

She settles for the carousel.

'What did you mean by that?' I demand. 'About the match.'

Dad doesn't meet my eyes.

'We've got two households to run now, Terry. We're really strapped for cash.'

Not so strapped he isn't buying himself new clothes.

'So?'

'So I've had to let our season tickets go.'

A rush of horror corkscrews through me.

'You've done what!'

'I couldn't afford to renew them.'

'Oh, Dad, tell me you're joking!'

'I was struggling to afford it last season,' he says hurriedly. 'It's an expensive day out, son, it really is. What with the separation, there's no way we can do it.'

All I can do is stand there, staring in disbelief. I see Schmeichel turning a somersault, I see Fergie holding up the Champions League trophy, finally I see me and Dad dancing down the Ramblas singing *Championes* and suddenly it's all one big sick joke.

'Dad, how could you?'

Without another word, I turn on my heel and walk away. I hear Dad yelling after me.

'Terry. *Terry*!'

Saturday 24th June
5.30 p.m.

On the way home Dad has his music on loud. I'm glad. I don't want to talk to the man who's just shut me out of the Theatre of Dreams. After the third play of *Born to Run* by Bruce Springsteen, Amy rebels.

'Can't we have the radio on?'

'Why?'

'Your stuff is so *old*.'

Dad pulls up outside the house but he leaves the engine running.

'Aren't you coming in?' asks Amy.

By now, Mum's on the doorstep, smiling thinly. She wraps her cardigan round her, as if trying to hide her belly.

'No, not tonight, love. I've got to get off.'

As he pulls away I hear someone saying my name.

'Hi, Terry.'

I turn to find myself looking right into Julie Carter's eyes. They're brown and bright. You'd almost think she was glad to see me.

'Oh, hi, Julie.'

She's wearing a red and white tracksuit. She looks cool and athletic. I'm aware that I'm sweaty and dishevelled after a hard day's roller-coastering. I see myself in her eyes, a scruffy, ginger dwarf. I shift awkwardly from right foot to left.

'What brings you up here?'

'I've been round at Kelly's all afternoon. She only lives up the road.'

'Oh yeah. Forgot.'

We look at each other. I'm dying to say something brilliantly witty. Dying to, but failing.

'Time to go home to my parents and the three stooges,' says Julie.

'Huh?'

'My kid brothers.'

'What are their names?'

'Guess.'

'Huey, Duey and Louis?'

Julie laughs, which comes as a surprise. The moment I say it I'm trying to swallow the words back into my mouth.

'Not far off. It's Gerard, Josh and John-Joe.'

I feel encouraged. I mean, here's Julie Carter, the *gorgeous* Julie Carter, laughing and joking with me and she isn't bored or anything. She isn't even fidgeting or looking around. She actually seems to be enjoying my company.

'So there are four of you: Gerard, Josh, John-Joe and Julie?'

'Mm, my mum isn't very adventurous when it comes to consonants.'

I smile. Bobby was right. Julie is nice, and so easy to talk to. I don't feel tongue-tied at all. It would be no effort to ask her out right now. Do it, Terry, do it now. The words start to form in my mind.

'I'll have to run for my bus,' says Julie, glancing at her watch. 'See you in school on Monday. Kelly and I are going to watch you play Blackridge.'

Julie's thrown me off the scent. Don't let the moment pass, I tell myself, ask her. But I don't ask her. Instead I mumble something like:

'I'm only substitute. Fitz got past me too easily at practice.'

'I know,' said Julie. 'He's really good, isn't he?'

What have I done? Instead of asking her out, I've only reminded her that Frisky Fitzy is better than me! Just as I'm trying to salvage something, Amy appears at the door.

'Hurry up, Terry. Mum says tea's on the table.'

'Got to go,' I mutter.

'Yes, me too,' says Julie. 'If I miss my bus it'll be twenty minutes until the next one. It was nice talking to you, Terry. Bye.'

'Bye.'

I watch her walking briskly away, her plait bobbing.

5

'Terry,' says Bobby, 'you're one seriously sad little man.'

I look down at my feet like a kid getting told off.

'Just think about it. Destiny handed you the best chance you're ever going to get with Julie, and you passed up on it.'

'I got interrupted.'

'Do you want to know what you say the next time your sister interrupts you? Remember these immortal words, Terry: *Don't butt in, butt out.*'

'It sounds easy when you say it.'

Bobby sucks in his breath. He's getting frustrated with me.

'Terry, it *is* easy. You had Julie on her own. What does it take with you, a written invitation?'

'You weren't there. You don't understand.'

'Terry, *she* came up to you. *She* spoke first. *She* told jokes. Listen to me, because I'm only going to say it once: *She likes you, you big dope.*'

I catch my reflection in the long, black drama department window. What I see resembles a uniform hanging from a yard brush, topped with fluffy, flyaway ginger hair. A babe magnet I'm not.

'I don't know.'

Bobby leads the way into school, shaking his head. We make our way to our desks, but before Bobby has the chance to continue his interrogation in walks Six Guns.

'Good morning,' he says gruffly.

'Good morning, sir.'

Bobby digs me in the ribs.

'Look, he's got our placements.'

I strain to read the list on Six Gun's clipboard. Sure enough, it's

49

headed *Work Experience*. Six Guns takes the register then starts down his list.

'I'm afraid we couldn't place you all with your first choices,' he begins. 'Bobby Quinn, you're working at Lewis's.'

'Lewis's,' said Bobby. 'But that's a department store. What's that got to do with electrical engineering?'

'Maybe they'll let you change a light bulb.'

The comment draws loud laughter from the back.

'Michael Gavin, you'll be happy. You're at the Pooch Parlour in Bootle.'

Michael – now known as Mick the Dog – looks so happy I expect to see his tail wagging.

'Terry Payne...'

He runs his finger down the list then frowns.

'You're at Autumn Lodge.'

He flicks through the attached sheets of paper.

'Yes, here we are. Autumn Lodge, along with Chloe Blackburn.'

I ignore the wolf whistles that accompany Chloe's name. Autumn Lodge? Funny name for a fitness club.

'Sir,' I ask, 'What's Autumn Lodge?'

Fitz is straight in with his two pennyworth.

'Don't you get it? You're working in an old people's home.'

I give Six Guns a pained glare.

'That's about the size of it, Terry.'

'But I wanted a gym.'

'No problem,' chuckles Fitz. 'You'll get fit lifting the old biddies.'

He puts on his best old woman's voice.

'Change my bedpan, sonny?'

I stare at Bobby in disbelief.

'And you thought you drew the short straw.'

Six Guns continues down his list, finally reaching Fitz's name.

'Here's somebody else who's got his first choice,' he says.

I grip the edge of the desk. No, it's not possible.

'You're assigned to the pony sanctuary in Hale. You're with another of our pupils, Julie Carter. Maybe you can fix up joint transport, John. It's quite a trek.'

Fitz looks like the cat that got the cream. He's positively beaming.

'Are you all right?' Bobby asks me.

'Sure,' I tell him. 'For somebody who's just had their heart kicked out of their chest.'

Monday 26th June
12 noon

It's destiny. It's got to be. I'm at the front of the queue in the canteen and guess who arrives immediately after me?

That's right, Julie.

And that's not all. She's on her own. It's as though fate has drawn us together.

'No Kelly today?'

'Fifteen minute detention. She left her coursework at home.'

We're both smiling, big, shiny grins like we're telling the whole world how glad we are to see each other.

'Are you going to the end of year disco?' she asks.

OK, so how do I answer this one? If she's only making small talk I'd be mad to ask her to go with me. But what if she wants me to ask her and I don't? I mean, that's worse, isn't it? It's rejection. Oh God, why don't they do an instruction manual for this stuff. An A-Z of getting the girl. It would sell millions. I see Bobby come in behind Julie but he gives me the nod and goes off to sit by Caitlin. He's willing me to do the business. So what's holding me back? It's not like there's a force-field round her.

'Might do,' I say, playing it as cool as I can with a heat rash climbing my back. 'Bobby's band is playing. I've got to show my support. It's not my scene usually.'

I plump for chips and gravy followed by apple pie and custard. Julie goes for green salad and crusty bread with a pear to follow. The girl is a dietary saint.

'What about you?'

'I suppose I'll tag along with Kelly.'

She sounds disappointed. She does want me to ask her, I know it.

'Don't let on I've told you,' Julie says, leaning forward to confide in me, 'but she fancies Gary Tudor rotten.'

So that's why they were at footy practice. It wasn't to watch me, which I kind of knew already.

But it wasn't to watch Fitz either, which is brilliant. I smell Julie's hair and I feel giddy.

'My lips are sealed,' I tell her.

We hover awkwardly. Do I follow her to a table and sit next to her? It feels as if she willing me to do just that. But will I have enough to talk about if I do? I'm in an agony of indecision when Kelly arrives to make my mind up for me.

'Julie, Ju-lee! Over here, I've got something to tell you. Something amazing.'

Julie gives me a parting smile.

'Better see what she wants,' she says.

Is that a hint of regret in her voice? I'll never know. With a sinking heart I watch her go. Feeling suddenly very silly and very alone, I head for Bobby. He's my refuge in the storm.

'Well,' he says. 'Tell all, maestro.'

I glance at Caitlin. I feel uncomfortable talking with her around.

'There's nothing to tell.'

'Oh, you didn't let her slip through your fingers again!'

'Behave, will you. She wasn't in my fingers in the first place.'

If only, if only...

'Terry, Terry, Terry,' says Bobby. 'What will I do with you?'

'Leave it, eh?'

I chance a furtive glance in Julie's direction. She's in deep conversation with Kelly when Fitz arrives and makes a beeline straight for them. Kelly nudges Julie and the two of them greet Fitz with broad smiles. He's got everything on his side: the gym club connection, the Anfield connection, the beautiful people connection. And Fitz isn't hanging about, not like me.

'*He* doesn't let the grass grow under his feet,' says Bobby.

I glare at Fitz. I wish it would grow all over his stupid face.

I'm on the bench for the Blackridge game. Everybody's nervous. It's the latest we've ever played, a month after the end of the football season proper. It's all to do with exams and stuff, and building work after a minor fire in our changing rooms a few weeks ago. As a result, this final has been postponed twice. Fitz and Gary Tudor are over the ball waiting for the whistle. Julie and Kelly are about twenty yards away, giggling excitedly about something.

Not me, that's for certain. They haven't looked in my direction once since they arrived. The conversation in the dinner queue is ancient history. It may as well never have happened. Why, oh why, didn't I make my move? Am I trying to throw her into Fitz's arms?

'Which team's Knowsley Manor?' asks Amy.

I've had to run all the way to her school to pick her up, then rush her back here. Mum doesn't knock off until five-thirty, so I'm stuck with her.

'Ssh.'

'But I don't know who to cheer for.'

'We're in the Inter Milan strip.'

'Which is that?'

Sisters!

'Black and blue stripes and black shorts. Don't you know anything?'

'I know more than you do!'

'Come on, Knowsley Manor,' screeches Amy.

'Knock it off, will you? You're embarrassing me.'

'No, I'm not.'

'Amy, I think I know if I'm embarrassed.'

'Terry, you don't even know when you're stupid.'

Fitz gets the game underway. Amy is immediately jumping up and down, making more noise than all the other spectators put together.

'Who's this?' Fitz asks as he takes a throw in front of us. 'Your girlfriend? Like them young, don't you?'

'She's my sister,' I hiss, gritting my teeth.

Fitz tears off down the line to get the return ball.

'He's good,' says Amy.

Too good.

At half-time we're 1–0 down, a defensive mix-up.

'You stay right here,' I tell Amy.

'Why, where are you going?'

'I've got to go to the team talk.'

'But you're not even playing.'

'I might be, in the second half.'

'Bet you're not.'

I decide not to grace her with a reply and join the rest of the team, mentally executing my little sister for crimes against humanity in general and me in particular. To my disappointment, there are no team changes after the break.

'Just keep pressing,' says Six Guns. 'We don't deserve to be behind. Retain possession as we're doing and we'll get our chances.'

I search among the twenty or so spectators for Julie. She's standing alone, brushing her hair. Kelly's watching Gary Tudor. I watch Julie snap a purple bobble round the thick, glossy mane and long to run my hands over it.

'It's never going to happen,' comes a voice.

I turn. It's Kelly.

'I've seen you staring at Julie,' she says. 'Can't take your eyes off her. You don't think she'd go out with a Manc, do you? You've got no chance.'

It makes sense. Julie's the new girl, but in the gym club crowd she had a ready-made social scene. Plus they all support Liverpool. It was obvious she'd hang around with them. After all, I'm just a ginger Manc. I feel a rush of temper.

'That so?' I retort. 'Well, you've got no chance with Gary Tudor either.'

Kelly blushes to the roots of her California-blonde hair.

'Who told you I fancy Gary?'

Panic sweeps through me like a long and very violent shiver. What have I done? Julie told me in confidence and I've blurted it right out.

'Nobody. Look, I didn't mean...'

'You're stupid, you know that? And nasty. Don't you come near me, or Julie.'

I watch her stamp away and I want the ground to swallow me up. I see them talking. After a few moments Julie turns her head and glares at me. Her eyes are cold. She knows I've betrayed her.

54

I'm a ginger Manc all right; a *suicidal* ginger Manc.

I'm sorry, Julie.

Sorry, sorry, sorry.

I feel like I've broken a precious vase and I know I'll never be able to stick it together again, no matter how hard I try.

Sorry.

Monday 26th June
5.15 p.m.

'I'm hungry.'

Amy has started the moment we get home.

'Just give me a minute, will you?' I snap. 'Let me get through the door.'

'What's the matter with you?' asks Amy. 'You'd think you'd lost.'

In fact, we won 3–1. Gary and Paul got the first two and Fitz scored the third to put the game beyond Blackridge. It was a sickener watching him parade round the field holding up the trophy. It was even worse watching Julie jumping up and down, eyes sparkling, clapping fit to burst.

'And I don't want a butty,' says Amy. 'I had butties for dinner.'

'I'll do you chicken nuggets and chips,' I tell her. 'Just give me a minute.'

I march into the kitchen stamping on Fitz's face with every step I take. I stab four Frisky Fitzy chicken nuggets and put them under the grill. Finally, I put some chips in the oven, wishing Fitz was shrunk to six inches and trapped inside with them.

I imagine his guts and brains dribbling down the inside of the oven and his eyes popping like corn, but when the beeper tells me the chips are done, fat, steaming chips is all I see. No cooked up bits of John Fitzpatrick glistening on the metal tray.

'Here's your tea,' I shout.

'Aren't you having anything?' Amy asks.

'No,' I tell her. 'I don't feel like it.'

The truth is I feel sick.

Sick to the pit of my stomach.

6

'Keys,' says Mum. 'Has anybody seen my car keys?'

'On top of the freezer,' I tell her.

'The freezer,' she says. 'What were they doing there?'

'You put them down when you were sneaking that Crunchie ice cream.'

Mum glares at me, before prodding a finger at the corners of her mouth looking for chocolate crumbs. She obviously thinks nobody has noticed her secret nibbles. I think the theory goes something like this: *If nobody sees me eat it, it's got no calories.*

'Amy,' she calls. 'Are you ready?'

I hear Amy come thumping downstairs in her riding boots.

'See you, Terry,' pants Mum. 'We'll be back about eight.'

'OK.'

'And if you go out, put the alarm on.'

'Got it.'

I hear a sharp intake of breath.

'Are you listening to me, Terry?'

'Sure. Back at eight, put on alarm. I heard every word.'

'See you then.'

'Yes, see you, Mum. See you, Amy.'

Amy ignores me. She usually does these days. She doesn't like me picking her up from school. In fact, I'd go so far as to say she hates it. Can't say I'm wild about it, myself. I glance at the kitchen clock. Bobby said he'd be round about five. He's late. I can't wait to see him. It's been a long while.

What with work experience, I've hardly seen anybody and I'm desperate for news about Julie. Bobby gets to know everything through the grapevine. Julie tells Kelly. Kelly tells Pepsey. Pepsey tells

Caitlin and Caitlin tells Bobby. I remember what Caitlin said in the canteen: *Fitz is like an octopus.* I just hope he hasn't got his tentacles on Julie yet. I'm smashing a Frisky Fitzy lump of potato with my fork when the doorbell rings. There's Bobby on the doorstep with a grin as wide as the Grand Canyon.

'Hi, Terry, how's it going?'

'Come in,' I grunt moodily.

'Whew, somebody's in a good mood. Hey, new haircut.'

'Yes, I got it done yesterday.'

I'm feeling really self-conscious about it. I still remember saying the words I thought I would never utter:

I want it like Michael Owen.

'Did you know that in your lifetime you will grow nine hundred and fifty kilometres of hair? What's it supposed to be anyway? Paul Scholes?'

Part of me is disappointed that Bobby doesn't recognise the style. Another part is relieved that my intentions aren't too transparent.

'It isn't supposed to be anybody,' I tell him. ' Anyway, stop wittering and tell me what you know about Julie.'

Bobby perches on the arm of the couch and sips slowly from a can of Seven-Up. He's only doing it to build the suspense.

'You've blown it good style,' he tells me. 'That stuff about Gary Tudor. A definite own goal there, my son.'

'Yes, I know all that. But what about her and Fitz?'

'Which do you want first: the good news or the bad news?'

'Good news.'

'They're not going out yet.'

My heart gives a little skip for joy, though I don't like the way he added the word *yet...*

'And the bad news?'

'They're both working an extra day this Saturday. There's an open day at the Sanctuary.'

'You mean they're working an extra day when they don't have to? For free?'

Bobby nods.

'Be suspicious. Be very suspicious.'

'Fitz is about the most selfish person I know,' I say.

Actually, I don't really know what he's like, but I don't care. I hate him.

'He doesn't volunteer for things.'

'He does now.'

Bobby crushes the empty can and tosses it in the litter basket.

'So how're things?'

'Here? Pretty much the same. Dad's got himself a flat. Mum's on a diet, but she's stuffing herself on the quiet. I think she's missing him.'

'Tell her to get a new man. You burn 6.4 calories a minute through passionate kissing.'

He realises I don't want to think about Mum passionately kissing anybody and changes the subject.

'How was Wrinkly Dell?'

'It's called Autumn Lodge.'

'Whatever. How did it go?'

'It was all right, funnily enough. There was hardly any slobbering. I was working with Chloe Blackburn. We were a good team.'

Bobby winks suggestively but I ignore him.

'We got a really good report from the manager. Mum was dead pleased. How did your work experience go?'

'I was in the sports department.'

'What was that like?'

'Boring, but there were some nice perks.'

'Perks?'

'One perk actually. There was this girl from the south end.'

'Girl?'

'Rosie Ogunbiyi. She was on work experience too. I've already burned up about 120 calories on her.'

He's showing off. I bet it's more like 12.8 calories, then something else occurs to me.

'What about Caitlin?'

'What about her?'

'Have you two finished?'

'Course not.'

'So...?'

'So I'm dating two girls at once. Big deal. It's not like we're married or anything.'

Suddenly I'm seeing Bobby in a completely different light. He's a love-cheat!

'Bobby, that's rotten.'

'Behave yourself, what's rotten about it?'

'It's not fair on either of them.'

'Terry, it's a bit of fun. I'm fifteen, for crying out loud. Everybody does it at our age.'

'I don't,' I exclaim indignantly.

'Well, that's for sure. Terry, you don't even have *one* girlfriend.'

'Got to rub it in, haven't you?'

'Sorry, but I don't see what right you've got to judge me. I'm only doing what comes naturally.'

After a few moments of simmering silence I give him a playful punch on the arm.

'You're right. Take no notice. I'm all wound up over Julie.'

'You've only yourself to blame for that, Terry mate.'

Ain't that the truth!

Friday 7th July
8.00 p.m.

I see the car pull up and open the door for Mum and Amy.

'Was that Bobby I saw at the top of the road?' Mum asks.

'Yes, he came round to bring me up to date with all the goss.'

'He's going home early, isn't he?'

I close the door behind them.

'He isn't going home. He says he got a hot date.'

'With Caitlin?'

I hesitate, trying to picture Rosie Ogunbiyi. Bobby didn't say which one he was going out with.

'Yeah, of course with Caitlin.'

'So you're staying in?'

I nod.

'I don't want to play gooseberry to those two. Besides, they're going to see Mission Impossible 2. I saw it last week.'

'Did you? Who with?'

It was an Access Alley event, courtesy of Dad. A movie, then back to his new flat with take-away. The flat isn't much to write home about, a pokey two-bedroomed affair above a shop. I wonder what was so awful about living here to drive him to Grotland.

'Dad took Amy in to see that Stuart Little film about the talking mouse, and paid for me to go to MI-2.'

'That was good of him.'

She delivers the line heavy on the sarcasm.

'Have you two had an argument?' I ask her.

'Fat chance of that,' says Mum. 'We've hardly spoken for a fortnight. Mr Monosyllable, that's your dad. Oh, by the way, he wants you to phone him. It's about tomorrow.'

I'm about to give him a call when I notice a leaflet on the table.

'What's this?' I ask.

'Give that here!' shouts Amy. 'That's mine.'

'Hang on, I only want to read it.'

'Mu-um, Terry's robbed my leaflet.'

'Give it to her, Terry. I was going to take Amy tomorrow.'

'I haven't robbed it,' I tell Mum. 'I'm curious, that's all.'

'You?' says Mum. 'Since when were you interested in horses?'

Since Julie started work experience at the pony sanctuary, that's since when. I skim the details:

OPEN DAY

*Horse and Pony Sanctuary Lane Ends Farm, Hale Village.
Domestic and rare breeds, pony rides, bouncy
castle, and much, much more.*

It's the one Julie's at, all right.

'Tell you what, Mum,' I say, 'you have the day off. I'll ask Dad to take both of us.'

Mum does a double-take.

'You? With Amy to a pony sanctuary?'

'Yes. Why, what's up?'

Mum and Amy are staring at me open-mouthed like a couple of goldfish. As I pick up the phone I'm not altogether sure whether this is a good idea. It seems too much like snooping. But there's no going back now. It's something I've got to do.

Saturday 8th July
11.00 a.m.

'I hope you know who you look like with that haircut?' says Dad disgustedly as we walk down the path to the pony sanctuary. In his eyes, Michael Owen is Public Enemy No. 1 ever since an over-the-top tackle on Ronny Johnsen.

Amy stares at me.

'Who?'

'Only that little diver Owen.'

I can feel my face burning. It's as though I've betrayed the Red Devils.

'Don't be daft. I just wanted it short, that's all.'

'Mm.'

Dad's giving me suspicious looks all the way to the farm. Before you know it he'll be bringing me up on a charge of going soft on Liverpool.

Are you now, or have you ever been, sympathetic to Liverpool Football Club?

Maybe I'll plead the Fifth Amendment and decline to answer on the grounds that it might incriminate me.

Dad pays the admission and we go in. My stomach is churning, but there's no sign of Julie.

'Oh, isn't he beautiful!' cries Amy, heading straight for a Shetland pony.

'Just looks like a sawn-off horse to me,' I grunt.

'What's the matter with you?' asks Dad. 'This *was* your idea.'

I shrug my shoulders.

'Is it OK if I wander round by myself?'

'I don't see why not.'

I roam aimlessly around the stables and the various rides and stalls. There is no sign of Julie, though I bump into Dad and Amy twice. It's hard to avoid them at such a small event. At least Amy's having a good time. By the time I bump into them the second time, she's had a donkey ride and helped to groom a big Shire horse. Eventually I find myself at the far end of the grounds by a Dutch barn. I see Amy on the bouncy castle and give her a wave. She actually waves back. This treat has earned me a few brownie points.

61

'Are you lost, mate?' asks a man in his early twenties.

I'm obviously somewhere I shouldn't be.

'No, just looking round.'

That's when I hear a squeal – Julie's squeal. I turn round in time to see her come tumbling down the hay bales in the barn. She looks flushed and dishevelled. To my horror, Fitz comes tumbling after her. They're both covered in straw. So what did I expect? I've given the best-looking guy in school a free run and I wonder why he's taken advantage! Dufus Moronicus, that's me.

'Well, look who it isn't,' says Fitz, picking himself up and brushing himself down. 'And what have you done to your hair? Look at the state of him, Julie. He's always copying me.'

Copying you? Not exactly. We're both copying Michael Owen. Julie stares at me, her expression a mixture of suspicion and surprise.

'Are you spying on us, Payne?' asks Fitz. 'Because if you are, I think that's pretty weird. Don't you think he's weird, Julie?'

Julie is still picking the straw from her hair. She looks completely embarrassed by my arrival.

'What *are* you doing here, Terry?'

I wish I could just beam up and be a zillion miles away. This was a really bad idea. What on earth did I expect to achieve?

'I saw a leaflet, that's all. My little sister's really into horses.'

As I speak, my legs are turning to jelly.

'Pull the other one,' says Fitz. 'You're a stalker, that's what you are.'

He's really enjoying my discomfort. He knows I've built another obstacle between myself and Julie.

'Imagine that, Ju, you've got your very own stalker.'

I wince at the familiar *Ju*.

'I am not a stalker,' I retort. 'I didn't even know this was the farm you were working at.'

Which is when things go from bad to worse.

'Yes he did,' comes a familiar voice behind me.

My heart sinks. It's Kelly. The girl is glued to Julie. What is she, her personal bodyguard?

She's wearing a Chicago Bulls baseball cap that makes her look as annoyingly perfect as ever.

'He's had Bobby Quinn pumping my friends for info about you,

Julie. You don't want anything to do with him. He'll be rummaging in your bin next. Weirdo.'

I look around in panic. My scalp is prickling under this traitor's haircut and Kelly's jibes have penetrated right to the quick. The day has turned into a complete disaster. I want out.

'It's not true,' I stutter. 'I only...'

Compared to Fitz and Kelly, Julie is almost sympathetic. She speaks to me in a gentle, level way, more in regret than anger. But that doesn't make her next words any easier to take:

'Terry, why don't you just go?'

Saturday 8th July
1 p.m.

I'm going, all right, but only after I've endured Amy trying every single activity going. It's been awful. My flesh is creeping right off my bones. Fitz is really enjoying my embarrassment, of course. He keeps turning up, running his hand over his haircut, making out I'm trying to look just like him. Oh great, there he is again.

'Going so soon, Terry? And just when the fun was starting.'

He jerks his head in the direction of Julie. She's giving the little kids rides on one of the Shetland ponies. She's so nice, so perfect for me I could cry. I really hate Fitz.

'Do you know that lad, Terry?' asks Dad as he closes the farm gate behind us.

'He's at our school. He's here on work experience.'

I don't mention Julie. I think if I tried to say her name I'd give the game away. It's hard trying to sound cheerful when you've got stinging eyes and a lump in your throat, but I manage to sound composed. At least, I think I do.

'Did you have a good time then?' asks Dad.

'Oh Dad, it was lovely.'

Amy looks at me with shining eyes.

'Thanks Terry.'

At least I've got one girl on my side. Unfortunately, it isn't the one I want.

'Any time, Amy. World's greatest big brother, that's me.'

We get in the car and I give the pony sanctuary a last look. There's no sign of Julie and Fitz. Good job. I probably wouldn't like what I saw. Looks like I've left the way wide open for him. As we hit the M57 Dad puts a tape on. The first song is 'Is she really going out with him?' by Joe Jackson.

Amy immediately wants the radio on instead. Joe Jackson gives way to the latest tween pop band she's into. Thank goodness for little sisters.

7

It's the end of term. It's just crept up on me. The last twelve days have gone by in a haze. After the pony sanctuary fiasco I've been too gutted to notice the passing days.

'You're not doing it, Bobby. There's no way I'm turning up tonight if you do that.'

I'm talking about Bobby's little Alison speech. He still thinks his corny song dedication can salvage something with Julie. He's actually been planning to put me on the spot in the middle of the school disco. It's a good job I've rumbled his little plot.

'You need something to sting you into action, Terry. A bomb up the bum, something like that.'

'Look, I'm not having you playing Cupid. Stop interfering, Bobby. I can sort myself out, thank you very much.'

He gives me a sideways look as if to say: *Can you really?*

'Oh, get a life, Bobby.'

'I've got one,' he retorts smugly. 'Two, actually.'

There's a twinkle in his eye. He means Caitlin and Rosie, of course.

'Which one are you taking out tonight?'

'Oh, Caitlin, of course. It's got to be Caitlin around school. What do you think I am, stupid?'

'So when are you seeing this Rosie?'

'Tomorrow night. We're going bowling near hers.'

'You're going to get a reputation the way you're going.'

Bobby grins more smugly than ever.

'Don't worry about me, Terry mate, I know what I'm doing.'

'Are you sure about that?'

'Positive. Now tell me, if you don't want my help, how are you going to rekindle the gorgeous Julie's love for you?'

'What do you mean rekindle?' I reply. 'There was no fire in the first place. Not from her anyway.'

'I'm not so certain.'

My whole insides turn over.

'Have you heard something?'

'Not really. It's just, when I've seen her with you, there seems to be a bit of a spark.'

I shake my head.

'You're imagining it.'

But what if he's not? A chance, imagine if there's a chance.

'Hey, take it from your Uncle Bobby. I'm an expert in these things.'

'Well, this time you're barking up the wrong tree. You should have seen her face when I turned up at the pony sanctuary.'

Bobby shrugs.

'OK, so you dropped a brick there. You embarrassed her in front of everybody. But it was a tactical mistake, not a strategic defeat. It doesn't mean she doesn't like you.'

I'm dying to believe him. Sure, what's a tactical mistake between friends?

'Honest,' Bobby says. 'She'll have got over it by now.'

'Says you. Bobby, not everybody bounces back the way you do.'

'Are you saying I'm fickle?'

'Well, you have got two girlfriends on the go at the same time.'

'Terry, I'm hurt.'

He says it in a way that makes it obvious he isn't. He's loving every moment of it.

'So you don't want my help tonight?'

'Don't you dare.'

'Fine, it's your look-out.'

'Exactly,' I say. 'It's my look-out. Anyway, I've got to go. I'll be late for our Amy.'

As I turn away, Fitz walks past. Just as he's done every time he's seen me for the last week and a half, he pats his hair and winks at me, all superior. I really hate that guy. And to think, once upon a time I wanted to be him.

'Be at the school hall for half past six,' Bobby shouts after me. 'You can help us set up.'

'OK,' I answer. 'So long as you don't try to set me up. Oh, by the way. I'll have a surprise for you.'

'What's that?'

I glance in Fitz's direction.

'It won't be a surprise if I tell you.'

Thursday 20th July
3.45 p.m.

'But I'm hungry,' protests Amy.

'Look, I'll do the tea the moment we get in. Come on, it'll only take fifteen minutes.'

Amy looks doubtfully at the barber's.

'Look, I'll get you something from the newsagents. I'll pay for it out of my own money.'

'Like what?'

'You name it. Any sweet you want.'

I see the look in her face. She's wondering how much she can squeeze out of me.

'OK,' I say. 'Look, I'll go up to a pound. You can pick two things, one for now and one for after your tea. I won't even let on to Mum. Deal?'

Amy is thinking mega-sugar boost. Right now, she'll go along with just about anything.

'Deal.'

She nearly snatches my hand off.

'OK,' I say. 'You go to the newsagents and meet me back here. I want to get inside quick while there's no queue.'

By the time Amy returns, most of Michael Owen lies on the floor of the barber's. I see the look of horror on her face. Two minutes later the deed is done and I pay the barber.

'Mum will kill you,' says Amy the moment we're outside. 'You're bald.'

'I am not bald,' I say, viewing myself self-consciously in the chemist's window. 'It's only a number two.'

'Mum will still kill you,' says Amy.

'Don't be silly,' I tell her. 'She won't mind.'

Thursday 20th July
5.45 p.m.

'Oh my God!' cries Mum. 'You look like a convict.'

'It's only a number three,' I say.

'You said it was a number two,' says Amy, interrupting.

'I lied.'

'You're a skinhead. My son's a skinhead. Why didn't you ask me to cut it?'

'Because you wouldn't have cut it short enough,' I tell her.

'What was wrong with the way you had it?' Mum asks.

'I looked like Michael Owen,' I explain.

'So? He's a good-looking boy. Not a thug either, not like that Roy Keane.'

'Mum, Michael Owen's the enemy. He plays for Liverpool.'

'Oh, but why quite so short? You look like an urchin out of Oliver Twist.'

Honestly, first a convict, then a skinhead, now an urchin. Mum, you do wonders for my self-esteem.

'I felt like a change.'

That's not the real reason, of course. If the Michael Owen had done the trick with Julie, I don't think I'd have ever changed it.

Real reason number 1: It'll get Fitz off my back.

Real reason number 2: I won't feel like a traitor.

Real reason number 3: It's so short you can hardly tell I'm ginger.

'Are you going to the school disco like that?' asks Mum.

'No,' I say sarcastically, 'I'm wearing a blond wig. Of course I'm going like this.'

'Well, put some nice clothes on.'

'Mum, I'm quite capable of choosing my own clothes.'

'I just hope you do better with them than you have with your hair.'

Thursday 20th July
6.15 p.m.

I leave the house in a white T-shirt, smart trousers and the new trainers Dad bought me. Guilt money. Mum thinks I look nice – except for the hair. I catch my reflection in the chemist's again. OK, so it is a bit severe, emphasising my narrow face and prominent cheekbones, but at least Michael Owen is dead and buried. I smile with satisfaction at the thought of him being tossed in a black bin-bag and put out for the dustmen.

When I arrive at school *The Sons of Moe Szyszlak* are all but set up. Bobby's discussing input and output leads with the DJ while Caitlin sits dangling a pink shoe from the end of her toe.

I feel uncomfortable talking to her, knowing what I do about Bobby's other woman, but I make the effort.

'You look nice,' I say.

'Got to make the effort, haven't you?' she says, her eyes fixed on the top of my shorn head.

'I thought it would help me stay cool in the hot weather,' I say feebly.

'Mm,' says Caitlin unhelpfully. 'I preferred it the way it was.'

'Whoa!' cries Bobby, detaching himself from the DJ. 'If it isn't Fabien Barthez. So this is your surprise.'

I smile at the mention of the United keeper.

'It's not that extreme,' I say. 'Barthez is completely bald.'

Bobby grabs me and plants a kiss on my skull, just the way Laurent Blanc did to Barthez at Euro 2000.

'Let's see if Julie likes the hard man look.'

'Bobby,' I say. 'Do you really think an ectomorph can be hard?'

'Certainly,' he replies. 'As sure as I'm sitting here on this unicycle.'

I pull a face.

'Anyway,' he says, 'If you're not doing anything you can give me a hand with the speakers.'

Did I say I hate Fitz?

Well scrub that, I loathe him, abhor him, abominate him. You want to know why? Because he's everything I want to be.

He turned up about an hour ago in casual trousers and what looks like a red gym vest, just so he could show off his arms. He's all biceps and triceps and all sorts of other ceps I don't know the name of. His arms are like a bag of grapefruit, all macho and bulging.

I detest him.

And it isn't just what he looks like, it's the way he's acting. He's been on the dance floor for an hour. He knows every move to every song. You'd think he'd come across all nerdy and embarrassing, dancing with the girls like that. But he doesn't. He's the leader of the gang. Everybody's crowding round him, copying him. And just look at Julie. I mean, look at her! She's laughing and giggling at everything he does. He slides behind her during that corny *Grease* compilation, running his hands up and down her arms.

You're the one that I want.

He's the one that I hate.

He's everything I'd like to be: school football captain, top set in everything, boy-band good looks. Julie was bound to give in eventually. After a few minutes, Julie detaches herself from the Frisky Fitzy Appreciation Society and goes for a drink. Accidentally on purpose, I find myself next to her in the queue. I can't take my eyes off her. She's wearing the little black dress. Simple but effective; so effective I find it hard to breathe as I follow her to the hatch where they're selling cans.

'Julie, I just wanted to say sorry about the pony sanctuary.'

She smiles, not the full Colgate treatment, more diplomatic and reserved than that.

'Forget it. I have.'

'I didn't want you thinking I was, you know, weird.'

'Terry, I know you're not weird.'

Despite everything, I'm sure I can detect a little warmth in her voice. I hesitate. She says I'm not weird. Is that good or bad?

'Enjoying yourself?'

'Oh yes, Fitz is a real laugh, isn't he?'

Sure, just a little bundle of joy, our Fitzy.

'You ought to let yourself go, you know. I've seen you hanging round. I bet you haven't had a single dance.'

Ask me then, *please* ask me.

Then a little voice inside my head says: *Behave, it should be* you *asking* her. Little Voice is right; even now it isn't too late. Go on, Terry, ask her. But all I end up saying is:

'I feel stupid.'

What a chat-up line that is: *Look at me, I'm stupid.*

We reach the hatch and Kelly and Pepsey come over. Kelly gives me a daggers look.

'Two more Diet Cokes,' says Julie. 'And a Tango for Fitz.'

The bottom drops out of my world. She's buying him drinks now.

'Love the hair,' says Kelly sarcastically. 'First Michael Owen, now David Beckham. You like to ring the changes, don't you?'

I know I've gone bright red. I watch helplessly as Kelly and Pepsey whisk Julie away. I catch Fitz's eye. He pats his head then roars with laughter. Suddenly I know how it feels to be two inches tall. I walk away from the hatch holding my Diet Coke and trying not to look gutted when the DJ's voice booms out of the speakers.

'Right, that's all from me for a few minutes. While I take a break, the music's going to be coming from a band drawn from Year 10 and 11 students at the school. Give it up for *The Sons of Moe Szyszlak*.'

The lights go off. Then they come back on and the four members of the group appear wearing *Simpsons* masks. There's Moe Szyszlak, Barney Gumble, Bart and Homer Simpson. After a round of applause and cheering, off come the masks.

Bobby counts the band in and they launch into 'Heatwave'. I watch Fitz skipping across the dancefloor. He even knows what to do to the Golden Oldies. All the way through their set the dance floor's bouncing even though most of the dancers have never heard any of the numbers before.

Then I hear the words that make my heart turn to ice.

'This one's for my best friend, Terry. Here's hoping he finds his Alison.'

Loads of pairs of eyes pick me out. Oh, Bobby, no, I begged you. I

71

pleaded with you. I stand gobsmacked as everybody pairs up for this classic slowie. I want to get away from this place, but not until I see where Julie is. I scan the dancefloor. Where is she? Then I see her. She's got her arms round Fitz's neck and her cheek's touching his. I want to scream.

Now I know what it feels like to be one inch tall. Somebody save me.

'Terry?'

I look round. It's Chloe Blackburn. She's wearing black trousers and a shiny white top. Even the way I'm feeling I can't help noticing she looks nice.

'Yes?'

'Look, I don't know who your Alison is, but I don't see you dancing with anyone.'

She's the one. Chloe's come to save me. She takes my hand and leads me onto the dance floor. I follow her in a daze as the music wraps itself round me. I'm inside this cocoon of music and lights and the smell of Chloe's auburn hair. A girl has finally asked me to dance, but I hardly feel a thing. This isn't the girl I want to be with.

'Come closer.'

I do as I'm told. My hands are on Chloe's hips. She feels good pressed against me like this, but she's not Julie. I steal a glance to my left. There they are, swaying gently, Julie and Fitz. It's her eyes I catch first.

This is wrong, my eyes are telling her and, just for a moment, I feel she's saying the same thing back. Then it's Fitz looking back. He grins, wide and mocking, and squeezes Julie even tighter. Then I'm drowning, sinking in despair and music and the smell of Chloe's hair. So I cling to her...

...and she clings back.

Part Two

Between Two Girls

Or

Red Shirt, Red Face, Red Mist

1

Girls are like buses. You wait forever for one, then two come along at once.

'So what are you going to do?' asks Bobby, stealing a glance at Dad. Dad's chatting to a fisherman just along the bank. He's just arrived to pick us up from overnight fishing. Well, you can do that sort of thing when you're in the middle of your six-week summer break. In fact, it's about the only time you can do it. School is no respecter of freedom. Dad has news. Mum's given him Chloe Blackburn's phone number to pass on to me. At least hostilities could be suspended long enough for her to do that. Seems Chloe's just got back off holiday and she wants me to give her a call.

Gulp!

I'm staring at the phone number wondering how to answer Bobby.

'Chloe's a nice girl,' says Bobby, packing his olive-green bivouac. 'You could do worse.'

'You sound like my mum,' I tell him as I empty the last of the unused bait into the lake.

My emotions are wriggling more feverishly than those maggots. My head's in a spin. I stare at the piece of paper Dad's just handed me. Chloe's number is written on it in red biro. The colour makes it seem urgent: phone me! Yes, you with the ginger stubble on your head: PHONE ME! I haven't seen either Julie or Chloe since we broke up from school for the summer. Julie vanished to Huyton, probably with Fitz in hot pursuit, and Chloe went off on holiday to Portugal with her parents. For a fortnight life has been uncomplicated. Sure, I've thought about little else but Julie and Fitz and Chloe, but I haven't had to face them in the flesh. I've managed to put my heartache on the back-burner.

'You know what they say,' Bobby chips in unhelpfully. 'A bird in the hand's worth two in the bush.'

'What's that supposed to mean?' I demand irritably, packing my rod.

'Think about it,' says Bobby. 'You've had it with Julie, that's pretty obvious. She and Fitz are definitely an item. Time to forget her and get back out there in the field.'

Out there in the field! Bobby makes it sound like a game. Some game! I close my eyes. I can still see them at the disco, Julie with her head on Fitz's mesomorphic shoulder, him with his hands round her gym-conditioned waist. Just thinking about them, I feel like I'm boiling inside.

'It'll have to wait till home,' I say. 'I left my mobile on charge.'

'Here,' says Bobby, tossing me his. 'No time like the present. Give Chloe a call.'

Then Dad detaches himself from the angler and comes over.

'Hurry up and pack your stuff, lads. I want to get off home.'

Bobby starts to take his rod apart.

'I'll get a couple of choccie bars for the drive home while you're finishing off,' says Dad.

'Did you know that you will eat one hundred and sixty kilograms of chocolate in your life?' asks Bobby.

'No,' says Dad. 'I didn't, but I do now.'

He sets off the shop and I stare at the mobile. Bobby's mum insisted we brought it with us. She wasn't too happy about us spending the night at the lake. Neither was my mum. But Dad won them round, reminding them that we are nearly sixteen, and a spot of overnight fishing is a lot better than hanging round the streets. I expected Mum to start arguing with him, but she didn't. Not that it's a good sign. They've barely talked since Dad left at the end of June.

'Oh, come on, Terry,' says Bobby, jabbing a finger at the phone number. 'The girl phoned you the moment she got back off holiday. She's crazy about you. You'd be a mug to pass up the chance.'

'Yes, but...'

'But what? She's a girl, not a bad-looking one, and she likes you. She's made the first move, for crying out loud! The first *two* moves, in fact.'

I think about the way she approached me at the disco. I think about the way she pushed up against me, so close I could hardly breathe. I think about her auburn hair and the way it smelled. I run my eyes over the phone number. Bobby's right, I could do worse.

'Go on, what's holding you back?'

'Not everybody's the same as you, Bobby. We can't all turn our feelings on and off like a light switch. I still care about Julie.'

Bobby ignores the dig about Caitlin and Rosie.

'Yes, and she cares about Frisky Fitzy, you wussie. Face it mate, you've been dumped good style. Trust me, it's better to be a dumper than a dumpee. Don't be such a mug.'

He's right. I'm sure he is. I *know* he is. Chloe and I kind of match. Like me, she's on the skinny side, freckle-faced and red-haired. Not too tall, either. I wouldn't be worried about looking like a dwarf the way I do next to Julie. Chloe's like me in her ways too. She's quite shy, though not too shy to ask me to dance. What the heck, Julie's gone. What have I got to lose?

'Well?'

'OK, I'll do it,' I tell him. 'I'm going over there so I can have a bit of privacy. No eavesdropping.'

Bobby holds up his hands and comes over all innocent.

'Me, listen in on a mate's private telephone call? As if I would.'

I give him a knowing look.

'Just stay put, right there.'

Bobby does his obedient dog impression and I can't help but smile. I see Dad making his way back from the fishery shop and hurry away to a secluded spot overlooked by some weeping willows. I punch in Chloe's number and take a deep breath.

'Hello?'

It's Chloe. Thank goodness it isn't her mum or dad.

'Hi Chloe, it's Terry.'

'Terry!'

She sounds so glad to hear my voice it makes my skin prickle. I shouldn't be doing this, not the way I still feel about Julie.

'I got a message to call you.'

'Yes, I've been thinking about you. You know, since the disco.'

'But how did you get my number?'

She giggles. I do too, not quite sure what I'm laughing about.

'Ever heard of the phone book?'

I remember how we stopped by the bank on the way home. Caitlin and Bobby were a few yards away, snogging the faces off each other. Chloe looked up at me expectantly and I kissed her. It felt really good, but all the while I was thinking of Julie.

'I thought maybe you wanted to see me again.'

This is it, Terry. Remember what Bobby always says: *Just do it.*

'Yes, I'd like that.'

There, done it. I'm amazed at myself. Chuffed to bits, really. Before I know it, we're talking excitedly about where we're going on our first date (her words, not mine). We make plans to go to Southport on Saturday.

I'm standing there for a couple of minutes after she hangs up, with a stupid grin all over my face. I've got a girlfriend! My first proper girlfriend. One who is keen enough to do all the chasing.

Then the bushes behind me shake.

'Bobby, you promised!'

But it isn't Bobby. It's the fisherman Dad was talking to, an old guy in his sixties. He's smiling at me.

'Young love, eh?' he says.

I know I must have gone bright red.

Yes, young love.

Thursday 10th August
8.30 p.m.

We dropped Bobby off on the way back, so here we are sitting in Dad's flat among the coffee cups and the Chinese take-away wrappers. The *Mirror* is open at the football section *Mania*. I read a line highlighted at the top of the page:

mania: noun, mental derangement marked by great excitement and (freq.) craze: passion (for).

Mental derangement marked by great excitement. That's me and Man U all right. Me and Julie too, come to think of it. You can cut that out, I tell myself. You're with Chloe Blackburn now, so start acting like it. OK, so there's no mental derangement with Chloe. Big deal, I like her. She's pretty and nice and mad about me. That's enough, isn't it?

'What're you looking at?'

Dad glances at the headline over my shoulder. There's a picture of Liverpool's five summer signings and they're saying: *We're coming to get you Fergie!*

I already have the Day of Judgement in my head. December 17th. United v Liverpool at Old Trafford.

'Wishful thinking,' says Dad. 'It's our title again. The bookies have got us odds on.'

'I hope you're right,' I say. 'I just wish we'd signed five new players. I can't believe we haven't got a single new outfield player. I mean, our defence leaked forty-three goals last season, more than any other title contender.'

'I know what you mean,' says Dad. 'That's why we got knocked out of the Champions League. But just watch us in the Charity Shield. We'll batter Chelsea this Sunday. Fergie knows what he's doing.'

Fergie might, but do I? As I look at Nick Barmby grinning at the camera, I see Julie's head superimposed on that Liverpool shirt. Come December 17th, one of us will be on cloud nine, the other in the dead zone. My skin prickles with Julie-fever. Mental derangement, you can say that again!

'So who's this Chloe then?' Dad asks.

'Just a girl.'

Dad nods knowingly.

'Ah, just a girl.'

'Yes, just a girl. Can we leave it at that?'

'Sure. What do you want to do this Saturday?'

Saturday! I do a double-take. First, because everything Bobby predicted about our Access days has come true. It hasn't taken Dad long to run out of ideas. Second, because I've already told Chloe I'd go to Southport with her.

'Sorry, Dad,' I reply finally. 'I'm busy this Saturday.'

'Busy?' Dad asks, his face falling. 'Busy how?'

'Chloe,' I tell him. 'I said I'd go to Southport with her.'

'Ah.'

'You don't mind?'

'Course not. Nice to see that one of us is having some luck with his love life.'

I grimace to indicate I don't really want to know. Just because I hang around with him doesn't mean he's forgiven.

Dad nods.

'Looks like it's just me and Amy.'

'Sorry.'

'Don't be, son. You're growing up.'

'Anyway,' I say, feeling quite pleased with myself for finally having a girlfriend. 'I'd better be off.'

'Want a lift back?'

'No, it'll only take me ten minutes.'

I fold the *Mirror* and slide it into the magazine rack. That's where I find a copy of *Men's Health*. There's this bloke on the cover with biceps like Spanish onions and veins like pipe-cleaners.

'What's this doing here?' I ask, nodding at the old man's beer belly. My dad reading *Men's Health*? It makes about as much sense as Roy Keane with a knitting pattern.

'I've decided to get into shape,' says Dad.

A moment's hesitation then the confession: 'As a matter of fact, I've joined a gym.'

Now, just you hang on there, father of mine. Gym = membership fee = broken promises.

'You've what!'

There's horror in my voice. Anger too.

'What's the matter with that?'

'Do I need to spell it out?' I yell. 'You cancel our United season tickets, then you blow the money on some stupid gym.'

'Oh, now that's not fair,' Dad replies. 'It's nothing fancy, just a council fitness suite. It doesn't add up to a fraction of what it costs to go to Old Trafford.'

I shake my head. Right now, I don't want to hear balance sheets. Or reasoned argument. In short, I don't want to hear Dad. All I know is, he's traded in my treasured season ticket and now he's wasting the money trying to get fit.

All I get out of the arrangement is lousy Access days.

'So why do you want to get fit all of a sudden?' I ask. 'You've been

79

happy being a slob all these years.'

I see a flicker of embarrassment in his face. I'm thinking aftershave and hair gel. I'm thinking new gear from Next.

'You're after some woman,' I gasp. 'You're going out on the pull, aren't you?'

I think of Mum secretly working her way through a packet of cookies and wondering what she's done wrong and all of a sudden I'm seeing Dad through slime-tinted spectacles.

Home-wrecker!

Season-ticket canceller!

And now – womaniser!

'Dad, you're a dirty old man.'

I slam the door and stamp down the stairs. Seeing him open his door to call after me I shout up at him:

'Dirty old man!'

Thursday 10th August
8.45 p.m.

'That you, Terry?' shouts Mum.

'Nah, Jack the Ripper.'

She appears at the living room door. I notice the telltale Hobnob crumbs nestling in the folds of her top.

'Is it too much to ask for a normal answer?' she asks, brushing away the evidence.

'Probably.'

I see a flash of temper in her eyes and backtrack quickly.

'Sorry. I'm spending too much time with Bobby. Where's Amy?'

'She's at Katie's. She's sleeping over.'

'Oh yeah, I forgot.'

'Did your dad give you that girl's phone number?'

At the mention of Dad my cheeks start to burn, but I manage not to let it show.

'Yes, I phoned her.'

'And?'

'And we're going to Southport on Saturday.'

Mum's wearing this sickly smile.

'So who is she?'

'A girl, Mum, female of the species. Her name's Chloe.'

'When do I get to meet her?'

I take a deep breath.

'Mum, it's our first date. No need to buy a new hat quite yet.'

She looks away and I realise it's probably not too good an idea to make wedding jokes.

'You OK?'

'Of course,' she says, 'Why do you ask?'

I point out the Hobnob crumbs.

'I've been at a bit of a loss tonight,' she admits. 'It felt so strange being in on my own.'

She bites her lower lip.

'You know I even got two cups out when I made myself a coffee.'

'Dad, you mean?'

Mum nods.

'I just can't get used to him not being around. I've been part of *us* so long I've forgotten how to be *me*. You know what I am, I'm the clockwork key in everybody's back. I wind you and Amy up and send you off to school. I used to wind your Dad up and send him off to work. When I got married, I thought it was for good. Marriage was what I did. I cooked, I cleaned, I made a home. Now I don't really know what I am.'

I listen in silence. God, she sounds down.

'Terry, can I ask you something?'

'Fire away.'

'Has Geoff said anything? Has he ever told you why he left?'

I'm feeling uncomfortable. What does she think I am, a Relate counsellor?

'He did say one thing.'

Mum's looking at me all expectant.

'He said he didn't get the butterflies any more.'

She looks shocked. For a moment or two she doesn't say a thing. Then she looks annoyed. 'He said that! So that's why he's decided to walk away from seventeen years of marriage, is it? Butterflies! Well, believe you me, Geoffrey Payne, I haven't felt the butterflies for years, and *I* wasn't about to walk out.'

She stamps into the living room. I wander into the kitchen wishing I'd kept my mouth shut and return a couple of minutes later. There's only one thing for it. I hold out the biscuit barrel.

'Hobnob?'

2

'I don't believe this!'

'What happened to the marking? What was Johnsen doing leaving Hasselbaink clear?'

We're 1–0 down to Chelsea in the Charity Shield and it hurts. I hate Chelsea. I mean, I really hate them. They beat us 5–0 at Stamford Bridge last season and I wanted revenge today. It's not just the scoreline that bothers me. It's the way the two sides are playing. Chelsea have carved out three or four gilt-edged opportunities and we haven't even got off the blocks.

'Don't panic,' says Dad. 'Plenty of time to go. Keano will get them organised.'

But Keano doesn't even get himself organised. Hasselbaink treads on the United captain's ankle and Keano sees red. From then on it's only a matter of time before he goes into the ref's book. I see him moving up behind Gustavo Poyet and I hold my breath. The telltale signs are there. The red mist has descended.

'Don't do it,' I hiss, gripping the edge of the couch.

But he does it, does it with knobs on, hacking into the back of Poyet's left leg right in front of the referee. Yellow card, please let it be yellow. We don't want to go into the new season with Keano on a three-match suspension.

But it isn't yellow. It's red. Keano's off. I look at Dad. He shrugs.

'We lost the last two Charity Shields,' he reminds me. 'It didn't stop us winning the Premiership both times.'

Always look on the bright side of life, that's Dad's signature tune.

'Just think about it,' he says. 'Two years ago Arsenal beat us 3–0 in this fixture and we still won the Treble.'

Somehow it doesn't help. I'm watching my beloved Reds being taken to the cleaners by Vialli's bunch of international playboys and nothing can ease the agony. I imagine Julie and Fitz are sitting together on a couch somewhere right now lapping this up. Liverpool are playing a friendly against the Italian side, Parma. I just hope they're losing too.

'We might as well switch the TV off now,' I tell Dad.

'Give over,' he says. 'Have you forgotten when Keano got sent off against Arsenal in the FA Cup semi-final? We still won then.'

Always look on the bright side of life.

Dee doo, dee doo, dee doo, dee doo.

But it isn't going to happen this time. That evening, Ryan Giggs was on fire. This afternoon he's a damp squib. He looks like he's only come along to make up the numbers. With only one shot on target we look completely toothless. Things go from bad to worse when Melchiot slips the ball through Stam's legs. 2–0. When the final whistle goes, Dad and I bolt for the kitchen together. It's an unwritten law. We never watch the other side lift the trophy when we lose. Instead, we pretend it never happened.

'Toasted sausage sandwich?' asks Dad.

'Fine.'

'One or two?'

'One.'

When I'm gutted, I go all monosyllabic. It's better than crying. We switch the TV off and eat.

'So how did your date go?'

'It was good.'

The pain of defeat is easing. I'm up to three syllables already.

'What did you do?'

'You know, stuff.'

We did stuff all right. We went on the roller coasters, held hands, licked ice creams, drank Coke, ate fish and chips, kissed. We kissed straight after the fish and chips. Chloe's lips tasted of batter and vinegar. She could have tasted of petrol, I would still have enjoyed kissing her.

'Don't give much away, do you?'

I grin.

'Like father, like son.'

'Meaning?'

'Mum asked me if I knew why you'd walked out.'

'What did you tell her?'

'What you told me. That you didn't feel the butterflies any more.'

Dad rolls his eyes.

'I bet that went down well.'

'Not very. She was really annoyed.'

I look straight at him.

'So *is* that why you went? The butterflies, I mean?'

Dad sighs.

'Pretty much. Don't get me wrong. Your mother's great. I feel terrible walking out on her. Life was just so routine. Every day was the same. It felt like I was wading through treacle.'

'And that's it?'

'You don't understand, do you?'

That's an understatement. He breaks up a whole family because of a butterfly deficiency. I'm like Mum. I believe in one boy, one girl, happy ever after. Sad? Maybe, but that's the way I'm made.

'Look, do you get the butterflies with this Chloe?'

'Yes.'

It's true, I do. Little ones that creep up from the pit of my stomach until I've got a lump in my throat. But no matter how I try to tell myself otherwise, I know it's nothing to what I'd feel with Julie. With her, I'd have butterflies the size of vultures. Genetically-enhanced butterflies. Let's face it, I'm talking butterfly-mania!

'And it feels good, doesn't it?'

I remember the way we sat together on the platform at Southport station. Chloe rested her head on me and I felt like I'd won the lottery. I even forgot Julie for a while.

'Of course it does.'

'Then just imagine being with somebody for seventeen years. You wake up one morning and you think: am I never going to feel that way again?'

I feel disloyal to Mum just listening to him. I know that she's in the right and he's in the wrong. But I want to hear more. I mean, this could be my future.

'Mum says the butterflies went for her too,' I tell him. 'She says there's more to marriage.'

Dad shakes his head.

'Maybe for her.'

He looks sadly at his half-eaten toastie.

'When you first fall for a woman, you feel so alive. I just wanted that thrill again.'

I listen to him, but I don't quite know what to make of it. I look round his pokey flat. He seems to have given up a lot, just for a thrill.

'Believe me, Terry,' he says, 'There could come a time when you're with somebody, and no matter how good it feels, you find yourself wanting more.'

I think of Chloe and how warm and comfortable everything feels with her. Then I think of Julie and I know I would give it up right here, right now, if she only gave me one iota of encouragement.

Dad, I know the feeling already.

Sunday 13th August
6.30 p.m.

I'm walking past Prescot station when I hear it. Fitz's voice.

'So what was the score today, Terry?'

I look in the direction of his crowing voice and my stomach turns over. Walking towards me are Julie and Fitz, Kelly and Gary Tudor. They're all kitted out in their Liverpool shirts. Gary, Kelly and Fitz are wearing the home strip. Julie's wearing black pedal-pushers and the new gold away shirt.

'You know the score,' I grunt.

'Go on,' says Fitz. 'Just for me, say the scoreline.'

He puts a hand behind his right ear.

'How did the mighty Man U do today?'

Julie's watching me, wondering how I'll react. I need to stay cool.

'You know very well,' I tell him. 'We lost. 2–0.'

'Did Roy Keane have a good game?' asks Gary Tudor.

'Get stuffed!' I snap hotly.

So much for staying cool.

'No need to be like that,' says Kelly, cheeks dimpling under her

Liverpool baseball cap. 'We were just wondering how the Footballer of the Year got on.'

I turn to go. The back of my neck is prickling. I've got this neon sign flashing away in my head. December 17th. Manchester United v Liverpool. Suddenly it's situation critical. It's bad enough having four Liverpool fans on your back. But when one of them is Julie...

'You haven't asked how we got on,' says Fitz. 'We've just got back from Anfield.'

'You mean you went to the game?'

I glance from Fitz to Julie. I can just see them hugging as the goals go in. Please let it be a Parma win, or a 0–0 draw. Anything to keep his octopus-hands off her.

'Go on then. What was the score?'

'5–0,' chuckles Kelly. 'And that's against the likes of Cannavaro and Lilian Thuram. World-class defenders and they couldn't live with us. Not bad, eh?'

Five! That's five hugs. I can see Fitz holding her tight. So tight. Oh God.

'We were class,' says Fitz. 'Hamann got the first. Cracker of a free kick.'

'Our new signings scored too,' says Gary. 'Barmby and McAllister got on the score sheet. We've bought some good players in the close season.'

Don't rub it in. What have we got? Just Barthez and he was left exposed all afternoon by a threadbare defence. The neon sign flashes even more intensely. December 17th. Manchester United v Liverpool. I hear Houllier's words from the year before last: 'One day we're going to beat them.' Maybe this is the year. Armageddon.

'Who scored the other two?' I ask, dreading the answer.

Please God, not Michael Owen.

'Michael Owen,' Julie replies.

OK, ignore me then, God. Rub it in all you like.

'He's back to his best,' says Julie.

'That's right,' Kelly adds, knowing exactly which buttons to press. 'Back to his gorgeous best.'

Fitz lifts the club badge on his shirt to his lips.

'The best squad an Anfield manager's put together in ten years.

We're going to slaughter you this year,' he says.

December 17th. Armageddon.

'Just watch us take that title off you.'

'I'd like to see you try,' I reply, trying my best not to pout. I do that when I'm up against it.

'Man U have had their own way for ten years,' said Fitz, 'But look at our record. Eighteen league championships, four European Cups.'

He probably doesn't know it, but he's logging on to my worst nightmare. All good things have to come to an end. Is this the year Man U start to slide?

'Be worried, Terry, be very worried. When it comes to winning honours, there isn't another English club comes close to us.'

'We've won the most FA Cups,' I venture.

'Yes, and we all know what you think of the Cup. You didn't even play in it last year.'

Fitz gives a broad grin. He knows that's the killer answer. Without another word he snakes his arm round Julie's waist. He's reminding me who got the girl. Julie gives me a pitying smile – at least I think that's what it is – and they walk off up the road. It has started to rain and they're sharing an umbrella.

'By the way,' shouts Fitz, 'How's it going with that skinny bird I saw you with at the school disco?'

Skinny bird! Fitz doesn't half know how to put somebody down.

'Man, did she have the hots for you. What's her name? Yeah, Chloe.'

Julie scowls and pulls away from him. Refusing his hand, she walks off with Kelly. At least she doesn't want to join in Fitz's tormenting. Gary's another matter. Next minute he and Fitz are cooing her name:

'Chloe, Chloe.'

I ought to say something, but I don't. I just stand there, sick with powerless anger. When they get to the roundabout they're a foursome again, each couple sharing an umbrella. Julie's annoyance with Fitz hasn't lasted long. As they reach the corner, Julie glances back at me. I want to run after her and tell her she's too good for the likes of Fitz. I don't of course.

Instead, I just stand there while the pelting rain runs down my face.

3

Saturday 19th August
9.00 a.m.

'I'm making a new season's resolution,' I declare.

'What's that?' comes Bobby's voice, still thick with sleep.

I look down at him. Last night was band practice at the community centre with *The Sons of Moe Szyslak*, so he stayed the night. Now he's curled up in a sleeping bag on top of the inflatable bed. He sleeps over at mine as often as he can, usually when his mum is having her boyfriend over. You know the one, big guy, cocker spaniel. Bobby doesn't like him. The big guy, that is. He doesn't mind the cocker spaniel.

'No more divided loyalties,' I tell him. 'I'm going to stop thinking about Julie and just have the best time with Chloe.'

I've been thinking about this ever since the drumming rain woke me up about an hour ago.

'Good for you,' says Bobby.

What he means is: shut up and let me sleep. Bobby doesn't believe in crawling out of bed until eleven o'clock at the earliest. It's a habit he's developed while he's been off school. That way he avoids having breakfast with the big guy and his cocker spaniel. The big guy has bad breath and the cocker spaniel has fleas.

'I mean, Chloe's a lovely girl,' I say. 'You've said so yourself.'

'Yes, lovely,' grunts Bobby, burying his head in the sleeping bag.

'And Julie doesn't even know I exist.'

I can't help wanting Bobby to contradict me, remind me how she came up to me outside the house that time, how she smiled at me in the canteen, how she pulled her hand out of Fitz's when he was tormenting me. He doesn't say a word. Instead he yawns and rolls over. I stare at him in his sleeping bag, a shiny, red caterpillar on the floor.

'Are you listening to me?'

'Yeah, course I am. You're going to stop thinking about Chloe and make a go of it with Julie.'

I give an exasperated cry and boot the misshapen red caterpillar. Bobby corrects himself.

'Sorry, reverse that. Chloe yes, Julie no. She's a Scouser, she must go.'

He pokes his head out of the sleeping bag, very pleased with himself.

'Hey, I'm a poet and I didn't know it.'

'You're a wombat.'

Bobby scratches his head and sits up.

'I'm a hungry wombat. Is your mum in?'

'No, she's taken Amy to some horse thing. One of those gymkhanas. My dad's gone with them.'

Bobby's pulling on his jogging pants.

'Does that mean anything?'

'What, like them getting back together, you mean?'

Bobby nods.

'No chance. They're just putting on a show for Amy.'

'So we've got the house to ourselves?'

'Uh huh.'

'Well, you know what that means, Terry mate,' he says, pulling on his Adidas top. 'Monster breakfast coming up.'

Twenty minutes later we're wolfing down eggs, bacon and pancakes with Canadian maple syrup. Bobby even dips his bacon in maple syrup and runny egg!

'You're disgusting,' I tell him.

'No, I'm not.'

Twin streams of runny egg and maple syrup are spilling down his chin. Rather than watch his disgusting eating habits, I glance out of the window. The rain clouds are clearing and the sun is peeping out.

'Good conditions for the big kick-off,' I say.

Man U don't play until tomorrow but I can feel the tremor of excitement. The butterflies. I glance at the clock. This time last season, Dad and I were getting ready to steam down the M62. Even when United aren't playing, there's plenty to think about, psyching myself up, willing our closest rivals to trip up. This afternoon I'll be flitting through the sports channels, willing Sunderland to beat Arsenal, Bradford to beat Liverpool, West Ham to beat Chelsea, Everton to beat Leeds. As if he's just read my thoughts, Bobby chips in with:

'We could do you a favour this afternoon at Leeds.'

I grin. Bobby's a staunch Evertonian and it seems cruel to remind him that Everton have only won once at Elland Road since the end of World War Two. Hitler's got a better chance, and he's dead!

'Chance would be a fine thing.'

No, come ten to five the classified results will register wins for all the bad guys, leaving us with a job to do against Newcastle. I try to focus on Chloe and Man U, but for some reason a snowstorm of other images fills my mind: Julie in her leotard; *This is Anfield*; Fitz in his Liverpool home strip; 'You'll Never Walk Alone'; Julie at the disco with her head on Fitz's shoulder; Liverpool and their eighteen league championships and four European cups; Julie in her little black dress.

Julie, always Julie.

I clear the breakfast things, feeling like I'm letting Chloe down already, and give a long sigh.

'No wonder people break resolutions.'

Saturday 19th August
3.15 p.m.

Bobby and I are squatting on the wooden floor. There are four empty cans of Red Bull and two screwed up packets of crisps in the waste paper bin. You've got to keep up your energy levels when you're listening to football.

'Is this the way you imagined spending your Saturday afternoons?' I ask, insanely jealous of the hundreds of thousands of fans watching their teams on the first day of the season.

'Pretty much,' says Bobby. 'Only I didn't expect Chloe to turn up.'

'What?'

I see a fuzz of red hair at the window and hear the doorbell.

'Wonder what she wants?' I murmur.

'You, you sexy devil,' says Bobby.

He does this low growl just to wind me up.

'You can cut that out,' I tell him as I go to answer the door.

'Hi, Terry,' says Chloe. 'Doing anything?'

Her eyes light up the moment she sees me. I wish I could return the compliment, but right now she isn't really welcome. I don't tell her. I'm too much of a coward for that.

'No, Bobby and I are just hanging out listening to the match reports.'

Her eyes dull a little at the mention of Bobby. I told her Mum and Amy were going to be out so she obviously thought she'd have me to herself. Bobby curses loudly in the living room.

'Go on,' I say, 'What's happened?'

'Leeds 1, Everton 0,' he reports.

'Oh wonderful!'

'Why are you bothered?' asks Chloe. 'I thought you supported Man United.'

'I do,' I explain. 'Leeds are one of our rivals for the Premiership.'

Chloe's *Oh* of bewilderment reminds me she knows nothing about football, and cares even less. Try as I might, I can't stop Julie from popping into my head. She would never ask a question like that. She understands football. Minutes later the afternoon gets worse. Chelsea take the lead against West Ham.

'Is that bad?' asks Chloe.

Don't snap, I tell myself.

'Yes Chloe,' I tell her, desperately trying to shoo Julie out of my head. 'It's bad.'

Bad becomes disastrous for both me and Bobby just before half time. Leeds have gone 2–0 up.

Bobby sits dejectedly on the floor with his face buried in his hands.

'What's the matter with him?' Chloe whispers.

'It's called pain,' I explain, just about keeping control of my temper. 'All summer he's lived for today, just waiting for Everton to put on a good performance on the opening Saturday.'

'It's only a game,' says Chloe.

That does it. Julie won't be shooed. She would never say anything as dumb as that. She's got Shankly's words carved onto her heart:

Football is not a matter of life and death; it's much more important than that.

I see Julie next to Fitz at the Anfield Road End. The pair of them are wearing matching Liverpool home shirts. I glance at the scores in the right hand corner of the TV screen. At least they're not winning yet. At eight minutes past four there is actually a piece of good news.

Paolo Di Canio has equalised for West Ham against Chelsea. Seven minutes later it gets even better. Sunderland have taken the lead against Arsenal. Maybe this Saturday afternoon can be salvaged after all.

'Can't we go out somewhere?' asks Chloe.

'I can't go out now,' I tell her, appalled at the idea. 'You've heard the scores, haven't you?'

'Yes,' says Chloe, all sweetness and light. 'And it won't make any difference you being stuck in front of the TV.'

The words are no sooner out of her mouth than Chelsea retake the lead. I just stop myself from saying:

Now look what you've done.

I've hardly got over that disappointment when even worse news comes through. Liverpool have taken the lead against Bradford. Bobby groans and buries his head even deeper in his hands. He hates Liverpool almost as much as I do. As far as he's concerned there are only two teams on Merseyside, Everton and Everton reserves.

'Now what's up with him?' asks Chloe.

'His team are losing 2–0,' I explain, wondering if she's trying to be stupid, or if it comes naturally. 'And the old enemy across Stanley Park are winning.'

Chloe gives another of her *Ohs*.

By full-time, the news is almost universally bleak. Liverpool, Leeds and Chelsea have all won. The only shaft of sunlight is the news that Arsenal have gone down 1–0 and their star midfielder Patrick Vieira has been sent off.

'Come on now,' says Chloe, 'After all, it's only the first match.'

Bobby reacts as if somebody's slipped a firecracker down his pants. He shoots up and bolts for the hallway.

'I'm off home,' he says.

I follow him to the front door.

'Did you hear that?' he hisses, mimicking her slightly reedy voice. '*It's only the first match*. Typical comment from a female.'

93

I give a sympathetic smile.

'She means well.'

'Yes? Well, so did Genghis Khan. So did the rotten Spanish Inquisition. Terry, forget the resolution. The girl knows nothing about football. Julie yes, Chloe no, she's a dufus, she must go.'

Suddenly, despite all my efforts, Julie's face is looming larger than ever.

4

'Isn't Chloe a lovely girl?' says Mum.

She's talked about nothing else since yesterday. She and Amy came in from the gymkhana and caught me and Chloe kissing. Oddly enough, she didn't seem bothered. In fact, she seemed chuffed to bits. Somehow, she's got it into her head that if I'm going out with a *Nice Girl* – and as she keeps telling everyone Chloe's a *very* nice girl – then I'll let my hair grow again and be a *Nice Boy*. I don't quite know why, but if you've got a Number One haircut, it's route one to hell for you, my lad. After ten minutes of Mum interrogating me about Chloe, I'm high-tailing it to Bobby's for some light relief. There's no better way to warm up for this afternoon's match than a kick around. We recruit a few guys from up the street and head for the field. It's attack and defend with me in goal.

'Fabien Barthez!' I roar, the first time I make a decent save.

'You've certainly got the haircut for it,' says Bobby.

I pull a face and lob the ball out.

'Hey, look who's here,' says Bobby, as he measures up to defend the goal.

It's Julie and Kelly. Julie's in a purple dress and white trainers. It's her legs I notice most. They're sun-tanned, and they shine. I don't really register what Kelly's wearing.

'Hello, boys,' says Kelly.

There's a sarcastic sting in the tail of her *hello*. Julie gives a winsome smile. I get the weirdest feeling the smile is for me. Or is that wishful thinking? I wish some scientist would invent the Fancy-ometer, cast-iron proof of how a girl feels about you.

It would save a lot of embarrassing moments. Julie and Kelly stop to watch us for a few minutes.

That's my cue to launch myself into some spectacular saves. I'm out to impress the girl. I tip one shot over the bar with my fingertips. At least I would have done if there was a bar. Then I palm another away round the right hand post. Or, to put it another way, the right hand rolled-up sweater. Finally, I dive low to smother Bobby's drive, skidding across the uneven grass surface. Julie's impressed. She can't take her eyes off me. All of a sudden, I'm swelling up like a puffer fish.

She's looking at me. Julie's actually got her eye on me.

Bobby fishes a bottle of Fanta out of his bag.

'Five minute break,' he says, passing the bottle round.

I take a swig and turn to Julie.

'How's it going?'

'Good.'

'Did you go to the match yesterday?'

Julie nods.

Please, not with Fitz. Frisky Fitzy with his octopus hands.

'I went with my Dad and the boys.'

That's music to my ears. It gives me the confidence to make a joke.

'What, Huey, Duey and Louis?'

Julie giggles and Kelly gives her a sideways glance as if to ask what she's playing at. This is going well.

'Yes, that's them.'

I look into her brown eyes. They're sparkling and there are these cute little wrinkles round the corners where she's smiling. This is going really well. What I don't get is why Julie and Kelly seem to be looking at my chest all the time. It's not like I've got any pecs to speak of.

'I saw the reports on Sky,' I tell her. 'Rodney Marsh called it a 1–0 massacre.'

'That about sums it up,' says Julie. 'We were all over them like a rash. Just couldn't get it in the net. Good strike by Heskey though.'

'Yes, I saw it on Match of the Day.'

I resist the tendency to congratulate him for staying on his feet for once. This is going *so* well. It's like Fitz doesn't exist. Or Chloe. I start to feel guilty, but Julie's smiling face soon puts that right. When I'm talking to her there doesn't seem to be another human being on the planet. I just wish I knew why she keeps looking at my chest.

'Still in the gym club?' I ask.

It's a way of fishing for a progress report on her and Fitz. I remember that Fitz's kid sister's in the same club.

'Mm,' says Julie. 'We've started training three times a week, Tuesday, Thursday and Saturday.'

I know I shouldn't, but I mentally note the days.

'We're away in the Isle of Man for four days next week.'

Good. That's four days away from Fitz. I'm searching for something clever to say when Kelly sticks her oar in.

'How's Chloe?' she asks acidly. Though her family moved up the hill out of Liverpool when she was five, Kelly's your ultimate Scouse nationalist. She doesn't want her best mate getting chatted up by a Manc. The interruption earns her a glare from me and Julie. There's definitely something in the air, a connection, an electricity. I'm not imagining it. Please tell me I'm not imagining it.

'Fine,' I mumble.

The spell is broken and Julie starts to go.

'See you,' she says.

'Yes, see you.'

As they carry on across the field, ponytails bobbing, Bobby offers me the Fanta.

'She's such a nice girl,' I say. 'Too good for Fitz.'

'You still fancy her rotten, don't you?' says Bobby, digging me in the ribs.

I nod, which makes me feel even guiltier. What about my resolution? What about Chloe? But there's no sense in lying to Bobby. He's known me since we were in the nursery, fighting in the sandpit.

'And I suppose you think that went well?' he says.

I'm thinking me and Julie in matching pullovers pushing a trolley round the supermarket.

'Yes. Why, don't you?'

'I've just two words to say to you,' says Bobby. 'Dog poop.'

'What?'

I look down. To my horror, there it is – a huge streak of the stuff right across the front of my new top. I must have dived right into a big, steaming pile of it when I made that last save.

'Oh gross!'

Then I think of Julie staring at it while I rabbit on with this big, stupid grin on my face. No wonder she was staring at my chest. It was poop, not pecs, she was looking at.

'Oh God!'

I sink to my knees. There's me thinking she's smiling at me and all the time she's laughing at my pooped-on shirt. What an idiot!

'Why didn't you warn me?'

'What was I supposed to do? You wouldn't have thanked me for pointing it out while you were chatting up the lovely Julie.'

Julie and me and the dog poop makes three.

Ohmigod, ohmigod, ohmigod.

'I suppose that's the end of the game,' says Bobby. 'You'll be attracting too many flies.'

I hold the ball to my chest in a vain attempt to hide the stain.

'You're not kidding. I've got to go home to change.'

We leave the other boys at the top of Bobby's street and head for my house.

'You seem to have forgotten Chloe pretty quickly,' says Bobby.

'No, I haven't!'

Bobby's struck a chord.

'It isn't going far if your heart isn't in it,' says Bobby, sounding more like an agony aunt all the time. (Do they have agony uncles?)

'My heart *is* in it,' I tell him.

I try to sound convincing but it doesn't wash with Bobby.

'Yes? Tell it to the marines. This is your best mate you're talking to. I can read you like a book.'

I blush right to the top of my ears. Bobby's got me sussed, all right. But Julie and I are going nowhere, especially after the dog poop incident.

'I'm sticking with Chloe, all right?' I answer hotly.

'Whatever you say,' Bobby replies. 'Just do one thing for me. Tell me you're over Julie.'

I try to get the words out, but I can't. Instead I do what I always do when he's got one over on me. I insult him.

'Bobby, you're stupid.'

But he isn't. Not by a long chalk.

Yesterday counts as Amy Access, so today it's just me and Dad and the TV set. Mum told me to enjoy the match. Just goes to show she doesn't really understand about football. Enjoy definitely isn't the right word. From the moment I get up in the morning my whole system is turned upside down. Fear of losing is like a stream of hot lava bubbling through my veins. I spend the whole match on the edge of my seat, willing every opposition attack to break down, every United move to end in a goal. Today the stakes are high. We looked sluggish in the Charity Shield against Chelsea and yesterday all but one of our title rivals won well. Only Arsenal stumbled at Sunderland. We can't afford to drop points.

'Just look at that,' says Dad approvingly as the team take the field. 'Sixty-seven thousand fans packed into the Theatre of Dreams.'

I can't help but have a dig.

'Just a pity we're not among them,' I say.

Dad takes it on the chin. The tension eases as United launch attack after attack on the Newcastle goal.

'They're looking sharp,' says Dad, offering the Pringles.

'Yes, they're up for it.'

Just how up for it we discover in the twenty-first minute. Stam almost scores from a corner. A second corner on the run finds Ronny Johnsen clear and he heads home. Dad and I are on our feet, arms raised. It's almost like being at Old Trafford.

Almost.

We continue to pile on the pressure and when Giggsy is brought down in the penalty area we're screaming for a penalty.

'The only thing that worries me,' I tell Dad, 'is that we've had so many chances but are still only 1-0 up. It only takes one mistake and they're right back in it.'

Dad nods.

But in the seventieth minute I can finally breathe easily. Cole and Giggs exchange a neat one-two and Andy Cole fires the ball into the far corner.

'2-0,' chuckles Dad. 'Game, set and match.'

Thank goodness for that. If I bump into Fitz I can hold my head up. My mind is already fixed on the coming week. Liverpool visit Arsenal on Monday. We go to Ipswich on Tuesday. With a bit of luck we'll be three points clear of the old enemy by ten o'clock Tuesday night. But just when everything's rosy, the phone rings.

'Hello,' says Dad. 'Oh, hi.'

There's something about his voice that makes me sit up and take notice.

'Yes, I'll see you there. Eight o'clock.'

Dad glances at me then speaks again.

'Looking forward to it.'

His eyes are still on me. He's expecting the third degree but I don't ask him who it was on the phone. I'm not stupid. I know it was a woman.

'Anyway,' I say, 'I'm getting off.'

'OK, son,' says Dad.

I think he's relieved. He doesn't fancy explaining the mystery caller, and I'm in no hurry to find out. As I hit the street, I fish for some change in my pockets. I think I'll buy Mum a packet of Hobnobs on the way home.

Tuesday 22nd August
6.00 p.m.

It's boys' night. Me and Bobby playing badminton. I've spent the day with Chloe at Croxteth Park. Bobby was out with Rosie last night, and he and Caitlin tagged along to Croccy with us this afternoon. So we're getting a break from the girls. It's just the two of us knocking the shuttlecock back and forth. I glance around the main hall. There are three activities going on at the same time. It's judo club nearest the door, the badminton club in the middle, but it's the far end of the hall that concerns me. Behind this big partition net everything is set up for the gymnastics club. Yes, you've got it, it's Julie's gym club. Maybe I'm a pathetic loser, but I just couldn't stay away.

'Hey, Terry, pay attention,' says Bobby.

He's just whipped the shuttlecock past me.

'Sorry.'

I hear the door creak. It's two girls in tracksuits. They head for the gym area and unzip their jackets. Bobby follows them with his eyes.

'Hey, you,' I say, 'Aren't two girls enough for you?'

'Terry,' he replies, 'there aren't enough girls in the world for me.'

I swat the shuttlecock back at him and he grins broadly. Ever since he got off with Rosie he thinks he's God's gift to women. The grin fades a little the next time the door opens. In walk Julie, Kelly and Pepsey Cooper. I avoid Bobby's inquiring glance.

'Come on,' I say, 'Let's play.'

In the corner of my eye I glimpse the three girls whispering. They're staring in my direction.

'So that's your little game,' says Bobby knowingly.

'What are you on about?'

'Oh, come on, do you think I was born yesterday?'

More members of the gym club arrive, maybe twenty in all. The gymnasts are warming up. Julie's wearing a white leotard with a blue star on the shoulder. I'm finding it impossible to look away. This is what eyes are made for.

'Terry.'

Bobby's hissing at me.

'What?'

It's Fitz. He's just come in with his little sister, Hayley. He's telling her he'll pick her up in two hours when he spots me. Instinctively he looks over at Julie.

'What are you doing here, Payne?'

He says *Payne*, not *Terry*. There's no love lost. I brandish the badminton racket.

'What does it look like?'

'You know what I mean.'

He gives me a venomous look then goes over to Julie. They exchange a few words. I know what he's doing. He's saying: *She's mine*. That's a red rag to a bull. I hit him with the only weapon at hand, Liverpool's 2–0 defeat last night at Arsenal.

'So what was the score, Fitzy?'

'Get stuffed.'

I remember the way he wound me up over the Charity Shield. It's pay-back time.

'Two players sent off. You're hardly going to win the Fair Play award, are you?'

'The ref was a crackpot,' says Fitz, really rattled. 'He ruined the game.'

'Oh yes,' I answer. 'It's always the ref's fault, isn't it? Funny that, I thought it was because you played like a pub side.'

Fitz gives me a daggers look and walks up to me. For an instant I think he's going to swing for me. But that's not his intention. Instead he shoves his face right into mine.

'At least I'm not some saddo who hangs round somebody else's girlfriend,' he hisses.

'I'm here to play badminton,' I tell him, trying not to show he's got to me.

'Sure, and it's just a coincidence you booked the court when Julie's here. Kelly was right. You're a lousy stalker. At least you can't follow Julie round for a while. She's off to the Isle of Man for a week. Bet you didn't know I'd be going with her.'

I feel a knife going through my heart.

'That's right, when our Hayley goes to a display the whole family goes with her. We make a holiday of it. What do you think of that, Terry, me and Julie in the Isle of Man for four days. Sun, sea, sand and ... well, I'll leave that to your imagination.'

I know there's nothing in it. He's just boasting, but my mind is working overtime. Suddenly, it's *Titanic* just before the iceberg hits, with Julie as Kate Winslet and Fitz as Leonardo DiCaprio. He knows he's scored a direct hit.

'Jealous, are we?'

I shove him away. He reacts by raising a hand. For a moment I think it's going to turn into a punch-up, then Fitz gives his superior grin.

'What's the point in hitting you?' he says. 'Julie isn't interested anyway. See you, saddo.'

I'm dying to hit him with a stinging put-down but I can't think of a single thing to say. As Fitz walks past the judo club he gives his parting shot:

'You know, maybe I should tell that skinny bird of yours what you're like. Yes, I'm sure Chloe would be really interested.'

I pull a face but I don't feel too good the way things have turned out. I feel even worse when I see Julie peering through the partition netting. She shakes her head and returns to her warm-up exercises.

Tuesday 22nd August
8.00 p.m.

'Well,' says Bobby sarcastically. 'That went well.'

'Oh, knock it off.'

'No, I thought you handled yourself really well.'

'Bobby, shut up. I'm not trying to chat Julie up. I'm not a two-timer. Not like some.'

He ignores the dig.

'No? And what if Julie showed some interest?'

'I'm going out with Chloe. Full stop. End of story.'

If only. Why does everything have to be so complicated? I mean, why can't I just shut Julie out of my mind and settle for what I've got? What's so all-fired difficult about that? I turn my key in the front door and walk into the hallway. Bobby's right, of course. Turning up on Julie's gym night was really stupid, just like going to the pony sanctuary that time. On both occasions I was asking for it and I got it. Julie's with Fitz. All I've done is make sure she stays with him. Talk about own goals.

'That you, Terry?' calls Mum.

'No,' I answer. 'The Boston Strangler.'

'There's a plate of sandwiches for you and Bobby,' says Mum, ignoring the flip reply. 'I assume he's with you.'

'Hi, Mrs Payne,' says Bobby brightly.

'Hi, Bobby.'

He tucks into the sandwiches while I turn on the radio. We're playing Ipswich. 7.45 p.m. kick-off so by now we should be 1–0 up at least.

'And Beckham's bringing the ball away,' says the commentator. 'United are still trying to get back on level terms.'

I stare at the radio in disbelief. What's going on? We can't be losing, not to a bunch of turnip-heads! No, I've heard it wrong. Must have.

'Just to remind you of the surprise scoreline,' come the chilling words. 'Ipswich are 1–0 up against the Champions.'

Bobby sprays sandwich crumbs all over the table.

'You're losing,' he says. 'To flipping Ipswich?'

Suddenly I can't eat. The news has me pacing up and down the kitchen. Not only are we losing, we're getting overrun in midfield. Well, thanks a bunch United, I was relying on you to cheer me up after what happened at the leisure centre, and this is what you do to me. The minutes tick by and we only have one decent effort on goal.

'Oh, come on, lads,' I say, 'You should be stuffing this shower.'

But they're stuffing us. It's been a night for stuffing. Fitz stuffed me at the leisure centre, stuffed me good style. Julie's face told me that much. Finally, seven minutes before half-time, we draw level. Beckham puts in a free kick and Wallwork dummies the ball. A soft goal but they all count. I feel a huge sense of relief. We'll walk it in the second half.

'So what happened to the new season's resolution?' asks Bobby, tucking into the cookies during the interval. 'What happened to "I'm not dumping Chloe"?'

'I'm not.'

'No, but you can't get the lovely Julie out of your head, can you?'

'Leave it, eh?'

'Sure, it's your problem.'

Too right. And so are United. In the second half they never quite get going and it stays at 1–1.

'Disappointing result,' observes Bobby at the final whistle.

'Yes,' I say. 'Sometimes things don't turn out the way they're supposed to.'

I think about Julie. Then I remember Fitz's threat to grass me up to Chloe.

Do they ever?

5

Saturday 26th August
10 a.m.

Dad's just been to pick up Amy. He's taking her and her friend Katie swimming. He asked if I wanted to come. I told him I was seeing Chloe. He doesn't argue or look disappointed. I think he's relieved. He's long since run out of original places to go.

'Did I hear you say you were seeing Chloe?' asks Mum.

'S'right.'

I emit the lowest teen-grunt I can manage. Does she have to harass me like this?

'Going somewhere nice?'

Time for teen-grunt two.

'Dunno. Just out.'

The doorbell rings.

'Oh, hello, Chloe love,' says Mum.

Could she be more gushy? I'm half-expecting her to cut cucumber sandwiches and pour ginger beer.

'Hi, Mrs Payne,' says Chloe.

She sounds like she's glad to see Mum. How do people do that? How do they make everybody they meet feel important?

'Are we going?' I ask.

I feel tetchy and on edge. I can't get Fitz's threat out of my mind.

'OK.'

The moment we hit the street Chloe starts going on about how nice my mum is and what a shame people have to split up and don't I think honesty matters in a relationship. Guilt-mites are burrowing under my skin.

'I don't know how you can cover for Bobby the way you do.'

I stop dead.

'You know about Bobby?'

'I know he's seeing somebody. I think Caitlin does too.'

'But how?'

I suddenly realise I've just confirmed her suspicions.

'Just the way he acts,' says Chloe. 'He's a player.'

'You've been watching too many American chat shows,' I tell her.

I see her on an imaginary TV screen. Go Jerry, go Jerry.

'But I'm right, aren't I? He *is* seeing somebody else?'

We've reached Eccleston Street. We've been going nowhere in particular and ended up in the town centre.

'Promise you won't say anything to Caitlin.'

'Of course not. That's up to Bobby.'

'He met this girl on work experience, Rosie.'

Chloe shakes her head slowly.

'I think that's disgusting, don't you?'

It's like Fitzy is right here with us. This little Fitzy-devil is perched on Chloe's shoulder grinning at me, enjoying my discomfort.

'Terry?'

'What?'

'Don't you think it's awful when people cheat?'

The guilt-mites are making my skin crawl.

'Oh yeah, awful.'

I mustn't have sounded too convincing because Chloe continues the interrogation. All she needs now is an anglepoise lamp and a set of thumbscrews. Ve haf vays of making you squirm.

'You wouldn't ever do that to me, would you?'

By now it feels like the guilt-mites are drawing blood.

'No, never.'

'It would break my heart if you weren't honest with me.'

It's quiet at this end of the street. I pull her to me and plant a kiss on her lips. The next moment we're kissing hard, lips slightly parted. She doesn't know I did it to shut her up. She thinks I'm being romantic. In fact, I'm being desperate.

I wouldn't normally be out so close to kick-off, but I've got to warn Bobby that Caitlin's suspicious. OK, so he's been asking for it, but he's still my mate. I knock on the door. Bobby's mum answers. A cocker spaniel is scrabbling to push past her and jump on me. The big boyfriend must be there.

'Is Bobby in?'

'He's in his room.'

She turns and shouts up the stairs.

'Bobby, it's Terry.'

I climb the stairs wondering just how to break the news without incriminating myself.

'All right, Terry,' he says.

I look round the room. There are apple cores, yoghurt cartons and sweet wrappers everywhere. I shove two pizza boxes off a beanbag and sit down.

'Didn't expect you,' says Bobby. 'I thought you were out with Chloe.'

'I was. I came to tell you something.'

'Yes?'

'Caitlin's on to you.'

Bobby laughs.

'That all? So what's new? She's been quizzing me all week.'

'What did you say?'

'Nothing.'

I stare at him.

'How can you be so cool about it?'

'So she finds out. I've still got Rosie.'

'Bobby, you're disgusting.'

'Says who?'

'Chloe ... and me.'

Bobby laughs again.

'You don't sound too sure.'

'Sure I'm sure.'

I want to be like Chloe, one hundred per cent sure of how she feels. I'm trying to take the moral high ground, but it isn't easy when you're sinking into a beanbag.

'You ought to be faithful to one person, honest. You shouldn't cheat.'

'Who's that talking? You or Chloe?'

I get annoyed.

'Me, you lower life-form. I've always thought that.'

Bobby chuckles.

'Not a very good example of it though, are you?'

'Meaning?'

'Meaning there are things I could tell Chloe.'

I blush.

'No, there aren't! I've never gone out with anybody else. Not even kissed anyone else. She's the first one, the *only* one.'

'OK, so maybe you haven't actually gone out with anyone else, but you'd like to.'

'The difference between me and you,' I retort hotly, 'is that I can control myself.'

Bobby roars with laughter. I feel totally stupid. I have this picture of myself as a demented professor wrestling with a rebellious robot hand: I CAN control myself!

'Honestly, Terry, you take everything so seriously. You sound like a middle-aged man.'

He looks at his watch.

'Here's something you should take seriously. It's kick-off in ten minutes. If we go now we can listen to the footy round yours.'

'Why not here?'

'Slughead's here.'

I frown. Slughead?

'Mum's boyfriend.'

Of course. Big guy. Cocker spaniel. Slughead.

'Ours it is.'

Saturday 26th August
3.30 p.m.

It's mixed fortunes so far. Bobby and I have got good reason to be happy. Both Man U and Everton are winning, but so are Leeds,

Arsenal and Liverpool.

To make matters worse, Michael Owen's scored for Liverpool. Out on the Isle of Man, Julie and Fitz are probably hugging each other in celebration right now. Unfortunately, Chloe just came round so we're having to put up with her interruptions. When the Owen goal went in I cursed loudly.

'I didn't know you swore,' said Chloe, disapprovingly.

What is it with her? Does she have to be Miss Nice from Nice Avenue, Nicetown? Bobby is taking care not to look at her. Every time their eyes meet she gives him this searing glare.

She's definitely got him down as a love-rat. When Bobby goes to the toilet, she whispers into my ear:

'I think he's a bad influence. You act differently when he's around.'

When Chloe goes to get a can of Coke, Bobby whispers into my ear:

'She's going to make you as boring as she is.'

He mimics her voice:

'Terry, I didn't know you swore.'

I laugh, which makes Chloe scowl when she comes back with the Coke. Andy Cole makes up for it at West Ham. He's just put us 2–0 up. Everton are 2–0 up as well. Unfortunately, Liverpool have just taken a 3–0 lead.

'Why does it bother you so much if Liverpool are winning?' asks Chloe.

She sounds genuinely bewildered.

'They're the enemy,' I explain.

Of course, I don't explain about Julie and Fitz.

'It *is* only a game,' says Chloe.

Just how much it isn't a game she discovers in the closing stages of the second half. Everton squander their 2–0 lead against Derby.

Bobby starts calling his players all the names under the sun. Then in the final three minutes we throw it away as well, having to settle for a 2–2 draw. The only saving grace of a disappointing afternoon is that Liverpool have drawn as well, surrendering a three-goal lead to draw 3–3. Dad arrives with Amy and Katie. Stevie Wonder's 'Superstition' is playing. I tell him the score.

'We've got to do something about that defence,' he says, shaking his head. 'Fancy squandering a 2–0 lead.'

'We did the same,' says Bobby. 'Anyway, I'm getting off, Terry.'

'See you, Bobby.'

Chloe stands on the doorstep with her arms folded. She doesn't say anything to him.

'I thought I might come round tomorrow,' I say, deciding to be nice to Dad. 'Watch the Celtic–Rangers game with you.'

Dad grimaces.

'Sorry, son,' he says. 'I've got plans.'

I see Mum looking through the net curtains at us. I know exactly what plans he means.

'Who is she?' I ask.

'You'll meet her soon enough. I'll be in touch, Terry.'

'Yes, see you, Dad.'

Chloe has been listening. Later, when we're alone she says:

'First Bobby, now your dad. You wouldn't treat me like that, would you, Terry?'

No, Chloe, I never will. I've made up my mind. Come the start of the school year I'm not going to so much as look at Julie. The funny thing is, I can't quite come up with the right words to reassure Chloe. For the second time that day I can only think of one way to answer. I kiss her.

Part Three

The Girl

Or

Belgian Suicide

1

There's a kind of grudging admiration in Bobby's voice.

'I never thought you'd make it this far.'

Neither did I. We've been going out for nearly six weeks. We've started a new term together, moved up to Year 11 together, everything we've done together.

'I've told you, haven't I?' I say. 'It's me and Chloe, full stop, end of story. We're together.' We've just left Chloe and Caitlin at the bus stop. This afternoon is strictly boys only. We're going round to Dad's flat to watch the England–Germany game.

'And you never give Julie a second's thought?'

I couldn't say that. In fact, I find myself thinking about her most of the time. It's not like I ask her in, she just strolls through the back door of my mind. The last few weeks haven't been easy, watching her and Fitz talking in the canteen or the library, heads so close together they almost touch. But I've pretended not to notice. By steering clear of Julie, I may even have salvaged a little of my dignity.

'I'm with Chloe.'

Bobby smiles in that superior way of his.

'Let's get our skates on,' I say. 'We're going to miss the kick-off at this rate.'

Of course, there's no chance of that happening. Bobby takes the hint. Time to talk about something else.

'What's your prediction?' he asks.

'Score draw.'

'You're kidding! Did you see Germany at Euro 2000?'

'Did you see *us*?'

'Yes, but we've picked up since. Remember the friendly against

France? That was a new beginning.'

I'd love to believe that, but I'm a bit short on optimism just lately. United have gone three games without a win. It's the first time that's happened since 1992. We're actually in third place in our group of the Champions League. It doesn't bode well for England when you think the four United lads are the spine of the national team.

'We'll see.'

We invest in a bag of sweets and jog up the stairs to the flat. The door opens and we come face to face with a blonde woman in her early forties. I check the leather trousers and short bomber jacket and exchange glances with Bobby.

'Mutton dressed as lamb,' I sneer as she clatters downstairs on stiletto heels.

'More like mutton dressed as mutton,' says Bobby, eager to back me up.

That's when Dad appears. He gives us daggers. He obviously heard the exchange.

'Thats your new squeeze?' asks Bobby.

I wince. The last thing I want to hear about right now is Dad's *squeeze*.

'That's Muriel,' says Dad.

He looks about as uncomfortable as you can get without bathing in cold baked beans. It's the first time I've run into this Muriel, though I have found evidence of her from time to time. There was hairspray in the bathroom, a pair of tights stuffed behind a cushion and a bottle of nail varnish on the coffee table. She was in quite a hurry to leave. Looks like Dad was trying to chase her out before we arrived.

'Anyway, come in, lads. Make yourselves at home.'

I look round the living room for any evidence of Muriel's latest stay. There isn't any, not even a lipstick mark on the mugs.

'So how'd you meet her, Geoff?' asks Bobby.

I glare at him. He grins back in mock-innocence.

'We go to the same gym,' says Dad, taking a few Red Bulls out of the fridge and shaking out a king-size tub of Pringles into a bowl. 'We got talking and kind of clicked...'

He sees the expression on my face and trails off.

'So what's the scoreline going to be, lads?'

'I say 2–1,' says Bobby. 'Terry's going for a draw.'

'A draw? Come on, Terry, you've got to be positive. Beckham, Scholes and Cole. That's worth a goal or two.'

I shrug. I'm in no mood to banter with him. I'm still gagging on that woman's scent. Mum would have hated her. Muriel looked an inch or two taller and nearly a stone lighter.

'Oh, you've got to be kidding!'

Bobby's exclamation breaks the silence.

'What's the matter?'

'Have you heard Keegan's team selection? Southgate in midfield. What's he doing *there*? Why not give Joe Cole a chance? We need to be creative.'

Dad nods, still giving me the occasional wary glance.

'The fellow can't make his mind up. One minute it's Kev the Cavalier, then it's Mr Defensive. There's no pattern to his management.'

Dad's right there. There's no pattern to England's play, either. For the first ten minutes the Germans waltz round us. Then, on fourteen minutes, Hamann puts a free kick past Seaman.

'Where was the wall?' Bobby demands, 'Where was the flipping wall?'

'Where was the keeper?' asks Dad.

I just sit munching a chunk of chocolate. I told them.

'Might have guessed it'd be a Liverpool player who put us one down,' rants Dad.

I feel like pointing out that, as a German, Hamann is supposed to score against us. Only a Man U fan could manage to blame Liverpool for this fiasco, but, what the heck, anything to take a pop at the Scousers! For the rest of the first half, we slip and slide in the mud. Michael Owen is particularly useless. He's like a schoolboy running round aimlessly while the big German defenders look on, completely untroubled. Bobby's so gutted by the performance he sits out the final ten minutes of the half open-mouthed, the same Pringle perched unchewed on his lower lip.

'Rubbish,' he announces when the half-time whistles blows. 'Utter flipping rubbish.'

Nobody's arguing. There isn't even an inquest during the interval. When Bobby goes for a pee, Dad leans across.

'Sorry about Muriel,' he says. 'I meant to have her out of here before you arrived.'

'Forget it,' I say. 'No skin off my nose.'

'I just wanted...'

'Leave it, Dad,' I tell him. 'It's your life. You can do what you want with it.'

And that's the cue for Bobby to return.

'At least it can't get any worse,' he says, oblivious to the tension between us.

True, but it doesn't get much better. Becks plays himself into the ground and comes close to equalising. When he limps off with a knee injury, England's last hope goes with him. At the final whistle, Bobby and I bombard the TV screen with Pringles.

'Hang on there, lads,' says Dad. 'It's me that has to clean this lot up.'

Bobby gives him a long, hard look.

'You mean you clean up?'

'Of course I do.'

'Funny,' says Bobby. 'I thought men only did that to impress women.'

He sees me looking at him, and remembers Muriel.

'Oh yeah, I forgot.'

Saturday 7th October
6.00 p.m.

Even Bobby isn't insensitive enough to mention Muriel in front of Mum, so when we get back to my house, he restricts himself to a few comments about England's performance. He even asks Mum if she's lost weight.

'I wish,' she says. 'With my diets, it's a case of one pound off, two pounds back.'

'What was that about?' I ask Bobby when we get to my room.

'Come again?'

'Asking my mum if she's lost weight. You know she hasn't.'

'Dunno. I suppose I felt sorry for her. Something to do with seeing that Muriel.'

'What did you think of her?'

115

'Sad old slapper,' says Bobby, never one to be too subtle. 'See that tan? Straight out of a bottle.'

'Mm,' I say. 'But you can see why Dad likes her. I mean, you can tell she works out.'

Bobby nods and traces an hourglass figure with his hands.

'Doesn't look like your folks will be getting back together, does it?'

'No.'

'I told you what it would be like, Terry mate.'

'Yes, I know. Stuff happens.'

Just then, Mum shouts up the stairs.

'Have you heard the news?' she calls.

'What news?'

'It's Kevin Keegan. He's resigned as England manager.'

In stereo, we say:

'Stuff happens.'

2

I'm making my way home from Chloe's house. Her mum and dad asked me over for tea. Bobby laughed his socks off when I told him.

'You're too young for all that malarkey,' he said. 'At our age, girls are for fun. Save all that commitment stuff for when you're over the hill. When you're thirty, or something.'

Funnily enough, tea at Chloe's wasn't as painful as you might think. They were even watching the Derby–Liverpool game when I arrived. Thinking about it, I was the only one who showed much interest in it. Chloe probably got her parents to have it on. She's thoughtful like that. I have to admit to feeling a pinch of guilt. She's so thoughtful, so nice she makes me want to kick myself. How come I find her niceness so irritating? How come I don't feel more strongly about her? I'm fond of her, I really am. But is 'fond' enough? I've tried to make the feelings grow, but it isn't like cultivating a yucca. Some things you can water and water, and they still stay the same size. Even while we were sitting together on the settee, Julie was there, like Banquo's ghost. (In case you're wondering, we've just done *Macbeth*. I thought killing the old king was sick. Bobby thought it was a cool career move. Seems we're as far apart in our views on politics as we are in our attitudes to women. Unbelievably, he's still managing to string Caitlin and Rosie along. Frailty, thy name is Bobby. (And yes, I do know that isn't from *Macbeth*.)

I jog across the road by the police station and walk towards the Fusillier. I'm passing the library when I hear familiar laughter. It's Julie. I'd know her voice anywhere. It's always with me. For a moment, I think she's alone. Then I see him.

Fitz.

He unfastens his jacket and drapes it over her shoulders. Thinks he's gallantry personified, that one! Julie glances back at him and smiles. I find myself retreating into the darkness and watching them. I can feel the green monster clawing its way up my throat.

Fitz slips his arms round her waist from behind and she leans back against him. They look comfortable together. Disgust fills me like cold jelly. He's animated, skittish. He's obviously full of Liverpool's 4–0 thrashing of the Rams. United won too this weekend, but Liverpool's victory this afternoon has taken some of the gloss off our win at Leicester. The old enemy are tucked in just behind us in fourth place.

The old enemy. There's only one enemy in my life just now, and that's Fitz. He's got the girl. My girl. He's also got my place in the Year 11 team. I haven't played once this season. No, it's all Fitz. He's the star man. He can't put a foot wrong. I start planning horrible deaths. Just when I'm imagining him choking on a shredded Liverpool scarf, I see him lean forward and nuzzle Julie's cheek. His hands start to move up over her stomach, but she stops him with a playful slap.

'Oh no, you don't,' she says, but her tone of voice is too gentle for my liking. The least he deserved was a slap across the face.

I see her bus coming. She disengages herself from his embrace. She gives him a quick peck as it pulls up at the stop, but he wants more. He presses his lips against hers. I can feel my nails digging into my palms. I could do him some serious damage. Just give me the opportunity. Julie finally draws away from him and gets on the bus. She gives him a wave and starts to move down the bus. Fitz stands there for a couple of minutes like a cat that's had the canary. He sets off home with a spring in his step. I walk away with a heavy tread.

Wednesday 18th October
7.20 p.m.

Bobby's struggling to keep up. It's on account of the day I've had. For starters, I was woken by Mum hammering on the bedroom door.

'How many times?' she yells.

'How many times what?'

'How many times have I told you?'

'How many times have you told me *what*?'

I wasn't trying to be funny. I just didn't know what she was on about.

'Leaving loose change in your pockets, that's what! A ten pence piece is jamming the pipe in the washing machine. You've blocked it again. The stupid thing won't drain.'

So what do I say in reply?

'Didn't you check my trousers before you put them in?'

It was just about the worst thing I could have come up with.

'*Me* check them! Terry, you're fifteen, not five. I expect you to check them yourself.'

That was bad enough, but worse was to follow. After that dose of earache from Mum, I was so fed up, I left home without my English coursework. That meant a fifteen minute detention from Spotty. Then, living up to the old saying that disasters come in threes, Six Guns told us about the new PE timetable. We're going to get a lesson a week at the fitness suite at the sports centre, the one Dad goes to.

'What's wrong with that?' Bobby asked. 'It's a gym. A gym, Terry! Where else do you get to watch women sweat?'

'That's the point,' I reminded him. 'Julie will be there, but so will Fitz, rubbing my nose in it. I get to see the pair of them sweat.'

Bobby gave me a sideways look.

'And this is the man who's only got eyes for Chloe Blackburn!'

That last little jibe put me in a nark I still haven't got out of. So here I am, storming down the street with Bobby panting along behind.

'Are you sure your old man won't mind us landing on him like this?'

'I don't care if he minds or not,' I tell him. 'I'm not missing the Champions League, but I'm not staying in the house with *her*.'

Her is Mum. Not satisfied with having a go at me over the washing machine at breakfast time, she met me at the door tonight with a bag of washing.

'I got this out of your room,' she said.

'You went in my room!' I cried, all indignant. 'It's private.'

'It's a tip,' snapped Mum. 'Can't you put anything in the laundry basket?'

So what did I say?

'Oh, get a life, Mum. Dad has. I've met his new girlfriend. She doesn't go on about the laundry, and she doesn't have to OD on Hobnobs, either.'

I could have bitten my tongue off for saying it, but I soon stopped feeling sorry for her. Mum immediately launched into this mega-rant about disgusting teenage boys. I shouted back, and before you know it, there was civil war in the Payne household. So here I am, on my way to Dad's flat to watch United play PSV Eindhoven. I ask you, there's qualification to the second stage hanging in the balance, and Mum gives me aggravation over a few pairs of socks!

'Think your dad'll have anything to eat?' asks Bobby.

'Why, haven't you had anything?'

'No, Slughead's round ours.'

So that's why Bobby turned up on the doorstep. He's been turfed out by Cocker Spaniel Man and he needs somewhere to go.

'You need to eat properly,' I tell him.

Bobby shakes his head: 'Percentage of men who plan their meals: 25. Percentage of women who plan their meals: 90. It's in my genes not to eat properly.'

We ring the bell and Dad answers.

'Oh, Terry.'

'Yes,' I say. 'Terry. Your son, remember. I need a favour. I've had a row with Mum. Can I watch the match here?'

Dad hesitates, so I put on my best hangdog expression.

'Yes sure, why not?'

I'm settling down to watch the build-up when I hear water running.

'Cutting it fine, aren't you?' I ask, 'Do you think you've got time for a shower before kick-off?'

Dad's face goes as red as a United shirt.

'It isn't my shower.'

'So who...? Oh.'

Bobby gives a frown of incomprehension, then goes wide-eyed.

'Oh, Muriel.'

Which is the cue for her entrance. She pads in wearing a white towelling robe just as Terry Venables is predicting a narrow United victory.

'Oh, hello, lads,' she says. 'Geoff didn't tell me we had company.'

'We're not company,' I tell her. 'I'm family and he's...'

I'm not sure quite how to introduce Bobby.

'He's an Evertonian.'

To my horror, Muriel responds with this amazing donkey bray.

Hurrgh-aw, hurrgh-aw, hurrgh-aw.

Muriel! Mule is more like it.

The moment she leaves the room to get changed, Bobby winks.

'Didn't she make an ass of herself?'

Dad smiles thinly.

'That's her only drawback,' he says. 'The laugh from hell.'

But it's kick-off time, so who cares?

Wednesday 18th October
9.16 p.m.

'No!' I cry, holding my head. '*No!*'

Van Bommel's just equalised for PSV. We could be out of the Champions League. We were 1–0 up after eight minutes through Teddy Sheringham's header, and flying. Now we could be on our way out of the competition.

'Come on!' I yell as play restarts. 'You can't just throw it away.'

'Takes his football seriously, doesn't he?' says Mule.

She follows up with a manic bray: Hurrgh-aw, hurrgh-aw, hurrgh-aw.

Me and Dad give her daggers simultaneously. There are some things you don't joke about. Suddenly, United have shaken themselves out of their torpor. They're pouring forward. After six minutes, Paul Scholes bursts through, flicking the ball in the air before slamming it home. Barely five minutes later, Dwight Yorke streaks clear of his marker to score our third.

'Yaaarrgh!'

Dad and I are leaping all round the room. Bobby's polishing off the butterscotch ice cream.

'What a terrible noise,' says Mule, wincing at our celebrations.

Me, Dad and Bobby exchange glances then roar with laughter.

Mule looks confused.

Chloe has her uses. She's just brokered a peace summit between me and Mum.

'Sorry I blew my top,' says Mum.

'Sorry I mentioned *her*. Mum, she's not a patch on you.'

There's only one way to seal the peace treaty.

'Friday night sugar hunt?' I suggest.

Chloe looks puzzled.

'House tradition,' I explain. 'At the end of the week, we forget diets and dental hygiene and stuff ourselves with sweets. You game?'

Chloe laughs.

'Just you try and stop me.'

So we set off for the offie. It's a Caramel for Mum, Maltesers for Amy, a Flake for Chloe and a Mars bar for me.

'We'll need that lesson at the fitness suite after this,' says Chloe, linking arms with me.

Well, gee thanks for reminding me. My mind flashes to Julie and Fitz.

'Something wrong?' asks Chloe.

'No, why?'

'You went all serious.'

'Just thinking about the game against Leeds tomorrow,' I say, lying through my teeth. 'I'm getting psyched up for it.'

'You and your football,' says Chloe.

I think of Julie and Fitz cheering on Liverpool against Leicester.

'Yes, me and my football.'

Friday 20th October
10.30 p.m.

When I get in from Chloe's, Amy is already tucked up in bed. Mum's in the living room.

'What're you watching?'

'I don't know.'

I look at the TV screen.

'So what've you got it on for?'

'Background noise.'

'Why?'

Mum looks up. For the first time I realise she's been crying.

'Are you OK?'

'Not really, no.'

I give her a questioning look. Even as I'm inviting her to explain, I'm half-wishing she wouldn't.

'I'm lonely, Terry.'

'But you've got us. Me, Amy...'

She smiles.

'I know, and you're great kids. But I need more, I need...'

'Dad?'

She closes her eyes for a moment.

'I thought I did. Did you know he's the only lad I've ever been out with?'

'You're kidding!'

Which is rich coming from me.

'It's the God's honest truth. Until this summer I never even thought about our marriage. It was just there. Now... Oh, I don't know what to think.'

'But you'd have him back?'

'I think so.'

Only *think* so!

'You would, wouldn't you?'

'Terry, this other woman, I don't know any more. Nobody wants to be second best.'

'You're not!'

Mum shakes her head.

'Tell your dad that. He wants her, this Muriel.'

She gets up and walks towards the door. The way she does it tells me she doesn't want me to follow.

'He certainly doesn't want me.'

Saturday 21st October
1.40 p.m.

'So,' Chloe asks, hands on hips, 'Can we go out *now*?'

'I just want to hear what Fergie's got to say,' I say, waving her away like a troublesome fly.

I ignore her snort of indignation and strain to catch the great man's words.

'This is stupid,' says Chloe. 'You've seen the match. Isn't that enough for you?'

'No,' I tell her. 'A big match is an event. Build-up, game, inquest. If you're a footy fan, you buy into the whole package. It's the pattern of life.'

Chloe shakes her head. I don't know why she's so put out. If United–Leeds hadn't been an 11.30 a.m. kick-off, she would never have got me to town. As it is, I'm making a big sacrifice. I'm giving up an afternoon of willing Arsenal, Newcastle and Liverpool – especially Liverpool – to lose.

'*Now* are we ready?' she asks.

I drag myself away from the TV. When you beat Leeds 3–0 you want to milk every glorious moment.

'Are you off?' calls Mum.

'Yes, just going.'

'Have fun.'

Chloe winks.

'We will.'

She will. I can't believe I agreed to this. We're going shopping. That's right – shopping! Chloe wants a new pair of jeans, and she expects me to stand like a lemon while she tries on a zillion pairs. I know what it's all about, of course. It's this couple thing. She wants us to traipse round Liverpool proclaiming: 'Look at us, we're an item.' All of a sudden, I'm finding loads of little faults with Chloe: the pinched face, the freckled nose, the reedy voice.

Why can't she be ... why can't she be Julie?

We're waiting at the station when I hear familiar voices. I look up and see a blur of red and gold on the pedestrian bridge. Julie and Fitz, Kelly and Gary. They stand talking just along the platform. It's like they haven't seen us, but I know Fitz has. Suddenly he's talking loudly. I know it's for my benefit.

'Leicester, we'll sweep them aside. Move over, Mancs, now it's our turn.'

I lean forward, stealing a look at Julie. She looks dazzling in her Liverpool away shirt. I'm vaguely aware of Chloe rattling away in my left ear. She's just asked me a question.

'Yes,' I answer.

'Yes!?'

The tone of Chloe's voice tell me I've said the wrong thing.

'I mean no.'

'Are you listening to me, Terry?' she asks.

She spots Julie and gives me a lethal stare. I think she's always had an inkling how I feel. It's the cue for Fitz to come over.

'Well, if it isn't Terry and Chloe,' he says, heavy on the final syllable.

I'm squirming. He's got something on me and he'll have no qualms about using it.

'Got yourself a catch there, Chloe,' he says.

Gary and Kelly laugh appreciatively.

'Oh, clear off, Fitz,' says Chloe.

'Keep your wig on, girl,' says Fitz.

The train pulls up.

'One piece of advice, though,' he says as he boards. 'Keep an eye on Terry here. I hear he's a bit of a lad.'

'What was all that about?' asks Chloe.

'Ignore him,' I tell her. 'He's just trying to wind us up.'

Trying, and succeeding. All the way to Lime Street it's 'Trust matters' and, 'I couldn't stand it if you turned out like Bobby' and, 'There definitely isn't anything you want to tell me?'

No, Chloe, there's *nothing* I want to tell you.

For the next two centuries I trail round the shops after Chloe. Between shops, I clock the latest scores. It's bad news: West Ham 1 Arsenal 2; Liverpool 1 Leicester 0. Arsenal are breathing down our necks with Liverpool neatly poised in third place.

'Haven't you made your mind up yet?' I complain.

'I think so,' says Chloe. 'I'm going back to that first shop.'

'The first shop!' I groan. 'So why didn't you get them right away and save us all this wandering round?'

'You don't understand women, do you?' she asks.

I think of Julie snuggled up to Fitz and shake my head.

'No, not one bit.'

Tuesday 24th October
7.45 p.m.

I hear the doorbell ring and close my eyes, willing it to be for Mum or Amy. Not Chloe, please not Chloe.

'Oh, hello, Chloe love,' says Mum.

The girl's timing is impeccable. She manages to arrive just as the United–Anderlecht match kicks off in Belgium.

'Oh, not football *again*,' groans Chloe. 'But it's Tuesday night.'

'Champions League,' I explain. 'If we win tonight, we qualify for the next stage.'

'I see,' says Chloe, who clearly doesn't.

So there she sits at the kitchen table while I listen to the game on the radio. I don't know anybody with digital TV so this is the best I can do. I've been looking forward to the match all day, but it doesn't go according to plan. For starters, there's Chloe with a face like a smacked bottom. Then there's the little matter of the score.

Anderlecht 1, Man United 0. Despair.

Anderlecht 2, Man United 0. Disbelief.

Anderlecht 2, Man United 1. Relief.

Dennis Irwin's penalty just before half-time is a glimmer of hope.

'How much longer?' asks Chloe, bringing me a Coke.

'Forty-five minutes. You know, the second half.'

That face again. A pinched bottom.

'Look, Chloe,' I say, 'You don't have to stay.'

'Is that it?' she says. 'Do you want me to go?'

Say yes, you dope. You know this isn't working. Be brave for once.

'No, of course I don't want you to go.'

Coward!

'I just mean, you look bored.'

'I *am* bored, Terry. It's a wonder that stupid Bobby isn't here too.'

'No, he's out with Rosie. Or is it Caitlin?'

I pick up the *Mirror* and start scribbling on a piece of scrap paper.

'Now what are you doing?'

'Adjusting the Group G table to see how we stand if the score stays the same.'

'Terry,' she says, 'That is so ... *sad.*'

I ignore her. The teams are out for the second half. In the opening exchanges, it's all United. But is the damage already done? Have our defensive frailties in the first half cost us the match? We're on top, all right, but no breakthrough.

'I don't believe it,' I murmur, with a quarter of an hour left. 'We're not going to make it.'

I catch Chloe's eye. Maybe she's thinking the same about us.

Fergie throws on Solskjaer for Irwin, an attacker for a defender.

'He's going for it,' I hiss.

But Anderlecht hold out. I slump against the freezer in despair. There is only one flicker of hope on a bleak evening. At least PSV Eindhoven have been held to a draw in Kiev. That means we hold on to second place in the group.

'Can I talk now?' asks Chloe.

'Sure,' I say, reaching to switch off the radio.

That's when everything falls apart. The presenter announces a correction. PSV have *won* in Kiev. That puts us third and on course for elimination. I bury my face in my hands. Belgian suicide.

'Oh, grow up, Terry,' says Chloe. 'It's only a game.'

'Do you ever think before you open that stupid mouth?' I snap.

Chloe's face drains of colour. Moments later, she bursts into tears. Let it go, I tell myself. Remember what Bobby says: sometimes you've got to be cruel to be kind. This relationship isn't working. So do us both a favour and do nothing.

'Terry, I didn't think you could be like this.'

Instinctively, I offer her a tissue. She shrugs my hand away. Don't do it. Remember, cruel to be kind. But I ignore my inner voice.

'Go on, take it.'

Then, the fateful words:

'I was upset about the match. I didn't mean it. Honest.'

You did mean it, Terry Payne, and you're not being honest. Chloe takes the tissue and gives me a thin smile, like she's reminding herself she likes me. I can't stand seeing her miserable, so I do the nice thing, the coward's thing. As if trying to prove I don't understand her, or myself, I do the only thing I ever do when we hit a crisis.

I kiss her.

3

'This is agony,' I whisper.

'Are you feeling all right?' asks Bobby.

No, Bobby, I'm not feeling all right. The cause of my agony is Julie. She's right there in front of me, just a heartbeat away. Bobby and I are on the row of cross-trainers behind her, pushing pedals, pulling handles. Julie and Fitz are side by side on the treadmills, pounding the track in unison. That's right, it's the first of 11S's sessions at the fitness suite.

And it really is agony.

I don't mean the exercise, either. The wall in front of us is mirrored, so here I am looking at the girl of my dreams from two angles at once. Julie Carter is jogging. No, whatever she's doing, you couldn't call it jogging. She's running hard, taking long, athletic strides. But it seems effortless. Her feet hardly seem to touch the treadmill. She's hovering, that's what she's doing, hovering over the moving track, her arms moving as gracefully as featherless wings. I've tried not to look at her, but there isn't a thing I can do about it. My eyes have taken on a life of their own. They're drawn to every movement of her body in her black and violet body-suit, every flick of her plaited, coal-black hair. She's an eye-magnet. But here's the reason for my agony. She's not my girl. She's with Fitz. And doesn't he want to rub it in! Every time I steal the slightest glance at her, he's flashing a knowing look my way, as if to say:

Dream on, loser. The girl is mine.

But still I look, and every time I look his eyes meet mine.

The girl is mine.

Julie seems totally unaware of my interest, but she must have noticed. All I want is a glance, the ghost of a smile, anything to say there is something between us.

What am I saying?

She's got her boyfriend right there beside her and here I am, Dufus of the Century, willing her to give me the come-on. As if the humiliating presence of Fitz isn't enough, Chloe will be back any minute. Her group is getting the guided tour. Small weights room, aerobic suite, spa bath, sauna, steam room.

'Nice bum,' says Bobby, just a little bit too loud.

Fitz glances round, not at Bobby but at me. And he's grinning. Like a cat that's licked the cream.

Nice bum, his eyes are telling me. *Too right.*

And it's mine.

She's mine.

Which has me dreaming up The World's Most Appalling Gym Accidents:

Promising footballer shredded in treadmill horror.

Teenager sucked into extractor fan. Bloodstains found as far as Huyton.

GCSE student strangled in gym. Over-long trainer laces to blame.

But nothing can touch Frisky Fitzy. The boy's fireproof. The Teflon kid, that's him.

I'm still scraping the gore from my imagination when Chloe returns. She gives a little frown when she sees how close I am to Julie.

'Nearly done?' she asks, a definite coolness in her voice.

'Yes,' I say. 'I'm going for a shower.'

'Cold one?' asks Bobby.

The joke goes down like a lead balloon. As Chloe stamps towards the female changing rooms, I give Bobby daggers.

'What?' he asks, all innocent.

I push past him and take a shallow breath. It's been a tough hour.

Like I said earlier:

Agony.

Fitz and Gary Tudor have taken over the changing rooms. They're laughing like hyenas and flicking each other with towels. I find myself scowling.

'What's up with you?' asks Fitz, spotting the look on my face.

'Nothing that couldn't be put right by you falling down a lift shaft,' I tell him, flushing beetroot at being rumbled.

Fitz smirks.

'Watching the match tonight?' he asks.

'Yes, what of it?'

'I hope you get stuffed,' he says. 'I hope Kiev put five past you.'

He's touched a raw nerve. United need to win to qualify for the next stage of the Champions League. We've thrown it away before. Against Gothenberg, Monaco, Borussia Dortmund. I couldn't stand another disappointment.

'I can't see that happening,' says Gary Tudor. 'But Kiev might get a draw. If that happens, the Mancs still go out.'

'Dream on,' I say, trying to sound more confident than I feel.

They give these big, forced laughs and head for the showers.

'You're going out, Manc,' they chorus. 'Ki-ev, Ki-ev.'

'Ignore them,' says Bobby. 'What's the difference between a Liverpool fan and a kettle?'

'Don't know.'

'A kettle can sing.'

Bobby makes me feel better, but not for long. A couple of minutes later, Fitz and Gary are back. Fitz is showing off a photograph and looking round at me.

'Let's have a butcher's,' says Gary.

Paul Scully and Jamie Sneddon join the huddle. Scully gives a low whistle.

'Lucky dog,' he says.

'Show the Manc,' says Gary. 'Let him know what he's missing.'

Fitz flashes the photo. It's of Fitz and Julie. I knew they went to a Halloween party a week last Sunday, but I'd never seen their costumes. In the pic, Fitz is dressed as an executioner. As for Julie, she's...

She's...

Ohmigod, she's stunning!

She's wearing a red miniskirt and top, red tights and shoes and little red horns. My angel, dressed as a gorgeous devil.

'Put it away,' I tell him.

'Got any of Chloe?' asks Gary. 'What did she go as?'

'Stick insect,' says Fitz.

'No, with that hair and that figure she could pass for a matchstick,' says Scully.

'Get stuffed!'

'Oo-ooh!'

'Poor old Terry,' says Fitz. 'Stuck with the wrong girl and about to get booted out of Europe.'

'At least we're in Europe,' I retort.

I'm acutely aware that I'm not defending Chloe, and I feel terrible.

'What about you? Beaten by Leeds and struggling to qualify in the UEFA Cup against some Czech no-hopers.'

Fitz shakes his head.

'And what about the great Michael Owen?' I ask, following him to the changing room doors.

'He's injured,' says Fitz. 'He had to have a brain scan after a head injury.'

'Two,' I say, correcting him.

We're out in the foyer.

'What?'

'Owen had two brain scans,' I tell him. 'And do you know why?'

'No, but I'm sure you're going to tell me.'

'Because they couldn't find his brain the first time.'

I'm warming to my theme.

'Let's face it, he isn't the sharpest blade of grass in the lawn. I bet there are cauliflowers with a bigger IQ. That's right, he's got the intelligence of a brussels sprout!'

For some reason, Fitz is grinning. I turn round and my heart turns to blancmange. Julie's looking right at me. There's me having a whale of a time slagging off her hero, and she's been listening the whole way through. That's one thing I have to say for myself. My timing is brilliant...

...Just brilliant!

I'm watching the match at home.

Alone.

Dad's gone out for a meal with Mule. Mum's taken Amy to a friend's birthday party. Bobby's gone out with Caitlin. Or is it Rosie? Either way, all I've got for company is a can of Red Bull and a packet of crisps.

'Come on, lads. Bury them.'

I can just hear Fitz if we fail to win.

'Ki-ev! Ki-ev!'

These Ukrainians have just become honorary Scousers.

We start brightly, taking the game to them. The first fifteen minutes are played completely in their half. Giggsy's running the show, turning their defence inside out with his mazy runs. But with a quarter of an hour gone, we still haven't scored. I'm getting anxious.

'Come on!'

After eighteen minutes United turn up the heat. Sheringham clears out of defence, the ball bounces around the penalty area for a few seconds and Teddy's on hand to stab it home.

'Sher-in-gham!'

Take that, Fitzy. We'll bury them now.

Only we don't. Just before half-time, Giggsy limps off with a hamstring injury. From then on, it's cat-on-hot-bricks-time. Mum and Amy come in just after half-time. I'm on the edge of the sofa, willing United to keep them out.

'You're winning then?' says Mum.

'Yes, 1–0, but we're making life difficult for ourselves.'

'Best leave him,' Mum tells Amy. 'Football.'

Amy nods.

Football.

We've lost momentum and Kiev are attacking. Barthez has had nothing to do in goal, but at 1–0 you're always vulnerable.

'Come on!'

Just a couple of minutes to go.

'We're going to do it.'

'Terry,' calls Mum.

'What!'

'It's Chloe.'

'Not now.'

'Aren't you going to speak to the girl?'

'Not... now!'

'But...'

'Tell her I'll phone her back.'

'OK.'

Mum's voice is disapproving. I don't care. Bodnar's just crossed low from the right. The substitute Demetradze sprints through to meet it. For a moment the world stands still. It's easier to score than to miss.

A draw and we're out.

'No-o-o...'

Demetradze shoots in slow motion.

'...o-o-o...'

He misses.

'Yiss! You camel, you great big Ukrainian camel!'

Three minutes of extra time.

'What? Where did you get three minutes from ref?'

But we hold firm. We're through. Take that, Fitz. I live to fight another day.

'Are you going to phone Chloe back?' asks Mum.

'Can't I just hear what Fergie has to say first?'

'Please.'

'OK.'

I dial Chloe's number.

'Yes?'

It's her. Her voice is flat.

'Sorry I couldn't come to the phone. It was a big moment in the match.'

'You never have time for me,' says Chloe.

A moment's pause, then the killer.

'I saw how you were looking at Julie.'

'I never! I wasn't!'

Truly, I protest too much.

'When you've made your mind up what you want,' says Chloe, 'tell me.'

Time for courage, Terry. End it now.

'Just be honest, Terry. What do you want?'

As usual, my courage fails. I just can't stand the disappointment in her voice.

'I want you, Chloe. You.'

'See you tomorrow, then.'

'Yes, tomorrow.'

I put the phone down and walk back into the living room. They're rerunning the Sheringham goal. My heart is full. Unfortunately, it's not on account of Chloe.

135

4

Friday 17th November
8.00 p.m.

So this is how it stands. With a month to go until the United v Liverpool game and five weeks until Christmas, life is really starting to suck. In fact, this winter is turning out to be the suckingest season that ever sucked. I've got a girl, but she's not *the* girl. When I'm out with Chloe all I can see is Julie, Julie and Fitz. Fitz with his Michael Owen haircut and his Liverpool shirt.

Which makes me feel guilty.

Which makes me feel bad.

As if that wasn't enough, my parents are getting divorced. Yes, the paperwork has finally started to go through. Mum left the envelope on the kitchen table this morning. Some family! Dad's going out with this old slapper with her bottled tan and her laugh like a jackass, and Mum's eating for England.

The Hobnob champion of Prescot.

Which makes me feel guilty.

Which makes me ... Well, you get the message.

I mean, what happened to happy? Just a few months ago I was a season ticket-holder with a full set of parents and an unbroken heart. You know what, you ought to be able to live your life over twice, once as a rehearsal and the second time for real. Wouldn't that be brilliant? Looking back, I can see where it all went wrong.

So I just rerun my life to one Saturday in June. I'm on my doorstep and Julie's got her liquid brown eyes trained on me. I untie my tongue and say the words that could change my life: 'Would you like to do something tomorrow?'

But life's a single take. You only get one go at it. Typical. I throw myself back on the bed and stare at the ceiling. Chloe's gone to her nan's and Bobby's out with Caitlin. Or is it Rosie? Anyway, I'm all on my lonesome.

An REM song drifts up from the living room. 'Everybody Hurts'. We're soulmates, me and Mum. Two human beings twenty-one years apart, but only a packet of Hobnobs between us. A few minutes later she's playing: 'Losing my religion.'

At least I've got that. United: the one true religion, the once and future champions. We play City tomorrow at Maine Road, the first derby match in four years. My mind dredges up a date: 23rd September, 1989. Manchester City 5, Manchester United 1. I was only four when it happened, but my skin still burns with humiliation at the thought of it. We've a score to settle tomorrow. A thumping victory might take my mind off Julie and me.

Might.

Saturday 18th November
11.20 a.m.

I'm at my dad's. I've got Bobby in tow. Caitlin's gone to town with her mates and Rosie is away seeing family. So Man City v Man U on Sky gets the nod. While the old man is making toasted sausage butties for in-match sustenance, we inspect the living room for signs of Mule. Nothing, not a lipstick, not a hairbrush, not a nail varnish. The whole place has had a Mule-ectomy. Bobby raises an eyebrow.

'You don't think...?'

'Beats me. To be honest, I'm past caring.'

It's not true, but it has a finality about it. It helps keep Bobby off the subject of the divorce.

'Hey,' says Bobby. 'I didn't tell you, did I? Fitz and Julie have had a tiff.'

My heart skips a beat.

'Of course, you won't want to know.'

His eyes twinkle with mischief.

'You're so loyal to Chloe.'

I scowl.

'Let's have the details, Bobby. Cough.'

'Caitlin told me. They were waving their arms about and shouting at each other.'

'Any idea what it was about?'

Bobby gives a shake of his head.

"Fraid not, but maybe, just maybe, all isn't well in paradise.'

I think of Julie and feel hope. I think of Chloe and feel guilt.

Maybe...

...just maybe.

Dad comes in carrying a tray. Toasted sausage sarnies, two cans of Coke, a mug of tea.

'Tea man, are you, Geoff?' says Bobby.

'Yes, coffee's too bitter.'

'Bet you don't know which country is the world's number one tea drinker.'

'No, I don't, but I'm sure you're going to tell me.'

'Irish Republic. One thousand, four hundred and twelve cups per person per year. It just pushes the UK into second place.'

'Well, fancy that.'

Dad delivers the line in a bored monotone. Something's up. I think about Mule's laugh and the absence of her stuff and wonder.

Maybe...

...just maybe.

Imagine. What if it all came together? Fitz splits with Julie. Dad dumps Mule. Me and Julie, Mum and Dad, the order of the universe restored. Send me a sign, oh gods of football. A win for United to tell me everything is going to be all right with the world, after all.

Saturday 18th November
11.32 a.m.

'Goallllll!'

David Beckham shoots from thirty-five yards. The shot travels at 68.2 miles per hour. Unsighted, Nicky Weaver in the Manchester City goal takes a step to the left. In an instant the ball has sailed past his flailing arms into the net.

'A sign from the gods,' I murmur.

'What's that?' asks Bobby.

'Oh nothing.'

Saturday 18th November
2.00 p.m.

Mum greets me at the door.

'Good, you're back. Oh, hi, Bobby.'

'Hi, Sharon.'

'I've got to nip out to the shops,' says Mum. 'Would you stay in with Amy?'

'Sure.'

'How did United get on?'

'Won 1–0.'

'Well, that'll make half of Manchester happy.'

Bobby immediately heads for the kitchen.

'Sorry, Bobby,' says Mum. 'I didn't buy any biscuits, so you're out of luck.'

'Cakes?'

'No sweet stuff of any description.'

Bobby and I exchange glances.

'You mean...'

'That's right,' says Mum. 'I've made up my mind. Look out world, I'm getting into shape.'

I give silent thanks to the gods of football. Today's victory is an omen. I can see it all. Dad dumps Mule. Mum loses weight. Dad comes back to Mum. Julie dumps Fitz. I ask her out. Clouds of apple blossom shower us as we walk into the sunset. Life has a purpose after all.

Maybe...

...just maybe.

Sunday 19th November
4.00 p.m.

I'm at Chloe's house.

I know, I know. Here I am thinking almost non-stop about Julie and whether she's broken up with Fitz, and at the same time I'm sitting on Chloe's settee, holding Chloe's hand and watching Chloe's television. I guess that makes me a pretty lousy human being. Well, I'm not proud of what I'm doing. I admit it. I'm a coward, a bona fide, yellow through and through coward.

(But at least Chloe's got Sky Sports).

And having Sky Sports is a real bonus, because – guess what? – the gods of football have continued to smile on me. Get this, not only did United win yesterday but all the obvious challengers lost. That's right, Arsenal, Leeds and Aston Villa all got beaten. I've convinced myself that everything's going my way. Which makes my behaviour stringing Chloe along even more disgusting. But I continue to play the game.

The conversation goes something like this:

Chloe: 'So why are you watching this match?'

Me: 'Liverpool are playing. They're one of United's main rivals for the title.'

Chloe: 'So you're supporting Tottenham?'

Me: 'Yes.'

Chloe: 'And you like them?'

Me: 'No. I *hate* them.'

Chloe: 'I don't think I'll ever get the hang of this.'

Ten minutes into the match she's got her head on my shoulder. For crying out loud, you don't cuddle during football! She really hasn't got the hang of it. The conversation resumes:

Chloe: 'Terry, can I ask you something?'

Me (thinking): 'No!'

Me (speaking): 'Go on.'

Chloe: 'Have you got feelings for Julie Carter?'

Me (thinking): 'Not half.'

Luckily, I don't have to answer her. At that very moment Robbie Fowler scores for Liverpool.

Me (relieved at the let-off, but sickened by the scoreline): 'Look at that! The Tottenham defence just went AWOL.'

I sit there uncomfortably, knowing she's bound to bring up the subject of Julie again. Gods of football, why have you forsaken me? Chloe's about to ask again when they finally smile once more.

Ferdinand equalises for Spurs. Two minutes later I go on a turbo-driven celebration. Sherwood has put the Londoners in the lead. At full-time Liverpool have gone down to a 2–1 defeat. It's been a weekend to remember.

'Happy now?' asks Chloe.

I count my blessings. United five points clear at the top of the Premiership; Julie and Fitz quarrelling; the Dad–Mule thing cooling; Mum kicking out the Hobnobs. Happy? I'm delirious. It's just too good to be true.

Monday 21st November
9.00 a.m.

It *was* too good to be true. I should have known as much. The moment I got to the end of the street it lashed it down. By the time I got to the school gates I was soaked to my undies.

I phoned Dad last night. He was on his way out – you've guessed it – with Mule. They haven't split up after all. Then I caught Mum opening her secret Hobnob stash. Diet, my eye! But that isn't the worst of it. I've just seen Julie and Fitz. She looked lovely with raindrops sparkling on her eyelashes. Then she went and spoiled the effect by going up to Fitz and giving him a peck on the cheek. Nothing passionate, you understand, but enough to tell me they haven't broken up.

Gods of football?

Who am I kidding?

5

Why do I bother?

I mean, why do I rotten well bother?

As usual, I've run all the way to Amy's school to pick her up and dragged her all the way back, protesting at the top of her whiny, little voice, just so I can get a game for the Year 11 team.

But do I play? Do I heck!

Six Guns thinks the sun shines out of Fitz. He's always first on the team sheet. Captain, playmaker, top scorer. No rotation here. Week in, week out yours truly sits kicking his heels on the subs' bench. I haven't started a single game this term. My only appearance has been five minutes taking Paul Scully's place when he got an elbow in the face. It wasn't even enough time to get my shorts mucky.

Amy doesn't help either.

'Why do you keep coming?' she asks. 'They never pick you.'

'I'll get my chance,' I growl, burying my face in my tracksuit top.

'When?'

Yes, when? I'm way down Six Gun's pecking order. That's me all right, lower than birdseed.

'Lucky last night, weren't you?' Fitz asks as he leads the team out.

'Lucky?' I snort. 'We won 3–1.'

Against Panathinaikos, that is, the Greek champions. Second phase of the Champions League.

'Oh, you won all right. But if they'd taken half their chances you'd have got battered.'

I stare after him. Why didn't I taunt him about Liverpool losing at Spurs? Why didn't I remind him they're nine points behind us in the Premiership? Why didn't I say *something*?

I'll tell you why. Because he's with Julie and that means he'll always get one over on me.

Bobby comes over and sits next to me. He isn't even a sub this evening. Six Guns says he's out of condition. Putting on the beef is the way he puts it.

'Noticed anything?' Bobby asks.

'No.'

'Look around you.'

I look. The penny drops.

'Julie, she isn't here.'

'Got it in one, Sherlock.'

'So where...?'

'That's the million dollar question. Something's going on.'

'But I saw them kissing.'

'And Caitlin's seen them arguing. I tell you, it could be the beginning of the end. Fitzy might just be losing her.'

I feel like yelling out loud, but just then Chloe puts in an appearance. Even though she hates football, she always turns up to support me. Usually that just means watching me sit on the bench. Chloe doesn't mind, though. I grimace with guilt. She's such a heartbreakingly nice person.

'Maybe next time,' she says.

'Yes, next time.'

Maybe...

...Just maybe.

Friday 24th November
8.00 p.m.

Cinema night. I've been dragged along to some lameoid films in my time, but this chick flick really takes the biscuit.

'Well, what do you want to see?' asks Chloe.

'It's all right,' I tell her. 'I'm cool.'

I'm buying a couple of tubs of ice cream, when I feel Chloe squeeze my arm.

'What's up?'

143

'Seen who's here?'

It's Julie. She looks great. Black leather trousers and a strapless top. I mean, gulp! For a moment I can't see Fitz and my spirits rise. Then I spot him getting the tickets. Lousy mesomorph. He sees me and sarcastically blows a kiss. I want to stuff it back down his stupid throat.

'What does she look like?' says Chloe sourly.

A million dollars, I think. Her mane of glossy black hair is cascading over her bare shoulders.

A fifteen-year-old Cleopatra.

'Dunno,' I say.

Obviously, I'm not convincing Chloe of my disapproval.

'You don't like that sort of thing, do you?' she asks.

Which means: *You don't like* her, *do you*?

I restrict myself to a casually shrugged shoulder, but inside I'm anything but casual. I'm like a can of Coke that's just been shaken within an inch of its fizz.

'You OK?'

'Sure,' I say. 'I'm fine.'

Chloe darts a glare at Julie. I'm not fooling her one bit.

Every now and then in the film theatre I steal a glance at Julie and Fitz. They're sitting five rows in front of us. Chloe catches my eye twice and snuggles up possessively. I squeeze back. What am I doing? Why can't I just be honest and tell her this isn't working? Because I'm a coward, that's why. Yellow right through. If I ever had any bottle, it's gone the way of the ten green ones.

'Is there any Fanta left?' asks Chloe.

I grunt and pass it. Just as I'm handing it over, Julie gets up and runs up the aisle and out of the cinema. Fitz races after her. I follow them with my eyes. I feel like going after them.

'I wonder what that's all about?' says Chloe.

I disguise my interest with another mock-casual shrug, but my mind is working overtime.

Is it the beginning of the end?

Closure.

That's what the Americans call it, closure. I saw it on *Friends*. Tying up the loose ends, putting your mistakes behind you, opening a new chapter in your life. Yes, I really do want closure.

Mum and Dad back together.

Closure.

Me back in the school team.

Closure.

United secure as Premiership Champions.

Closure.

Most of all, Julie free of Fitz. Then I can tell Chloe. Gently, but finally.

Closure.

But life isn't like that. Life's open-ended, contradictory, confusing. I haven't got the foggiest idea what my parents are up to. All I get from Mum is: 'It's with the solicitor.' And from Dad, 'it's your mum's move next.' He's keeping tight-lipped about Mule, too. I haven't heard her bray for a few days, but that doesn't mean much. Maybe he's just hiding her away. Suddenly, I can't even rely on United either. Just when things are looking hunky-dory, with the Red Devils eight points clear at the top of the Premiership, disaster strikes. Last night, Fergie fielded a scratch side against Sunderland in the Worthington Cup. It was a practice match, that's all. Or so I thought. But Dwight Yorke goes and gets himself sent off, doesn't he? Now he's going to miss the Liverpool game. That's right, the mother and father of all battles, the grudge match of the season. Andy Cole is already sidelined with an injury so we're down to just two fit senior strikers.

And to cap it all, I'm completely in the dark about Julie and Fitz. Everything tells me their relationship is on the rocks; the rows I've been told about, that walkout at the cinema. But there they are right in front of me on the treadmill, together as if nothing has happened. They're jogging side by side, the beautiful couple, the item. I hate this lesson at the gym. I have to run alongside Chloe, pretending to have eyes only for her, and all the time there's Julie.

Lovely Julie.

Making my heart jump.

Making my flesh crawl with the lies I'm telling Chloe each time we kiss.

So there's no closure.

Only hurt.

Wednesday 29th November
11.45 a.m.

I step out of the shower and right into Fitz's path. I take in the mesomorphic chest and shoulders, the Michael Owen haircut.

'It was criminal, that tackle of Yorke's,' he says. 'Could have finished that player's career.'

'It was mis-timed,' I reply. 'Dwight isn't that sort of player.'

'Got your just desserts though, didn't you?' Fitz continues regardless. 'You're out of the Worthington Cup.'

'Fergie was only playing the reserves,' I point out.

'*You're* the reserves,' says Fitz, earning an appreciative chuckle from Gary Tudor. 'How long is it since you played a game?'

I hold my tongue, mainly because I can't think of anything to say.

'What do they say on that quiz programme on telly? Yes, you are the weakest link. Goodbye.'

'Missing link's more like it,' says Gary.

Fitz grins.

'Come to think about it, you are a bit Neanderthal, Terry. Dragging your knuckles on the ground doesn't help you play football, you know.'

'Get lost,' I say, shoving past.

'Come to think of it,' Fitz says. 'I don't know why you bother to turn up at all. Face it, Terry, you'll never get a game with me in your way.'

I think of him playing in place of me.

I think of him holding Julie's hand, kissing her...

...in place of me...

'You are the weakest link.'

...holding her...

...in place of me...

'Goodbye.'

6

'Happy birthday, Terry.'

Mum greets me at the bottom of the stairs.

'Thanks.'

'Sixteen, eh? Growing up fast.'

Does she have to do this? I mean, I didn't mind it when I was six. Lapped it up. Wanting to be the big man. It's a bit much at my age. It's a wonder she doesn't pinch my cheeks and tousle my hair!

'My present to you is on the coffee table.'

Change of voice.

'So's your dad's.'

I see the two identical parcels, slim packages in gold paper. Mum's the one who wrapped them. Obvious. They've got that female neatness about them. I get fifty quid and a CD from each of them.

'Thanks, Mum.'

Amy wanders past in her dressing gown and tiger slippers.

'I know what Chloe's got for you.'

'Oh no you don't, young lady,' says Mum, ushering her into the kitchen. 'You're not spoiling the surprise.'

The words are barely out of her mouth when the doorbell rings.

'It's Chloe,' says Mum, twitching the net curtains.

Chloe! At 10.00 a.m. on a Saturday. Doesn't the girl sleep? She'll be cooking breakfast for me next!

'Happy birthday,' she says, simultaneously kissing me on the cheek and shoving a parcel into my hands.

'What's this?' I ask.

'Open it.'

Her eyes are sparkling.

'The United away shirt!' I cry. 'Thanks.'

Chloe grabs my hand.

'And...'

Inside the shirt I discover the video of 'Manchester United: Beyond the Promised Land.'

'I left the receipt in the bag,' says Chloe, 'in case you want to change them.'

'No,' I say, 'Everything's brilliant!'

She's just spend over sixty pounds on me, or her parents have. In the middle of the delight I feel a wave of guilt. This is the girl I'm thinking of dumping.

'You shouldn't have,' I say, my insides twisting with shame. 'It's too much.'

'Not for you, Terry,' she says, giving me a hug. 'Not for you.'

That surge of guilt is becoming a tidal wave.

Saturday 2nd December
3.15 p.m.

Amy lets Dad in. He finds me and Chloe listening to the United–Spurs match on the radio. At least, I'm listening. Chloe's humouring me. She's taking sneaky peaks at her GCSE Revision Guide on the sly. I glanced at it a few minutes ago. She was reading a page called Factorising a Quadratic. Doing a what to a what? I mean, it sounds really painful! It just reminds me how bad I am at maths.

'Happy birthday, son,' says Dad, chasing the Factorised Quadratic out of my head.

'Thanks, Dad.'

For the present and the chased Quadratic.

He's looking round the kitchen as if he's never been here before. I can't remember the last time he was in the house. Mum hovers in the kitchen doorway, darting accusing looks his way. Dad looks uncomfortable.

'Told our Terry about tonight, Sharon?'

'No, I was waiting for you to arrive.'

'Tonight?' I ask.

'We're going out for a Chinese meal,' says Chloe excitedly.

'We?'

'You and me, Bobby and Caitlin, Amy, your Mum and Dad.'

I stare. Mum ... and Dad! He senses my shock.

'That's right, the seven of us.'

He changes the subject.

'So who got you the shirt?'

That's right, I'm already wearing it.

'Chloe.'

Dad gives a knowing look. Chloe blushes. Why did she have to go overboard? Why does she have to be so rotten nice?

'So what's the score?' asks Dad.

'0–0.'

'Liverpool?'

'1–0 up.'

Dad scowls.

'There's one bit of good news. Leeds are losing 3–0.'

Dad nods approvingly.

'I see where you get it from,' says Chloe.

'Sorry?'

'Your football mania.'

That's not all I get from him. Imagine if Chloe knew how I've been feeling. She'd be so betrayed. Suddenly the shirt is making my skin burn. I want to feel the same way you do, Chloe, I really want to.

I want to, but I can't. Not towards you, anyway.

'Amy and I are going to the shops, Chloe,' says Mum. 'Want to come and leave the boys to their match?'

Chloe slips on her coat and follows Mum to the door.

'That girl's mad about you,' says Dad.

United are pressing. The comment is *de*pressing.

'I know.'

'What about you?'

What do I say? The truth? That she's OK to be going on with. Until Julie's free. It makes me sound so mercenary. Luckily, Paul Scholes is surging forward, dispensing with the need to reply.

Goooaallll!

I use the good news from Old Trafford as an excuse to ignore Dad's question. What can I say? What about me?

Saturday 2nd December
9.00 p.m.

I've been in more uncomfortable situations, but I can't remember when. Present around the table at the Chinese Garden are seven people. Of the seven, only one, Amy, is blissfully unaware of the tensions pulsating around us. That's hardly a surprise, of course; she is only nine.

It's all about what those present are trying *not* to do:

Mum and Dad trying not to mention the divorce.

Bobby and Caitlin trying not to mention The Other Girl, who he insists doesn't exist but obviously does.

Me and Chloe trying not to mention Julie.

All that Amy has to avoid saying is that she would have preferred to go to McDonald's. Life's easy when you're nine.

'Well,' says Dad, finishing a half of lager, 'That's another million brain cells killed off.'

'Actually,' says Bobby, gulping down the last of his crispy duck and entering the database of useless facts that is his brain, 'the theory now is that we grow brain cells throughout our lives.'

He goes on to mention something called the hippocampus which sounds like a big university but probably isn't.

'When did you swallow that encyclopaedia, Bobby?' asks Dad.

Detecting the sour note, Chloe dives in the way she has all evening. She is determined to make us all:

a) Get along

b) Stay cool

c) Look happy

Whether we actually *are* happy is irrelevant. Chloe must have been genetically-engineered in Disney World. Her constituent parts are ninety-nine per cent niceness and one per cent sweetness.

She brings the perfect presents, laughs at my lamest jokes and does her best to make everybody feel good about themselves. She's got to be the perfect girlfriend. So why on earth do I still think about Julie?

Bobby tries to kick-start the conversation:

'So how's Mu–'

I kick him under the table.

'Mu – Manchester United? Still winning?'

'Yes, we beat Spurs 2–0.'

A lamer attempt at recovering the situation we couldn't have engineered. Mum's eyes narrow. Dad tugs at his shirt collar. Caitlin gives Bobby daggers. I think she's just been waiting for an excuse. Finally, Chloe gives this high-pitched giggle.

'The last pancake, anybody?'

Pancake.

That about sums up this birthday.

Pancake.

As in as flat as.

Saturday 2nd December
9.45 p.m.

I'm in the Gents' washing my hands when Dad comes in.

'Well,' he sighs, 'It's nearly over.'

'Pretty awful, eh?' I say.

He nods.

'Feel that Arctic wind sweeping in from your mum?'

'Chloe means well,' I say.

Another nod.

'You and Mum still at war?' I ask.

'That's just it,' he tells me. 'I want to patch things up. I've finished with Mule ... Muriel.'

My senses swim. This is brilliant.

'No way!'

'You're not going to believe this,' says Dad.

'Try me.'

'I'm starting to realise how I feel about your mum. Maybe comfortable isn't such a bad thing after all. I think I've made a terrible mistake.'

My heart skips a beat.

'Have you told her that?'

'I'm trying.'

Closure, he's talking about closure.

'Then try harder.'

As we return to the table I glance at Chloe. Typical. Here's Dad wondering how to get Mum back, and all the time I'm wondering how to get shot of Chloe.

Doesn't anybody ever get anything right in this world?

7

'Some mistake!' I say, reminding him about Saturday night.

Dad and I are sitting in his shoebox of a living-room with our fish and chips on trays on our knees. We're supposed to be listening to the football phone-in. United play Sturm Graz tomorrow in Austria. But somehow we can't keep our minds on the game. We're thinking about Mum.

'Why couldn't you have worked this out earlier?' I ask.

Dad shrugs.

'I know, I know,' I say, beginning to feel sorry for him. 'I've heard the song. You don't know what you've got till it's gone. What I don't understand is why it's taken you so long? For goodness sake, the divorce is already on its way through. Talk about taking it down to the wire! So why?'

'Dunno,' he says. 'Male vanity, I suppose. When I met Mule...'

I burst out laughing.

'When I met *Muriel*, I just couldn't believe she was interested in me. Let's face it, she's a good-looking woman.'

I grimace. I'd rather not face it, thank you very much, Dad.

'It had been nearly twenty years since another woman showed an interest in me. It took time, but in the end I realised she wasn't the one.'

He lowered his eyes.

'One simple reason: she wasn't your mum.'

'So you want to walk round Asda in matching pullies after all?'

Dad smiles.

'Yes, I suppose I do.'

'And you've told Mum that?'

His expression changes.

'Not in so many words.'

'Then tell her. Tell her tonight.'

Dad frowns.

'I don't know if I can.'

'Why not?'

'Maybe it's a man thing,' says Dad. 'We're all emotionally illiterate. You won't believe this, but when I was your age I was always so tongue-tied with girls. I could never pluck up the courage to talk to them.'

I don't believe what I'm hearing. That's me he's describing.

'Then once, just once, I managed to say what I felt. That's how I got your mum to go out with me.'

He shakes his head.

'The way I see it, finding the right person is a lottery. Once, maybe twice, in your life you come across The One. And you know what, if you don't seize the moment right there and then, you can end up regretting it for the rest of your life.'

There's the sound of a million pennies dropping. Once, maybe twice, in your life! I could be blowing the only chance I'm ever going to get. At sixteen, I could be condemning myself to a lonely bachelorhood! Ohmigod, sixteen years old and I'll never be loved! I've got to tell Julie. It's what Bobby's been telling me all these months. Why didn't I listen? Why couldn't I just do it? So what if she turns me down? Maybe she isn't one bit interested, but I'll never know unless I try.

'Something the matter?' asks Dad.

'No,' I say. 'There's something I have to do.'

And do soon. The mocks are next week, so we're only in school part of the day, just for the exams.

'It's now or never.'

Dad looks confused.

'Now or never, what is?'

I think of Chloe. Suddenly I'm talking to myself.

'That's two things I have to do.'

'What are you on about?'

'Nothing. You just made me understand something about myself. Listen, Dad, I'm going after the thing I want most in the world. You've got to do it too. Tonight. You hear me? Right this minute.'

He's looking at me like I'm speaking fluent Bulgarian. But I don't care. I'm full of energy. I know what's got to be done. So things can be settled. So there can be The Happy Ending. So I can have closure.

'Now Dad. You're going to see Mum right now.'

Dad's still staring in a slightly bewildered way when I run out of the flat and on to the street.

Tuesday 5th December
7.00 p.m.

This is the hardest thing I've ever done. Chloe's looking right at me, eyes brimming with tears. Her pinched, pretty little face is red and blotchy.

'But why, Terry? What have I done wrong?'

'Nothing. You haven't done anything wrong.'

We're sitting on a wall at the top of her street. The blustery wind is whipping round us, showering us with icy raindrops. I zip my jacket up to the chin. I find myself biting on the zip, wishing I was somewhere else. What's going wrong? On the way up here, I had it all worked out. I've seen it in the movies. Boy meets girl. Boy loses girl. (To Fitz, rotten lousy mesomorphic stinkbag Fitz! OK, so that isn't in the movies, but what the heck, I had to get it off my chest.) Finally, boy wins girl. Life has a pattern. Love is written in the stars. Closing credits begin to roll with star billing to Manchester United. Happy ending.

'Then why do we have to split up?' asks Chloe in this whining, sniffly little voice that makes me want to scream. She grips my sleeve.

'Is there somebody else?'

Now she's dragging it out. I had this worked out too. She was meant to thank me for the good times and wish me well for the future. So why's she pulling my arm off and dribbling with misery?

'It's Julie Carter, isn't it?'

'No, she's got nothing to do with this...'

My voice trails off. I'm not sorry for her any more. I resent every reddened blotch on that pasty face of hers, every snotty sob from that pointy little nose. I'm impatient, angry. In fact, I want to run, to get away. I never wanted to hurt anybody. I made a mistake, a big one. I just want it put right, that's all. Why's she got to be like this?

The truth, it's the only way to set things right.

'OK, I really like Julie. It's always been her.'

Chloe lets out this miserable sob, but I carry on regardless. I'm talking to me now, not her.

'She probably doesn't know I exist, but...'

Chloe's got her face buried in her hands and her shoulders are shaking. I did that. Me! I never dreamed it could be this way. I thought that, if I ever split up with somebody, I'd be the one to end up heartbroken. Weird the way things turn out. Now I'm feeling sorry for her again.

'Chloe, don't. I'm not worth it, you see.'

I nearly burst out laughing. The stupidity of it. in the middle of this big scene I've just quoted a line from a song. Paul Young, I think. Some wrinkly from the eighties. Dad plays it when he's fed up. At my words, Chloe makes a noise like a wounded animal and her nose starts to run again. I pass her a tissue. She pushes my hand away.

'I don't want your rotten tissue!'

All of a sudden her voice sounds stronger. It crackles with resentment and wounded pride.

'I should never have trusted you, Terry Payne. You boys are all the same.'

I feel offended. Me, the same as Bobby? Me, the same as Fitz? Never!

'No, we're not. *I'm* not.'

'Yes, you are. You're like dogs.'

Dogs! So I'm a flipping Labrador, am I?

'You can't stay loyal to one girl.'

But I can! I really can. I'm a good dog. But it's got to be the *right* girl. And that's what I say.

'I could stay loyal to Julie.'

Chloe's eyes fill with horror.

'I hate you, Terry.'

But that I can't take. I really am a good dog, the best dog. I could win Cruft's, I'm so good. I didn't want to hurt her. I don't want to be hated.

'Don't be like this, Chloe. We can still be friends.'

She gives an exasperated screech.

'No, Terry. No, we can't.'

She gets up to go.

'Hang on, Chloe, I've got something for you.'

I hold out the Man United Superstore carrier bag. Now I'm an expectant St Bernard. She stares at it as if I've just handed her a tin of Chum.

'I want you to have my presents. The receipt is still inside. You can get your money back. Buy something nice to cheer yourself up.'

Which is about as bad a line as any guy anywhere ever used to break up with a girl. Chloe stares in disbelief at the bag.

'You don't understand women, do you Terry?'

She slaps it away.

'Keep your stupid shirt.'

She walks away and stops outside her house.

'You know what, I hope you lose to Sturm Graz and I hope Liverpool batter you too!'

Which is the most she's ever said about football!

'Chloe...'

'I hope Michael Owen scores a hat-trick.'

Now that's in bad taste!

'Chloe...'

'And I hope Julie tells you to get stuffed.'

She goes inside and slams the front door behind her. Knowing my luck, Julie will probably do the same!

Wednesday 6th December
3.10 p.m.

Terry Payne, you have fifty minutes to save the universe.

Fifty minutes.

Three thousand seconds.

Three thousand six hundred heartbeats.

Listen to me, I'm starting to sound like Bobby. And the maths is probably wrong anyway! But the top and bottom of it is this: I have to pick Amy up from her school and rush her back to Knowsley Manor in time for footy practice. Tonight is the last practice of the year and I'm determined to stand up to Fitz, show him I'm not the weakest link. And somehow, in the middle of all that, I have to see Julie.

Tell her how I feel.

Before it's too late.

Wednesday 6th December
3.20 p.m.

This is too good to be true. I'm halfway up the hill, jogging past the police station, when I see Julie.

And she's crying.

Because of him?

It's got to be.

I run across the road with my sports bag in one hand and all my hopes and dreams in the other.

'Julie,' I stammer. 'Are you all right?'

It's the second time in two days I've been face to face with a girl in tears. I offer her a tissue, the *same* one I offered Chloe. Unlike Chloe, she takes it.

'What's the matter?'

3.21 p.m. Nine minutes to pick up Amy. Thirty-nine minutes to save the universe.

'Nothing.'

'Come off it, you're crying.'

'It's nothing. I'm feeling a bit rough. I must be coming down with a cold.'

She does sound a bit under the weather, but that doesn't account for the tears.

'There's something else though, isn't there?'

'If you must know, it's Fitz.'

My heart feels like it's going to burst. Bobby was right.

'He can be such a pig. On my birthday too.'

'It's your birthday!'

Why didn't I know that? Why didn't somebody tell me?

3.22 p.m. Eight minutes to pick up Amy. Thirty-eight minutes to save the universe.

'What's he done?'

'He just comes on so strong. So pushy. Thinks he can order me around. He was so lovely at first. Now ... just because we're going out, it doesn't mean he owns me. Boys can be such...'

I remember what Chloe said.

'Dogs.'

Julie stares at me and laughs.

'What a funny thing to say!'

She says it so nicely I want to wag my tail. I remember the Huey, Louie and Duey crack. She thought that was funny too. Well, here goes nothing.

'Fitz doesn't deserve you.'

'No, and who does?'

There's a twinkle in her eye. She's teasing me. But in a nice way. There's a lump in my throat as big as a match ball. I can hardly swallow.

'Me. *I* deserve you.'

She stares at me for a second. Like I just landed from the Planet Loony Toon.

'You?'

'Yes, I really like you, Julie. I've always liked you.'

There, I've finally plucked up the courage. I've said it.

'What about Chloe?'

'It wasn't right. I finished with her. So I could ask you out.'

Now for the rejection, the big heave-ho. I close my eyes. But there's no rejection. I feel her hands on my shoulders! I feel her lips pressed against mine! It isn't a peck, either, this is a real, lingering, stay-in-the-mind smackeroo. Her fingers move down my chest, sending shivers of joy through me. I finally open my eyes.

'What was that for?'

'For being you. I just wish you'd said something earlier. *Four months earlier!* I didn't think you were interested. When you didn't make a move, I kind of let Kelly fix me up with Fitz. Everybody acted like it was going to happen anyway.'

Of course it was going to happen. Hasn't she seen all those American high school movies? They'd be favourites for King and Queen of the Prom. But she's saying she'd have... I'm not imagining it, am I? She would have gone out with me! If I'd just asked. If only I'd asked. I stare at her, the moist, brown eyes, the full lips, the slightly reddened nose, the mane of raven hair.

'Me, not interested! I couldn't have been more interested. Didn't you see me looking at you? I couldn't take my eyes off you.'

Do I sound too needy? Oh, who cares? I *am* needy. I need you, Julie.

Julie smiles. A lovely smile. A heart-stopping smile. She liked me all the time! I think of all the wasted months, the pain of seeing her with Fitz. I'm such a loser.

'Are you and Fitz...?'

'Finished? I don't know.'

I feel the air go cold between us. Julie seems to be having second thoughts. Let's face it, if she dumps him she loses the whole social circle around him.

No, don't have second thoughts. Stick with the first thoughts.

'Maybe I shouldn't be doing this.'

First thoughts!

First thoughts!

'No. You should! You should!'

She laughs. Her fingers are still on my chest. I can feel them right through my shirt, making my skin tingly and alive. I glance at my watch. 3.25 p.m. Five minutes to pick up Amy. Thirty-five minutes to save the universe.

Julie finally pulls away. I remember the scent of her hair, the press of her body. I can't let her go now.

'I don't know what I'm doing,' she says. 'This isn't fair on either of you.'

'But you're not meant to be with him. It isn't right.'

Julie smiles sadly.

'I don't know. Maybe you're right. Oh, Terry, why didn't you say something earlier? Fitz can be a pain sometimes, but he really is a nice guy. He knows everybody. I don't want to hurt him, I don't want to hurt anyone.'

No, NO! You were doing fine when you said he was a pain. Hurt him. He's big and ugly enough.

'Terry, I'm confused.'

Confused! What's to be confused about? We're meant to be together. The kiss, Julie, remember the kiss.

I glance at my watch again. 3.26 p.m. Four minutes to pick up Amy. Thirty-four minutes to save the universe.

'Are you in a hurry?' she asks, a bit put out.

'No... Yes, I've got to pick up my little sister.'

Another own goal. Make a mental note: when you're opening your heart to the girl you love never, but never, look at your watch!

'You'd better go then. Here's my bus, anyway.'

I see the bus coming up the road. In my mind's eye, it's transformed into a steam train wreathed in clouds of white smoke. Julie and I are wearing matching trenchcoats and in the distance guns are booming. I know, I know, I've seen too many old movies, but somebody had to be there to hand Mum the Kleenex.

'Julie, don't go.'

'I've got to.'

She starts to run. I feel the burn of that kiss on my lips, every contour of her body against mine.

'You've got to finish with him, Julie. You've got to. We're meant to be together.'

There's a cluster of first-years at the stop. They giggle and point at me. They don't see the trenchcoats, so it must be the words that have set them off. Julie climbs on the bus. I watch it pull away. I search for her face in the windows.

In vain... She's gone... No, there she is, smiling, waving. There's a chance, a real chance for us. I glance at my watch. 3.29 p.m. A minute to pick up Amy. Thirty-one minutes to save the universe. But it's half-saved already. I told Julie how I felt and she didn't think about Man U and Liverpool, and a love between two warring tribes. She didn't call me a loser or a weakest link. She didn't laugh.

She didn't do any of those things.

She kissed me.

Kissed ... ME!

'I don't know why you bother,' sniffs Amy.

'It's because I'm going to get back in the team,' I tell her. 'Because...' I think of Julie.

'Because I'm better than Fitz and I'm going to prove it.'

'It isn't even a proper match,' says Amy.

She's right. It's a practice match, but I don't care. Even if I were out on the pitch playing for United against Sturm Graz it couldn't be any more important. I've got to stand up to Fitz. I'll show him who the weakest link really is.

'OK, lads,' shouts Six Guns, clapping his hands. 'Gather round.'

We're glad to. It's cold and wet and we just want to get started.

'Six-a-side. It's your mocks next week so we won't be getting together again until January. What I want to see tonight is commitment. We're playing Blackridge again on the 10th, so if you want to be in the side, show me what you're made of.'

When he comes to pick the sides, there's an A-team and a B-team. The A-team's got Fitz, Gary Tudor and Paul Scully. All we've got is Jamie Sneddon, Bobby and me. Hardly the sort of selection to make the earth move. As the game kicks off I see Kelly watching me. She's looking as gorgeous as ever, but she doesn't crack a smile. California Ice, that's Kelly Magee. She's glaring at me. I wonder if she senses that something's happened between Julie and me. She's always known that Julie felt something too. Of course, that's why she gave me such a hard time because she knew it was a two-way thing!

But there's no time to worry about that now. Gary Tudor's coming towards me.

'Go to him, Bobby,' I shout. 'I'll take Fitz.'

Gary lays it off before Bobby can close him down. It's a straight contest between me and Fitz. Just when it looks like he's getting away from me, I wrap my leg round the ball and force it out for a throw-in. Fitz looks put out. From the throw-in, he tries to go past me again, but I'm ready for him. He tries the nutmeg.

'You are the weakest link,' he says.

But I get the block on. There's no goodbye. He has a dig at me as he walks away.

'I saw that,' says Bobby.

'Forget it, Bob,' I tell him. 'Just shows he's not getting his own way.'

Two minutes later Fitz is through again. I'm the last man. He chips the ball over my head and goes after it. I don't have his pace, but I'm not letting him get away. I lean into him and throw him off balance.

'Foul!' he roars, but Six Guns isn't having any.

'Play on.'

The moment Six Guns turns away, Fitz elbows me in the ribs.

'You've had it,' he warns.

I shove him away.

'Rattled?' I ask.

I remember Julie's lips pressed against mine. Who's the weakest link now, Fitz?

It's some time before we find ourselves in the same area of the pitch again, but this time we're both fired up. We go for a fifty-fifty ball. Nobody is going to pull out of this challenge. I see his studs go up. The idiot, he could do me some serious damage.

'You are the weakest link,' he hisses.

But I'm not backing down. I raise my feet just as high as he has. We're on a collision course.

'Goodbye!'

The crunch is sickening. My shin hurts a bit as I hop away from the collision, but I've come through pretty much unscathed. I see the ball bobble away. There's a strange noise coming from underneath me, but I can't quite focus on it. I'm too excited. I did it. I put one over on Fitz. But just as I'm picking myself up I hear the scream. It's him. He's underneath me, lying awkwardly.

And he's screaming.

He's not faking it, either.

He's in agony.

'Look what you've done!' roars Gary Tudor, facing up to me. 'You did that on purpose. You maniac!'

I look around. Everybody is staring at me eyes cold with anger and accusation.

'It was fifty-fifty,' I protest. 'He raised his studs first.'

They're all shouting, all of them except Bobby.

'Knock it off, will you?' yells Six Guns. 'You're not doing anybody any good. Run for the school secretary, somebody. This looks bad. I think he's broken his ankle.'

Broken it? Oh no, not that!

I look down at Fitz. What have I done?

I see Kelly on her mobile. I know who she's phoning. It's Julie. It's got to be. I can just see her nursing her cold and hearing this. What's she going to think? On no! Not this, not now. Not when everything was going my way. I can feel the other lads jostling me, letting me know what they think of the tackle. But I don't care. It's not just Fitz who's lying broken on the ground. It's all my hopes. Julie will never believe it was an accident. She'll never believe me.

I *am* the weakest link.

Goodbye.

Thursday 7th December
9.00 a.m.

'What do you mean, you're not going? My band is playing again.'

'I mean, I'm not going. Not after last night.'

The last place I want to be tomorrow is the Christmas disco. I'd be the rotten turkey. Not only did I put Fitz in hospital and wreck things with Julie, but Mum told Dad she wasn't interested in getting back together. You know what she told him: *You've hurt me too much.* United beat Sturm Graz 2–0 last night and I hardly even noticed!

'People will soon forget.'

I indicated Paul Scully and Jamie Sneddon. They're shaking their heads. I know it's for my benefit.'

'Do they look as if they're going to forget?'

I see Kelly and Gary Tudor coming the other way. No sign of Julie. 'How's Fitz?' I ask.

'What do you care?' snaps Gary. 'That tackle was out of order.'

'I didn't do it on purpose,' I protest.

'That's not what Fitz thinks,' says Kelly. Then, with venom: 'Or Julie.'

'Where is she anyway?'

'She's got a heavy cold. She's staying off till Monday. She wants to be better for the mocks.'

'What did she say?'

'About you? Nothing. Who do you think you are?'

'I don't believe you, Payne,' says Gary. 'Doing something like that to a team-mate, just because you're jealous.'

'I'm not jealous!'

'Not much you're not,' says Kelly. 'Julie's told me about you following her around.'

Julie told Kelly! She wouldn't. Not after what she said to me last night.

'You're off your head,' says Gary, walking away.

'Kelly,' I say, as she starts to follow.

'What?'

'What did Julie really say?'

Kelly shakes her head.

'Gary's right. You are off your head.'

And that's it. I'm standing with a face like a smacked behind. Chloe walks past and adds her own two-pennyworth.

'Happy now?' she asks. 'Dumper gets dumped, eh?'

Right now, I want to be anywhere but here in the school corridor.

'What was that?' asks Bobby.

'What?'

'Pleading with Kelly like that. Haven't you got any pride?'

Maybe not. So I stand among the jostling kids feeling like I've had my guts kicked out. Just yesterday afternoon everything seemed to be going my way. How could it all go so wrong so quickly?

Thursday 7th December
9.30 p.m.

'Mum,' I ask. 'Are you serious?'

'Serious about what?'

'Dad, of course.'

Mum looks up from her book.

'Yes, Terry, I'm serious. I don't see any way back for us.'

'But he's...'

'What?'

'He's sorry.'

'Sorry! That's a good one. Terry, you say sorry for dropping a plate. Sorry is nowhere near good enough after what he's done to me. I built my life around that man. Don't you understand? I put everything into this family. I lost track of most of my friends. I didn't need them, did I? I had Geoff. Well, I look pretty stupid now, don't I?'

'Don't be like this,' I say.

'So how do you want me to be?' Mum demands. 'I dare say you'd like me to welcome him back with open arms.'

She lays on the sarcasm with a trowel.

'Hello, honey, welcome home. Sorry I don't give you the butterflies any more. I'll try to get my act together. How many pounds would you like me to lose? Thirty? I'll do my best. Sit down, my lord and master, while I get you a cup of tea.'

'But he's dumped Mule.'

'Well hallelujah!' cries Mum. 'Now he's dumped two women. Doesn't that make me feel better!'

I throw back my head. She sees the look on my face and places a hand on my shoulder.

'I'm sorry, Terry, I shouldn't pile all this on you, but you have to understand, Geoff's hurt me. It isn't something you can put right just like that.'

Amy comes downstairs.

'Are you two arguing?'

'Arguing?' says Mum, 'No, love. Just talking.'

'Funny,' says Amy. 'You talk to Terry like you used to talk to Dad.'

We watch her going back upstairs.

'Not daft, is she?' I say.

'No,' says Mum. 'She's growing up fast.'

Friday 8th December
7.00 p.m.

I'm standing in the drenching rain where I kissed Julie three days and a whole lifetime ago, reliving the joy, the hope. Across the road,

I can see kids making their way towards school to the Christmas disco. Gary and Kelly are jogging, sharing an umbrella. Paul Scully and Pepsey Cooper are just behind them. Everybody has somebody, everyone but me. Then I get another shock.

I see Jamie Sneddon coming up the road straight towards me. I know the girl who's with him too.

'Chloe?'

'Well, if it isn't Terry,' she says acidly. 'Julie not coming tonight? Oh no, I forgot. She'll be feeding Fitz a bunch of grapes and signing his plaster cast.'

Jamie hangs around waiting for her. He looks uncomfortable. When you catch a girl on the rebound, you don't want to be too close to her ex.

'How does it feel to be a loser, Terry?'

She comes closer.

'Maybe now you understand how you made me feel.'

With that she links arms with Jamie and clatters away on her high heels.

'Great,' I say out loud. 'Just great.'

What happened to the pattern, the Happy Ending?

At that very moment I see Bobby crossing the road towards me.

'Was that Chloe?'

'Yes, Jamie's taking her.'

'She doesn't let the grass grow.'

I nod.

'Caitlin told me you were here,' says Bobby. 'What do you think you're doing?'

I shrug.

'I'm not quite sure myself.'

'Come to the disco.'

'Joking, aren't you? There's no Alison for me tonight.'

Bobby chuckles.

'You needn't worry. We're not playing it tonight. Come on, you'll enjoy yourself.'

'I doubt it. Chloe's just had a pop at me.'

'Big deal. Girls come and girls go. You're taking it all too seriously. Come on, Terry. Check out the talent. Emma Holland's all right you know, and she's unattached.'

'I don't think so, Bobby.'

I turn to go.

'Snap out of it, Terry. These things happen.'

As if to add to my misery, a car passes playing Travis' 'Why does it always rain on me?'

'Don't listen to it,' says Bobby. 'Who needs victim rock?'

'Victims,' I say pointedly.

With that, I set off home, leaving the spot where I very nearly made Julie mine.

Saturday 9th December
2.50 p.m.

Dad lets me in.

In the background I can hear 'Don't Dream It's Over' by Crowded House. He's getting into the victim rock as well.

'That bad, huh?' I ask.

'She just blew me out, Terry, told me she wasn't interested.'

'You walked out on her, remember.'

'But I thought...'

'She'd be falling over herself to take you back? You're forgetting the little matter of a woman called Mule. Mum's got some pride, you know. Nobody wants to be second-best to somebody who uses Permatan.'

'But you told me to go and see her.'

'And I was right to. You can still get her back.'

'I don't know,' he says, shaking his head. 'So how's Chloe?'

'I broke it off.'

'Yes?'

'Yes. I finished it and told Julie how I felt.'

'Julie?'

'The girl I really care about. I must have told you.'

Dad frowns.

'Can't recall. So you're going out with this Julie now?'

'No. I crippled her boyfriend.'

'What?!'

I manage to explain, after a fashion, just before kick-off.

'I don't think either one of us is much of a Romeo,' says Dad. 'Let's see if we can do better at football.'

United are at Charlton. I'm at a low ebb after the Julie debacle. I need a good performance. At least the Red Devils can come up with a Happy Ending. Just minutes into the match, it doesn't look like I'll get it. Charlton score the opening goal and it could be three. Our defence is all over the place.

'Nothing's going right,' says Dad, hurling a shoe across the room. I notice that he's got a hole in his sock.

Who's arguing? He's right, nothing is going right. I can't get Chloe's words out of my head. In my mind's eye, I see Julie feeding Fitz grapes and adjusting his pillow. We're 1–0 down, our nearest challengers Arsenal are 2–0 up, Mum's sent Dad away with a flea in his ear and I've blown it with Julie. Not the best two days of my life.

'Come on, United!'

We steady the ship and launch wave after wave after attacks, but with half-time approaching we're still behind.

'Come on, lads. Fight for it!'

Which is just what they do. Suddenly we score twice in thirty-five seconds, Giggs and Solskjaer. In the second half Roy Keane hits a screamer.

'3–1! Ye-e-e-ss!'

Fight for it! That's what I've got to do with Julie. Forget the way I behaved last night, I refuse to lie down.

'We'll stay eight points ahead of Arsenal,' I say, but I've spoken too soon. Fergie has taken Keane and Beckham off, saving them for the Liverpool game next week. Is it too soon? Looks like it. Charlton pull one back. 3–2 and a jittery last ten minutes.

'It's not over,' says Dad.

Oh no, even when you fight for it things go wrong. And they do go wrong. Big style. Charlton equalise.

'I don't believe it,' groans Dad.

Neither do I. No matter what I do, everything just falls apart. The pair of us sit there, staring disaster and possible defeat in the face.

'Fight for it, lads,' I shout, as much for me and Dad as for United.

We're into injury time. Three minutes added on. Backs to the wall.

Fight for it.

Giggs fizzes a shot wide.

Sixty seconds left.

Fight for it. For goodness sake, fight for it.

There's no time left. We draw 3–3 and lose ground at the top.

'I feel sick,' says Dad.

'Me too,' I admit. 'Now we've got to beat Liverpool next Sunday, or Arsenal could be just three points behind us.'

I think of the old enemy, then of Julie and Fitz.

I *will* fight for it.

8

The build-up starts here.

I take a deep breath and walk into school. The hall and the dreaded Maths paper are waiting for me at the end of this corridor. Julie too, if she's feeling better. What do I say to her? How do I make her understand? If I could get her on her own, maybe, just maybe, I could get her to listen. Fat chance of that, though. Kelly's bound to be there protecting her form the Mad Manc (my new nickname). I haven't even got Bobby for company. He's late.

'Here goes nothing,' I murmur to nobody in particular.

In the event, it's even worse than I'd been expecting. Julie hasn't just got Kelly round her, but Fitz is there too. Look at him, milking the attention for all he's worth. He's standing propped up on his crutches, holding court to Gary and Paul. Before you can say wounded hero, Pepsey rolls up to sign his cast. Then, just to pile on the agony, Jamie and even Chloe join the admiring crowd.

'Look what the cat's just dragged in,' scoffs Gary.

'Maimed anyone today?' sneers Paul.

He pretends to fall over.

'See that, he just chopped me.'

Everybody's laughing, even Chloe. Especially Chloe. No, scrub that, Julie isn't laughing, but who knows whether that's a good thing or a bad one. Her face is completely expressionless.

'Now now,' says Fitz, surprising everybody by his response. 'Go easy, eh? It was a fifty-fifty ball. I was unlucky, that's all.'

Gary's mouth is hanging open.

'No hard feelings, Terry.'

With that, Fitz makes his way to his table. The heads of his

171

entourage turn to follow their hero. He's stunned them to silence. Me too. As I sit down and stare at the test paper lying face down in front of me, I hear the hall door open. It's Bobby, closely followed by Caitlin. I frown questioningly.

'Don't ask,' Bobby hisses. 'Just don't ask.'

He and Caitlin sit at opposite ends of the hall, about as far apart as they could get.

'Settle down, please,' says Six Guns.

He's no need to say that, the place is like a mausoleum already. He runs through the usual preamble, then gives the fatal order:

'Begin.'

I flick through the paper.

Finding the nth term.

Gulp.

Three-letter Angle Notation.

Eek.

Combinations of Transformations.

Come again.

Vectors.

Mayday, mayday, the *SS Terry* is sinking fast.

Loci and Constructions.

Latest news. *SS Terry* is lost with all hands. Next of kin have been informed.

I look around. Fitz is beavering away already. Julie is writing too. Caitlin meets my eye then looks away with a toss of her reddish hair. I realise with horror that everybody knows what they're doing except me.

SS Terry hits the ocean bottom.

Completely sunk.

Monday 11th December
11.15 a.m.

'How do you think it went?' asks Bobby.

'What?'

'The exam, you idiot.'

'It didn't,' I say. 'It was rock hard.'

'Funny, I don't think it was that bad,' he says.

'It wasn't,' I tell him, 'so long as you've got a brain. Which I haven't.'

I mime opening my skull.

'See, cranial cavity completely empty. Anyway, what's with you and Caitlin?'

'We're finished,' says Bobby. 'Cheeky little cow. She only nicked my mobile and found Rosie's number.'

'You mean...?'

'That's right, now they've both dumped me.'

'I did warn you,' I say, but Bobby's miles away.

'Bobby, are you listening?'

'Back in a minute,' he says.

'But where...?'

Now I know where. He's gone over to talk to Emma Holland, the one he tried to pair me off with on Friday. I don't believe that guy! He doesn't stay dumped for long. Now what's he doing? He's writing something down. She's given him her phone number!

He looks round and grins before walking out towards the bus stop with Emma. I'm still marvelling at his ability to bounce back from a dumping when Fitz arrives. We're alone in the corridor.

'Thanks for what you said...' I begin, before he cuts me off.

'That was for my public,' he says. 'Now for the authorised version. You're a mad get, you know that? I had a trial this week with Liverpool and you've put me out for weeks. I hope you're proud of yourself.'

'But you said...'

'I know what I said, and Julie will love me for it. She's into all that forgiveness stuff. Not me. Believe me, you're going to pay for what you did, Payne.'

He checks the corridor then shoves his face into mine.

'I know you've been hanging round my girl. Well, forget it. You're pond-life, Payne, and I'm going to make sure Julie knows it. Before I've finished, she'll think you're responsible for the Ebola virus, the thinning of the ozone layer and global warming! My dad's treating us this Sunday.'

He pulls a couple of tickets

'Man U v Liverpool. That's right, I'm taking Julie, and we're going to watch the boys stuff your lot. You're a loser, Payne, always were,

173

always will be.'

There's more to come, but just as Fitz is warming to his theme Julie and Kelly start walking towards us. Fitz takes a step backwards and his voice changes completely.

'So like I say, no hard feelings. It could have been you in a plaster cast.'

He shoots out a hand and pumps mine.

'See you, Terry. Oh, and good luck this Sunday.'

He winks.

'You'll need it.'

Julie walks past me without saying a word. It's only when I hear the main door slam that I realise I should have said something, anything, to put my side of the story.

Now it's too late.

Thursday 14th December
12.30 p.m.

So much for the pattern of life. I had it all worked out: Boy meets girl. Girl meets sleazebag. Girl ditches sleazebag for boy. Boy and girl live happily ever after. Well, if there's one thing I've learned about the pattern it's this:

THERE IS NO PATTERN.

Stuff happens. Not just good stuff, either. Bad stuff, stupid stuff, stuff to make you squirm, stuff to make your toes curl, how-on-earth-could-that-happen stuff.

Just stuff.

'Penny for them,' says Bobby before stuffing half a burger in his mouth.

'I was just thinking,' I tell him. 'All this Happy Ever After rubbish. It's a complete con. What you get in real life is just any old Ever After. Happy doesn't come into it.'

We set off towards school. It's French this afternoon. Sacré flipping bleu!

'Is this about Julie?' Bobby asks, 'Or Liverpool beating Fulham last night?'

I grimace. I sat through Liverpool's victory sinking deeper and deeper into despair.

'Both.'

It's all the same thing. Not only did Liverpool win, but Julie's hero Michael Owen bounced back from injury to score the opening goal. When he scored, it was like watching Fitz celebrate. Just what I needed only five days before the United–Liverpool match. I remember what Chloe said: *I hope he scores a hat-trick.*

'You know your problem?' says Bobby. 'You take things too seriously. Just have a laugh, like me.'

I see this cartoon picture of Bobby being booted out of one door by Caitlin and Rosie only to bounce right back into another door opened by a smiling Emma Holland.

'I'd definitely be happier,' I admit. 'But I wouldn't be me, would I?'

'I suppose you're right,' says Bobby. 'You're the loyal, decent sort. All sincerity and moral dilemmas.'

Then, with a mischievous grin, he adds: 'Poor sod!'

We reach the school gates. There's Fitz sitting on a bench. Julie and Kelly are sitting either side of him. Gary, Pepsey and Paul are standing.

'Poor performance,' Gary's saying. 'I mean, Fulham might be top of the Nationwide, but they out-passed us for half the match.'

Fitz sees me coming.

'Maybe,' he says, 'But at least we showed a bit of steel. Patient for ninety minutes, then bam, bam, bam, three in extra time. We didn't throw late goals away.'

Unlike United at Charlton.

'And Owen's back. Lethal weapon.'

'So you think we'll turn United over on Sunday?' asks Kelly, also aware of my presence.

'Flatten 'em,' says Fitz. 'Oh, hello, Terry, didn't see you there. Did I mention that Julie and I were going to Old Trafford? Have you got a ticket?'

'You know I haven't.'

'Well, just stay in front of the TV. You might even see us on the screen. We'll give you a wave.'

I glance at Julie but she doesn't return the look. I've been tried and convicted before a no-jury kangaroo court.

CHARGE: That you, Terry Payne, on or about 16.40 hours on Wednesday, 6th December, did, with malice aforethought, break the ankle of one John Fitzpatrick.

VERDICT: That the above-mentioned rotten, lousy Manc is guilty of actual bodily harm, driven by acute jealousy and general low character.

SENTENCE: That you, Terry Payne, be left unloved and unwanted for the rest of your natural life. On the lesser charge of being a rotten, lousy Manc you are further sentenced to watch your team getting thumped by a resurgent Liverpool FC.

What I need now to put Fitz in his place is a magnificent riposte, a gem of wit and repartee.

'Fitz,' I say, after a moment's thought, 'Get stuffed.'

Friday 15th December
3.30 p.m.

'Oh, give it a rest, will you?' says Bobby. 'All you talk about is Julie, Julie, Julie. Get over it, will you?'

'I don't want to get over it,' I shoot back. 'She likes me, I mean really likes me. We could be good together, special. It'd be criminal if she stayed with a slimeball like Fitz just because of a misunderstanding.'

'I think,' Bobby says, correcting me, 'that it's because of the broken ankle.'

'I wish I was the one with the broken ankle,' I say wistfully. 'Then everything would be all right.'

'You have got it bad, haven't you?' says Bobby. 'OK, if you won't move on, why not talk to her?'

'How?' I cry. 'I can't get her on her own. If it isn't Fitz hanging round her, it's Kelly. There's always somebody on guard.'

'Phone her,' says Bobby.

'I don't know her number. And she's ex-directory. I checked.'

Bobby scrolls down the addresses on his mobile.

'There you go,' he says, flashing the screen at me.

'What are you doing with her number?' I ask suspiciously.

'I got it when she started at our school,' says Bobby. 'She's a looker.

I was interested too.'

I give him daggers.

'Hey, you should be thanking me. The moment you told me how you felt, I backed off.'

'You *were* going out with Caitlin at the time,' I remind him.

'OK, that too. Look, do you want this number or not?'

I write it down. I read the magic numbers. Time to take the plunge.

Friday 15th December
4.00 p.m.

My mobile isn't charged so I have to wait for Mum to get off the phone.

'Oh, come on,' I say.

'She's talking to Dad,' says Amy.

'Really?'

'They've been talking for ages.'

'What about?'

'He's asking to come home.'

'How do you know?'

'I was listening on the upstairs extension until they chased me.'

I smile. I always thought Amy was getting along just fine with our semi-detached family. Seems she's as keen as me for them to get back together.

'Think there's much chance?' Amy asks.

The words are no sooner out of her mouth than Mum slams down the receiver.

'That answer your question?' I say.

Amy retires to her room. I wait until Mum's gone before punching in Julie's number.

'Hello?'

It's a boy voice. Either Huey, Duey or Louie. I mean, Gerard, Josh or John-Joe.

'Is Julie there?'

'Who's asking?'

'It's Terry.'

'Oh, you're the Mad Manc, aren't you? Fitzy's told us all about you.'

177

'So can I speak to her?'
'No. And, by the way, we're going to flatten you on Sunday.'
The line goes dead.

Friday 15th December
4.45 p.m.

With any luck, Julie's three-headed guard dog will have gone out by now.

'Hello?'

It's the second head, another boy's voice, deeper than last time.

'Could I speak to Julie, please?'

'Who's asking?'

'Terry.'

'Oh, the...'

'Yes, the Mad Manc. Now could I speak to her?'

'No chance. You're going to get battered this Sunday.'

Friday 15th December
5.15 p.m.

I've got to have more luck this time.

'Hello.'

Damn! The third head. The youngest by the sound of it.

'Could I speak to Julie, please?'

'No, you can't, you Mad Manc...'

'I know,' I say, cutting him short, 'We're going to get hammered this Sunday.'

This time I hang up myself.

Friday 15 December
6.00 p.m.

I run to answer the phone. Maybe Julie's seen the light. It's got to be. Yes, that's it, she's slipped to the phone box to escape the attentions of her brothers. (I can dream, can't I?)

But it's only Bobby.

'Oh, hi.'

'So,' he asks. 'How did it go?'

'It didn't. I keep getting her brothers on the line.'

'Why don't you ring her mobile?'

'You've got her mobile number!'

'Sure have.'

He must have fancied her more than he's been letting on. I don't say anything. I just want the number. He reels it off.

'Why didn't you give it to me in the first place?'

Bobby sounds apologetic.

'I didn't think. Anyway, I've got to go. I'm taking Emma out.'

I hang up and phone Julie's mobile. My heart misses a beat. It's ringing and there are no brothers to field the call. But there is Fitz. I'd know his voice anywhere.

'Hello?'

I can't think what to say.

'Hello?'

I hear him talking to Julie.

'I just answered your mobile, Ju, but they're not speaking.'

There's a moment's pause then a note of suspicion enters his voice.

'That isn't the Mad Manc, is it?'

I can hear Julie in the background. So near and yet so far. I hang up without answering.

Saturday 16th December
3.50 p.m.

I've felt lower, but I can't remember when. I'm round at my dad's, and that's about as much fun as putting my leg through a bacon slicer lately. He took me and Amy for a pizza earlier. We had plans to take a walk round Sherdley Park or something but it's throwing it down as usual, so Amy wanted to go home. I look out of the window at the downpour. Why *does* it always rain on me? I read the footy pages again. Every time I look at the Liverpool line-up for tomorrow they look stronger. I mean, those three strikers, Heskey, Fowler and, of course, Owen. And we still look shaky at the back. Those three goals we shipped against Charlton. Then there's the shortage of strikers on our side. Cole injured, Yorke suspended. Oh, stop torturing yourself, Terry. It's the mighty Reds at Old Trafford. Unbeaten since dinosaurs walked the Earth. It's ten years since Liverpool turned us over there. March 1990. But the record's got to go some time. Why not tomorrow?

'Got myself in a right mess, haven't I?' says Dad, breaking the silence.

'Come again.'

'Walking out on your mother. What was I thinking of?'

'Maybe it's going to take time,' I say, feeling more than a bit impatient.

If I've had to put up with his whingeing once, I've had to listen to it a thousand times. I ought to say something but I can't pluck up the courage.

'Nobody likes to feel second best,' I tell him.

I feel a pang of guilt as I remember the night I dumped Chloe.

'Is that what she said?'

'She didn't have to, Dad. Mule was everything Mum wanted to be. She could get in a size 12 for a start, and she had you.'

Dad buries his head in his hands and puts on his suicide tape. He's done this compilation of misery-rock: the Verve, Crowded House, REM. That's it, if he's going to wallow in self-pity, I'm off. With United playing tomorrow, I can't even distract him by putting the footy on the radio. As I hit the street I zip my jacket up to my chin and pull my cap low over my eyes. It's sheeting down and it's cold. I squint through the silvery, flickering rain and look ahead to the holiday.

Julie and Fitz at Old Trafford.

Julie and Fitz exchanging presents on Christmas Day.

Julie and Fitz exchanging kisses at the stroke of twelve on New Year's Eve.

I see her lovely face at all the high points of the calendar and I know she'll be doing them all without me. For a moment I feel like going back to listen to the suicide tape with Dad. But I've sworn that I'm not going to give in. Somehow, some way I'm going to fight for her. She's too good for Fitz. She doesn't even really want to be with him. That stupid challenge! It pushed her back into his arms. One moment of madness, and my life's gone pear-shaped.

'I'm depending on you, lads,' I say out loud.

I can't bear the thought of Fitz triumphant. If Liverpool wins tomorrow he'll have it all. A victory over my team, my place in the school side, my girl by his side.

'You can't let me down,' I say.

I'm walking down Oliver Lyme Road. This old dear gives me a suspicious look. People get really paranoid about boys who talk to themselves. I let her get further up the road before clenching my fists and announcing to the world:

'You've got my happiness in your hands, lads. You've got to beat them, tank them, flatten them, murder them!'

Got to.

Sunday 17th December
11.14 a.m.

I have a bad feeling about this. They've just announced that Teddy Sheringham is out with a hamstring problem. That leaves us with only one fit striker, Ole Solskjaer. Liverpool will never have a better chance of turning us over.

'Another injury,' groans Dad. 'Doesn't anything ever go right?'

I'm dying to tell him to stop moaning, but I feel kind of sorry for him, so I bite my tongue. Besides, I'm too busy scanning the Old Trafford crowd for some sign of Julie and Fitz. The TV presenters keep repeating Gerard Houllier's words: 'We're going to beat them one day.' One day, but not today. Please not today.

'If we lose,' says Dad handing me a bowl of crisps and cashew nuts, 'my life won't be worth living. It's all Liverpool lads at work.'

'I know,' I say through gritted teeth. 'You keep telling me.'

Doesn't he ever stop moaning?

The match kicks off. For the first half hour it's like a game of chess. Liverpool are defending deep and stopping us playing. We can't get our natural rhythm going.

'Great,' says Dad. 'Even United are letting me down now.'

Letting you down. Since when was it about you, Dad? Stop rotten moaning!

He's right about one thing, though. We're not playing well. The only decent chances go to Liverpool. We're not opening them up at all. With forty minutes gone, Fitz and Julie will be well pleased. Liverpool are holding their own at Old Trafford.

'Too many passes going astray,' says Dad. 'If we lose...'

Stop moaning!

A couple of minutes before half-time things take a big turn for the worse. Gary Neville handles the ball outside the penalty area. It's a free kick in a dangerous position. Danny Murphy hits a curving shot just inside the post. We're 1–0 down. I flop back in my chair. I can just see Fitz with his arms round Julie. I'm just wishing that voodoo dolls worked when my mobile goes.

'What's the score, Terry?'

It's him, Fitz. He's called me from Old Trafford just to wind me up.

'Make sure you stay tuned at half-time,' he chuckles. 'You do want to see the goal again, don't you?'

I hang up on him. How did he get my number anyway? Stupid question, I suppose. After all, I got Julie's.

'Who was that?'

'Nobody.'

A big, grinning nobody.

There's no respite after the interval. After just one minute Michael Owen hits the bar.

'This is going from bad to worse,' says Dad.

Honestly, I've never really noticed until the last few weeks, but he could whine for England!

Stop moaning, stop moaning, stop moaning!

A minute later Solskjaer almost scores at the other end, our first meaningful attempt on goal.

'It's not our day,' whines Dad. 'We're not going to do it.'

Quit it, quit it, quit it!

Westerveld comes off his line to thwart Scholes.

'We can't lose, not to them.'

For goodness' sake, Dad, shut up.

We press and we press, but there's no penetration. After a frustrating second half we're seconds away from our first home defeat to Liverpool for ten years. Sure enough, the whistle goes and that's it, we've lost. If Arsenal beat Spurs tomorrow night we'll only be three points clear at the top of the table. That's when I see them. It's Fitz and Julie all right, wearing matching Liverpool away strips. The Sky Sports cameramen do this, zooming in on a cute girl. Only the cute girl they've chosen today is having the face kissed off her by my mortal enemy. He looks straight at the camera and holds up his fingers to signal 1–0. I know it's meant for me. It's what he promised. I stare at Julie. I wouldn't say she looks unhappy. How could she be? Her team has just won a famous victory. But there's a tension. I'm not kidding myself, am I? Even here, amid scenes of jubilation, she's not quite sure if it's him she wants to be with. Am I reading too much into a slight change of expression? I'm starting to know you, Julie Carter, and you don't really believe he's the one, do you? In the midst of despair I give a half-smile.

'What are you grinning at?' demands Dad. 'Don't you realise what's just happened? This is the worst day of my life.'

And, at long last, I say it:

'If this is the worst day of your life, you've had it pretty easy,' I snap. 'Just stop whining, Dad.'

He stares in disbelief.

'Whining? I've lost the woman I love, I'm living in a dump and now my team's lost to Liverpool.'

'It's true. You've lost Mum, but whose fault is that, Dad? Nobody asked you to walk out. Stop looking for excuses. You did it, nobody else. So stop whining and do something about it.'

I'm halfway to the door when he grabs my sleeve.

'You've no right to talk to me like that,' he says.

'Haven't I?'

I'm feeling strong. Even here, even after the bitterest setback of the season, I know it's not over. We're still top of the Premiership and

Julie's still the same girl who said she had feelings for me.

'We're all responsible for our own actions, Dad. You made a mistake, so put it right. Things happen because we let them. Well, I'm not going to lie down and die. I'm going to fight for what I want. Maybe you should do the same.'

Dad stands open-mouthed. I've said what I wanted, so I turn on my heel and jog down the stairs to the street. As I walk past the library and the museum I can feel the hurt of the defeat and of Fitz hugging Julie like that. But I won't let it end this way. Julie and me, we're meant to be together. I know it and somewhere, deep down, I think she does too. You want the Happy Ending, Terry Payne? Well, it won't just drop into your lap. Like you said to the old man, you're going to have to fight for it.

Eveything's still to play for.

Part Four

Giving the Girl the Cold Shoulder
Or
All Over Bar the Shouting?

1

Saturday 23rd December
3.10 p.m.

So what next?

The Reds are no problem. They've returned every ounce of love I've given them, and more. With every flowing, pulsating attack, with every telling pass and every goal, they tell me I matter. I'm part of the Red Tribe; a winner. It's different with Julie. With every flick of her glossy, black mane of hair, every sulky glance from those deep brown eyes, she cuts me to the quick, tells me I'm nothing.

'Any score, Terry?' shouts Mum.

She isn't really bothered about football; it's more a matter of moral support. She knows what I'll be like if we lose.

'Still 0–0,' I tell her.

I'm pacing the kitchen floor, listening to United–Ipswich on the radio. After three thousand, two hundred and forty minutes of football, two hundred and ninety-six fouls, twenty-eight bookings and one hundred and thirty-three goals, we finally lost our two-year unbeaten home record to Liverpool last week. It's vital we bounce back with a win today.

'Amy and I are nipping down to the shops,' says Mum, sticking her head round the door. 'I don't think we've got enough milk for the holiday.'

'OK.'

Mum's had a surprising change of heart recently. For months after Dad left, she was the needy one, wanting him back, wishing he'd reconsider. But in the last few weeks I've noticed something different about her, as if she's taken a long, hard look at herself in the mirror and decided to take hold of her life. Good for her, scary for Dad.

The doorbell goes. It's Bobby.

'Room for a little one?' he asks, with the usual twinkle in his eye.

'I thought you'd be out with Emma,' I grunt.

Emma Holland, that is, who's now his girlfriend. Quick work.

'She's in Liverpool, shopping with her mum and sister. What's the score at Old Trafford?'

'0–0.'

'Everton?'

'Losing 1–0.'

He doesn't look surprised. Well, who would?

'Liverpool did you a favour this morning, didn't they, Terry?'

Not half. After beating us last week at Old Trafford, and very nearly cutting my soul to ribbons, they've just hammered our closest rivals Arsenal 4–0 at Anfield. Weird thing, football. Your worst enemies can become allies overnight. Nothing is ever black and white. A bit like life, really.

'Doing anything over Christmas?' asks Bobby.

'No, family stuff, that's all. You?'

'A couple of parties. I'm taking Emma. That's what I called round for, to see if you wanted to come. The first one's tonight.'

'What, and play gooseberry to you two? No thanks.'

'You can't just sit at home moping over Julie. You know your trouble? You think the sun shines out of her. You've put her on a pedestal.'

Put her there? She climbed up all by herself.

'She's a girl, Terry, not an angel, not a vision, a flesh-and-blood girl. There's plenty more just like her.'

Like Julie? No, Bobby, not for me.

'Get back out in the field. I did.'

Didn't he just! For weeks he was dating two girls at once. No sooner had they rumbled him and given him the elbow than he copped off with Emma. Mr Rebound, that's Bobby, an elastic-band Romeo. It's all a game to him. He doesn't see how you can set your heart on just one girl. He's never fallen for anyone the way I've fallen for Julie. Love at first sight means different things to different people. For me it means wanting Julie until it hurts. For Bobby it means loving himself.

'Forget it, Bobby,' I tell him. 'I'm not interested.'

The roar of the crowd alerts me to a goal-scoring opportunity. 1–0. Ole ... Gunner ... Solskjaer. I dance round the kitchen, arms raised.

The Reds … returning the love. I wish Julie was. But she's still with Fitz, and she's totally out of my league.

Solskjaer's through again. 2–0. He is my Solskjaer, my Ole Solskjaer.

'We're back,' I crow. 'We're back.'

I'm back too. Last week, I was dead and buried. I'd lost my girl and we'd lost to the arch-enemy, Liverpool. Can there be a worse place to be a Man U fan than here in Prescot on the eastern rim of Merseyside?

I was gutted, humiliated. Now, just a few days later, I can hold my head up, and it's all down to the Reds, returning the love.

'Sure you're not coming tonight? Emma's got a couple of mates…'

I wrinkle my nose.

'Nah, don't feel like it.'

'It's your funeral. I'll give you a ring tomorrow.'

'Yes, see you, Bobby.'

He bumps into Mum and Amy at the front door. I hear them talking.

'Why don't you go to that party?' asks Mum, emptying the shopping bags. 'It'll do you good.'

'I don't want to, OK?'

Mum holds her hands up.

'Only asking. I still don't know why you had to finish with Chloe. She's such a lovely girl.'

Yes, she is a lovely girl. But she isn't Julie.

'You know why,' I retort. 'I like somebody else.'

'Who?'

'Julie Carter.'

'You're a silly lad,' says Mum. 'It's obvious this Julie's not interested.'

But that's the thing, Mum, she *is* interested. I can't quite believe it, but she's got feelings for me too. She told me so only last week. What did she say? *Why didn't you tell me four months ago?* Before she went out with Fitz, that is.

I had hope for us then, real hope. And now she's back with Fitz, lousy, smirking Fitz. Plastic Scouser Fitz.

'Mum, it's my life.'

That's right, it's my life, and I'll cock it up my own way.

If that's Christmas, you can keep it.

It was the tale of two turkeys, three if you count my dad. I had Christmas dinner with Mum and Amy and Gran and Grandad Thompson. The turkey was moist, the sprouts were firm and my thoughts were elsewhere ... with Julie, where else?

Is she with Fitz? Is she happy?

I had Christmas tea with Dad and Amy in his scabby flat. The turkey was burnt and the sprouts had dissolved into a green mush, so we had TV dinners on our knees and I was still thinking about Julie.

Do they have mistletoe? Are they kissing?

That was Christmas Day. It came, it went, it was rubbish. Still, at least life's halfway back to normal now. There's a full football programme today. Arsenal have already kicked off. They're 1–0 up against Leicester through Henry. I suck in my breath. If they run out winners, we've got to beat Villa away to keep our eight-point lead at the top.

'Oh, it's not football again,' moans Amy, walking into the living room.

My little sister doesn't understand The Beautiful Game.

'I'm afraid so.'

'I wish you and Dad still went to the match,' she says.

You and me both, Amy, but family finances just don't run to it any more. I have to make do with Sky Sports instead. The Villa–United game starts with relentless United pressure.

Giggs, Solskjaer and Butt all have good chances. After twenty minutes we've had sixty per cent of possession, but it's still 0–0.

Zero progress, like Julie and me.

At Highbury Arsenal are running away with it. They're 3–1 up. At Villa Park, Paul Scholes goes close with a header. Another newsflash from Highbury. Now it's 4–1. The pressure is on us to come up with a goal. We reach half-time. United's possession stands at seventy per cent, astonishing for the away team, but no breakthrough.

Same as Julie and me.

Meanwhile, the news from Highbury has got even worse. Arsenal have battered Leicester 6–1. I'm on the edge of my seat, willing the Reds to score, but as the minutes go by I'm becoming more and more tense. All that possession and nothing to show for it. Beckham's crosses don't have the usual zip, Ole Solskjaer's killer instinct seems to have deserted him.

'Come on, lads.'

Six minutes to go and I'm losing hope.

Then the breakthrough comes. Beckham crosses, Solskjaer scores with a sweet header. How could I have doubted them?

Villa 0, United 1.

We've broken their unbeaten home record and hung onto our eight-point lead. Suddenly, it dawns on me, there's a lesson in this. United haven't had it all easy this season. We got turned over by Chelsea in the Charity Shield. We lost to Arsenal and Liverpool, but did we fold? Did we heck! We had that bit of steel. Keep your nerve, hold on to what you know to be true, and things are bound to turn out all right in the end. Keep your nerve, that's it! I've done enough chasing round after Julie. Who wants somebody who acts all forlorn and desperate?

I'm not going to be a little, lovesick puppy any more, trailing round after her, embarrassing myself. The lovelorn bit hasn't worked, so I've got to change tack. I'm going to salvage some dignity. I'll take a leaf out of United's book. What I need is tactics, a strategy. I'm going to play it cool. Wouldn't that be a novelty? No matter how often she glances round, she won't catch me looking at her soulfully. No matter how much I'm tempted, I'll be looking the other way.

Thursday 28th December
8.30 a.m.

I'm woken by Amy squealing her head off. Her best friend Katie slept over last night and she's squealing too.

'Mum, Terry, come and look. It snowed in the night.'

I stagger to the window in my boxer shorts. Amy's right. It's a total white-out. Everywhere's covered in a blanket of snow, two or three inches at least. I watch for a few moments then climb back into bed. My mind starts playing a game of What Ifs.

What if you could win the Double or win Julie? Which would you choose?

What if you could get Mum and Dad back together or win Julie? What then?

I shake my head. Even if life was like that, how could I choose?

But what if life turned out the way it ought to? Me and Julie together, United winning the Premiership and the Champions League, Dad back where he belongs, that would be my idea of heaven on earth. The trill of my mobile breaks in on my thoughts.

'Hello?'

'You up yet, misery guts?'

It's Bobby. I didn't think he knew half past eight existed!

'Get up, you lazy dog.'

This is Bobby calling me lazy! We're talking pots, kettles and the colour black.

'I'm calling for Emma on my way to yours,' he says. 'You're going to enjoy yourself, and that's an order. Snowtime!'

'But...'

It's too late to tell him I'd rather stay in and feel sorry for myself. He's already hung up.

'Terry love,' Mum calls, 'Would you take Amy and Katie to the park? They're really excited.'

'But I was going out with Bobby.'

'Where?'

'Snowball fight.'

'Perfect. You can take the girls with you.'

Her voice changes. She's obviously talking to Amy and Katie.

'Terry will take you to the park.'

The announcement is met with deafening cheers.

Thursday 28th December
10.00 a.m.

'I know,' shouts Bobby. 'Snow angels.'

He throws himself on his back, flapping his arms to make wings in the snow. Before I know it, Emma, Amy and Katie have joined him, laughing like mad things.

'Come in and join us, Terry. The snow's lovely.'

Oh well, in for a penny, in for a pound. I flop down, flapping my arms.

I take my eyes off the others just long enough for them to pound me with snowballs.

'Right,' I declare, clawing up handfuls of snow. 'You're dead.'

Within moments I'm in the thick of a furious snowball fight. My ears and cheeks are burning with the cold and slowly melting snow is running down my back, but I couldn't care less. I'm having fun.

'Who wants to help me build a snowman?' asks Emma.

Amy and Katie are jumping up and down, shouting: 'Me, me!'

'She's good with them,' I say, watching Emma organising the girls.

'Yes, she's great,' says Bobby approvingly.

'Are you going to do the right thing by this one?' I ask.

'Meaning?'

I'm thinking about his exes, Caitlin and Rosie.

'No two-timing her.'

Bobby winks.

'You never know, Terry mate, you never know.'

He jogs over to help with the snowman. I shake my head. The sun's come out and it's gleaming on the spire of Prescot parish church in the distance. It's a picture postcard scene. A gang of boys are playing football. My thoughts go back three weeks to footy practice. At a quarter to four that Wednesday afternoon Julie had all but told me she was going to dump Fitz. By half past my hopes were dashed. I close my eyes and I'm there on the pitch. Fitz is goading me: *You'll never take my place in this team. You are the weakest link.* We go for a fifty-fifty ball. He's got his studs up. *You are the weakest link, goodbye.* I refuse to pull out. I will not back down. There's a sickening crunch, then a loud scream. It's Fitz. I've broken his ankle.

It was an accident, Julie, an accident.

But she'll never believe that now. And that's why she's with him, because he's a victim, and I'm a thug.

But it wasn't like that, Julie. It wasn't like that at all.

'Hey, Terry,' shouts Bobby. 'Get over here. You don't think you're leaving all the hard work to us, do you?'

I smile and join in. As if by magic, Bobby has just produced a carrot for the snowman's nose and a couple of two-pence pieces for the eyes when I hear familiar voices. Kelly Magee and Gary Tudor, Fitz and ... Julie.

Gary's the first to say anything: 'Well, if it isn't Chopper Payne.'

I scowl.

'It was an accident, Gary.'

'Yes, sure it was. You're such a little innocent, just like Roy Keane.'

Fitz lets his mate do the talking. He stands propped up on his crutches, enjoying my discomfort. He's clever like that. He knows the best way to Julie's heart is to play the victim. And, boy, doesn't he milk it! Look at him, all blue eyes and Michael Owen haircut; you'd think butter wouldn't melt in his mouth. I can feel Julie's eyes on me, but I refuse to meet them, even though it's killing me. These new tactics, I never thought they'd be so tough to put into action.

As they turn to go, Fitz stumbles. Julie puts an arm round his waist to support him.

'He did that on purpose,' says Bobby. 'For your benefit.'

'Tell me something I don't know,' I say.

'Move on,' says Bobby. 'You're flogging a dead horse.'

I watch Julie and Fitz crossing the park. Now that she's got her back to me, it's safe to look. Flogging a dead horse? Maybe. All these months and I'm no closer to taking her out.

But I can still remember her words before the practice match when it all went wrong: *If only you'd told me four months ago.* And she kissed me. I'm not imagining it. It happened. I can still feel the press of her lips on mine.

There's something there. I know there is. Fitz isn't right for you, Julie. You're not happy with him. If only I could talk to you alone, just for a few minutes, if only I could explain. But I won't plead and I won't beg. I'm not going to run after you, Julie Carter. I've got my pride. No matter how hard it is, every time I see you I'm not going to give myself away.

I knew this was a mistake. I knew it the moment Bobby persuaded me into it. Going to a New Year's party in my frame of mind. Am I mad? For starters, the moment we arrived Bobby left me on my own to dance with Emma. Then Chloe showed up with Jamie Sneddon. Every time I turn round, she's there with him. I think she's trying to tell me what I'm missing. As if I haven't suffered enough, Fitz has just arrived with Julie. I might have guessed they'd be here. I'm sticking to my promise, though. Every time I come near Julie I'm Mr Cool, at least on the outside. I said I wouldn't go trailing after her, and I'm not. So here I am sitting on my own in a corner watching everybody else either dancing or copping off. Whoever said you never feel so lonely as when you're in the middle of a crowd got it dead right. I become aware of somebody talking to me:

'You haven't seen Bobby, have you, Terry?'

It's Emma.

'No, I thought he was with you.'

'He was. I got talking to one of my mates and he just disappeared.'

Oh oh, no, Bobby, you wouldn't.

'I've been all round the house looking for him.'

Not right under her nose. Bobby, you wouldn't.

'He's probably just in the loo.'

Emma smiles thinly. I think she's got an inkling.

'Yes, maybe.'

That's when I hear pandemonium in the kitchen.

Please, not Bobby.

A voice rasps over the beat of the music:

'I'll have you, Quinn. Outside, now!'

It's Paul Scully. He's lashing out at somebody, or at least trying to. Gary Tudor's pulling him back. That's when I see Bobby. He's got a red mark above his eye, and he's looking a bit embarrassed. Paul's still trying to get at him.

'Snogging my bird, the dirty little get.'

I catch sight of Pepsey Cooper, Paul's girlfriend. She looks upset, you know, caught-at-it upset. Her mascara's running. Bobby, you idiot. Right under Emma's nose, and Paul's. Talk about asking for it. Paul gets a hand free and thumps Bobby smack on the nose. It takes Gary and a couple of other guys to restrain him. I glance round at Emma. Her eyes are welling up. Oh great! Now I'm going to have to take care of her. She turns and heads for the door.

'Emma!'

I glare at Bobby. This was bound to happen some time. I'm about to follow Emma when I come face to face with Julie. Am I mistaken, or is she following me round? I'm tempted to speak to her. My God, are the tactics working? Great, here's Julie pursuing *me* and I've got my hands full with Emma. Aaargh!

'Emma, you can't go home alone, not when you're upset.'

Even as I'm saying it, I'm actually hoping she can. She looks at me.

'How could he do that to me, Terry? How?'

I notice Julie standing on the doorstep, watching us. What do I do? I just want to dump Emma and run to Julie. But Emma's suffering. Bobby's done the dirty on her and she needs a friend. That's what I'm good at, being a friend. This is killing me, Julie, just killing me. I take Emma's arm and lead her away.

'Come on, Emma, I'll walk you home.'

What am I, some sort of rotten saint?

Emma smiles.

'You're a nice guy, Terry.'

Yes, that's me, nice guy, but you know what they say about nice guys? They never get the girl. Emma kisses me on the cheek. My face starts to burn. What if Julie saw us? What if she takes it the wrong way? As Emma and I walk off down the street, I'm dying to know if Julie's still watching. Did she want to talk to me? And what about? But I don't look back. I'm not going to chase after her like a lovesick kid. I'm doing the right thing. I know I am.

Aren't I?

Monday 1st January 2001
One minute past midnight

I'm on my own again. I have been since eleven o'clock. Emma and I were just turning into her street when Bobby came panting up. It was all a mistake, he said, a misunderstanding. Just let me explain. And Emma let him. That's how I left them, with Bobby in grovel mode and Emma slowly thawing. He'll win her round. That's what he does, Bobby. He charms people.

Since then I've been wandering round, killing time. I must have relived every moment of my pursuit of Julie, the first sight of her in the school gym, the time she got together with Fitz at the school disco, the time she kissed me. I told Mum I'd be home by half past midnight. See in the New Year and come straight home. So I wasn't about to turn up an hour and a half early. I don't want her thinking I'm a loser.

Which I suppose I am. Especially if Julie thought Emma and I...

It's nagging at me. Not another misunderstanding. I mean, that's two to explain, and I'm no Bobby. I don't do charm. It's a relief to see the fireworks and hear the strains of Auld Lang Syne. Now I can head home and put a brave face on a disastrous evening. I turn into our street and groan.

It's Dad. He's rotten drunk and he's shouting his head off:

'Just give me another chance, Sharon. I love you.'

Except it comes out *Ahlurrvya*.

He says it over and over again:

Ahlurrvya, ahlurrvya, ahlurrvya.

Then he sinks to his knees on the pavement.

Oh, Dad!

All the neighbours are looking. Mum's at the window too.

'Terry, would you get him out of here?'

'Dad, get up,' I plead. 'I'll take you home.'

'But I love her,' he says.

It comes out *Ahlurrverr*.

Ahlurrverr, ahrlurrverr, ahlurrverr.

'I know you do, Dad,' I say, guiding him in the direction of his flat. 'But this isn't the way to show it.'

'Then what is, Terry?'

As we stagger away I lift my eyes to the sky. I remember Emma kissing me on the cheek. Then I think of the way I ignored Julie. It seemed a good idea at the time. Now I'm not so sure.

'Tell me, Terry, what is the way to show it?'

I have to give him an honest reply.

'I don't know, Dad. I just don't know.'

2

Strategy, I call it. Keeping my dignity, I call it. Hah? Suicide is more like it. What was I thinking of? The very idea of me, the skinny ginger nut with the number one skinhead crop, the many-freckled failure, Mr Won't-Get-Any-GCSEs, deciding to ignore somebody as drop-dead gorgeous as Julie Carter. As if she's even noticed! She's too busy with her Michael Owen lookalike boyfriend and her bimbo best mate Kelly.

It's been the best part of a month I've been ignoring her, and, in all that time – every single one of the twenty-eight days I've kept up my *strategy* – I'll bet she hasn't given me a second thought. All I've done is leave the way wide open for Fitz. Some competition I am. Just when the strains in their relationship are starting to show I start pretending she doesn't exist. Nice one, Terry! As I head over to Dad's flat to watch the FA Cup fourth-round tie against West Ham, I try to get my head straight. What on earth do I do now? She hasn't even spoken to me in a month, never mind decided to dump Fitz for me. My mobile goes. For a crazy split second I fantasise that it might be Julie on the other end of the line. It isn't. It's Bobby.

'Where are you?'

'Here.'

I hear his sucked-in breath.

'And where's here?'

'I'm on my way to my dad's, to watch the match.'

'Well, du-uh.'

'Do you want to come over and watch it?'

'Forget it. Did you know that people in the UK spend an average two hundred and fifteen minutes a day watching TV?'

197

I didn't.

'Anyway,' says Bobby. 'I've sworn off football. Bad for my health.'

That's on account of Everton getting battered 3–0 at home by First Division Tranmere Rovers. Bobby just can't take the humiliation. Or the heart palpitations.

'Do you want to do something later?' he asks.

'Sure. Where's Emma?'

'She's sleeping over at a friend's house. Girl thing.'

So he obviously needs me for a boy thing.

'Call in at mine about five. I'll be back by then.'

'And through to the fifth round of the Cup,' says Bobby. 'You'll murder West Ham.'

I hope he's right. Somehow, I'm pretty relaxed about it. We beat them 3–1 in the league just twenty-seven days ago, and should have scored more. They were as limp as week-old lettuce. We could have got into double figures.

'See you later, then.'

'Yes, see you, Terry.'

As I jog up the stairs to Dad's flat I can hear the strains of 'Don't Let the Sun Catch You Crying' by Gerry and the Pacemakers. It must be centuries old, from the Record Collection that Time Forgot. When is Dad going to pull himself together? I find the door open. For a moment, I feel quite spooked. I'm thinking Marie Celeste.

'You there, Dad?'

'Yes, come in, Terry.'

Phew, he hasn't slipped into a parallel universe or anything like that.

I look around for a place to sit. Dad seems to have forgotten his resolution not to have a guy-flat. When he first moved in, he used to keep it neat but suddenly there are microwave meal trays and drinks cans on the coffee table, there's a pair of undies on the stereo and the carpet doesn't look like it's been vacuumed in weeks. He's obviously stuck in yearning mode. Message to brain: Don't mention Mum in front of him.

'I thought you'd have the match coverage on,' I say.

'It's ITV,' says Dad. 'Who wants to listen to Terry Venables rabbitting on?'

Funny, Dad's always rated El Tel, even if he is a Cockney. I decide his behaviour has got more to do with male auto-destruct than his real verdict on TV football pundits, and let it pass without comment.

'So can I put it on now?'

'Go ahead, I need a win to cheer me up.'

Just lately, Dad whines louder than a pair of Boeing 747 engines. And he's got less lift.

Be patient, I tell myself. It's a phase he's got to get through.

Sunday 28th January
4 p.m.

Some phase! Suddenly Dad's going into overdrive.

His job's rubbish, his flat's rubbish, now his team's rubbish. Only he doesn't say rubbish – somebody pass the swear box.

His self-pitying whine reaches a crescendo in the seventy-sixth minute of the match. This is how he descends into emotional meltdown:

Paolo Di Canio beats United's offside trap as Kanoute's pass dissects our defence.

Moaning reaches 7 on the Richter scale.

The United defenders stand appealing for offside.

7.2 on the Richter scale.

The linesman's flag stays down.

7.8.

Barthez in the United goal continues to appeal. He looks like a schoolboy asking for the loo.

8.0.

Di Canio puts the ball in the net. Now Barthez looks like a schoolboy who's forgotten his homework.

That's a big 9.5 on the Richter scale. Any minute now he'll go off the scale altogether.

'Rubbish, absolute rubbish,' is Dad's verdict.

Boing!

When I dare to contradict him, pointing out that we outplayed the Hammers in the first half, that we're thirteen points clear at the top of the Premiership and well-placed in the Champions League, not only does he not stop whining, he actually accuses me of *not caring!* What's he on about? Even when I was at nursery school I cared. One Monday morning the teacher asked each of us to sing our favourite rhyme. You know what I chose? Glory, Glory Man United!

'Me!' I retort angrily. '*Me*, not care? Who cancelled our season tickets, Dad? Go on, who put his gym subscription before the Reds? We could have been there today at the Theatre of Dreams. But you wanted to get fit, just so you could cop off with Mule.'

Dad doesn't like being reminded about Muriel. The memory of him going out with a size 12 Permatanned gym bunny is the biggest obstacle to Mum taking him back. What woman likes being dumped for a younger, slimmer model?

'Oh, rub salt in the wounds, why don't you?' he snaps.

'Dad, the only wounds you've got are entirely self-inflicted. What did you expect? That Mum would take you back with open arms the moment you got fed up of your...'

The word *floozy* pops into my head. It's a word Mum might use, but it would sound ridiculous coming from me.

'My what?'

'Your ... your ... MULE!'

We stand glaring at each other, veins bulging, eyeballs popping.

An imaginary exchange goes through my mind. It ends with Dad calling me an ungrateful pup and me calling him a loser. Luckily, we both keep our mouths shut.

'I'm going,' I say.

'Fine,' he says.

'Fine.'

'Fine.'

'Bye.'

'Yes, bye.'

Sunday 28th January
5.15 p.m.

'Do you want to know the Cup draw?' asks Mum.

'No,' I say.

'No way,' says Bobby.

Who cares? Our teams are both out of the competition. Amy giggles. Bobby and I give her daggers, as if reminding her that little sisters can be easily kebabed.

'Another bacon butty?' asks Mum.

She's obviously trying to console us after the football catastrophes of the weekend. What becomes of the broken-hearted? I'll tell you: they gross out on rashers of prime back bacon.

'Wouldn't mind,' says Bobby.

Does he ever? The boy's got the digestive system of a great white shark. One of these days he'll cough up a car number-plate.

'Anyway,' says Bobby, 'what's that you're eating, Mrs P?'

'She's on Carol Vorderman's detox diet,' Amy informs him.

'Oh,' says Bobby. 'Stale buns and rabbit food. My old lady had a go at that.'

'Did she lose weight?' asks Mum hopefully.

'Nah, just friends. It was all those sprouts. Gave her gas.'

Mum frowns. I'm not sure whether it's because of the mention of gas or because the diet hasn't got a hundred per cent approval rating. She's desperate for a quick fix.

'I think that must be a different diet,' she says.

'Talking of gas,' says Bobby. 'Did you know that, on average, people break wind fifteen times a day?'

'Yes,' says Mum, wrinkling her nose. 'I saw the advert on telly. And before you say anything, I still think men are a lot worse than women.'

'Not according to the statistics,' says Bobby.

'Bobby,' says Mum, 'I'll bet you it's men who come up with those statistics.'

'Could be,' says Bobby. 'It's a man's world.'

'Mm,' says Mum, 'that's half the problem. In fact, it's the whole problem.'

I grimace. For him, maybe. He's had more girlfriends than most kids have had zits. But the world doesn't belong to this particular guy. I take after Dad, a loser in love.

'Anyway,' says Mum, 'seeing as you lads are going to inherit the Earth, you won't mind doing the washing-up. I've got a phone call to make.'

She's about to go when she turns round.

'Would you baby-sit for me on Wednesday, Terry?'

'No problem,' I say. 'We're playing Sunderland away. I'll be listening to the match on the radio anyway. So what're you doing?'

There's a brief pause.

'You *are* joking!' she says, walking out.

I stand in a puddle of bewilderment. Now what have I done?

'Parents' evening, you dope,' says Bobby.

Fancy forgetting that. It's like a turkey getting amnesia about Christmas.

'Got any biccies?' Bobby asks.

'None in the house,' I say. 'Mum doesn't want any temptation, so we're all on a diet.'

Amy nods ruefully.

'That's right. There isn't even ice cream.'

'So what do you have for afters?'

'Fruit or yoghurt.'

Bobby looks unimpressed.

'We'll go down the offie later,' he says. 'Stock up on illicit chocolate.'

All of a sudden I know what Al Capone got out of Prohibition.

'Will you get me something?' asks Amy, brightening.

'Sure,' says Bobby. 'Raid the piggy bank.'

'I've got a steel cash box,' says Amy stuffily. 'To stop him getting in.'

By *him* she means *me*. I act all offended.

'When did I ever raid your money box?'

'Four years ago when you wanted that Man U annual.'

'Oh yes, I forgot. Sorry.'

We wash up then head down to the offie.

'So how's it going with Emma?' I ask. 'Has she stopped bringing up the Pepsey Cooper incident yet?'

'Just about,' says Bobby.

There's a twinkle in his eye as he adds:

'It was worth it though. She's got lips like a limpet, that Pepsey. Snogs the gob off you.'

'Bobby, you're disgusting.'

'What, just because you're not getting anywhere?'

That's a low blow.

'How long is it since you last talked to the lovely Julie?'

'You know very well. It was New Year's Eve.'

'Still ignoring her?' he asks mischievously.

'OK,' I admit. 'So it was a dumb idea. What do you suggest?'

'I suggest,' says Bobby, nice and slow so it sinks in, 'that you forget all about her.'

Monday 29th January
12.45 p.m.

I'm sitting on one of the new benches near the sports hall. They're meant to be for anyone who wants to read or sit quietly. Of course, the moment Fitz lays eyes on me, he has a different interpretation.

'Found the Billy-No-Mates seats, have you?' he sneers.

Gary Tudor and Paul Scully laugh appreciatively, egging him on to have another dig.

'Did you enjoy the match?' he asks. 'I know I did.'

I knew this was coming. Kicked out of the FA Cup in the early stages. I feel so humiliated.

'Get stuffed.'

'Funny,' says Fitz, 'I thought that's what happened to United.'

'Did you see Barthez standing with his arm up?' chuckles Paul. 'What a divvy.'

'Please, Mr Di Canio,' says Gary in a really stupid, whining voice, 'don't kick the ball past me.'

He's trying to sound French, but it's more Welsh than anything.

'You can't be onside. You're playing Man U.'

The next minute, the three of them are standing with their hands up.

'Go on,' I grumble. 'Have your fun.'

'Oh, I intend to,' says Fitz. 'Especially now the plaster cast's off.'

I wince at the memory of my mis-timed tackle, not because it hurt Fitz, he was asking for it, but because it pushed Julie back into his arms. Fancy feeling sorry for that moron. I wish I'd broken his neck as well.

'I'll be playing again in a month to six weeks,' he says. 'Then I'm taking my place back.'

I thought that would be getting to him. I did well in training last week and Six Guns is going to give me a start in the team in our next match. It's great, I'm replacing Fitz.

I intend to make the most of it. What wouldn't I give to put one over on Frisky Fitzy.

'You're going to have to fight for it,' I tell him, managing a cosmetic yawn of contempt.

Fitz's eyes narrow.

'You wait, MnM,' he says.

(That's my new nickname, MnM, short for Mad Manc).

'I'll fight you all right.'

Gary and Paul think Fitz means competition on the pitch, but I know what really happened in our collision.

I know which of us put his studs up first and which of us meant to do damage. No, when he says fight he means it. We're talking GBH. Fair enough, if that's the way he wants to play it.

'Two home defeats in a month,' says Fitz. 'Do you think the wheels are coming off the Man U bandwagon?'

'You wish,' I say defiantly.

'Aw, diddums lose to ums nasty Cockneys?' taunts Fitz.

It's his parting shot. They move away, laughing and pushing. I stare at my feet.

'Penny for them,' says a voice.

I look up.

'Oh, hi, Emma.'

Emma's smiling. Smiles suit her. I'd forgotten how attractive she is.

'Seen Bobby?'

'No. That's why I'm sitting here. Nothing to do.'

I remember what Fitz said: the Mad Manc in his Billy-No-Mates seat.

'You can talk to me.'

She sits down next to me.

'How did your mocks go?'

My shoulders sag.

'They didn't.'

'That bad, eh?'

'They've put me in a booster class for Maths. Mum will go mad.'

'I don't see why,' said Emma, 'You can't be good at everything.'

'I'm not that good at anything,' I say. 'Me and exams don't mix. It's a bit like sincerity and politicians.'

'Bit like me then,' says Emma cheerfully. 'I've got a brain the size of a pea.'

'I'm sure that's not true.'

'All right,' she says with her heart-stopping smile. 'A broad bean then. Honestly, I'm not very academic.'

It's my turn to smile. When I'm around Paul and Gary, and especially Fitz, I feel really inadequate. They're all in the top set for everything, same as Julie. You know who I am: Billy-No-Brains in his Billy-No-Mates seat.

'I'm Bobby's dream woman,' says Emma. 'Pretty but dim.'

Actually, she's more than *pretty*. If it wasn't for Julie ... and the fact that she's my best mate's girl...

'You're not dim!' I protest.

'Thanks.'

She brushes a loose thread from her skirt. Her knee touches mine. A mild electric shock shudders through me.

'Listen to us,' she says. 'We sound like card-carrying members of the Low Esteem Club. You know what we need, a booster class in self-confidence.'

Personally, I can't see that she's short on self-confidence at all.

'To tell you the truth, Emma,' I say, 'I couldn't take much more boosting. I think I'm all boosted out.'

She laughs. It reminds me of the times I've made Julie laugh. It's nice making a girl laugh. It makes you feel ... somebody.

'Does Bobby talk about me much?' she asks.

Suddenly I don't feel somebody any more. I'm just somebody's mate.

'All the time,' I fib.

'Liar.'

She can obviously see right through me. What am I supposed to do, tell the girl the truth, that she's his latest *squeeze*, OK to be going on with but nothing serious?

'You don't need to stick up for him, you know,' she says. 'I know exactly what Bobby's like. I haven't forgotten New Year.'

I'm starting to feel uncomfortable. Where's this going? She soon tells me.

'Bobby's a laugh, but we're going nowhere fast. I'm beginning to wonder whether I went out with the wrong friend.'

She gives my hand a squeeze. The mild shock is replaced by seismic Death Row convulsions.

Oh my God, I'm being squeezed by the squeeze! My skin prickles and my throat goes dry. This I didn't expect!

'Emma,' I stammer, 'Bobby's my best mate.'

'Yes, and you're very loyal. I'm not sure if he deserves you. I don't know whether he deserves either of us.'

She has inched closer. I can smell the sweet mixture of perfume and girl-hair. Oh crumbs!

'You were lovely to me at New Year, a real gentleman.'

Gentleman, *me*? I don't feel much of a gentleman right now. I feel hot, bothered, confused, tempted. Emma's looking right into my eyes. I don't know where to put myself.

'I needed a friend that night. Thanks.'

With that, she gives me a peck on the cheek. And, would you believe it, just as her lips touch my skin, Julie walks out of the sports hall accompanied by Kelly McGee. Dinner-time gymnastics club. How did I forget?

No-o-o-o!

Julie stares at me like I'm some slavering dog on heat, then jogs towards the library. I can't help stealing a look at her legs. Kelly, self-appointed secretary of the No-to-Mad-Mancs Society, scowls at me then trots after Julie. No doubt she'll soon be sticking the knife into me. Emma Holland, your timing's incredible!

'Oh, wonderful,' I groan. 'Just wonderful!'

'Still carrying that torch for Julie Carter, are you?'

Emma sounds disappointed.

'What do you think?'

'I might just have done you a favour,' she says.

'How do you work that out?' I bleat.

'I might just have made her jealous.'

I shake my head. Chance would be a fine thing!

Mum knocks on the bedroom door.

'Can I have your duvet cover for the wash?'

'Hang on.'

I start unbuttoning the cover. Mum pops her head round the door.

'You need to do a tidy up in here.'

'Yes, in a minute. One thing at a time.'

I'm wrestling with the duvet and the duvet's winning. My mobile goes. Mum passes it to me. It's Bobby.

'I think I'll let it ring,' I say, finally overcoming the duvet's resistance.

'Have you two fallen out?' Mum asks.

'No, of course not.'

'Then why aren't you answering?'

I go all hot.

'Don't feel like it.'

Mum gives me a sideways look. It suddenly strikes me that her face looks thinner. Would you believe it, her diet is actually working.

'Anything you'd like to tell me?' she asks.

Normally I'd die rather than confide in Mum, but I'm short of shoulders to cry on. Dad's suffering from a terminal case of Self-Pity Syndrome and I can hardly tell Bobby that his girlfriend's got the hots for me, can I? Pathetically, that just about exhausts my list of confidants.

'It's a bit embarrassing.'

'Go on.'

'You know Emma?'

'Bobby's girl, Emma?'

'Yes. She kind of came on to me today.'

'Oh dear.'

I thought Mum would be appalled. Since Dad's fling with Mule, she's really down on love-cheats. Not that she ever had much time for them in the first place. Very straight-laced, my mum. But just lately, every time infidelity is mentioned on TV or in the paper, she jumps on her soapbox.

Really bitter.

'Is that it? "Oh dear"?'

'What did you expect?'

'Dunno. More than "Oh dear".'

'It happens.'

I snort.

'Not to me, it doesn't.'

'I don't see why not. Don't put yourself down. You're a good-looking lad.'

'Behave.'

'No, you are.'

Come to think of it, Chloe Blackburn liked me, and Julie sort of ... kind of ... now Emma, she definitely likes me. That's three really cute girls. Maybe I'm not such a loser, after all.

'So what do I do about it?'

Mum smiles.

'The question is, what *did* you do about it?'

'Nothing. Bobby's my best mate.'

'Then I think you did the right thing.'

I smile.

'Nothing, you mean?'

'Exactly. You didn't let anybody down. Not Bobby, not Emma, not yourself. You were a good friend.'

That again!

'Yes, you're right, Mum.'

'It doesn't matter if other people want to behave badly,' she says. 'You've got to be able to look yourself in the mirror.'

I think of Bobby. He behaves badly on a regular basis and he has no trouble looking in the mirror. He loves himself to bits. He could look like the Elephant Man and still put on as many airs as Brad Pitt.

'What are you two talking about?' asks Amy, arriving with her duvet cover.

'I was just saying what a good-looking lad your big brother is,' says Mum.

Amy lets out this paint-stripping shriek of laughter.

'Him!'

Go on, I think, build my self-confidence, why don't you?

'I think you ought to ring Bobby,' says Mum, leaving with the laundry. 'After all, you didn't do anything, did you?'

'You're right, Mum. Thanks.'

I ring Bobby back. While I wait for him to answer I think about what Mum said.

No, I didn't do anything.

I never do.

3

'Good performance, lads,' says Six Guns, applauding us off the pitch.

We've just won 2–0 against St Thomas Aquinas. I had a good game, clearing off the line when it was still 0–0 and setting up our first for Jamie Sneddon. He didn't thank me for the assist, of course. I still haven't been forgiven for breaking Fitz's ankle. Jamie just ran across to the touchline and waved to Chloe. They started going out the moment I dumped her. The rebound effect. Or is it the *Up yours* effect?

'Good goals, Gary and Jamie,' says Six Guns. 'Busy work in midfield, Terry.'

A couple of pairs of eyes turn in my direction. Any recognition for my efforts is pretty grudging, but it is there. Maybe, just maybe, memories of what happened back in December are beginning to fade. One person who'll never forget is Fitz. He's watched the whole game from the touchline, with Julie by his side. His brooding presence makes sure nobody actually congratulates me.

'I won't be long,' I tell Amy who is standing shivering all by herself in the drizzle.

I feel quite sorry for her, really. It must be boring just standing there, not knowing anyone. I've got to get a move on. It's parents' evening tonight and Mum is going straight to the school after work.

'Hurry up,' says Amy, 'I'm freezing, and it's starting to rain.'

When I come out of the changing room, I get a surprise. It's throwing it down. That isn't the surprise. It's done nothing else this year. No, what I didn't expect was to see Amy sheltering under Julie's umbrella.

'She was getting drenched,' says Julie. 'This isn't really fair on her.'

'I know,' I say, 'But Mum is working. No alternative.'

'You could get a baby-sitter,' says Julie. 'Lots of us do it for extra cash.'

Is that some sort of offer? My pulse rate accelerates.

'Thanks for sheltering her,' I mumble, not quite sure what to say next.

'Where's Fitz?' pops out inevitably.

'Talking to Gary and Jamie somewhere.'

There's something in the tone of her voice that gives me hope. She isn't quite the adoring girlfriend.

'Looking forward to tonight?' asks Julie.

'Parents' evening?' I ask. 'No chance.'

Julie will be all right. She's in top set for everything. University material. I've only made it in English and French. The conversation sags between us. Questions hang in the air, but they remain unanswered. Amy stands between me and a meaningful conversation. Fitz appears and waves to Julie. Julie acknowledges him.

'Hang on,' she says as Amy and I turn to go. 'Here.'

She produces a rolled umbrella from her bag.

'It's Kelly's. You can borrow it for tonight.'

'Thanks.'

I stare after Julie, wondering if they mean something, the umbrella and the mention of baby-sitting.

'You like her, don't you?' asks Amy.

'Don't be daft,' I say.

Daft? She's anything but.

Wednesday 31st January
8.05 p.m.

'How long will Mum be?' asks Amy.

She picks her times, my little sister. It's Sunderland (third in the Premiership) against United (first), what they call a six-pointer. Kevin Phillips has just pulled the trigger for the Black Cats and it's backs against the wall for United.

They're putting pressure on us, breaking up our play, giving us no time on the ball and...

...Amy starts asking some stupid question.

'Well?' says Amy impatiently.

'Well what?' I ask.

Why can't she just go and watch TV or something?

'When will Mum be home?'

I put my hands over my ears and try to shut her out.

'Oh, I don't know. Soon.'

Mum's still at parents' evening. Dad too. She's summoned him to do his paternal duty. I've been dreading this all week. They'll find out about the booster class ... and me going down a Maths group ... and the mock results. In a way I'm kind of hoping they'll have a bit of an argument. At least that way the heat is off me. Oh, what am I saying? That's wrong. Wrong and downright selfish. I want them back together. I want that more than anything. I never thought they'd be apart this long. I mean, Mum and Dad, that's the natural order of things. Like United and Alex Ferguson. But all things pass. Even Fergie. He retires next season. The thought makes me uneasy. It's like the ground is shifting under my feet.

'I don't know why they bother with your parents' evening,' says Amy sulkily. 'They never come home happy.'

'Oh, shut up, pipsqueak,' I snap. 'Just because you like school.'

Like it? She *adores* it. Teacher's pet, our Amy. Can I do a job for you, Miss? Can I have some extra homework, Miss? Love you, Miss. Three bags full, Miss.

'*I* get good reports,' says Amy.

Oh, quit it, you little pain. Sheringham's just gone close. We're getting back into the game.

'I get good reports,' I mimic in a nasal, whiny voice.

Amy puts her tongue out and goes back to the living room. At last. United go on the attack again, but the ball runs through to Tommy Sorensen, the Sunderland keeper. I'm just making myself some toast when the front door opens. Mum appears first, followed by Dad. He enters uncertainly, as if he's walking on eggshells. We've got a free kick just outside the area, but I don't get to hear the outcome. Mum stamps over to the radio and turns it off. Dad and I exchange glances. Here it comes.

'I was *so* embarrassed!' she begins.

Sorry.

'Some of your grades have actually gone down. Mr Shooter says you just don't try.'

Sorry.

'You didn't even have the decency to tell me you've been put in a remedial group.'

Sorry, sorry, sorry.

'So what have you got to say for yourself?'

'Sorry.'

And on and on she drones.

'Don't you realise this is GCSE year?'

'Yes I do.'

'Don't you care about your future?'

'Of course I do.'

'Don't you have anything to say?'

'I said I'm sorry.'

'I don't mean you,' says Mum. 'I was talking to your dad.'

And guess what Dad says?

'Sorry.'

Mum gives an exasperated shriek.

'Can I put the football back on?' I ask.

Mum darts an accusing look at Dad, then throws her arms in the air.

'That's all you two care about,' she says, climbing the stairs to get changed out of her posh, parents' evening clothes. 'Eleven men chasing a ball around.'

'Put it on, son,' says Dad. His voice is a strangled whisper.

It's half-time. 0–0. Liverpool are 1–0 up at Man City. Arsenal won last night. If we don't get all three points tonight we'll lose ground in the Championship race.

'Aren't you going to have a go at me, too?' I ask.

'It'd be a bit rich coming from me,' says Dad. 'I didn't do much at school. At least you're good at three subjects.'

'Three?'

'Yes, English, French and IT.'

I never knew I was good at IT.

'So what is it with Maths and Science? Is it because you find the work hard or because you're bored off your box?'

'Both,' I say.

'That's how I was. Don't worry, your mum will calm down.'

'What about you two?' I venture. 'Anything new?'

'No, she still wants the divorce. Looks like it's a done deal.'

'Oh.'

Amy comes in and gives Dad a big hug. He swings her up to the ceiling. She squeals with delight. Life's easy when you're nine.

'I'm going to bed now,' she says. 'Night, Dad.'

'Night, petal.'

She ignores me.

Mum walks back into the kitchen. She's wearing leggings. I haven't seen her in them for ages. Then I realise why. She stopped wearing them when she developed bumps that shouldn't be there. But the bumps have gone. I've got a new, bumpless Mum.

'You've lost weight,' I gasp.

She forgets she's angry with me long enough to smile.

'Thanks for noticing,' she says.

'I noticed too,' says Dad lamely.

She ignores him completely. Her body language says he's no right to be looking any more.

'I'm making coffee,' says Mum. 'Do you want one, Geoff, or do you have to go?'

The way she says it leaves Dad in no doubt that he ought to go. Immediately.

'No, thanks,' he says sadly. 'See you, Sharon. See you, son.'

As Dad closes the front door behind him I realise that this is no temporary separation. It really could be over.

Wednesday 31st January
8.53 p.m.

It's Bobby. He's in his school uniform.

'What are you wearing that for?' I ask, horrified.

'Mum dragged me along to parents' evening,' he says. 'She thought it would look better if I went in uniform. I feel a right prat.'

'You look like one.'

'Thanks for the vote of confidence.'

I'm about to say something else when Paddy Crerand goes ape on the radio commentary.

'1–0 to United. Goal king Cole!'

Andy Cole's put us in the lead.

'Ye-e-e-sssss!'

'And Michael Grey's having a go at the referee. He's off. Michael Grey's been sent off for foul and abusive language.'

'Ye-e-e-sssss!'

United ahead and Sunderland down to ten men. Just what I need after the roasting Mum gave me.

'So how are the Blues doing?' asks Bobby. 'Or shouldn't I ask?'

'You shouldn't ask,' I say sympathetically. 'You're 1–0 down.'

'Liverpool?'

'Were 1–0 up. It's 1–1 now.'

'That's something, I suppose.'

But just as I'm dancing round the room, Andy Cole and Sunderland's Alex Rae square up. It's handbags at forty paces but the ref sends them both off. United down to ten men, Sunderland down to nine. The crowd's going mental. This is crazy.

'Referees,' I say, shaking my head.

'Referees,' says Bobby, rolling his eyes.

He changes the subject.

'Have you spoken to Emma lately?' he asks.

My stomach flips inside out. I know I must have gone red. What's this about?

'We've spoken,' I say guardedly. 'Why?'

'Dunno. Can't quite put my finger on it. She seems a bit lukewarm, that's all. Any idea why?'

How do I answer this? Maybe I should plead the Fifth. In the event I manage a half-decent reply:

'No idea. A slow burn from New Year?'

'Nah. She's forgiven me for that.'

'You sure about that?' I ask.

Bobby squints thoughtfully.

'Has Emma said something?'

'She has mentioned your snog with Pepsey.'

'One slip,' says Bobby indignantly. 'One little mistake. I'd forgive her for one mistake.'

I doubt that, but I don't say so.

He shakes his head.

'Women!' he says.

'Women!' I say, not because I agree with him, but because I want to put him off the scent.

We exchange news.

His love life's gone sour, mine doesn't even exist.

He got a great report, I got ... a report.

His mum's buying him a new mobile, mine's throwing darts at a picture of me.

'Have you walked under a ladder or something?' he asks.

'Must've,' I say.

'Still, at least United are winning.'

I nod.

Wish I was.

Wednesday 31st January
9.25 p.m.

'Has Bobby gone home?' asks Mum.

'Yes, he cleared off when Middlesborough went 2–1 up.'

'Sorry I lost my temper,' she says. 'I was so disappointed, that's all.'

'You made that pretty clear.'

I'm not in the mood for a heart-to-heart. United and Sunderland are still playing.

'You *will* try though, won't you, love?' she asks.

First the roasting, now the guilt trip.

'Yes, Mum, I'll try.'

'That's all I want, Terry. Just do your best.'

She's on her way out of the room when I call her back.

'Mum, is it definitely over? You and Dad, I mean?'

There are three minutes left in the match. I want a quick answer.

'It's over,' she says.

'He *is* sorry,' I say.

'There are some things sorry can't put right.'

I watch her go. United are winning. I'm not. There are four minutes of extra time, four minutes to maintain our lead at the top of the table.

Do it for me, United. My life's going down the tubes, so for God's sake hold on.

Oh no, hand ball on the edge of the area. Barthez saves the free kick. Fifty seconds to go.

Corner to Sunderland. Phillips loops the ball over the bar.

Go on, United. Salvage something out of this mess.

Varga goes for goal for Sunderland. Barthez holds on to the ball. That's it. The full-time whistle goes. Sunderland 0, United 1.

So what if I got a lousy report? So what if Julie's still with Fitz? So what if I'm getting the come-on from my best friend's girl? United are always there like a rock.

Returning the love.

Thursday 1st February
12.45 p.m.

I'm standing outside the canteen holding the umbrella Julie gave me last night. I've been trying to return it all morning. That isn't quite true, I suppose. It's Kelly's umbrella, after all, but I haven't gone near her. No, it's Julie I want to give it to, on condition I catch her on her own. I don't want an audience when I'm making an idiot of myself. All that time I ignored her and now I just want to hear her voice. Bobby comes up with Emma. He sees me holding the umbrella and looks up at the ceiling.

'Where's the leak?'

'What?'

He points to the umbrella.

'It was a joke. At least it was meant to be.'

I just want him to go away, him and Emma. She's putting me in a difficult situation. I haven't forgotten the kiss outside the sports hall. My skin burns at the thought of it.

'So when did you start carrying an umbrella?' asks Bobby. 'Not turning into Mary Poppins, are you?'

He puts on a Dick Van Dyke Cockney accent: 'God bless you, Terry Payne.'

For the second time in as many minutes I fail to see the joke.

'It's Kelly's umbrella.'

'So what are *you* doing with it?'

'Julie gave it to me.'

Bobby looks genuinely confused. Emma isn't. She's got the situation sussed straight away. The moment she sees Julie coming down the corridor, she taps Bobby on the arm.

'Let's leave him to it.'

Bobby sees Julie and the penny drops at last.

'I've got the umbrella,' I announce hurriedly as Julie approaches. She's got her long, raven-black hair in a single plait. Her skin appears sun-tanned, but it can't be, not in February. I don't think it's a sunbed tan, either. However she does it, she looks wonderful. All the better for being alone. No Fitz and no Kelly. I hold out the umbrella.

'Thanks.'

She pauses and looks around.

'Was that Bobby and Emma?'

'Yes.'

'So what's going on there?'

'I don't...'

I do, but I can't think of a way to explain.

'Bobby and Emma. *You* and Emma. Is this a little love triangle you've got going?'

'There is no *me and Emma*.'

'No? What about outside the sports hall? What about New Year?'

'We're friends.'

'Just good friends, eh?'

There's a mischievous twinkle in Julie's eyes.

'I said I'd walk her home from the party. It was a thank-you peck on the cheek.'

I get the feeling that, deep down, she knows that's all there is to it. She's enjoying teasing me.

'And outside the sports hall?'

'It was nothing.'

'Does Emma know it's nothing?' says Julie. 'Does *Bobby*?'

218

I've probably gone bright red by now. If I had a spade I'd dig a hole, jump in and bury myself.

'I told you, there's nothing between me and Emma. Bobby's my best mate, for goodness' sake! I wouldn't mess with his girl.'

I'm burbling, sinking into a quicksand of embarrassment. And yet Julie's still smiling. Why does she find my discomfort so amusing?

'You're funny,' she says.

'I am?'

I don't feel particularly funny. It's not like I've grown a red nose or a pair of outsize feet.

'It doesn't take much to wind you up, does it?'

'No, clockwork boy, that's me.'

There, done it again, just when I should be explaining what really happened when Fitz broke his ankle, I start telling dumb jokes. Why am I such a gimp?

'Julie...'

'Yes?'

'There's something I've got to tell you.'

She smiles broadly. Look at that, I ignore her for a whole month and she still smiles at me. I watch her lips part, and I dissolve inside. Great, my innards are made of Disprol. Any minute, I'll be no more than a fizzy patch on the floor.

'It's about...'

Oh no, Kelly's just come out of the canteen with Gary Tudor.

'Go on,' says Julie, obviously intrigued.

And there's Fitz coming the other way with Jamie Sneddon. It's a pincer movement. I look around for an escape route and find it in the shape of the side door that leads outside.

'No,' I say, bolting for freedom. 'It was only that Mum might be looking for a baby-sitter. It doesn't really matter.'

I escape into the frosty air. What do I mean, 'doesn't matter'? The most beautiful girl in the world doesn't matter! Of course it matters – more than anything. I didn't want to talk to her about baby-sitting. If only she knew what really happened between me and Fitz. I didn't set out to hurt him. He was going to get me. I haven't got an aggressive bone in my body. Well, except for this sudden desire to beat Fitz's brains out with Kelly's umbrella!

Thursday 1st February
8.00 p.m.

'Terry!'

I hear Mum calling me, but I don't really register. Her voice comes through a dream haze. I've been thinking about Julie. I see her the way I saw her the first time, in the gym, in that royal blue leotard ... running. Boy, was she running! It was rhythmic, mesmerising, soft-focus running. I'm supposed to be doing my homework, but I'm seeing that back tuck of hers in glorious slow motion, and I'm doodling her name over and over again on my jotter. Julie, Julie, Julie.

'Terry!'

Mum's still not punching through the dream haze. Blue leotards take precedence over harrassed mums any day of the week.

'*Terry!*'

I look up. Mum and Amy and her best mate Katie are standing next to me.

'What?'

'I've been shouting for you for half an hour.'

I frown. She's got to be exaggerrating.

'OK, about a minute, but why don't you answer?'

'That's why,' says Amy, snatching the jotter off me. 'Terry's in lurrvve.'

'Give that back!'

Amy skips out of reach.

'Mum, tell her to give it back.'

A torrent of emotions rages through me: embarrassment, anger, humiliation.

'What's it say?' asks Katie. Her eyes widen. 'Julie Carter! She's my baby-sitter.'

More emotions: interest, passion, panic.

What if Katie rats on me? I'd never be able to look Julie in the face again.

'Yours!'

'Yes, she's been doing it for ages, since before Christmas.'

I remember that Katie lives in Huyton, near the Bluebell. Not ten minutes from Julie's house. It could be true.

'Wait till I tell her.'

I make a grab for my jotter. I snatch it back at the second time of asking.

'Don't!'

'Oh, Katie, you've got to,' chuckles Amy.

I fix Katie with pleading eyes.

'Please.'

I feel like the wuss of the century. I'm pleading with a nine-year-old. How sad is that? It comes out *Purr-leese*.

'What's it worth?' asks Amy.

Mum laughs.

'Mum,' I groan. 'Tell her.'

Mum smiles.

'Don't get so uptight. Nobody's going to rumble you, Terry. Amy and Katie are just winding you up.'

'You won't tell, will you?' I say, the slightest hint of a shake in my voice.

Katie pulls a face, as if weighing up her options.

'Your secret's safe with us,' smirks Amy in that flesh-creepingly superior way of hers.

'If you girls have stopped teasing Terry,' Mum says, 'I'd like you to get in the car.'

She squeezes my shoulder. 'That's what I was trying to tell you. We'll be about half an hour.'

'OK,' I croak, dying inside.

I hear the door go. I stare at the doodles on my jotter. How could I be so stupid? My fate is in the hands of a nine-year-old. Could I *be* more vulnerable?

4

Wednesday 7th February
3.50 p.m.

This morning's *Daily Mirror* got me thinking. If United can team up
with the New York Yankees, maybe that's what I need; a collaboration.
I can just see it: Terry Payne meets Romeo, Ginger Nut links up with
Casanova, Mad Manc joins forces with David Beckham. Let's face it,
it's the only way I'm going to get anywhere with Julie, especially if
Katie drops her bombshell. It doesn't seem to matter what I do, the
result's the same every rotten time, the mathematics of misery.

Terry Payne minus Julie Carter equals heartache.

Julie Carter plus John Fitzpatrick equals jealousy.

As for Terry Payne plus Julie Carter, that would quite simply add
up to heaven on earth. It would also be a miracle.

'What are you grinning at?' asks Amy, noticing the Julie-induced
smile.

She always moans on footy practice night. She has to shiver her
socks off for an hour while I train. Next week's an away fixture and
Mum has actually been wondering whether Amy can go on the bus
with the team! I told her it was a non-starter. Six Guns would go
ballistic at the thought of it. He isn't exactly crazy about me having to
drag her along to practice every week.

'Can't condemn a man for smiling,' I say.

'But what are you smiling *about*?' asks Amy.

'Wouldn't you like to know?'

I can't resist teasing her.

'You're stupid!' she says. 'I'm going to tell Mum on you.'

'So,' I say, ignoring my own advice, 'tell her.'

Now wasn't that mature! Amy pouts.

'If I say you've been horrible to me, she'll stop you going to football.

You'll just have to take me home instead. Or...'

She gives her superior smirk.

'I'll get Katie to tell Julie about you.'

Damn! I forgot Amy had the whip hand. One word from her and I'm dead. Another victory for Fitz. There's only one way to sort this. Bribery.

'OK, what do you want?'

Amy scratches her chin theatrically. She wants to keep me hanging on.

'Dunno. You'll have to make it worth my while.'

'Come on, I know you've got something in mind.'

'Well, there is this art magazine. I saw it on telly. It shows you how to shade fruit.'

'Go on, how much?'

'Three pounds.'

'Three quid!'

I could shade gold bullion for that!

'So should I have a word with Katie?'

'Don't you dare!'

But Amy knows when she's on to a winner. No amount of shouting is going to put her off. She cuts me short with a cheeky: 'Bribe please.'

We nip into the newsagents by the school gates. When we come out Amy is one art magazine richer, I'm three pounds poorer. That leaves me with one pound fifty to last till Friday. It isn't a complete disaster though.

The two-minute delay buying Amy's stupid magazine means we walk in on a full-blown row between Julie and Fitz. What's three pounds compared to the promise of heaven? We're too far away to catch the drift, but it's obvious that not everything's hunky-dory in paradise. After a couple of minutes Julie throws her hands up and storms off. I watch the long legs, the black, swinging ponytail. If only ... if only...

'Quick,' I hiss, shoving Amy round the corner of the sports hall, 'she's coming this way.'

'Hey, stop pushing!'

'Amy, please,' I beg, 'pipe down.'

Julie breaks into a run. Her hair whips up off her shoulders like the tail of a black panther. I watch, enthralled. I've been crazy about her for months and still the thrill of seeing her hasn't faded a bit. She's half the reason I get out of bed in the morning. Man U's the other half.

'Run, Julie, run,' I murmur.

Amy gives me a funny look. Brain to mouth: Turn down the volume.

'Julie,' Fitz calls after her. 'Don't go. I didn't mean it.'

He's about to say something else when he notices me and Amy watching him. He goes bright red.

'What's the matter with you, MnM?' he snarls.

I've rarely seen him looking so uncomfortable. I wish this moment could last for ever.

'Nothing,' I say, revelling in the reversal of fortunes. 'Nothing at all.'

Wednesday 7th February
8.00 p.m.

I'm sitting on a wall with Bobby.

'What's the matter with you?' he asks. 'I thought you'd be over the moon. Julie and Frisky Fitzy at each other's throats, what more could you want?'

'Nothing.'

'So why the long face?'

'I think I'll have to miss the next match.'

Mum's just broken the news.

'Why?'

I bury my chin deep in my jacket.

'It's away. I've got to look after our Amy. It's OK taking her along to Knowsley Manor but she can't come on the minibus to an away match. Six Guns won't stand for it.'

'What about your mum and dad?'

'Both working late.'

'There's got to be somebody.'

There is. Julie. But I couldn't ask her. I wouldn't dare.

'Grandparents?' says Bobby.

I shake my head.

'No go. I'm snookered. Just when I'd got Fitz's place in the side.'

'I could baby-sit.'

'You!'

'I'm not in the team any more, and my band's broken up.'

Now there are two theories about why Bobby's band broke up. One is musical differences, the other is him lusting after the drummer's girlfriend.

'Why shouldn't I baby-sit?'

Because it would be like putting an arsonist in charge of a firework factory, that's why!

'I don't think Mum would fancy you doing it. She hasn't forgiven you for the time she caught you smoking in our bathroom.'

'It was only the once. I don't do it any more.'

'It was once too often.'

Bobby ponders for a moment or two.

'Got it,' he says.

His face lights up. It's an Archimedes and bathwater moment.

'Emma! She'll do it.'

I remember Emma nudging along the bench, pressing close to me, the smell of her hair, her perfume, the touch of her lips. All that stuff about going out with the wrong mate. No, that really would be asking for trouble.

'No,' I say, rather too hastily, 'not Emma.'

Bobby's face clouds over.

'Why not?'

Yes, why not? Think, Terry, think. An excuse, I need an excuse. But what?

'She's your girlfriend.'

'Meaning?'

Yes, what do I mean? Trust me to blurt that out. I've given the game away this time. Come on, there's got to be something I can say. Not just anything, either. It's got to be watertight. No sieve-style explanations.

Got it!

'I don't want you inviting yourself round. I can just imagine it. There's you and Emma snogging in the living room and our Amy walks in. Mum would hit the roof.'

It works. If there's one thing that's guaranteed to work on Bobby, it's flattery. He likes nothing better than being portrayed as some sort of love god.

'Aw, you've got me sussed. Anyway, there must be other baby-sitters.'

'There is one,' I say doubtfully.

'Who?'

'Julie.'

'*The* Julie? She baby-sits?'

I nod.

'This is destiny,' Bobby gasps. 'It's got to be.'

'No,' I say. 'It's stupid.'

Bobby shakes his head.

'Why is it? Stop being such a wuss. Just ask her.'

I look at him, allowing hope to flare.

'I could, couldn't I?'

Friday 9th February
7.00 p.m.

Masterplan about to be put into practice. I'm standing in the kitchen trying to look cool. This is good, I'm leaning against the fridge, swigging from a can of Red Bull and flicking through a GCSE study guide. It's just the right balance to strike. Nonchalant *and* studious. But will Mum buy it? Oh, hurry up. Phone Julie. She's had the number since yesterday when I handed it to her. I didn't ask Julie, of course, I couldn't pluck up the courage. I'm hoping Mum will do the job for me. She's phoned Katie's mum. I think she got a good reference. I'm determined not to remind her about it. I don't want to sound too keen. Not good for the image. Besides, she'll smell a rat and get another baby-sitter instead, somebody with braces and a wooden leg.

This weird little voice fills my head:

'Phone Julie.'

Then it goes frantic.

'Phone Julie, phone Julie, phone Ju-leeee!'

'Do you remember where I put that phone number?' Mum asks.

This is it. Sound unconcerned.

'What number's that?'

'You know which number. Julie the baby-sitter, the one you've got a crush on.'

Ouch. I've been rumbled.

'It's by the phone.'

'You sure?'

I should be, I put it there.

Mum goes into the hall.

'Here it is. It fell behind the phone table.'

I make a mental note. Next time Blutak it to the stupid table. Nail it down if you have to.

I hold my breath as Mum punches the number.

'Oh, hello. Is Julie there?'

Please be in, please be in, please be in.

'Julie? Hi, this is Mrs Payne.'

She's in! I punch the air. Yiss!

'That's right, Terry's mum.'

There's a pause, while Julie asks a question. That's right, be suspicious!

'That's right,' says Mum. 'Terry suggested you.'

I find myself edging towards the kitchen door. Say you'll do it, Julie, *please* say you will.

'You can. Oh, that's such a relief. Boys and their football.'

Mum laughs at something Julie's said. Oh no, don't say they're laughing at me!

'That's arranged then. Our Terry will take you to the school to pick up Amy, you know, introduce the pair of you... Oh, you have. Well it won't hurt for you both to meet her the first time. Then he'll go off to his football and you'll bring Amy home.'

It's a ten or fifteen minute walk from my school to Amy's. That means Julie and me together all that time. There's a lump in my throat the size of a duck's egg. Masterplan complete.

When Mum hangs up I fly back to my station and continue flicking through the study guide. OK, so she knows Julie the baby-sitter and Julie the crush are one and the same, but at least I can try to look cool.

'It's all fixed up,' says Mum. 'Oh, and by the way, your book's upside down!'

There's Julie. She's just ahead of me, making her way through the crowd of kids at the school gates.

'Are you still on for tomorrow night?' I ask, catching her up.

It's a miracle. She's on her own. No Kelly and no Fitz either. Both her minders have gone AWOL. Come to think of it, I haven't seen her with Fitz for days. Mentally, I cross my fingers.

'Yes,' says Julie with a smile.

She gives a low, throaty chuckle.

'Just like I was still on yesterday and the day before.'

You idiot, Terry, I tell myself. You're coming across all desperate again.

'I was just checking,' I say, trying to recover. 'I don't want anything going wrong, you know, with Amy.'

'I know exactly what you mean,' says Julie, emphasising the *exactly*.

She looks right at me, through me, and I dissolve in her lush, brown eyes.

'Sorry,' I say.

'What are you saying sorry for?' she asks.

Anything you want.

Sorry for being a pest.

Sorry for having ginger hair.

Sorry for being thick.

Sorry for being a Mad Manc.

Sorry for not being good enough for you.

But I'm not sorry for loving you.

'Dunno,' I say with a nervous giggle. 'Sorry.'

She laughs too. It's a lovely sound. There is nothing cruel or malicious about her. She can tease me without humiliating me. I can't believe how strongly I feel about this girl.

'So I'll see you at home-time tomorrow,' she says. 'And we'll pick Amy up together.'

There's a hidden goodbye in there somewhere. Then I see the reason why. Kelly is jogging towards us. I watch them walking away together. Kelly turns to Julie as if to say: I don't know why you give him the time of day.

Neither do I.

But I'm glad she does.

Tuesday 13th February
8.30 p.m.

'Stupid men!' says Mum as she walks through the front door.

She's been to the supermarket with Amy. As they start to pack the shopping away, I venture a cautious:

'Why are men stupid?'

I figure I might learn something about the female mind. I'm not too good on all that Venus and Mars stuff. I'm astronomically challenged.

'You should have seen them,' says Mum. 'Queuing up with their Valentine's Day love baskets. All with the same, pathetic, embarrassed look on their faces.'

Valentine's Day! Of course, tomorrow's Valentine's Day.

'And not one of them means it. They only do it to stay out of the dog-house.'

'How do you know they don't mean it?' I ask.

I'm not defending the male species, just this particular member of it.

'Your dad didn't mean it, did he? Bought me flowers every Valentine's Day for seventeen years, then he just walked out on a whim. So much for romance.'

She finishes putting the shopping away. Pasta, vegetables, low-fat this and high fibre that, but not a Hobnob or a Crunchie in sight. The diet continues. I look at her. She's definitely losing weight.

'You're getting thin,' I say.

I'm not sure I like it. Mum's always been cuddly, lived in. Now that the fat's moved out, she looks different, and I don't just mean thinner.

'Good,' she says, 'and I'm going to get even thinner, with your help.'

'My help?'

'That's right. I've joined a running club. Monday and Friday evenings, seven till nine. You're baby-sitting. Don't worry, I'll pay you.'

'What if I want to go out?' I ask.

229

'Simple,' says Mum with a twinkle in her eye. 'I can always phone Julie.'

Mum thin, Mum running, Julie in my house. It's a brave new world and I'm not sure I can cope with it. I'm on my way upstairs when my mobile goes.

'Oh, hi, Dad.'

'I rang you on your mobile so your mum didn't hear. Are we safe to talk?'

I carry on into my room. Privacy among the litter.

'Yes, fire away. Is it about tomorrow night?'

I mean the match. Champions League. United v Valencia in Spain.

'Yes.'

Only Dad isn't talking about football, as I discover from his next sentence.

'I got your mum a Valentine's Day present.'

'You're joking!'

'Why?'

'Because she doesn't want to know. You'll only make things worse.'

'She always liked a bit of romance.'

Dad, I think, groaning inwardly, don't do this to yourself.

'What have you got her?'

It can't be what I'm thinking.

'I picked it up at the supermarket.'

Dad, you dufus.

'It's called a love basket.'

Basket-case is more like it.

'Do you think it's worth a try?' he asks.

'Sure,' I say, 'If you fancy open-heart surgery without anaesthetic.'

'That bad, huh?'

'Dad, you don't know the half of it.'

There's a long silence at the other end.

'Are you coming over to watch the match?' he asks plaintively.

I don't really want to commit myself. What if Julie's in no hurry to go after baby-sitting?

'Terry?'

I'd be a mug to go to Dad's.

'I'll be there,' I tell him.

I know, I'm a mug. But at least I'm a loyal mug, a mug who can look himself in the mirror in the morning.

Wednesday 14th February
12.20 p.m.

'Have you got Emma anything?' I ask Bobby as we walk past the shops.

He grins.

'A big, sloppy kiss.'

'Anything else?'

'Yes, I got her a card. A rude one.'

'How rude?'

'Oh, a real cheek-slapper.'

'What did she think of it?'

'Dunno. I haven't given it to her yet.'

He fishes it out of his blazer pocket and hands it to me. I read it.

'You can't give her that!'

'Why not?'

'She's a nice girl.'

I remember the way she snuggled up close. Are nice girls supposed to do *that* to their boyfriend's best mate?

'Why do you ask?'

I take a deep breath. Here goes nothing.

'I was thinking of buying Julie something.'

'Is this why you dragged me out of school for dinner?' asks Bobby.

I give an embarrassed nod.

'What were you thinking of getting her?'

'That's just it, I haven't got a clue. I thought you might have some suggestions.'

I give him his card back. Those sort of suggestions I don't need. We find ourselves outside a florist's. It's heaving with bouquets and balloons, hearts and teddy bears. I look at some of the price tags. My heart sinks.

'Dear, aren't they?' says Bobby.

I nod miserably. I couldn't afford a ventricle, never mind a whole heart.

'Come on, let's get back.'

We're turning to go when Fitz makes an unwelcome appearance.

'What's this, MnM, buying something for your Valentine?'

Gary's with him. He chips in with his two-pennyworth:

'Bobby, you're a lucky guy.'

'A match made in heaven,' says Fitz.

Before we can stop him, he's pinched both our cheeks.

'You young lovebirds!'

Then he's gone.

'If Julie's ditched him,' Bobby says, rubbing his cheek, 'he's taking it well.'

There are a few rose petals on the pavement. I watch them blow away, just like my dreams.

Wednesday 14th February
3.15 p.m.

'OK,' says Julie, appearing out of a scrum of kids, 'I'm all yours.'

My heart lurches. If only that were true. I notice Kelly glaring at me.

'See you later, Julie,' she says.

We turn right. She turns left. She must hate leaving Julie with me. The Scouse princess and the Mad Manc.

'How's your gymnastics going?' I ask.

'It must take dedication.'

'I suppose it does,' says Julie. 'I'm used to it now. It's just like doing homework.'

I grimace.

'I wouldn't really know about that.'

'You're not keen on school, are you?'

I shake my head.

'So what are you doing next year?'

'I'm going to college,' I answer. 'Can't wait to get away from this place.'

I wince. That came out wrong. There's at least one person I don't want to get away from.

'What about you?' I ask.

'I'm going into sixth form,' she says, 'so long as I get the grades.'

'You'll get the grades,' I say. 'You're dead clever.'

She laughs, completely unaffected.

'Thanks.'

I'm dying to ask her, what about Fitz? I do it in my usual roundabout way.

'Had any Valentines?'

'A few.'

A *few*! So I'm not Fitz's only rival...

'You?'

How do I answer this?

'Oh, you know, one or two.'

'Is that one or two?' she asks, smiling.

'None,' I mumble.

I'm not sure honesty is the best policy.

'Aw, poor Terry.'

Funnily enough, she sounds like she means it. We've almost reached Amy's school. The time has flashed by in an instant. I had so much to say, too. But it will have to remain unsaid.

'There's your Amy now,' says Julie.

I nod.

'See you then.'

I don't move.

'Haven't you got to get back?'

I just stare dumbly.

'The match.'

I look at my watch. I've got to be on the bus in ten minutes.

'I'll see you later,' I say, turning to go. 'See you, Amy.'

By the time they answer, I'm running back towards Knowsley Manor.

As I turn into our street, my heart is pounding. I've run all the way from school, a mixture of elation, hope and excitement. The elation was provided by a 3–0 win. I made one and scored one. Julie's providing the rest. When I get to the door I fumble for my keys and drop them on the pavement. By the time I've retrieved them, somebody has opened the front door.

Let it be Julie.

It isn't.

'Oh, it's you.'

'Who did you expect?' asks Amy. 'Oh, I get it. You thought Julie would still be here.'

'You mean she's gone?'

'Half an hour ago, when Mum came in.'

I follow Amy inside and throw my bag on the floor.

'Temper, temper,' says Amy.

By way of reply, I scowl.

'That you, Terry?' asks Mum.

'No, the Amazing Spiderman.'

'Well,' Mum quips in return, 'spin your web into the kitchen. Something came in the post.'

'For me?'

'Yes, Terry, for you.'

'What is it?'

'How should I know? Do you think I steam your letters open?'

The moment I walk into the kitchen, my heart does a somersault. It's a card. In a red envelope.

A Valentine's Day card.

I open it and read:

'To a nice guy. Lots of love.'

I try to remember what Julie's writing looks like, but I don't remember ever seeing it. I scrutinise the message for hidden meanings.

A nice guy...

...lots of...

...love!

Lots of, not just bits of.

Let it be from her. *Please* let it be from her.

Wednesday 14th February
7.20 p.m.

Though it has been frosty all day, I walk to Dad's flat embalmed in a warm glow.

I see the message on the card. Lots of love!

'You look pleased with yourself,' Dad says when he answers the door.

'I got a Valentine,' I explain. 'From *her*.'

'Oh, this Julie you've been telling me about?'

'I think it's from her.'

It's got to be. Who else would send me one?

'At least one of us has had a Valentine,' says Dad glumly.

I spot the love basket sitting on the coffee table. The rose petals are already withering, and the little teddy bear looks like he's seen better days.

'You didn't send it then?'

Dad shakes his head.

'No. You were right. Sharon would only have lost her temper. There's no point making things even worse. I'd better face it, this divorce is a done deal. I'll be a free man any day now.'

He smiles unconvincingly, then admits:

'Can't say I'm looking forward to it much.'

I imagine him fishing in the Meals-for-One cabinet at the supermarket. For the want of anything better to say I tell him:

'Mum's taking up jogging.'

Dad does a double-take.

'Is this the same Sharon Payne we're talking about?'

'I'm not making it up. Every Monday and Friday. She's lost loads of weight with the diet. Once she starts running there'll be nothing left.'

Dad stands with his mouth open, like a codfish in slow motion. It's really starting to sink in now. He's beginning to understand just what he's thrown away.

'Have you got the right channel on?' I ask.

'Yes. It'll be starting any minute.'

We settle in front of the TV just in time to hear the strains of the Champions League anthem. I listen while Des Lynam sets the scene. Mestalla stadium ... bucketing down all day ... water lying on the pitch.

Then the size of the task before United: Valencia have the best defensive record in the competition; they are unbeaten at home by foreign opposition since 1992; United have never beaten a Spanish side on their own soil. We're playing last year's runners-up on their own turf. It isn't going to be easy.

'Don't worry,' says Dad, sensing my anxiety. 'We took four points off them last year.'

Weird how, when it really matters, all we can talk about is football. That laminated leather ball must have been designed to fill the hole where men's feelings ought to go. The match gets off to a cracking start. Both sides are going for it. After five minutes Giggsy nutmegs a defender and finds Cole in the box. After ten Valencia put the ball in the net, but it is ruled offside. Twenty minutes in, Beckham almost gets on the end of a Giggs cross.

'Giggsy's got the beating of Angloma,' says Dad.

But on the half-hour it's Valencia who are turning the screw. During a period of relentless pressure Wes Brown denies Mendietta. Two minutes later Scholes comes close with a great half-volley. Two heavyweights are throwing bombs at each other, but at half-time it's still 0–0.

'Let's just take a look at those terrific wins for Leeds and Arsenal last night,' says Des Lynam.

'Let's get a snack,' says Dad, rocketing out of his chair like it's an ejector seat.

No self-respecting Red is going to sit around and watch the opposition do well. It's only fun watching Liverpool, Leeds or Arsenal when they lose.

'Are you wishing you could turn back the clock?' I ask. 'Over Mum I mean?'

'I never think of anything else,' says Dad. 'I can't live down my mistake. It's with me every minute of every day.'

'So why did you walk out in the first place?'

'You really want to know?'

'Yes.'

'What set me off was this lad at work. He got divorced and met a girl ten years younger. I envied him. I mean, it was all routine with your mum. I only started to realise that I needed our routine when I moved out.'

Dad shakes his head.

'I'm one brain-dead plank.'

So who's arguing?

By the time we return to the living room it's the ad break.

'Want to put a bet on the score?' asks Dad.

'No.'

It would be tempting fate.

'Here's my prediction, for what it's worth,' says Dad. '1–0 to United.'

But with half an hour to go it is Aimar and Mendietta for Valencia who are starting to boss the game. It's a Thrilla at the Mestalla, a game of slick, one-touch passing with half-chances by the bucketful. But at the full-time whistle there is still no score.

'A draw will suit United,' says Dad. 'One more win and we're through to the quarter-finals.'

'That'll do me,' I say, with more than a hint of satisfaction in my voice.

'So this Julie, are you really serious about her?' asks Dad.

'I'd like to be. I don't know how she feels though.'

'Well, don't just stand there wishing,' says Dad. 'Decide what you want and go for it.'

I give a half-smile.

'Yes, I know it's a bit rich coming from me, but it's good advice all the same.'

I walk to the door.

'Think about it, Terry,' says Dad.

I already have. I'm going to phone Julie on the way home.

Wednesday 14th February
9.45 p.m.

I try her mobile. It's switched off. Great. Now I've got to ring her at home. I daren't postpone this. I'll never pluck up the courage again. I listen to the ringing tone. Getting Julie is a six to one shot. Any of them could pick up. Her mum, her dad, one of her three brothers: Gerard, Josh or John-Joe. If I get Julie it's got to be a sign; destiny.

I listen to it ring.

Let it be her, please let it be her.

Somebody picks up and speaks.

It *is* her. Oh my God, what do I do now? What on earth do I say? Why didn't I plan this better?

'Hello?'

Tell her you love her, you wimp.

'Hello?'

Say it. *Say something*.

'Is that you, Fitz?'

What do I say?

My mind races through the possibilities:

I love you? Too dramatic.

I care? Too needy.

Do you want to go out with me? Too ordinary.

I'm trying to come up with more permutations when Julie loses patience. She hangs up. I stand at the top of our street, beating my head with the mobile.

One of the neighbours is out walking his dog. He gives me ever such a funny look. The dog's suspicious too.

I'm about to go through the front door when I notice I've got a text message. The words make a chill run down my spine:

Did u like my card? Emma.

Emma!

Emma sent me the Valentine!

I stare at the mobile in disbelief. I've just come within a hair's breadth of making a complete idiot of myself.

5

'You mean you hung up without saying *anything*!'

I've just told Bobby about the abortive phone call to Julie. I keep quiet about Emma's text message and the Valentine, of course.

'You've got to get in there, Terry mate, before somebody beats you to it.'

'You've lost me.'

'Do you walk about in a daze or something? It's the talk of Year 11. Julie's finally done it, she's given Fitz the heave-ho.'

I always thought that, when their break-up finally happened, it would be a real big deal. There would be advance warning, then a huge, theatrical bust-up followed by an extensive post-mortem. We're talking sirens and lights, crashing waves, thunderbolts and lightning. In the event, the Fitz and Julie roadshow just got shunted quietly into the sidings.

'Are you sure about this?' I ask.

My voice has gone all quavery.

'Sure I'm sure.'

'Then how do you explain that?'

Fitz's posse has just come round the corner. There's Gary Tudor, Kelly Magee, Paul Scully, Pepsey Cooper, Jamie Sneddon and ... Julie.

'I said her and Fitz had stopped going out. I didn't say they were mortal enemies.'

This I find hard to take. I've heard about people staying friends when they break up. I didn't think it actually happened. It's certainly not like that with Mum and Dad. Amy and I feel like we're tip-toeing round emotional razor wire.

As the group walk past I catch Julie's eye. I give a half-smile. It sets

Fitz off.

'What are you grinning at, MnM?' he snaps, eyes bulging with anger.

I take his over-the-top reaction as proof of Bobby's news.

'See.'

I watch them as they head for double Maths. Julie glances over her shoulder at me.

'What more do you want?' asks Bobby. 'See the way she looked at you? Fitz is history. Go for it.'

Thursday 15th February
12.50 p.m.

I eat my dinner with Bobby and Emma.

'I don't know why it's such a big deal,' says Emma. 'Julie's dumped Fitz. So what?'

'What Emma says seems to make sense,' says Bobby. 'After all, people make love one hundred and twenty million times around the world every day.'

I meet Emma's look and feel distinctly uncomfortable. No way are we going to make it one hundred and twenty million and one!

'But,' says Bobby, oblivious of the exchange of glances, 'there's nothing ordinary about a man in love.'

Oh God, Bobby, pass the sick bag.

'Terry's been carrying a major torch for Julie for months. It's a big deal to him.'

'I can't see why,' says Emma, a bit too huffily for my liking. 'She's not so wonderful. Her bum's too big.'

Mee-ow!

'Just drop it, will you?' I say.

Actually, I think Julie's got the world's number one bum. The bum to die for.

'Happy to,' says Bobby. 'By the way, I didn't tell you my news, did I?'

'What news is this?'

'Slughead's proposed to Mum.'

I picture Bobby's mum's boyfriend. Big guy. Cocker spaniel.

'When?'

'Valentine's Day. They went out for a curry and he poppadomed the question.'

I pass over the stupid pun.

'So how do you feel?'

'How do you think I feel?' says Bobby. 'Gutted. The guy's a complete moron. And he's got sweaty feet. His socks stink the house out. Plus he's a Liverpool fan.'

It's something Bobby and I have in common, our hatred of all things Liverpool, him from an Everton perspective, me from a Man U one.

'What difference does that make?' asks Emma.

'All the difference,' says Bobby. 'And his dog hates me. It puked in my bed.'

I try not to dwell on images of a vomiting spaniel.

'So when's the wedding?' I ask, also trying not to make eye contact with Emma.

'Next month, I think. Registry office do. But he's moving into our house permanently this week.'

Bobby glances at his watch.

'Anyway, I've got to go. I've got IT.'

Emma and I have Maths. Booster Maths.

'See you later.'

'Poor Bobby,' I say.

'Poor Bobby nothing,' says Emma. 'Slughead ... I mean, Phil, he's OK.'

'And the cocker spaniel?'

'Poor little thing. She had an upset stomach. Lady wouldn't puke in Bobby's bed on purpose.'

We're wittering on aimlessly like this when Julie and Kelly walk by. Julie gives Emma a sideways glance and carries on out of the canteen. I get a sinking feeling.

'I just know she thinks there's something going on between us,' I say.

'Maybe we should really give her something to think about,' says Emma, putting her hand on mine.

I snatch my hand away as if she's just touched me with a cattle prod.

'Emma!'

She smiles mischievously.

'Time for Maths,' she says. 'Coming?'

I follow reluctantly. Like a man on his way to the electric chair.

Thursday 15th February
1.45 p.m.

I'm on my way to my next lesson when I bump into Julie. From somewhere I get a sudden attack of boldness.

'Is it true about you and Fitz?' I ask.

This simple sentence is the culmination of hours of agonising: ask her, don't ask her, ask her, don't ask her... In the event, I can't believe I've actually asked her.

'Yes, it's true. Why?'

Did she have to ask me that?

'No reason. Just being nosy, that's all.'

No! That isn't all. Tell her, you dope. Say how you feel.

'I never thought you were right for each other.'

'No?' says Julie.

'No.'

I thank my lucky stars she didn't go all sarcastic, you know, ask me when I became a Relate counsellor. But the monosyllabic question has thrown me. Now what? I stand, shifting my feet. In the end, I come up with this:

'There's nothing between me and Emma, you know.'

'Did I say there was?' asks Julie.

'No, but...'

Maybe I'm protesting too much. Why did I have to say that anyway? There can only be one reason for telling her that. So why not go the whole hog? I can almost hear Bobby's voice: ask her out, for crying out loud! But before I can open my mouth, Julie says something that completely disarms me.

'I should never have gone out with Fitz. Don't get me wrong, he's a great guy...'

I bite my bottom lip. This, I don't want to hear. He's not a great guy.

If the world had an armpit, its name would be Fitz.

'But I knew weeks ago it wasn't working.'

This, I do want to hear.

'I think I'm going to take my time before I jump into another relationship.'

No, you were doing so well. Don't spoil it.

'Anyway, I've got to get to my next class.'

And, with a turn and a whiff of perfume and a flick of the ponytail she's gone. She doesn't need another relationship! Have I been reading the signs all wrong? Doesn't she like me *at all*?

I stand in the corridor for a long time.

A *very* long time.

Thursday 15th February
11.30 p.m.

I'm in bed, but I can't sleep.

I've made up my mind. Tomorrow I do it. It's the last day before half-term so I've got to do it, or else lose a whole week of my life.

Tomorrow I ask Julie out.

Friday 16th February
11.30 p.m.

In bed again, still unable to sleep.

I messed up. I saw Julie three times but I didn't once ask her out.

I hate me.

6

Monday 19th February
11 a.m.

I've just crawled out of bed. The house is empty. Mum took Amy round to Katie's on her way to work. The sneakiest nine-year-old blackmailer in Prescot is spending the day there. On her way out Mum shouted something about me not sleeping the day away. I was going to get up about ten, but as soon as I heard that I stayed between the sheets an extra hour, just to spite her.

Stupid Mum.

Stupid half-term.

Most of all, stupid ME.

Six months I've spent kicking myself for not asking Julie out. Now I'm repeating the same pathetic mistake all over again. Maybe I should ask somebody else to kick me. It might make more of an impression.

'Pillock!' I say loudly.

I pass the hall mirror.

'*Pillock!*' I say again, this time with feeling.

I'm also a hungry pillock, so I get myself a bowl of Shreddies. I notice an official-looking letter on the kitchen table. I run my eyes over it. It's Mum and Dad's divorce. It's through. The end of an era. Or is it the end of an error? I'm licking the sweet gunge from the bottom of the bowl, consoling myself with sugar, when the doorbell rings.

It's Bobby.

'Emma's two-timing me,' he announces, walking right past me.

'Morning, Bobby,' I say, by way of reminding him about his manners, and also to give myself time to think.

'Did you hear what I just said?' he demands irritably. 'Emma's seeing someone else.'

I feel like I've gone all red and blotchy. After all, it's me she's seeing, or would be if I'd agree to see her back. This is crazy, week after week I've been doing the decent thing and it looks like I'm still going to get slaughtered.

'How do you know?' I ask nervously.

And *how much* do you know?

Bobby takes a quick swig from the can of Coke he's taken from the fridge, and answers.

'Caitlin told me.'

'Caitlin did!'

'Yes, she couldn't wait to spill the beans. It's the first time she's spoken to me since the split, and didn't she come over all smug and superior! You know what she said: *What goes around, comes around.*'

'Meaning?'

'Meaning I'm getting a dose of my own medicine. And I damned well deserve it.'

I feel like carnivorous worms are eating me alive, from the inside.

'Did she say who it was?'

He takes another swig of Coke. The tension kicks in. I lean forward, dreading what he'll say next.

'No.'

Phew. Relief sweeps through me like Vicks Vapour Rub through a blocked nose.

'But,' says Bobby, and it sounds like a big but, 'Caitlin says mine wasn't the only Valentine Emma sent. She's sweet on somebody.'

I see something new in Bobby. He's always been one of these *All's fair in love and war* types. He has never really cared how things were going in a relationship. He could always find somebody else. This time he's angry. No, not angry. *Incandescent.* I'm wondering how to point out that he has cheated on three girls this year, including Emma, when he says:

'I know what you're thinking. I did the dirty on Emma, snogging Pepsey like that, so what have I got to whinge about?'

Couldn't have put it better myself. Bobby looks at me, misery written in his eyes. How can I tell him the truth? It would be like kicking a puppy.

'Well, you're right. I've been a pig. But when I nearly lost Emma at New Year I started to realise how much she means to me.'

I don't believe it. Bobby's sounding just like Dad!

'Whoever it is,' he says. 'I'll kill him.'

Some week this is turning out to be. Mum and Dad have just got divorced, Liverpool and Arsenal both won, I've failed dismally to make any progress with Julie, and now my best mate is on the trail of the object of Emma's desire – me!

'Are you sure you're not getting this way out of proportion?' I ask. 'I mean, what's a Valentine? People send them for a laugh.'

'Well, this is no joke,' says Bobby, agony twisting through his voice. 'I'm going to find out who's messing about with my girl, and when I do...'

He doesn't finish the sentence. Instead, he crushes his Coke can.

'He'll wish he'd never been born.'

I close my eyes for a moment. Don't worry, Bobby, he already does!

Tuesday 20th February
11.45 a.m.

We're at the Blue Planet Aquarium. As a concession for half-term, Mum and Dad have each booked a day off work. Today is Dad's day. He told me and Amy we could both bring a friend. Amy asked Katie. I made an excuse about Bobby. I'm kind of avoiding him at the moment. The thought of him finding out exactly who Emma has the hots for has me squirming in my socks.

'So what's Bobby doing again?' asks Dad as we watch the sharks gliding overhead.

'He's out with his girlfriend,' I lie.

'What's happening with this girl you've set your sights on?' he asks.

'Not a lot.'

'How come?'

'I keep trying to ask her out but the words just won't come.'

'Still?'

A raised eyebrow.

'Still.'

'Well, don't dither much longer, or you're going to watch her get snapped up all over again.' I watch the circling sharks. Suddenly they've all got the faces of guys in my year. I know Dad's right. But how do I do it? How? I've never actually made the opening move. Chloe went first, and so did Emma.

'I always mean to say it,' I tell him, 'but it just doesn't come out.'

'Then make it,' says Dad. 'Make it.'

He's about to say something else when he notices the girls heading for the gift shop.

'Yikes,' he says. 'Better intercept those two before they bankrupt me.'

I watch while he tries to explain why that gorgeous, cuddly shark, that cute 3-D seaworld diary, the adorable dolphin balloon and the unputdownable teddy bear purse are more than his bank account can bear. Standing there, negotiating limply, he's hardly setting an example of decisiveness, but so what? He's right about Julie. I have to say something. And soon. Before the sharks come any closer.

Tuesday 20th February
2.00 p.m.

Oh great. Bobby's waiting for me when Dad drops me off outside the house.

'You missed a good day, Bobby,' says Dad. 'Go somewhere nice with that girlfriend of yours?'

Bobby frowns.

'I haven't seen Emma today,' he says.

It's Dad's turn to frown. He looks at me but I turn away.

'Anyway,' says Dad, 'You can fend for yourself, Terry. I'm going to drop Katie off.'

Bobby and I watch him pull away.

'What was all that about?' asks Bobby.

'Beats me,' I say. 'You know what my dad's like.'

That seems to satisfy Bobby. But, as I open the front door, we slip right back into the discomfort zone.

'I challenged Emma about what Caitlin said.'

Heart sinking, toes curling, legs turning to jelly, spots before my eyes, rushing sound in my ears. It's a multi-sensory embarrassment experience.

'And?'

'She denied it. What do you expect?'

I seize on this in desperation.

'Maybe Caitlin's making it up.'

'She's not like that,' says Bobby. 'If she was going to do something like that, why not months ago? No, Emma's got something to hide. I can tell.'

Why's this happening to me? I haven't done a thing to encourage her, but here I am feeling guilty as hell. I could lose my best mate ... over nothing.

'Still planning to sort out whoever it is?' I ask.

'Too right,' says Bobby. 'What would you do?'

'Spend six months trying to pluck up the courage to say something, but what's that got to do with it?'

'I tell you,' Bobby says purposefully, 'no matter how long it takes, I'm going to track him down. If he was here right now I'd flatten him.'

He is here right now, and he's flat enough as it is.

Tuesday 20th February
4.00 p.m.

OK, so maybe this wasn't the cleverest thing to do, but I've called on Emma. I just had to clear the air. We're walking down Scotchbarn Lane, talking. Emma's wearing a black pencil skirt and a sleeveless top – in the middle of February! She's got goosebumps the size of golfballs. The price of looking good. For all my anxiety that Bobby might see us, I'm enjoying her company. She is one really cute girl. I've just finished telling her how upset Bobby is.

'Look, Terry,' says Emma, 'You mean well, but I think I know how to handle Bobby.'

'But I've never seen him like this,' I say, interrupting. 'He's dead jealous. He's *never* jealous.'

'Good,' says Emma. 'Now he knows how I felt at New Year. It was a rotten thing to do.'

I agree. It was. But that isn't what I say.

'But Emma, you can't hold that against him forever!'

She stops and plants her hands stubbornly on her hips.

'Why not?'

For a few moments I can't think what to say. How would I feel in her place? In the end I manage a feeble:

'You just can't!'

'Terry, if you're going out with somebody, you don't kiss another girl, not right under your girlfriend's nose.'

'But this doesn't help,' I say. 'Two wrongs don't make a right.'

'Don't they?' says Emma. 'What's sauce for the goose is sauce for the gander.'

When we finally finish swapping idioms I say something she needs to know.

'He wants to know who the other guy is.'

'Well, I'm not telling him,' says Emma. 'And he's no right to ask after what he did. If he keeps going on about it, he'll lose me anyway.'

She's not telling him who she fancies. Well, that's something.

'I mean, I'm flattered,' I say. 'But this isn't going anywhere.'

Emma gives me a sideways look. She's got this weird expression on her face, like I've just started speaking Arabic.

'What isn't going anywhere? Terry, what *are* you on about?'

'You and me. The Valentine.'

Emma gives my cheek a friendly pinch.

'Oh, I get it now. *That's* why you're so excited. Oh, Terry, you idiot.' She laughs.

'There is no You and Me. I was flirting, that's all. I do it all the time. And I send lots of Valentines. I even sent one to Six Guns, and Adrian McAllister.'

He's the fat kid in Mr Spottiswood's form. Half blimp, half doughnut.

'It's a laugh, that's all, a bit of a wind-up.'

Now I'm completely lost.

'So I've no need to worry?' I burble.

A reassuring shake of the head.

'I'm not the one...?'

Emma mouths the word 'No' through smiling lips.

'Bobby's not going to...?'

Emma gives me a playful hug. I feel every curve of her body and go hot all over.

'Poor Terry,' she says. 'No, you're not the one. And no, Bobby hasn't got any reason to fall out with you. Far from it, you're the best friend he could have.'

'Great,' I say.

But I don't feel great. I feel bewildered, totally and completely confused. I watch Emma walk past the swimming pool and turn right into St James Road. That's when a thought strikes me.

If not me, then who?

Tuesday 20th February
7.10 p.m.

I'm on my way home when I bump into Bobby.

'Where are you off to?' I ask.

I do it to give myself time to think of a reason why *I'm* here.

'Emma's,' says Bobby. 'What about you?'

For the first time, I see a glint of suspicion in his eyes. He's obviously never even considered me a candidate for the dirty, rotten scoundrel awards. Doesn't that make me feel good? I finally decide to do what I should have done all along. Tell him the whole truth. Now I know I'm not the one Emma's had the hots for, it's a lot easier. So that's what I do, I tell him: about the New Year's peck on the cheek, about the kiss outside the sports hall, about the Valentine's Day card. Then I take a deep breath and wait to hear what he has to say.

'You wally,' he says. 'Of course I didn't think it was you.'

'Good,' I say with a relieved smile, then a hurt: 'Hey, why not?'

'Because you're my mate, and mates don't do the dirty on each other.'

'Not because I'm a skinny ginger guy, then?'

'No.'

'Oh,' I say, 'that's all right then.'

'But it isn't all right, is it?' says Bobby, his face as long as one of Beckham's cross-field passes. 'There is somebody, isn't there?'

What can I say? Emma admitted as much not half an hour ago.

'Yes,' I say. 'You're right about that. There is somebody.'

'But who?' says Bobby, kicking a wall. 'Who?'

'I haven't got a clue,' I tell him. 'But I know one thing. You shouldn't go confronting her over it.'

'Why not?'

This is a bit rich. Me giving Bobby advice.

'She'll keep bringing up Pepsey Cooper. Why not just leave it for a bit?'

'Because,' says Bobby as he prepares to say words I never expected to hear from him, 'I love her.'

Tuesday 20th February
7.40 p.m.

In the end I left Bobby and Emma to it. Let's face it, there's nothing I can say that's going to make an ounce of difference. Besides, I had to get round to Dad's flat to listen to the match with him. He keeps promising to get digital TV, but he hasn't got round to it yet so it's United–Valencia at Old Trafford, live on Talk Radio.

'Cutting it fine, aren't you, son?' says Dad.

'Bit of business,' I say.

'Girl business?'

'Kind of.'

'Good on you,' he says with a wink.

I don't tell him it isn't the girl he means. Instead I say:

'You sound brighter.'

'How do you mean?'

'You know, with the divorce going through.'

'Oh that. Well, you've got to move on, haven't you?'

The conversation is interrupted by a Ryan Giggs run, followed by a Killy Gonzalez counter-attack for Valencia.

'Close at both ends,' says Dad. 'It'd be nice to win this one. Get through to the quarter-finals with two games to spare.'

I nod but I can't help but think he's not as chirpy as he's trying to make out.

'Go on, Gary lad,' says Dad as Gary Neville goes on a run.

It's a good effort but it stays 0–0. No score. A bit like Julie and me. But hang on… wait just one minute… Cole… Andy Cole!

One–nil!

That's it, it doesn't have to be no score. I *can* talk to Julie. I *can* ask her out.

I will.

I'll do it.

Thanks United.

For returning the love.

As always.

Thursday 22nd February
2.45 p.m.

OK, so Wes Brown ended up scoring an own goal and Valencia got a 1–1 draw. It doesn't change a thing. United have spoken to me again, they've told me what I've got to do.

I've got to seize the opportunity, grasp the nettle, take the bull by the horns. Come to think of it, the way I feel I'd seize any opportunity, grasp anything, take any animal by the horns. You name it, I'd take it, grasp it, seize it. I'm reincarnated as Get Up And Go For It Man. *I will*, I'll go for it. No more Mr Wimp, no more being tongue-tied and trodden on. Nobody will ever take my dreams away from me. Never again. Nobody's going to walk all over me or kick sand in my face. Let the sharks circle, a new Terry Payne is born.

Except ... every time I so much as think of asking Julie out there still seems to be an awful lot of the old Terry in me.

God, I'm a loser.

Oi you, Wimp – *no!* Get thee behind me, weak and snivelling fake Terry.

This is the real Terry, forged in the fire of lost love, steeled by the suffering of seeing her going out with Frisky Fitzy, made strong by a thousand slings and arrows. (That's right, we've just done *Hamlet* at school.)

You've got to tell her how you feel, Terry, and tell her now.

But how?

And when?

I lie back on my bed, head resting on my laced fingers, and watch the rain streaming down the window pane.

That's the question, when?

What if the sharks move in? What if Julie goes out with one of them? I couldn't stand it happening again. I couldn't take the rejection a second time. No, I've got to act, and I've got to do it now.

But when? When can I see her?

'That's it!' I yell.

The gymnastics club, it's tonight. Saturdays, Tuesdays and *Thursdays*.

For a moment I think of phoning Bobby, asking him if he wants to play badminton. But I've done that before. Julie can see straight through it. I just come over as a sad stalker. No, this time I'm going to be straight with her. I don't need anybody to hold my hand. I don't need any strategies and subterfuges. Just me and the girl and the God's honest truth.

Sounds good.

I just hope it works.

Thursday 22nd February
5.50 p.m.

I'm standing in the rain in the leisure centre car park. I've done this before, the night of the school dance, standing in the rain waiting for Julie. But that time I was a saddo. Now I'm reborn, a super-hero: Get Up And Go For It Man. So why are my legs turning to jelly? Why's my skin tickling and prickling? Why's there a lump the size of a dodo egg in my throat? Get Up And Go For It Man wouldn't behave like this. He'd be cool, steadfast and strong. He'd take the girl in his arms, look in her eyes and say...

Oh God, what *do* I say?

On the way over here I had it all worked out. Had it all prepared, I did, a speech, no, an *oration*. I should have written it down. No, you sad sack, you can't read something like this from a script! Maybe I should go. Yes, that's it! I'll sneak away under cover of darkness. Too late, there she is, getting out of a car. Come on, Terry, you can do this:

...cool...

...steadfast...

...strong.

Kelly sees me.

'Oh, look who's here, the Prescot Stalker.'

I want to dissolve, merge with the rain and trickle down the nearest drain, but I stand my ground.

'Hi, Kelly,' I say, 'I want to talk to Julie. Privately, if you don't mind.'

What was that? Did you hear what I just said? I was cool, I was steadfast, I was strong. I am the strongest link. Hello!

Kelly and Julie exchange glances. To my amazement and absolute joy, Julie nods. Kelly walks reluctantly into the leisure centre foyer.

'Fire away, Terry,' says Julie. 'I'm listening.'

I look at her face, illuminated by the centre's floodlights. She's stunning, her long, black hair bound in skull plaits, her brown eyes looking into mine.

Gulp!

I've just forgotten how to talk!

'Terry?'

What do I do now?

I've never given it much thought until now, the ability to talk. It's natural, you dork. Well, it isn't natural now! I know it's got something to do with the jaws, the tongue, most of all the brain. But how do you engage them all at once? Suddenly the faculty of speech seems so far beyond me I could be a squid or a warthog.

What the hell do I do?

Then I remember, the prepared talk, the oration, all the things I've got to say, and it comes out in a stream of consciousness babble, a tumbling waterfall of words:

'Look, Julie, you know I've always liked you. Always. Ever since I saw you the first time at school. You were wearing blue. I know, I know, it doesn't really matter what you were wearing. Well, it does of course. I'm not implying I've thought of you wearing nothing...'

Aaaargghh! What am I saying? My mouth's just been invaded by aliens from the Planet Gobbledygook. They're making me come out with complete gibberish! Quick, focus. Cool, steadfast, strong.

'No, what I mean is, I was gutted when you went out with Fitz. I just couldn't find the words to ask you out myself, but I like you,

Julie. I really like you. I know you probably think I'm a complete and utter loser, and I'm only in the top set for English and French and I bet you think they don't count, and I'm a Man U fan and you support Liverpool, but crazier things have happened.'

Name one? asks a secret voice inside my brain. But I'm not about to be sidetracked. I've been waiting for this moment for seven lousy months and, no matter what it takes, I'm going to say what I feel. That way, at least I've gone down fighting.

'There's never been anyone but you, Julie. I know I went out with Chloe for a bit, but that's because you were with Fitz. And she asked me when I was down, when I was *vulnerable*. It just kind of happened, but I ended it. She wasn't you. She just wasn't you. And Emma, you got that all wrong. I'd never mess around with her. All you saw was a friendly peck on the cheek. She's Bobby's girl.'

Isn't that a pop song? the secret voice asks, something I've heard round Dad's flat. *I wanna be, duh duh, Bobby's girl.* Who was it, Cilla Black, Dusty Springfield? Dad would know. Shut up! Shut up! There's a nerd in my brain. Get out of my head, will you? I take a deep breath.

'There's one last thing, I didn't break Fitz's ankle on purpose. He went for me first. I know you don't want to listen, but it's the truth. It really is.'

She's staring at me, eyes wide and with no discernible expression on her face. My eyes flick away for a second and I see her legs. They're shapely and they look tanned. She's wearing shorts. She's fantastic. Stop it, Terry. Focus. What's she thinking? I try to replay the speech to myself and it comes out as complete gibberish. Oh God, she thinks I'm mad. I'm the Mad Manc and I'm ogling her legs. I force my eyes away from her legs and back to her face and I make my last bid for happiness.

'Look, you probably think I'm a complete loony toon by now, but it's just because...'

Deep breath. Here goes nothing, just my whole life.

'... I like you so much. Will you go out with me?'

Would you? asks the secret voice.

Of course I would, I'd take pity on a nice guy – even if he's dumb as a mule and crazy as a coot – and I'd say yes. But I'm not Julie. She's already told me she doesn't want to rush into another relationship right away. What's she going to say? It's going to be no. I just know it.

For the next split second time stands still. The rain stops falling, the car tyres stop hissing on the rain-drenched streets, the trees bend their heads to listen, and Julie says:

'OK.'

OK! O for Omigod, K for Kerrumbs.

That's it, OK? All that yearning and wishing and hoping and she just comes out with it like that?

OK!

'Look, Terry,' she says, her words barely audible over my erratic heartbeat. 'I've got to go inside now. We're preparing for a big display and I can't be late. Call me after ten o'clock. We'll arrange something.'

'Ten o'clock,' I say. 'Is that when you finish?'

'No, it's when the Liverpool–Roma coverage finishes on telly. I'll be home in time for the second half.'

Without another word, she puts her bags down, slips her arms round my neck and kisses me full on the lips. The kiss burns through me like a brand, scalding me with joy and relief.

She said yes. The most beautiful girl in the world just said yes!

I notice that she's standing on tiptoes to kiss me. I don't believe it. I've always thought she was taller than me, but she isn't. I just felt that way, a case of The Beauty and The Dwarf.

'You won't forget to ring me, will you?' she says, pulling away.

'I'd forget to breathe first,' I say and she giggles.

I'm stunned. I've actually said something halfway romantic. I watch her run up the steps. By the door she turns round and waves. Even after she's gone I carry on standing and watching, imagining her there by the door.

Returning the love.

Part Five

With the Girl
Or
Theatre of Dreams

1

You won't believe the movie Julie wanted to see. *What Women Want*, it was called. Like I've got the foggiest idea! But I'd better cotton on quick. All these months I've sort of thought that history ended once the girl said yes, I'll go out with you. Then you just had to settle down for the Happy Ever Afters. What was I thinking of? This is where the difficult stuff really begins. I'm not going out with a dream of Julie, I'm going out with Julie. Maybe she's feeling the same way, wondering what the real Terry Payne is like. We're walking in the rain, dodging the cars as they head for the main road, when Julie slips her arm through mine.

'Walk me to the bus stop?' she says.

'I'd walk you all the way back to Huyton,' I tell her.

'The bus stop will do,' she says, laughing.

I remember the time I saw her at the same bus stop with Fitz. My skin catches fire at the thought. But I've got to be strong. Don't mention him. Don't act jealous. I'm on strict orders from Dad and Bobby. Cool is good, obsessive is bad. Each of them in their own way has been coaching me on being with The Girl.

'This is great,' I say. 'Being with you. Can I see you again tomorrow?'

'Sorry,' says Julie. 'I can't.'

'Oh.'

It's a big, disappointed *oh*, as heavy as a stone. She stops and turns my face towards her with fingers chilled by the night rain.

'Hey, I've really enjoyed this evening,' she says. 'You're not like Fitz. I don't have to fend you off.'

I remember Fitz's reputation. Somebody, Caitlin I think, once described him as a sex-mad octopus. A bit too graphic a description for my liking.

'I'm not turning you down,' says Julie. 'I won't be in Liverpool, that's all.'

'Where will you be?'

'Cardiff, of course. The Worthington Cup Final.'

'You mean you're going?'

It must have been a dream when Julie ceremonially burned her Liverpool scarf and became a Man U fan.

'We all are. Me, Mum, Dad, my brothers. Terry, this is Liverpool v Birmingham, our best chance of silverware for years. We're going on a coach and staying overnight in a hotel in Cardiff. One of the parents in the gymnastics club arranged it.'

'You're not telling me your family can fill a whole coach?'

'Of course not, there's a crowd of us.'

'Do I know anybody?'

'One or two,' says Julie.

Her voice falters slightly.

'Such as?'

'Kelly, of course. Gary, Paul, Pepsey, Jamie...'

She takes a little breath despite herself.

'... and Fitz.'

Remember what Dad and Bobby said, don't get jealous. Jealousy is the ultimate turn-off for a girl.

'Oh.'

Yikes! That sounded pretty jealous.

'You're not going to make a fuss, are you?'

Me, make a fuss about her going away to Wales with her ex? Of course not.

'No.'

I try to sound breezy and careless, but it comes out about as breezy and careless as an Eminem song. Julie stands on her tiptoes and kisses me. It's everything I've heard about in a kiss. Chloe's kisses were nice but they never made me feel this way. Julie's lips press firmly against mine. Her mouth opens just the slightest bit and she gives a little sigh. My skin tingles, my stomach fills with butterflies, heat floods through me. I feel like I'm floating up towards the stars. But, as she pulls away, there's this nagging doubt at the back of my mind. I've done this. I used to kiss Chloe this way when she started asking too many questions. It's the ultimate tactical shut up.

'You've nothing to worry about with Fitz, you know,' says Julie, squeezing my upper arms.

'Of course not,' I say, struggling not to pout, not to be jealous. 'You just went out with him for seven months.'

'And I would have gone out with you if you'd only asked.'

'Really?'

'Of course, really. You should have seen how many times I put Fitz off. But you never said a word.'

If I could kick my own backside, I'd be doing it now.

'I saw you looking at me.'

'You did?'

So much for those discreet looks of mine.

'Why didn't you say something?'

'I was ... oh, this sounds stupid.'

Julie is looking at me with this amused expression on her face.

'Go on, what?'

'I was shy. You're so ... you know. And I'm so...'

'Well,' says Julie, throwing her head back and laughing that rich, strong laugh of hers, 'that explains everything.'

She's teasing me, but I don't care. Julie teases the way most people caress: softly, gently, beautifully.

'You're lovely,' I say, still trying to explain. 'You're good at sport, you're popular, you're in the top set at everything, all the boys are after you...'

'Are they?'

'Are you kidding?'

'I thought it was Kelly,' says Julie.

'No way,' I say. 'Have you seen you?'

Julie kisses me again, pressing her body up against me. I don't want this evening to end.

'Terry, you're doing just fine.'

Saturday 24th February
2.00 p.m.

I've been in more embarrassing situations, but I can't really remember when. I've come down to see Julie off. She doesn't mind. She says it's 'sweet'. Everybody else seems to mind, though.

Kelly said: 'I don't know what you see in him. Loser.'

Fitz said (on the quiet, when Julie wasn't around): 'Think you're so clever, don't you, nicking my girl. Well, don't get too comfortable, MnM, I'm not finished, not by a long chalk. I'm nearly ready to play again. I'll have you, Manc.'

Gerard, Josh and John-Joe said, (one after the other and independently of each other): 'I thought our Julie had better taste. A Mad Manc!'

Gary said (to Fitz, but for my benefit): 'Watch he doesn't kick you again.'

So it's a relief when Julie takes me by the hand and leads me round the corner where nobody can see us, and says: 'Kiss me. This has got to last me the weekend.'

I'm just planning my Kiss-that-Will-Last-the-Weekend when Julie takes the initiative and I feel the warmth of her lips on mine. No matter how much I try not to listen, I find myself haunted by the secret voice saying: I wonder if she kissed Fitz like this? There's no point my saying anything like that to Julie so I kiss her back hotly, running my fingers through the cascade of raven black hair, then squeezing her back, letting my hands slide down to her hips.

'Have a good weekend,' says Julie.

What, on my own in Prescot?!

'Yes, you too,' I say, without that much conviction.

It's not only because Man U fans find it hard to wish Liverpool well, but because I can't get Fitz's face out of my mind. Julie might say it's over. I'm not so sure he thinks so.

'I'll phone you from Cardiff,' she says, jogging towards the coach.

'Have you got my number?' I ask, as she jumps on board.

'Both of them,' says Julie. 'Home and mobile. Your mum gave them to me.'

Mum, have I ever told you I love you?

'Don't forget,' I say.

'I won't,' says Julie.

As the coach pulls away she blows me a kiss. And it isn't sarcastic or anything. It's for real. As for Fitz, he gives me a two-finger salute, and it's not because he thinks he's Winston Churchill!

Saturday 24th February
4.30 p.m.

Alex Nyarko has just been sent off so Everton are down to ten men against Ipswich. Bobby starts kicking seven bells out of my bedside cabinet. The alarm clock falls to the floor and starts to bleat pitifully.

'Hey, go and kick your own furniture!'

'That was a nothing challenge,' says Bobby. 'Do these stupid refs want us to go down?'

I don't know how he can be so sure it was a nothing challenge. We're listening to the game on the radio! United don't play until tomorrow.

'Do you know how many players this ref's sent off this season?' rants Bobby. 'Seven!'

Something tells me this isn't just about Everton's prospects of survival. The uncertainty over Emma is getting him down.

'Have you had another argument with Emma?' I ask.

Bobby nods.

'She won't tell me who she's been seeing.'

'Why, did you think she would?'

'She says it was nothing, just a way of getting even with me for New Year, so I should drop it.'

'Maybe you should.'

'That's a bit rich,' says Bobby, 'coming from somebody who's going mad about his girlfriend being in Cardiff with Fitz.'

'Who's going mad?'

'Well, you're not happy.'

He's right. I'm not. I just know everybody will be trying to poison her against me. Especially Fitz.

'She isn't there with Fitz,' I retort. 'She's with a load of people.'

'Yes, including Fitz.'

Just then Everton go 1–0 down. Serves Bobby right for bringing up Cardiff!

He punches the bedside cabinet.

'What *have* you got against my furniture?' I ask, protecting the alarm clock from further punishment.

Bobby shrugs, and immediately Everton go 2–0 down.

'Look at that,' he groans. 'One minute we're coasting to a 0–0 draw, the next the ref sends Nyarko off and we're losing 2–0.'

'So are you going to drop it?' I ask, meaning him and the Who's-Emma-Been-Seeing? investigation.

'Would you?' he asks pointedly.

No, I think.

'Of course,' I say.

Saturday 24th February
10.00 p.m.

She hasn't phoned.

Here am I sitting waiting for Match of the Day and Julie's out having fun with all her mates ... and Fitz.

'I'm making a coffee,' says Mum. 'Do you want anything?'

I shake my head. I'm too miserable to eat. There's snow on the ground outside. I hope United have got the underground heating on. I need a good win against Arsenal to lift my spirits.

Fitz! Why did he have to be born?

'Sure?' asks Mum. 'I bought biscuits.'

'No, thanks.'

'I'll have a biscuit,' shouts Amy from upstairs.

'No, you won't, young lady. Now lights out and go to sleep.'

'Why does Terry get a biscuit?'

'He's seven years older.'

'That's not fair!'

'Who said life was fair? Now go to sleep.'

The phone goes and I bolt for it. It's only Dad asking whether I'm going round for the match tomorrow.

Of course I am, I tell him.

'How was the big date?'

'Great.'

I'm being monosyllabic so he will get off the phone. What if Julie is ringing me right now?

'I'll see you tomorrow then.'

'Yes, goodnight, Dad.'

'Waiting for Julie to phone?' asks Mum.

'Does it show?'

'Oh yes.'

She sits down. She's got a coffee but no biscuits.

'You're very disciplined,' I observe.

'It's seeing the weight come off,' she says. 'Gives me the encouragement to give the biccies a miss.'

I nod absent-mindedly.

'Don't take it too much to heart if she can't ring you,' says Mum. 'She's with all her family and friends.'

'I know,' I say.

But it isn't what I want to hear. If I mean anything to her, if she cares, then she'll phone.

Saturday 24th February
10.45 p.m.

She still hasn't phoned.

I never thought I would say this, but I can't keep my mind on Match of the Day. Come to think of it, I don't even know which game I'm watching. There's only one thing on my mind.

Where is she? Why hasn't she rung?

'Sure you don't want a biscuit?' asks Mum. 'Hobnob?'

I smile. It always used to be me comforting her with Hobnobs.

'Go on then.'

I think they call it comfort eating. I'm on my fourth biscuit when the phone rings.

'Terry?'

'Julie!'

Except it comes out *Zurrbleee* on account of the Hobnob. Crumbs

264

pebble-dash the phone table.

'What's the matter with your voice?'

'Hobnob.'

'I beg your pardon?'

'I was eating a biscuit.'

'Oh. Are you missing me?'

'Loads.'

I almost tell her I couldn't eat, but the Hobnob is making a liar out of me.

'I thought...'

No, not the guilt trip. Not attractive to a woman. Note 3 from Dad's Compendium of Advice on Females. I keep shtum, but Julie rumbles me.

'... That I wouldn't phone? Hey you, Reliable's my middle name.'

And Jealous is mine.

'We've been out for a meal.'

'Yes, who's "we"?'

'Just the family ... and Kelly.'

Oh joy! No Fitz.

'Nobody else?'

Stupid. That is definitely jealousy. Let's hope she hasn't noticed.

'Fitz went out with his mates,' says Julie pointedly.

She's teasing in that gentle way of hers.

'Anyway, here's wishing you really bad luck for the game against Arsenal,' she says.

'Yes, same for you against Birmingham,' I reply. 'I hope you get hammered.'

'Up the Gunners!' says Julie.

'Come on you Brummies,' I answer.

We both laugh. I never thought I'd be able to laugh about football!

'See you in school on Monday,' says Julie.

'Yes, see you then.'

I'm wondering whether it's too soon or too corny – or just too damned pathetic – to say 'I love you' when she hangs up.

Because I definitely do.

I'm so nervous I can hardly stand.

For starters, there's the match: United v Arsenal. First and second in the Premiership. If they win then, maybe, just maybe, they stand a chance of catching us. The gap would be down to ten points. So if we lost at Leeds and Liverpool ... I start doing the Maths ... then went down at Spurs ... More Maths. I might not be in the top set, but I can tot up the League table. And lost to City ... Oh crumbs, our monster lead doesn't seem quite so impregnable when you put it like that. The Gunners did it once before. Overmars scored the winner at Old Trafford and stood all cocky and superior after beating Gary Neville and Peter Schmeichel. After that, Dad and I hated all things Dutch, except for Jaap Stam, of course. We wouldn't let Mum buy Edam cheese and we wouldn't allow a tulip in the house! Arsenal went on to win the League and Cup double. It was a lousy summer that year. The signs aren't good for a midday showdown. Andy Cole and Ryan Giggs are unavailable. I've got a bad feeling about this.

Then there's Julie and me. Don't get me wrong. Everything seems to be going fine. Better than fine, we're talking Walk on Air Wondiferous. I can smell her hair just thinking of her.

She's so open and sweet and affectionate. Boy, is she affectionate! You wouldn't think she was the most gorgeous girl in the whole school. She could pick anybody and she's going out with me.

Me!

Which is half the problem, really. I mean, what on earth does she see in me? If I was a girl, I wouldn't go out with me. Too shy, too skinny, too ginger, too... too... TOO TERRY PAYNE! Put me next to Fitz and there's just no competition. He's all muscly and mesomorphic, he's sickeningly clever and everybody thinks he's Mr Wonderful. Most of all he's down there in Cardiff with her. What's to stop him rekindling the flame? Not me, that's for sure.

I can hardly stand.

So I sit down.

Heavily.

'Hey,' says Dad, 'watch the chair. The springs aren't too good.'

'Sorry.'

'So how's Julie?'

'In Cardiff.'

'Oh dear, missing her, are you?'

'There's more to it than that. Fitz is down there at the Cup Final.'

'Fitz?'

'Her ex. I told you.'

'Sorry. Head like a sieve. Still, I wouldn't worry. She dumped him, didn't she?'

'Yes, but...'

'But what?'

'I'm a loser.'

Dad's eyes flash with anger.

'Now you can cut that out. I'm the world's expert at feeling sorry for myself and I tell you, Terry, it gets you nowhere. If she's decided to go out with you, then you must have something going for you.'

I look up hopefully.

'You reckon?'

'Definitely.'

Sunday 25th February
1.02 and 47 seconds.

I've got something going for me, all right. Dwight Yorke has scored. A Paul Scholes step-over, a one-two with Dwight and I'm in seventh heaven.

Sunday 25th February
1.15 and 26 seconds.

No-o-o-o-o-o-o-o...

o-o-o-o-o-o-o-o-o-o-o-o...

o-o-o-o-o-o-o-o-o-o-o-o-o-o-o!!!!

Arsenal have equalised. Thierry Henry. That's it, chuck out the garlic. I hate everything French, except Mickael Silvestre and Fabien Barthez, of course.

Sunday 25th February
1.17 and 10 seconds.

Ye-e-e-e-e-e-e...
　　e-e-e-e-e-e-e-e...
　　e-e-e-e-e-e-e-e-e-e-e-e-s-s-s-s-s!!!!!
Seventh heaven again! Two for Dwight Yorke.

Sunday 25th February
1.22 and 30 seconds.

A-a-a-a-a-a-a-...

Sunday 25th February
1.22 and 40 seconds.

O-o-o-o-oo-o-o-o-...
　　Wah-hooooooo!!!
　　It's a Dwight Yorke hat-trick.
　　Is there an eighth heaven?

Sunday 25th February
1.24 and 15 seconds.

Un...
　　be...
　　liev...
　　a...
　　ble!
　　Roy Keane makes it four.
　　I'm in ninth heaven, and Andy Gray sums it up: 'Arsenal are on the end of a spanking.'

Sunday 25th February
1.37 and 46 seconds.

Now it's five – let me repeat that – five goals to one.

Ole Gunner Solskjaer, the baby-faced assassin.

Sunday 25th February
2.45 p.m.

Terry to Universe, Terry to Universe, I have just witnessed Big Bang Two. Manchester United 6, Arsenal 1!

Ready, Teddy Sheringham.

It's the twenty-second time in the history of the Premiership that United have scored five or more goals in a game, and we've never handed out a more satisfying thrashing.

'Happy now?' asks Dad.

Oh yes.

Sunday 25th February
5.00 p.m.

By the way, Liverpool have won the Worthington Cup.

Sunday 25th February
8.00 p.m.

The phone goes. It's Julie. It's a bit different to the last call. There's loads of shouting in the background.

'Where are you?' I ask.

'Motorway services. Did you see it?'

'Yes, 6–1.'

'Not United, Terry, *Liverpool*.'

Terry Payne's match report. Birmingham should have won. They were robbed. A blatant penalty turned down in extra time. I don't say that, of course. This *is* the girl I love.

'Yes, you did OK.'

'OK? We won the Cup!'

There's a noise like a rhino breaking wind.

'What's that?'

'Fitz.'

That flatulent rhino.

'Oh.'

It's my lead balloon *Oh* again.

'Go away!'

Julie's talking to somebody next to her. She is obviously trying to hang on to her mobile.

'I said, clear off!'

'Julie?'

'It's OK, Terry. They're excited, that's all.'

Oh, Fitz will be excited all right, excited about you, Julie!

I hear something like a door slamming.

'Terry, can you hear me?'

'Yes.'

'I'm in the ladies' loo. Nobody can get to me in here.'

A lavatory never sounded so romantic! For a moment I wonder whether to say the three little words. I'm dying to, but I don't want to be premature, or off-putting, or stupid. I've asked Dad and Bobby what they think. When do I say *I love you*?

Dad: When you're sure she's the one.

Bobby: Never.

I'm sure she's the one, but in the end I don't manage anything better than:

'Have you had a good time?'

'Oh, Terry, it's been fantastic.'

But what, what *exactly* has been fantastic?

'I'll tell you all about it in school tomorrow. I got you a present.'

She's got *me* a present. That isn't right. I should be buying her presents.

'Julie, you shouldn't.'

'Yes, I should. I definitely should. Anyway, got to go.'

'Bye, Julie.'

Maybe I should just say it. Go on, what harm will it do? Three little words. What's so hard about that? I open my mouth but as I form the words the phone goes dead. We're out of time.

2

This must be the best week of my life. It started when Julie gave me this naff cuddly red dragon she brought back from Cardiff. But so what if it was naff? It was from her, the first present between us. I've got it hanging over my bed.

Bobby was disgusted when he saw it: 'You going soft on me?' he asked.

'Definitely,' I told him.

Julie was made up when she saw it. I think she had a sneaking suspicion I would chuck it in the bin. I think putting it on display like that has kind of convinced her I'm in touch with my female side.

We've been inseparable all week. I think Kelly is feeling really put out by it all. Tonight, we're baby-sitting Amy together. Mum's gone to her jogging club. Julie and I are sitting on the couch. Amy is curled up in the armchair across the room. She gets to stay up until ten o'clock every Friday night.

'Shouldn't Mum be home?' asks Amy.

I glance at the wall clock.

'She's only five minutes late,' I tell her. 'Nothing to worry about.'

Just then the phone rings. It's Mum.

'Hi, Terry, is it OK if I go for a drink with some of the members?'

Some of the members? Somehow that doesn't ring quite true.

'I was going to walk Julie to the bus stop,' I say.

'What time is she going?'

'We have to leave the house at half past ten.'

'I'll be home by then,' says Mum. 'And if I'm not, I'll run her home.'

'Fair enough.'

I hear a man's voice in the background.

'Who's that?'

'Oh, just one of the members.'

That again, 'one of the members'. She's definitely up to something.

'That was Mum,' I tell Amy.

It's the adverts.

'Anybody want a snack?' I ask.

'Can I have Cheerios in here?' asks Amy.

It's one of Mum's rules. No breakfast cereal in the living room. I've spilt mine down the couch twice. She went mad.

'Yes,' I say. 'So long as you sit on a cushion on the floor.'

Amy goes wide-eyed with surprise.

'I like you going out with Julie,' she says. 'You act nice when she's around.'

I glance at a smiling Julie. She's definitely good for me. She's even got me doing some Maths revision.

'Yes, I suppose I do.'

Julie follows me into the kitchen. It's the first time we've been out of Amy's sight. While I pour out the cereal Julie slips her arms round my waist and squeezes gently. I stroke her forearms. God, this feels good, like we're a proper couple.

'Mum should be back for half past ten,' I tell her. 'She'll run you home if she's any later.'

'No problem,' says Julie. 'What's she doing anyway?'

'She's gone out with some of the members of the jogging club.'

'Sounds like a feller to me,' Julie observes.

'That,' I murmur, wondering what Dad would say, 'is exactly what I thought.'

Friday 2nd March
10.35 p.m.

We're at the bus stop, having a cuddle while we wait. There are four other people waiting. They've all got their backs to us. Funny that, how people don't like watching you when you're getting all lovey-dovey.

'Your mum looked a bit flustered,' says Julie. 'It's definitely a feller.'

'You think so?'

273

'Terry, I know so.'

I've got this mental picture of a tall, lean man in jogging bottoms and a London Marathon T-shirt. Mum with a boyfriend. Weird!

'I saw you here with Fitz once,' I say.

Julie stiffens.

'When?'

'Months ago. I was over there watching.'

Julie looks up at me.

'Did you follow us?'

I remember Kelly's stalker jibes and shake my head quickly.

'Of course not. I was on my way home, that's all. Fitz was trying it on.'

Julie laughs.

'He was *always* trying it on!'

My face must be giving me away because Julie immediately says:

'Oh, don't go all jealous on me, Terry. I made sure he behaved himself.'

'I try not to be jealous,' I say. 'It's just...'

'What?'

'He's so good at everything.'

'Don't put yourself down, Terry. You're worth two of Fitz.'

'So how come you still hang round with him?'

Julie frowns, obviously frustrated with me.

'Terry, he's a mate.'

'Are you going to the match together?'

'Well, not tomorrow. We're away at Leicester. The next home game we will be, but there's a gang of us: me, Kelly, Gary. My dad and our Gerard go as well. It's not like it's just the two of us. You can't want me to stop seeing my friends.'

I wish I could! I confine myself to a lukewarm, 'No, of course not.'

'Because I'm with you now, Terry. One hundred per cent.'

We kiss to seal the bargain.

'Anyway,' says Julie, 'here's my bus.'

I'm watching her climb on board when this old dear smiles at me.

'She's a lovely girl, son. You hang on to her.'

I smile back. I just hope I can.

'Seen this girl of yours?' asks Dad.

'Not today. She's gone to her gymnastics club, then she's going into town shopping.'

'Ninety-three per cent,' murmurs Bobby, who has been conspicuous by his silence.

'What?'

'Ninety-three per cent. The number of teenage girls who say that store-hopping is their favourite activity.'

'Oh.'

The three of us are watching Leeds–Man U on Dad's TV. It's a tight game with few chances. At half-time Dad makes some butties.

'Your mum OK?' asks Dad.

I must have hesitated.

'Terry?'

May as well be honest, I tell myself.

'I think she's seeing someone.'

Dad looks at the plate of sandwiches for a moment, then recovers himself and shrugs.

'She's a free woman now. She can do what she wants.'

I lead the way into the living-room, but not before I let him know I'm not fooled:

'Now say it like you mean it.'

United look like they are going to hang on to an undeserved 1–1 draw until Wes Brown turns a cross into his own net.

'Oh no!'

But the linesman saves our bacon. It's ruled offside.

'Lucky,' says Bobby. 'Very lucky.'

This time he meets our disapproving glare.

'Well, I've got the right to my opinion, haven't I?'

In unison, Dad and I roar 'No!'

I'm following Bobby out of the door when I lean across to Dad.

'Are you OK?' I ask. 'About Mum?'

'It's a matter of having to be,' he says.

I leave it at that and catch Bobby up.

'You're in a funny mood today,' I say. 'Something happened with Emma?'

'She says either I stop interrogating her about this other guy, or we're finished.'

'So why not drop it?' I ask. 'She isn't seeing him any more, is she?'

Bobby frowns.

'I don't think so.'

'Then leave it, Bob. You're driving her away.'

'It's hard,' he says. 'I just can't get it out of my mind. Who do you think it is?'

This is becoming an obsession with him.

'Bobby, I've no idea.'

'No, of course you haven't,' says Bobby, with a touch of dark humour. 'I mean, you thought it was you, didn't you?'

I shrug.

'We all make mistakes.'

'Are you seeing Julie tonight?' Bobby asks.

I nod.

'What are you doing?'

'You're not going to believe this.'

'Go on, try me.'

'I'm going to her house for tea.'

'Are you nuts?! They're all mad Liverpudlians. What are you going for?'

'Julie wants me to.'

'Mum, Dad, three brothers, all Kopites. They'll eat you alive.'

'It can't be that bad,' I say.

'You sure about that?'

Actually no.

Gulp!

I've been wandering around for ten minutes. Julie said get there at five-thirty, and I don't want to arrive too early. But something changes my mind. A couple of guys start sizing me up. I don't like the look of them. Ten minutes isn't *too* early, I decide. I make a move. The two guys follow me for a while then lose interest. I wonder if they can smell Mancunian – even an adopted Manc like me. I find Julie's house. Double glazing, hanging basket, new car outside. The family doesn't seem badly off. I ring the doorbell and wait, confidence draining out of me. I hope Julie answers. I see somebody in the frosted glass. It isn't her. When the door opens I find myself looking at a tall, gangly thirteen year old. This must be Huey, I mean Gerard. Duey and Louie will be lurking inside, plotting the downfall of the Mad Manc.

'Hi,' I say, as brightly as I can manage.

'Ju,' he shouts, ignoring me, 'It's your Manc.'

Julie shoves past, swatting him with a copy of the *Echo*, and waves me in.

'Ignore him, Terry. Come in.'

I follow her. I find myself thinking about condemned men and their final walk. I glimpse a long Ikea table set for seven people. Julie leads me past the kitchen and into the living-room.

'Terry, this is my mum.'

Dad once told me that, if you wanted to know whether to settle down with a girl, take a look at her mother. That's what she'll be like in a few years. So I take a look. Mrs Carter is tall, slim and tanned-looking. More than Julie, even. She has oval brown eyes and a full mouth. She passes the acceptable mother test.

'This is my dad.'

'Alright there, Terry,' says the thick-set, middle-aged man in a strong Scouse accent. 'Lucky this morning, weren't you?'

'A draw was a fair result,' I say defensively.

I keep quiet about Liverpool going down 2–0. Bad etiquette to gloat, I reckon.

'This is Josh,' Julie says.

Gerard's smaller version ignores me.

'And this is John-Joe.'

He ignores me too. Julie rolls her eyes.

'I hope you like Italian,' says Mr Carter.

'Love it,' I say.

'Good, because my wife's Italian.'

I glance at a smiling Mrs Carter. I suppose that explains Julie's bronzed skin, though you'd think it would have been bleached a bit by the Merseyside drizzle.

'We play your lot on the thirty-first, don't we?' says Mr Carter.

'Yes, that's right.'

'We'll get the double over you this year,' says Josh.

'Batter you,' says John-Joe.

I glance at Julie. What do I say? I decide not to rise to it.

'We'll see,' I say. 'Should be a good game.'

As if I care whether it's a good game. I want us to win, that's all!

'Well,' says Mr Carter, 'Shall we eat?'

I follow them, hoping I get to sit next to Julie. John-Joe steals my place. On purpose, I think.

'Hey you,' says Julie. 'Shift!'

'Why, want to sit next to lover boy, do you?' sneers Gerard.

'Now stop teasing,' says Mrs Carter.

She sounds pretty Scouse for an Italian.

I eventually get to sit next to Julie.

'Do you like spaghetti carbonara?' asks Mrs Carter.

'Probably,' I say.

Julie and her parents laugh, the three boys scowl. I spend the next ten minutes trying not to trail spaghetti against my shirt. It isn't easy. The food is lovely, though. I've been living on microwave meals since Dad left. Mum's always in a rush. I complete the meal with only two minor food streaks, and they match my top so it doesn't really matter. Thank goodness it wasn't bolognese. Mr Carter asks me about school. The conversation turns to the football team.

'I hear you're quite useful,' he says.

I glance at Julie and smile.

'Useful at breaking people's legs,' snorts Gerard.

Julie glares at him.

'Terry says it was a fifty-fifty ball.'

I look at her. She believes me!

'Besides,' says Julie, 'these things happen.'

Or maybe she half-believes me.

'It's a hard game.'

Or maybe she doesn't believe me at all!

'I'm afraid my three boys are secretary, treasurer and president of the Fitz Fan Club,' says Mr Carter.

Now that's a name I didn't want to hear over tea. I bet Fitz could eat spaghetti Doo-Dah without smearing it all over his shirt. To reassure me, Julie squeezes my leg under the table. I prickle with pleasure.

'Yes,' I say ruefully. 'He's dead popular.'

Saturday 3rd March
7.00 p.m.

We're going bowling. I'm glad to get out of the house. Huey, Duey and Louie have been hard work all evening, always trying to make me look like an idiot. And they dropped something into the conversation that's got me really worried.

'That wasn't too bad, was it, Terry?' asks Julie as the bus pulls away from the stop.

'No,' I say, 'It wasn't *too* bad.'

'Go on,' says Julie in that long-suffering way of hers. 'What's bothering you now?'

'What did Gerard mean?' I ask. 'He said something about Easter. Just after we'd eaten. You and Fitz and Easter.'

'Oh, take no notice of our Ged.'

'But what did he mean?'

Julie gives that little sigh of hers, like a mum having to explain to a little kid why the windows steam up in cold weather, or where babies come from, or why the cat couldn't get up again after it got run over.

'I'm in the gymnastics club, right?'

'Yes.'

'And Hayley Fitzpatrick is in the same club.'

'Yes.'

I don't like where this is heading. I've seen Fitz at the leisure centre picking his kid sister up, so it isn't exactly news to me.

'And you know we do displays in different parts of the country?'

'Of course. You've got that Ministrada thing next weekend.'

'Right. Well, not only do gym clubs from all over the country come to Liverpool. We go to them too. And at Easter we go to Edinburgh for the next competition.'

It rings a bell. They all went to the Isle of Man last year.

'And...?'

'And,' says Julie, starting to look uncomfortable. 'Hayley's whole family goes to support her.'

'Including Fitz,' I say.

'Yes,' says Julie. 'Including Fitz. His parents don't feel they can leave him alone in the house. I don't blame them really, he is a bit wild.'

While I'm wondering just how wild he got with her, Julie continues.

'Oh, Terry, I wish you'd stop worrying about him. It's over. To be honest, it's basically been over for months. I just couldn't bring myself to tell him.'

She takes my left hand between hers.

'Listen, if this is going to work you've got to trust me. Half the reason I broke up with Fitz was because he was so jealous.'

'What was he jealous of?'

Julie chuckles.

'Why, you of course.'

'Me!'

Now this is starting to get interesting.

'Yes, didn't you know?'

'Of course not. What's he got to be jealous of? I don't get it.'

'Every time he saw us talking he would go mad. He's very insecure that way.'

Fitz insecure! Now I've heard everything.

'So are you OK about Edinburgh?'

'Yes,' I say. 'Of course I am.'

I sit there looking OK about Edinburgh. I look out at the street lights snaking into the distance. I think I pulled it off pretty well. But OK about them being in Scotland together? I wish.

'See anybody we know?' says Julie, when we get to the bowling alley.

She means anybody *she* knows. Mr Popular I'm not.

'Not yet,' I grunt.

It's not like I'm trying very hard. I just want it to be Julie and me. I mean – Kelly, Gary, Paul, Pepsey, Jamie, my ex Chloe, I don't fancy hanging round with them all night. They're all members of the Fitz fan club.

'Hang on,' says Julie. 'That's Pepsey, isn't it?'

She leads the way. It's Pepsey Cooper all right. I can't help picturing her crying at the New Year's party after Paul caught her snogging Bobby. That certainly knocked the fizz out of her!

'Hi, Pepsey, anybody around?'

The moment she lays eyes on us Pepsey's face goes as white as a sheet.

'Where's Paul?' Julie asks, looking round. There are two cans of Coke on the table Pepsey's sitting at.

There's one of those long continental-film silences.

'He's ... er ... gone somewhere with Jamie and Gary. Boys' night out.'

'So where are the girls?'

'Not sure,' says Pepsey.

'So who are you with?'

'My ... cousin,' says Pepsey lamely.

She looks at me. She seems very nervous. She seems to be looking over my shoulder at somebody. She gives the merest hint of a nod. Julie catches the gesture and glances round.

'Anyway,' says Pepsey, definitely uncomfortable. 'I'm just off.'

With that she heads for the exit.

'Whoever she's with,' says Julie, 'it isn't her cousin.'

Saturday 3rd March
10.30 p.m.

We hold hands all the way back on the bus. Julie gets off soon. Four stops before me.

'I wish tonight could go on forever,' I say.

'A bit of a romantic on the quiet, aren't you?' says Julie.

I shrug, embarrassed. I'm still dying to say the three little words, but I'd come over really pathetic if she doesn't want to hear them.

'Was *he* romantic?'

'Fitz? Give over!'

I'm glad he wasn't. I don't have anything to live up to.

'Have you had any other boyfriends?' I ask.

'No,' says Julie, 'Fitz is it. Unless you count Mark Huxley in the Infants. We starred in the Christmas play together. He was Joseph and I was Mary.'

'Just the one boyfriend? You? Never!'

'I'm telling you the God's honest truth.'

I can't help it, I just lean over and kiss her.

'What was that for?'

'For being you.'

She laughs.

'You're funny, you know that?'

'Funny ha-ha or funny peculiar?'

'Both.'

'Why am I peculiar?'

'Well, you don't try it on.'

'Did Fitz?'

'Not half, I was forever fending him off.'

That I like to hear. I'm careful not to ask if she *always* fended him off. I know Dad is right. Jealousy is definitely unappealing.

'What about you?' she asks. 'How many girlfriends have you had?'

'Just the one. Chloe. Which is none really.'

'What do you mean, none?'

'It was a non-relationship. Rebound stuff. Because of you and Fitz.'

Julie smiles her heart-stopping smile.

'I have to admit I could never see you two together.'

'There's a good reason for that,' I tell her. 'It was a mistake. You know when we got together?'

Julie nods.

'The night of the school disco.'

I smile sadly. The night she got together with Fitz.

'I watched you,' she says.

I shake my head.

'I've been a real idiot,' I say. 'I should have asked you out seven months ago. All that wasted time.'

She moves closer.

'Still, you can start making up for it now, can't you?'

I see those wonderful brown eyes drawing me in. I love you, Julie Carter.

Saturday 3rd March
10.45 p.m.

I'm about to turn into our street. I feel tipsy, intoxicated by the smell of Julie's hair, her perfume, her skin. This is too good to be true. The most beautiful girl in the world with her olive skin and her mane of black hair, and she wants to be with me. In all the movies it's just at this moment, when you think you've finally made it, when life couldn't taste any sweeter, that the mad axeman arrives to cause mayhem. So where's the mad axeman going to come from? I look for grey clouds on the horizon. There's only one; Julie going away to Edinburgh at Easter, and Fitz being there with her.

'I know there's nothing to be worried about,' I say out loud. 'I know it.'

But knowing something isn't the same as believing it, and deep down inside something is gnawing at me.

'Stupid,' I announce to the empty street.

I'm putting my key in the lock when something makes me pause. There's another thought chewing away at the back of my mind, making me uneasy. It doesn't have anything to do with Julie and me, at least I don't think so, but it's these odd occurrences. Emma's little fling for one, and the owner of the other Coke that Pepsey was guarding. They're bothering me for some reason. I'm sure they add up to something. But what?

3

Tuesday 6th March
10.15 p.m.

'That you, Terry?'

   'No, Keanu Reeves.'

   'I wish.'

I take my jacket off and hurry into the living-room. The legs of my jeans are soaked right through.

   'Oh, Terry, is that all you had on, a thin jacket? Where's that coat I got you?'

It's at the back of my wardrobe. I wouldn't be seen dead in it. Only hard-core nerds wear a Nanook of the North coat. I'd rather get soaked than be seen in that thing. She'll have me driving huskies next.

   'Well, what have you done with it?'

   'Dunno.'

She snorts but steers away from a row.

   'How was revision?'

I've been revising round at Julie's. I met her after gymnastics and we went to hers. She told me something interesting about Pepsey. That night we saw her at the bowling alley, there was no boys' night out, she'd told Paul she wasn't well. She begged Julie not to give her away, but wouldn't say why. Anyway, about tonight. Julie's been trying to get me to understand vectors. Now I know that there are four notations I've got to learn. I can't actually remember what they are, but I know there are four. I'd make a good Moses. There are ten commandments, I'd tell my people, I don't know what they are but there are definitely ten! So whatever it is you want to do, DON'T!

   'Good,' I say. 'Julie's been explaining vectors.'

   'Go on then,' says Mum. 'Explain them to me.'

Uh-oh, I didn't see this coming. I have to admit I spent most of

284

the time looking at Julie, the way she crossed her legs, the way a lock of her hair snaked down her throat, the way she ran the tip of her tongue along her upper lip when she was concentrating. OK, so it isn't homework, but it kept me happy.

'They're shown as lines with arrows,' I say with as much authority as I can muster. 'And there are four notations.'

I should have letters after my name. Terry Payne, MK. That's Master of Kiddology. Mum smiles. Easily pleased, my mum. Good job she doesn't have a clue about maths herself, or I'd be well rumbled.

'I'm glad to see you're making an effort,' she says.

Oh, I'm making an effort, all right, an effort not to kill Huey, Duey and Louie.

All the time Julie and I were sitting at the kitchen table they were blowing kisses and making sarcastic remarks. Julie was wearing a sleeveless blouse. I was running a finger down her arm when the three of them came in and started sticking their fingers down their throats and making puking noises. The only kiss Julie gave me all evening was when we stood in the porch on my way out. Still, it's one kiss more than I would have got a few weeks ago. It kept me going all the way home.

'You'd better change out of those clothes,' says Mum.

I nod. On my way upstairs I remember I haven't got any money for my school dinner.

'Have you got my two pounds fifty?' I ask.

'There's some change in my fleece,' says Mum. 'It's hanging up.'

I feel in her pockets and pull out three pound coins. Stuck between them is a scrap of paper.

It reads: 'Richard – 426 0010.'

Richard? I don't know any Richard. Then the penny drops. She went for a drink again last night, straight after jogging.

'Did you get it?' Mum calls.

'Yes.'

In fact, I got more than I bargained for. I slip the note back in her pocket.

Wednesday 7th March
7.35 p.m.

Bummer!

Just when I was listening to Des Lynam explaining the importance of Panathinaikos v United in the Champions' League, Dad prised it out of me, the identity of Mum's new boyfriend.

'Richard?' he says. 'I don't know any Richard.'

'I think he's in her jogging club.'

Dad must be picturing this really fit hunk, a cross between Jude Law and Linford Christie, because he starts sucking in his belly.

'At least it isn't one of my mates,' he says. 'I couldn't cope with that.'

'It's not like she's having an affair,' I say. 'You are divorced, remember. Mum's a free woman.'

I'm only repeating what Julie said to me in school. Somehow, I don't think I'm helping. For the next ten minutes Dad's really quiet. It's a relief when the match kicks off.

But not much of a relief.

I've been looking forward to this game. Tonight's the night we're supposed to show our class and sweep away the opposition. Tonight's the night we're supposed to book our place in the quarter-finals. Only it doesn't go to plan.

Twenty-four minutes into a game we seem to be treating as a friendly, Panathinaikos take the lead with a screamer of a shot from outside the area.

'What are they playing at?' groans Dad.

One thing's for certain. It isn't football. We can hardly string two passes together. We're listless and, frankly, the Greeks are playing us off the park. Time and again they slice open our defence. It's embarrassing. Football is supposed to give you a chance to be part of something bigger than you, a thing of pride. All I can think of when the half-time whistle goes is how I can hold my head up in school tomorrow. The Manc-baiters will be out in force, that's for sure.

The second half isn't much better. Even though we put a bit more pressure on, we still can't open them up and they keep launching sweeping counter-attacks that threaten to kill us off.

'I don't believe this,' says Dad, head in hands.

Just like he can't believe Mum is going out with a marathon-running hunk called Richard.

'That's the end of normal time,' I say, glancing at my watch.

We're into stoppage time. Four minutes added.

'Come on, lads,' I say. 'Remember Barcelona.'

Sheringham and Solskjaer. European Champions. Doing the conga down the Ramblas.

'There's still time.'

'No miracles tonight,' says Dad.

Fortunately he's wrong. After ninety-two minutes Paul Scholes hits a sweet shot into the back of the net. He's spared United's blushes with an undeserved 1–1 draw. The upshot of a disappointing night: so long as we don't lose by more than 2–0 at home to Sturm Graz next Tuesday, we're through.

On my way home I phone Julie. Just to hear her voice. I can't believe how wonderful she is, she doesn't even ask why I phoned, but she makes me glad I did. She puts a smile back on my face.

Saturday 10th March
10.00 a.m.

The car park is packed. There are coaches from all over the country. I'm here at Everton Park sports centre to support Julie ... and to keep an eye on Fitz. OK, I know what I said about jealousy being a complete turn-off but Fitz would do anything to split me and Julie up. So I'm not giving him a chance. He'll use the fact that his kid sister Hayley is taking part to come down and make a nuisance of himself, but don't worry, I have a counter-nuisance strategy prepared. It's called Don't Let Julie Out Of My Sight.

'Terry, you made it!'

It's Julie. She throws her arms round my neck and kisses me. Kelly rolls her eyes and makes gagging noises. Pepsey just looks on. She's been subdued ever since we saw her at the bowling alley. I'd love to know what her big secret is.

'What's he doing here?' asks Kelly. 'This isn't a boyfriend event. My Gary isn't coming.'

'He isn't interested,' says Julie. 'Terry is.'

Yes, interested in you.

In the foyer, Julie gets me a pass. I'm about to follow her through to the hall where the display is taking place, when my mobile goes.

'I'd better answer,' I say. 'See you inside.'

I step back through the doors.

'Yes?'

'It's me.'

'Hi, Bobby, what's up?'

'I'm outside the stupid registry office.'

Of course, it's his mum's wedding day. She's getting hitched to Slughead, the big guy with the cocker spaniel that pukes over Bobby's bed.

'You still don't like him then?'

What comes out of the phone isn't a reply but this really long BLEURRCH! sound.

'He's a complete creepazoid, Terry. This is the worst day of my life.'

'I thought that was when you found out Emma had been seeing someone else?'

'Thanks for cheering me up, Terry.'

'Sorry.'

'It's not your fault.'

'Is Emma with you?' I ask.

'No, but she's coming to the reception. You sure you can't come?'

They're having a big do in the evening.

'Sorry, Bob,' I say. 'It clashes with this gymnastics disco.'

'But they're holding it at Anfield! You can't go in there. It's like a turkey signing up to get stuffed.'

'I've got to, Bobby. You understand.'

He gives a long sigh.

'Yes, I understand. The lovely Julie.'

'Yes,' I say. 'The lovely Julie.'

It's Julie's turn to perform. I watch her and the nineteen other members of the club walk out in their shimmering silver leotards. Looking at Julie, I can't believe she's actually going out with me. I keep on saying that, don't I? I mean, this girl is incredible. All the way through the first part of the dance routine I've got my eyes glued to her, sleek, lovely Julie. Just once, her eyes meet mine and she smiles. It's a breathtaking smile, kind of proud and kind of embarrassed and one hundred per cent beautiful. I glance round at where Fitz is sitting, two rows behind me and to my left. He scowls. Mrs Carter, who is sitting next to me, notices and chuckles.

'You're making him very jealous,' she whispers.

'I know,' I say.

Then, jokingly but also deadly serious: 'Good, isn't it?'

Mrs Carter winks. She's the only member of the family who isn't a card-carrying member of the Fitz fan club. On the quiet I think she had him down as the lousy groper he is.

The second part of the routine has begun: *Heaven must be missing an angel*. It's got an *Aw* factor of nine, mainly down to the younger girls, and a palpitation factor of ten, totally down to Julie. When they're finished I clap until my hands sting. Fitz is still scowling.

I meet Julie outside. There's a little catering stall and we have bacon sandwiches, doughnuts and fizzy drinks.

'Aren't you gymnasts supposed to eat healthily?' I ask. 'Pasta and chicken, that sort of thing?'

Julie laughs, dabbing bacon fat off her chin with a paper napkin.

'Supposed to is right,' she says. 'I even tried to be a vegetarian last year, you know, but I couldn't resist the smell of bacon.'

'You were fantastic in there,' I say enthusiastically.

'Thanks,' says Julie, 'but it wasn't that good. We missed one of our balances.'

'Did you? I didn't notice.'

'That,' says Julie, teasing me in that gentle way of hers, 'is because you were staring at my legs.'

'I was not!'

'Were too! And that's not all you were staring at.'

I'm wondering what to say, when she gives me a hug.

'Don't worry,' she says, 'I'm flattered.'

Her voice drops to a whisper: 'I fancy you rotten too.'

She fancies me! Fancies me *rotten*! This girl is too good to be true. I see Fitz come out on to the steps in front of the sports centre. He sees us sitting on the wall and shakes his head before going back inside. Six Guns says Fitz will be at training this week. The showdown is coming.

Saturday 10th March
8.30 p.m.

Now I know what Luke Skywalker felt like when he penetrated the Death Star. I've just entered Anfield, heart of the Evil Empire. Mum's dropped me off so I've got to tread enemy territory all on my own. There are all these bouncers ushering people past the Bill Shankly this and the Bob Paisley that. I'm at the heart of the Beast. I'm looking around for Julie, but I can't see her. I'm hovering uncertainly outside the function room where they're holding the disco when Kelly and Pepsey walk through the doors. They're both dressed up to the nines and look much older than sixteen.

'You look nice,' I say.

I've got to butter them up. They're Julie's best mates.

Kelly gives me a withering glance which says: *Whose shoe did you come in on?* Pepsey keeps shtum.

'Have you seen Julie?' I ask.

'She isn't here yet,' says Kelly, before walking away without so much as a by-your-leave.

She's just about to disappear into the function room when she turns round and says to one of the bouncers, a particularly gorilla-like individual with a shaved head: 'See him? He supports Man U.'

Kelly may look like an angel, but she's got a voice like a flipping foghorn. Every head in the place turns to look at me.

To my relief, Julie walks in at that very moment. She's wearing black trousers which look like they've been painted on and a sparkly crop top (I think that's what they're called) that shows her bare midriff. My throat goes dry. We're talking Gobi Desert.

'Julie,' I croak, before clearing my throat. 'I mean, Julie, you look...'

'What?'

How do I answer this without drooling?

'Gorgeous.'

'That'll do nicely,' she says, doing a mock curtsey. 'Where are the others?'

'Dunno,' I say. 'I just got here.'

I don't tell her about Kelly. There's no point bad-mouthing her best friend.

'There they are!'

All of a sudden there are all these teenage girls flocking together, hugging and talking all at once. Suddenly I feel very left out.

'Terry,' says Julie. 'I'm going to have a couple of dances with the girls. You don't mind watching our stuff, do you?'

I shake my head and sit next to a chair piled high with coats and handbags. I've played gooseberry in my time, but never to a dozen females! Fitz enters with Hayley. Hayley repeats the flocking, hugging, talking at once routine with the younger girls and similarly disappears in the direction of the dance floor, leaving me and Fitz alone in a corner of the bar. We look at each other briefly, wondering what to do next. Eventually, Gary Tudor walks in and he and Fitz go to the bar. I crane my neck to see the girls but they're out of sight round the corner. Julie's couple of dances last twenty-five minutes, and even when they do return it's only to take liquid refreshment and disappear back to the dance floor.

'Sorry to leave you hanging on here,' says Julie. 'But I won't be long. You do understand, don't you?'

'Sure,' I say. 'You enjoy yourself.'

And I sit there with this big stone in my heart, wishing I'd never come at all. I look around and I can't see Fitz. What if ... no, don't even think it. Another twenty minutes have gone when he appears.

'Left you on your own, has she? Bad sign that, mate.'

Then he's gone again.

I can't remember when I felt more alone.

Saturday 10th March
9.15 p.m.

I can't see Julie or Fitz. My mind is working overtime. How could she do this to me? Another five minutes and I'm walking out of here.

Saturday 10th March
9.25 p.m.

OK, five *more* minutes.

Saturday 10th March
9.33 p.m.

Right, that does it. She's with him. I *know* she is.

Fancy me rotten, does she?

Well, it looks like it, doesn't it? I've made a complete idiot of myself this time.

Saturday, 10th March
9.34 p.m.

It's her!

'Oh, Terry, I'm so sorry. I didn't notice the time. Come on, you've got my complete and undivided attention for the rest of the night. Hey, Fitz.'

He gets up from a table. It seems that's where he's been all the time. I breathe a sigh of relief. I've been torturing myself for nothing.

'Watch the coats, will you? I'm going to have a dance with my feller.'

I watch Fitz's face. It's worth all the waiting. He looks crushed.

Bobby's been round to my house for some TLC. Mum's fed him and I've counselled him. I should be a priest. I do good confession.

'That bad, eh?' I say, doing my best to sound sympathetic, which is hard when you're hearing the story for the third time.

'Would you believe it?' Bobby says. 'She puked over my shoe.'

She is Lady, Slughead's cocker spaniel. Not Emma, you understand.

'Maybe she's got a delicate stomach,' I suggest.

'So why's it only delicate around me?' Bobby demands. 'And what moron brings his dog to a wedding reception?'

'The moron your mum's just married.'

'That's when it all started to go wrong,' says Bobby, burying his face in his hands. 'Emma stuck up for the dog, I mentioned the mystery boyfriend and she walked out on me.'

'Have you phoned her?' I ask.

'Three times,' says Bobby. 'She just hangs up.'

I check my watch. I've got to make a move soon if I'm going to watch the Tranmere–Liverpool game on TV with Julie.

'Look, Bobby...'

'It's over, isn't it, Terry?'

'Maybe, but Bobby...'

'I can't let it end like this, though.'

'No, Bobby.'

'You think she's worth it, don't you, Terry?'

'Yes, Bobby.'

'I know I'm a prat.'

'Yes, Bobby.'

He frowns.

'I mean, no, Bobby.'

'Have you been listening to me?'

'Of course I have.'

For two hours actually!

'So what do I do, Terry?'

I pull a face.

'I don't know, Bobby, but if you want my advice the last thing you

293

do is bring up this other guy. That's just suicidal.'

'You're right,' says Bobby, brightening.

He stands up and I reach for my coat. Just as quickly he sits down again. Reluctantly, I put my jacket down.

'But what if she won't see me? What do you think, Terry?'

You want to know what I think, Bobby? I think you're one pain-in-the-neck loser right now. I don't say that, though. He's the pain-in-the-neck loser who listened to me all those months I was pining after Julie. I do my duty and say:

'Why not run through it again for me, Bobby?'

Sunday 11th March
2.46 p.m.

Julie lets me in.

'Sorry I'm late,' I say. 'I had to nursemaid Bobby.'

'Is this about Emma?'

I nod.

'You're just in time for the second half,' she says, leading the way into the living-room. On my way down on the bus I had this picture in my head of Julie and me alone in the living-room. I'm sorely disappointed. The whole family is glued to the screen. I have to sit on the carpet with my back against the leather couch.

'What's the score?'

'Two–nil to Liverpool.'

I grimace. I just can't help it.

'You'd better keep him quiet,' says Gerard, noticing.

He talks about me as if I'm a naughty puppy, or a particularly foul-mouthed parrot.

The match has hardly resumed when Yates meets a terrific cross and heads home for Tranmere.

'Yiss!' I shout, raising my fist.

Gerard, Josh and John-Joe raise their fists, and not in celebration.

Five minutes later Steven Gerrard puts Liverpool 3–1 up. The living-room erupts and I get mobbed. Everybody's rubbing my head and hitting me with cushions and asking me the score.

'All over bar the shouting,' says Mr Carter, making no effort not to gloat.

It isn't. After fifty-seven minutes the Tranmere substitute Allison scores with his first touch.

'Yiss!' I shout.

Tranmere two, Liverpool three.

Gerard, Josh and John-Joe glare at me.

'Can't you shut him up?' they ask.

Brain to mouth: If you know what's good for you, you'll keep quiet.

After seventy-six minutes Tranmere are denied an obvious penalty. There's no way I'm keeping quiet.

'See that?' I say. 'Hyypia was all over Allison. Blatant penalty.'

Gerard, Josh and John-Joe snarl menacingly.

Brain to mouth: Shut up, shut up, shut up.

Two minutes later Tranmere are denied a second penalty for hand ball.

'Oh, I don't believe this,' I protest. 'What's that ref's name, Gerard flipping Houllier?'

Brain to mouth: That's it, I'm off home. You're on your own.

Then, in the eightieth minute, McAllister goes down and is awarded a penalty. Robbie Fowler scores. Four–two to Liverpool and game over. Ten minutes later the ref blows the final whistle.

'Go on,' says Gerard, 'say something. Anything. Make our day.'

Say nothing, absolutely nothing.

'You only won because of the ref,' I say.

Next moment I'm buried under three Scousers all belting me with cushions.

'Had enough?' asks John-Joe.

'Tranmere should have...'

More battering.

'... had a...'

Bludgeoning into submission.

'... penalty.'

They finally let me up. Julie and her mum and dad are laughing themselves silly. I can't help but join in.

Sunday 11th March
9.00 p.m.

Julie and me at the bus stop. Drizzle. Kisses. The smell of coconut on her hair.

'You smell nice,' I say.

'It's my conditioner,' she says. 'Have you recovered from your ragging?'

'Just about,' I say.

'I think they're starting to like you,' says Julie.

'*That's* liking me!'

Julie nods.

'And I like you too, a lot.'

This is it. The time to say the three little words. I'm still trying to pluck up the courage when my bus comes. We kiss and I climb on board. I wave to Julie through drizzle-flecked windows and kick myself all the way home.

4

I walk to school through driving rain. I still won't wear my Nanook of the North coat so I'm making do with my fleece and a baseball cap. They don't give me much protection against the downpour, but at least I don't look like a nerd. Something else insulates me against the storm. United dispatched Sturm Graz 3–0 last night. We're through to the quarter-finals of the Champions League. I look down the hill towards Liverpool. It isn't much more than a puddle of grey under the rain, but suddenly the sun comes out from behind the clouds, a brilliant gleaming sphere riding the banks of purple. It turns the half-deserted streets into a giant mirror. The few pedestrians who are struggling up the hill are no more than silhouettes against the blinding sunlight. When a bus stops more silhouettes start to make their way across the road.

'Terry!'

One of them is Julie. I shield my eyes and smile to see her running towards me. She draws me under her umbrella and we kiss, faces illuminated by the eerie light. She warms me against the chill of the morning. Kelly is standing a couple of steps away. All I see is her shoes, but I know it's her. The shoes seem to snarl at me. Besides, I can hear the resentment working through her, like the hiss of air brakes. She's never far away from Julie, guardian of the Scouse flame. The three of us walk towards the school gates, Julie and me arm in arm, Kelly kind of semi-detached and hissing.

'Do you fancy coming round tonight?' I ask. 'I'm baby-sitting our Amy. Mum's going out again with the jogging club.'

'I thought that was Mondays and Fridays.'

'It is. Seems they've got a club meeting.'

Julie pulls a face.

'Meeting? About jogging? Sounds fishy to me.'

Funny, I've had the stench of haddock in my nostrils too. I'm guessing the attendance of this meeting will be a grand total of two: Mum and Richard.

'So do you fancy it?' I ask. 'We can watch Arsenal against Bayern Munich. You know, support the Germans.'

'How romantic!' sneers Kelly.

Julie winks at me. I love that. She's pulled me into a conspiracy of two.

'It's a date,' she says, 'so long as Mum and Dad don't mind. We can do some simultaneous equations before kick-off.'

At the thought of the approaching exams I feel the angel of death passing over me.

'Do we have to?'

'Terry Payne, I'll get you through GCSE Maths if it's the last thing I do.'

I see a tombstone. Julie Carter RIP. She died, broken on the rock of another's stupidity.

'Deal?'

'OK, it's a deal.'

Just then Kelly spots Gary and detaches herself. I watch her go then turn to Julie.

'She still doesn't like me, does she?'

'She'll come round,' says Julie.

'Sure about that?' I ask.

'Yes, sure as I'm sitting here on this unicycle.'

Wednesday 14th March
7.45 p.m.

'What an awful match,' I say.

'They're all awful,' says Amy.

She looks at Julie as if to say: *How can a girl like football?*

Arsenal have scraped through, so that's three English teams, three Spanish teams, one German and one Turkish team in the quarter-finals of the Champions League.

'We'll be joining you next year,' says Julie. 'Houllier's got us sorted.'

'Maybe.'

It's something I've always dreaded, Liverpool catching up with Man U. Dad's told me what it was like in the eighties, living in their shadow. We don't want to go back to that. But, with every week that passes, they seem to be catching us up.

'Fancy coming round again for the Liverpool–Porto game?' I say.

'Can't,' says Julie. 'It's the gymnastics club tomorrow night. It's less than a month before we go to Scotland.'

'Oh yes, I forgot.'

I feel the stab of a single icicle in my heart. Edinburgh, where Julie will be for three days. Fitz too.

'What do you do in the evenings?' I ask.

I hope she doesn't notice the green-eyed monster rearing its ugly head.

'The first night we just crash out. It's a heck of a coach ride.'

'And the second?'

'It's like the Ministrada. There's a disco for all the gymnasts.'

That's what I was afraid of. I remember Julie and Fitz dancing a slowie that terrible night last year when they got together. The icicle becomes a shard of glass slicing through my peace of mind.

'And you don't need to worry,' says Julie, 'I won't be dancing with any of those big Scottish hunks.'

Scottish hunks! Who said anything about Scottish hunks?

It was bad enough worrying about Fitz, now Julie's being courted by a mob of Bravehearts. I see all these hairy guys with blue faces. Gross!

'Anyway,' says Julie. 'I've got to go. I promised Mum I'd be home before half past eight.'

'I'll walk you to...'

I remember Amy.

'It's all right,' says Julie. 'You stay with Amy.'

I look at Amy, willing her to go to her room. She fails to take the hint.

'Amy,' I say, 'haven't you got anything to do?'

She stands, looking at me.

'No.'

'Homework or something?'

'No.'

'Anything?'

The penny drops.

'Oh,' she says, 'you want smoochies.'

Julie giggles at my obvious discomfort.

'I'll make myself scarce then,' says Amy, grinning mischievously at Julie.

'I hate girls,' I seethe as she runs upstairs giggling.

'Even this girl?' asks Julie, nibbling at my bottom lip.

'No,' I say, 'just little girls.'

'I was a little girl once,' says Julie.

I smile and run my hands over her ribcage and hips.

'That was a long time ago.'

Friday 16th March
12.10 p.m.

'Have you heard the draw?'

I press my mobile to my ear and smile. It's Dad. No: *Hi, Terry.* No: *How's your day been?* He just cuts to the chase. The draw for the Champions League quarter-finals.

'Not Real Madrid?'

'No, but not much better. It's Bayern Munich.'

A rerun of the final two years ago. Bayern will be up for that one. Hungry for revenge.

'Grudge match,' I say.

'Definitely. Oh yes, and Liverpool have drawn Barcelona in the UEFA Cup.'

I pass the news on to Julie who's standing next to me just outside the school gates. She purses her lips.

'Tough one.'

'That your girlfriend?' asks Dad.

'Yes, say hello, Julie.'

Julie shouts a breezy greeting.

'I never believed a son of mine would end up going out with a

Scouser,' says Dad.

I smile at Julie.

'Dad, I know what you mean.'

'How's your mum?'

'Fine.'

There's a silence at the other end. I know what Dad wants to say: *Any more on this Richard?*

'I'll see you tomorrow,' I say. 'We can listen to the United–Leicester game.'

'Yes, see you then.'

My face must betray my emotions because Julie asks:

'Is he going on about your mum and her boyfriend again?'

I nod.

'I think it's getting serious. I've been trying not to believe it, but you can tell, can't you?'

'Can you?'

'She comes in all flushed. She looks ... younger.'

'Sounds like love all right,' says Julie.

'So how do I tell Dad?'

Julie doesn't get to answer because Bobby and Emma arrive. I see Emma's face fall. For some reason she doesn't like Julie one bit.

'Fancy going into town for half an hour?' asks Bobby.

I glance at Julie. She shakes her head.

'I've got a couple of things to do in the library,' she says.

I look at Bobby and shrug my shoulders.

'Fair enough,' he says. 'See you later.'

The moment they're out of earshot I turn to Julie.

'What was that about?' I ask. 'You haven't got anything to do in the library.'

'No, it's Emma. She's got a real downer on me.'

'Any idea why?'

Julie shakes her head.

'I don't know what I've done wrong, but she doesn't want to know me at all.'

I look down the road. Bobby and Emma are just turning the corner. What *is* going on?

I'm in worry mode.

For starters, Barthez has done his hamstring. It was the one blemish on an otherwise satisfying afternoon at Old Trafford. The Reds dispatched Leicester 2–0 to go 17 points clear at the top of the Premiership. But now Barthez could be missing against both Liverpool and Bayern Munich.

Which brings me on to Worry Number Two. We visit Anfield the Saturday after next. I just couldn't stand it if they did the double on us.

And so to Worry Number Three. Dad is really down about Mum and this Richard bloke. That's right, he managed to prise it out of me at half-time.

'What's he like?' he asked.

'Dunno.'

'What does he do for a living?'

'Dunno.'

'How serious is Sharon about him?'

'Dunno.'

Actually, I've got a pretty good idea. Mum didn't get in until half past eleven last night. Her face was flushed. She was glowing like a lamp with a red shade. She's spending more and more time with him. I may be making a mint from the baby-sitting money, but I can't say I like it.

Then there's Worry Number Four. Bobby came round this morning. He's really cut up about Emma. He thinks she's still seeing this other guy. I can't believe this is the same Bobby. He didn't even give me the statistics for cheating by sixteen-year-old girls. Suddenly he's had a good mood-ectomy. He's really got it bad for Emma.

The more convinced he gets that she's messing him around, the more he wants to be with her. Confused? Me too.

Finally, there's Worry Number Five. The big one. That, of course, is Julie. You're probably wondering what I've got to worry about. But does she still feel something for Fitz? I mean, they did go out for seven months. That's got to mean something. How can you be sure what's going on in somebody else's mind? How do you know they feel the same about you as you do about them? I can't get it out of my mind. Three weeks tonight, Julie will be up in Edinburgh, and you can be sure Fitz won't be far away. And it isn't just Fitz. What about all those blue-faced Bravehearts queuing up for a dance? I remember that gymnastics club from Glasgow Julie was raving about at the Ministrada. They'll be there, all hunky and hormonal.

'A penny for them,' says Dad.

'I beg your pardon?'

'I was wondering what you were thinking. You were miles away.'

'Oh nothing.'

'Doing anything tonight?'

'I'm going to the cinema with Julie.'

'I hear she's a good-looking girl,' says Dad, with a wink. 'You'd better keep your eye on her.'

My head snaps round.

'What do you mean?'

I said that a bit too quickly, and a bit too loud.

'Whoa,' says Dad. 'Only joking, son.'

I look away quickly.

'Is everything all right?'

I think so. I *hope* so.

5

I forgot Worry Number Six, Fitz getting match fit again. Well, he's over the broken ankle and I reckon he'll be gunning for me tonight in training. I loosen my tie and unbutton my school shirt. I notice Fitz watching me. He's got this slight curl of a smile on his thin lips like he's got something in store for me. Gary's got his eye on me too and he is also smiling. I've got used to getting changed on my own and being left out of the dressing room banter. It's been my punishment for injuring Fitz at Christmas. But until tonight there has been a bit of a thaw. Some of the guys have actually been talking to me. Not tonight. I'm back on the outside looking in. The boy who crocked John Fitzpatrick. Mr Unpopular. Paul Scully goes over to Fitz.

'Make sure you've got your shinpads on properly,' he says.

It's meant to be overheard. I finish getting changed. The only thing that is going to get me through the next hour is the thought of Julie back home baby-sitting Amy. She'll be there waiting for me when I get in. There's nothing Fitz can do that can take the shine off that, the promise of Julie's brown eyes.

'Come on, lads,' shouts Six Guns. 'Look lively.'

Nobody's in any hurry to get out on the field. Sleet has been flickering through the air all day and now that it's late afternoon it's turning to snow.

'Look lively!' snorts Jamie Sneddon. 'He should have called it off.'

'I heard that,' shouts Six Guns from outside. 'You lads are too rotten mollycoddled. Get out there and warm up.'

We go through the motions. Jogging, various exercises, tuck jumps. But what everybody's looking forward to is the five-a-side. Everybody except me. The sympathy is all for Fitz, back from injury. I'll be lucky if I get a single pass.

Wednesday 21st March
5.00 p.m.

I got more than a pass. Fitz ran his studs down the back of my calf, really sneaky, then five minutes later he caught me on the ankle. I think Jamie saw him but he probably thinks I had it coming. I sit rubbing my calf, then ease my sock over my gashed ankle. Finally, I get dressed. Fitz is outside. The others are halfway across the field.

'What do you want?' I ask.

'I'm letting you know,' says Fitz. 'That's just for starters. I'm going to get my own back for what you did.'

'What I did! You know it was an accident. You were trying to do me.'

Fitz sneers.

'What if I was? It's my word against yours. I still ended up missing weeks of the season. I'm going to get you. You can count on it.'

He is setting off towards the school when anger flares inside me.

'I know what's eating you,' I call after him. 'Julie's with me, and you're jealous.'

Fitz spins round. I know I've struck a chord.

'Think what you want, slimeball,' he says. 'But believe me, that isn't over either.'

He hoists his bag over his shoulder.

'Not by a long chalk.'

Wednesday 21st March
5.15 p.m.

I'm at the Fusilier before I notice how far I've walked. I haven't been aware of my surroundings at all, only Fitz's words:

That isn't over either.

Suddenly all I can think about is Edinburgh.

I bet he's bluffing. He's got to be. It's all talk. Julie wouldn't do that to me. But they've got history. I remember something Mum said once: *You never get over your first love*. And that was Fitz. Julie's first love was John stinking, dog's breath, dirtbag, weasel eyes Fitzpatrick.

And whose fault is that? Mine. All the time she was waiting for me to ask her out I just stood there like a wet Wednesday with my foot in my mouth. If she does go back to him I've only got myself to blame.

But she can't go back to him! She can't. She mustn't. For a few moments I imagine myself begging her not to go to Edinburgh. But what good would that do? It would just make me look like even more of a loser than I already am. Jealousy – the biggest turn-off. No, I can't do it. I'd be telling her I don't trust her. She'd be hurt. And I do trust her. I love the bones of the girl. And yet ... that little voice won't go away.

It isn't over.

Wednesday 21st March
5.25 p.m.

'Are you all right?' asks Julie.

I'm not putting my full weight on my right ankle. That tackle by Fitz didn't just break the skin. I think it's swelling.

'Yes, just a little something from Fitz.'

'Oh, you two haven't been at it again, have you?'

'Us two! What do you mean, us two? I didn't do anything.'

Julie tries to laugh it off.

'It's not funny,' I say. 'Julie, trust me over this. I didn't break Fitz's ankle on purpose. He went for me. Now he's doing it again. Well, do you believe me or not?'

'Terry, it isn't a big deal.'

I shake my head furiously.

'It is to me. Fitz started it. You've got to believe me.'

I can see by the look on Julie's face that she wants me to drop it. But I can't. I hate myself for doing it, but I carry it on, insisting that she believes me. Then I really drop a brick.

'Don't tell me you're taking sides with Fitz,' I say.

'Don't be stupid,' says Julie.

She's getting impatient. But do I take the hint? Of course not. I just keep on at her, like a dog with a bone, until I really shoot myself in the foot.

'You've still got a soft spot for him, haven't you?'

Julie stares at me. Her eyes have gone hard.

'Is that what this is all about? You think there's still something between me and Fitz?'

Don't answer, says my better self.

'You went out with him for long enough.'

D'oh!

'I've told you what happened,' says Julie. 'I never really fell for him.'

Let it drop, says my better self.

'Yes? Is that why it took you six months to dump him?'

D'oh!

'Terry, if you're going to be like this I'm off home.'

Now let it drop, you dufus. But I don't. No, I open my fat mouth and say the stupidest thing I can imagine.

'I bet he can't wait for Edinburgh.'

D'oh, d'oh and double d'oh! The moment the words are out of my mouth, I want to stuff them back in. Julie's looking at me, really hurt. Tears start to well up in her brown eyes and she turns suddenly, grabs her coat and runs for the door.

'Julie,' I cry. 'Don't go. I didn't mean it.'

'So why say it?' she sobs.

With that, she's gone.

Wednesday 21st March
5.35 p.m.

I'm still standing in the hallway, my body slack with shock, my arms limp by my sides, when Mum comes in.

'Was that Julie I saw running down the street?' she asks.

I nod. I feel numb all over. It's our first row.

'Is something wrong?'

I explain what's just happened.

'Oh, Terry, you silly lad. Go after her. She might still be at the bus stop.'

I don't need telling twice. I fly out of the house and into the blowy darkness. I'm only wearing a T-shirt, jogging pants and trainers. The wind cuts through me but I don't care. I've got to get to Julie before the bus does. I'm sprinting for all I'm worth, the sleet stinging my face. Why couldn't I pay attention to my inner voice? There he was, the real me, telling me to behave myself. But would I listen? No. Instead, I have to take notice of the green-eyed monster. What if I've ruined everything? I'm running round the bend in the road within striking distance of the stop when the bus overtakes me.

Please let there be a lot of other passengers. Anything to hold the bus up.

But Julie's the only one at the stop.

'Julie!' I cry.

She doesn't hear me. Or maybe she does. Either way she gets on the bus without turning round.

'Wait.'

The doors start to close. Oh no you don't! I fling myself at the doors and sprawl full length on the floor.

'What the...?'

The driver looks shocked. I shove my hand in my pocket and drop some loose change in his hand. Without waiting for the ticket I walk towards Julie. I'm aware that my clothes are steaming.

'But where are you going?' asks the driver.

'I don't know yet,' I say as I stand panting by Julie's seat.

Look at me. Please look at me.

'I'll have to issue you with a ticket,' says the driver.

Oh, shut up about your stupid ticket. My life's on the line here.

'Sure, whatever.'

I slide into the seat next to Julie. She's looking straight ahead.

'I'm really sorry.'

Still looking ahead.

'I'm an idiot.'

'You got that right.'

Oh joy! She's talking to me.

'Hit me,' I say, offering my chin. 'Go on, hit me.'

Julie turns towards me.

'You don't really think I'd...? Not with Fitz.'

'Of course not. I trust you. You know I do.'

That's not good enough, says the sensible voice. Talk to her. Tell her how you feel.

So that's what I try to do. Haltingly. Stumblingly.

'It's just... You get feelings. You don't want to, but they just come.'

We talk all the way to her stop. I answer all her questions. I talk till I'm red in the face. That's when I remember.

'Mum!'

'Pardon?'

'She thought I was only going down to the bus stop. She'll wonder where on earth I've got to.'

Wednesday 21st March
6.15 p.m.

'You're where?'

Mum's cry of disbelief almost takes the top of my head off.

'Julie's.'

For the second time in an hour I'm trying to explain myself, this time on the phone to Mum.

'But you haven't even got a coat. Aren't you freezing?'

I admit that I am. Right now, I'd even wear the Nanook of the North coat.

'Do you want me to pick you up?' she asks. 'Amy won't mind.'

I hear Amy's voice in the background: *Says who?*

'Julie's brother says he'll lend me a coat,' I say. 'I'll be back by half past seven.'

'See that you are,' says Mum.

I put the phone down and see Gerard coming towards me with a jacket. It's a couple of sizes too small, but that isn't the most important thing. It's the logo. Liverpool FC.

'I'm not wearing that!' I say.

'Why not?' he asks all innocent.

'Gerard,' says Julie. 'Get him something he can wear.'

Gerard climbs the stairs chuckling all the way. Josh and John-Joe join in.

'They're only winding you up,' says Julie. 'He'll find something.'

I pull her close.

'Am I forgiven?'

'Of course you are.'

I go to kiss her. She draws away.

'But, Terry...'

'Yes?'

'Don't ever do that again. Either you trust me, or we're finished.'

I nod guiltily.

'I'll be a good boy.'

I put on my best chastened toddler look. Julie giggles.

'OK. Now, let's have that kiss.'

Out of the corner of my eye, I can see Huey, Duey and Louie pulling faces. I don't care. I've got out of jail.

Just.

6

I never thought it would come to this, me and half a dozen Scousers watching England play. Yes, I'm round at Julie's. Dad wanted me to watch the Finland game round his, but let's face it, in two weeks Julie is off to Edinburgh so I'm determined to be as high-profile as I can. When she's surrounded by Fitz and all those blue-faced Bravehearts, I want her to remember her loving boyfriend back home. So hard luck, Dad. When it comes down to a choice between the High King of Victim Rock and the most beautiful girl in the world, you're always going to take second place. Dad took it OK, no big guilt trip or anything, but there was no disguising the disappointment in his voice. He's all out of luck. Since he ditched Mule and decided he was still in love with Mum, his life has taken a real nosedive. He just can't believe they're divorced. Just about the biggest thing that's ever happened to him and it kind of crept up while he wasn't looking. As for Mum getting into a size 12 and finding herself a hunky running-machine of a boyfriend, he's devastated. Not because she's got a size 12 figure, of course, but because she's showing off to somebody else. Suddenly he's the major loser.

'You OK?' asks Julie, budging up on the couch until her thigh's touching mine.

'I am now,' I tell her, putting poor old Dad to the back of my mind.

Poor old Bobby too. He wanted to watch the match round at Dad's. Anything to escape the rest of his life. Emma's still acting distant and Slughead's cocker spaniel's taken to peeing by the side of his wardrobe. Bobby says it's a vendetta. Of course, it could just be a weak bladder. You know what I told Bobby? *If your room smells like a kennel don't be surprised when the dog makes itself at home there.*

He might be my best mate, but if Dad isn't going to drag me away from Julie, Bobby certainly isn't.

'I don't think Beckham's the man to captain England,' says Gerard pointedly, as Beckham leads the side out at Anfield.

'No charisma,' says Josh, glancing in my direction.

'Doesn't talk enough,' says John-Joe, making a big, goofy face at me. '*Can't* talk enough.'

'Exactly,' says Gerard, 'IQ of a lobotomised sprout.'

I grit my teeth. Maybe I should have gone round to Dad's after all.

'I wonder which Manc's going to ruin our chances this time,' says Gerard.

It's as if Fitz is right here in the room, taunting me. Now, that's an uncomfortable thought, a bad omen for Edinburgh. Josh and John-Joe join in the Manc-baiting. They dredge up all the old stuff, how Beckham got sent off against Argentina and got us knocked out of the World Cup, how Phil Neville gave away that penalty and got us eliminated from Euro 2000. To hear them talk you'd think there was a Manc conspiracy against the national team! They even have a go at me about Gary Neville, Paul Scholes and Andy Cole being the only players who don't sing the national anthem. Like I give a damn! A few minutes into the game, Beckham is on the way to shutting them up.

'Not a captain, eh?' I say. 'So explain today's performance. He's playing brilliantly.'

But the anti-Manc hysteria reaches fever pitch in the twenty-seventh minute when Gary Neville deflects a Finnish header into his own net. 1–0 to Finland.

'Told you,' crows Gerard. 'Now both the Neville brothers have done it. No wonder they don't sing the national anthem. They're too busy playing for the other side!'

He makes up this stupid song called Finland, my Finland. Funny guy!

Fortunately, England end the first half on fire. Beckham and Neville combine to set up Michael Owen's equaliser.

'There,' I say. 'Two United players made the goal.'

'Yes,' says Julie. 'But it took one of ours to score it.'

I grimace. She thinks Michael Owen's cute. Five minutes into the second half the misery of Gary Neville's own goal is well and truly buried. David Beckham turns captain fantastic and drills home a superb right-foot drive. When the final whistle goes and England have won 2–1, I have the audacity to shout:

'Beckham, king of the Kop!'

While the others boo and hiss, I think of next Saturday's Liverpool–United match on the very same Anfield turf where England have just revived their slim chances of World Cup qualification. That's one game I'm definitely watching round at Dad's.

Wednesday 28th March
5.50 p.m.

Boys' night in at Dad's flat. England v Albania.

In attendance:

Dad, pining for Mum.

Bobby, pining for Emma.

Yours truly, not pining at all. But for the nagging doubt about Edinburgh I'd be feeling really smug right now. Compared to this pair of losers I'm quite the ladies' man.

'It isn't over, you know,' says Bobby, the moment Dad goes out to check on the chilli.

It's about the only thing he can cook. Chilli con carne and baked potato. He's on another of his *Men's Health* diets. No change in the waistline, but he produces lots of gas.

'What isn't over?' I ask, as if I didn't know. Emma's cheating heart is the only thing Bobby talks about. He doesn't even come out with useless facts any more. He's too *depressed*. I feel like telling him that it's a bit rich with his track record, but he is my mate.

'Emma and this guy. She's been seeing him again.'

'How do you know?'

'I called for her last night but she was out. When I asked where she was her mum got all flustered.'

'Wouldn't really stand up in court, would it?' I ask.

'She's seeing him, all right. You just know when somebody's messing you around. You get vibes.'

This vibe-getting might come in useful after Edinburgh. I mean, I know Julie wouldn't, but I need to know, just in case she did...

which she wouldn't...

...would she?

I want to ask Bobby about it but Dad comes in with our tea. It'll have to wait.

Wednesday 28th March
10.00 p.m.

I arrive home dead on time. Mum lets me stay out until ten o'clock on a week day, half past ten or sometimes even eleven at the weekend.

The moment I walk through the door I can feel that something is different. I wonder if this is what Bobby means by vibes.

'That you, Terry?'

I do my usual.

'No, it's the Pope.'

'How was the match?'

'England won 3–1. It was OK, that's about all.'

Just then Mum giggles, and not at my match report. She sounds all high-pitched and girly. So what's going on? I reach the living-room door and there's this man.

He's a six-footer; short, blond hair; smart casual clothes. They're sitting on the couch side by side. Mum looks flustered and her hair's dishevelled. Oh gross, she's been snogging Marathon Man right here in our living-room!

'Terry,' she says, the aftershock of the giggle still rippling through her. 'This is Richard.'

Richard stands up and holds out his hand for me to shake. I give him the cold fish treatment. He's shaking hands with a mackerel.

'Nice to meet you, Terry.'

I say nothing.

'Typical teenager,' says Mum, desperate to end the uncomfortable silence. 'They just stop talking. Why is that?'

Richard doesn't seem to know because he just stands there with this wrinkled grin on his face. 'It's getting late,' he says.

Mum accompanies him to the door. By the time she's finished

saying goodnight, I'm already in my room listening to music through my headphones. Mum takes the hint and leaves me to it.

Friday 30th March
11.00 p.m.

I walk through the door high on the smell of Julie's hair, the dab of perfume on her throat. We hung around the bowling alley most of the evening. Sure, it meant having to be polite to sour-faced Kelly and to Fitz and his mates, but my reward for putting up with the Scouse mafia was a kiss and a cuddle at the bus stop. With Julie that is, not the Scouse mafia. Actually, Fitz walked past while we were kissing. I'd give my right arm for a photograph of the look on his face.

'Ignore him,' Julie told me. 'He's only jealous.'

I smiled. All sorts of things were going on behind the scenes tonight. Fitz and I nearly came to blows at one point when he wouldn't stop ribbing me over United. Then Paul and Pepsey had this big row and Pepsey stormed off home. There at the bus stop I didn't care. I was with Julie and that's what counted. When we're together like we were tonight, when I smell her hair and taste her lips, I can't believe that anything will ever come between us. I don't just think, *I know*, that we're for keeps. Then, the moment I'm on my own again, shadows start to form in the backwoods of my mind. Shadows of Frisky Fitzy. Shadows of blue-faced Bravehearts. I know I'm probably being paranoid, but nothing I do can hold back the shadows. Then I'm scared, really scared, that Julie's out of my league. I think and I think, and the more I think the more I convince myself that I'm just a skinny nerd that no girl in her right mind would be seen dead with. Once I'm in this mood there's always something there to remind me of the bad times. The times when Julie and Fitz were together.

Tonight the trigger for the shadows is tomorrow's game at Anfield. The last time we played Liverpool we lost 1–0 and Sky Sports showed Fitz with his arms round Julie, smirking into the camera. It was the worst day of my life. It was like he'd stuck his hands into my heart and flipped it inside out. What's to stop it happening again, I wonder? They'll be part of the same gang going to the match. What if it brings back old memories? The next two weekends are vital. The two biggest tests for our relationship so far: Anfield then Edinburgh. They could set the seal on a dream come true or they could bring everything crashing down.

Saturday 31st March
12 noon

High noon. Liverpool v United at Anfield. Liverpool haven't done the double over us since 1979, but they look up for it today. They do a team huddle under the heavy, perpendicular rain. I feel nervous. We've only played well once since Christmas. It's as if running away with the Premiership title has taken the edge off our game. It isn't just the match, either. I'm still thinking about Julie and Fitz. That game at Old Trafford. The 1–0 defeat. The sight of Fitz hugging Julie right there on the TV screen. It was almost more than I could bear. And they're together again today. There's a gang of them at the match: Gary and Kelly, Paul and Pepsey, Julie and Fitz. While Dad makes the sandwiches and Bobby drones on about Emma and how she's hurting him so badly I concentrate on the crowd, as if I'm going to be able to pick them out from a crowd of nearly fifty thousand people.

Both sides come close in the first five minutes, Robbie Fowler for Liverpool, Dwight Yorke for United. In the next five minutes honours are still pretty even, a chance for Liverpool through Sami Hyypia, one for United through Wes Brown.

'Come on, lads,' says Dad. 'I don't want to be eating humble pie at work this time as well.'

That's when it all goes wrong. After sixteen minutes Barthez makes a poor clearance and Gerrard hits a wonder strike from thirty yards.

One nil to Liverpool.

Dad slumps in his armchair. I crane forward to try to get a glimpse of Julie in the heaving crowd. If Fitz dares ... No, I tell myself, don't let yourself down. I won't be jealous. I won't be conquered by the green-eyed monster. It's over between them. She's with me now. There's nothing to be jealous of.

After the first goal Liverpool have us on the rack.

'They've got you on the rack,' says Bobby, as if reading my mind.

Dad tells him to shut up. I lob a Coke can at him. He shuts up.

Then, forty minutes in, Fowler takes a Gerrard cross superbly and scores. Two–nil to Liverpool.

'Game over,' says Bobby.

Dad tells him to shut up. I lob the Coke can at him again. This time he doesn't shut up.

After sixty-six minutes something finally goes our way. The best move of the match is finished off by Dwight Yorke. Dad and I rise from our seats.

'Yes, 2–1. Here comes the fightback.'

That's when Bobby tells us the linesman has given offside. I throw the Coke can at him for the third time.

'What's that for?' Bobby complains. 'It wasn't me. It was the linesman.'

'I couldn't reach the linesman,' I explain.

Half an hour later it's gloom and doom here in Dad's living-room. Liverpool have become only the third team to do the double over us since the Premiership began.

'You'll have to play better than that against Bayern Munich,' says Bobby.

Dad and I scowl at him, but we both know he's right. We're getting a bad feeling about the game.

Saturday 31st March
11.15 p.m.

Special dispensation. Mum's letting me stay out till midnight. Julie knows this club called *Scene One*. It holds under-eighteen nights once a month. There's no booze allowed on the premises for these events. The management make a big deal about that to reassure parents. All it really does is make sure most kids stay well away. Still, I get to be with Julie, so who cares? Julie's dad is picking us up at 11.45 p.m. Mind you, I would feel better about being here if Mum wasn't having Richard round. Marathon Man's starting to get his feet under the table. The idea of that creep trying it on with Mum makes my blood boil.

The scoreline at Anfield has also taken a bit of a shine off tonight. I mean, it's great dancing with Julie, but I'm getting loads of grief off Kelly, Gary, Paul and Fitz over the result. Julie, Pepsey and Kelly clatter away to the loo leaving us guys hanging round like spare parts.

'What was the score?' slurs Fitz.

'Have you been drinking?' I ask.

Fitz bursts out laughing.

'What do you think? Everybody's at it.'

Everybody except me, it seems.

'We've got a stash of alco-pops hidden in the corner,' Fitz boasts.

'You'll get yourselves thrown out,' I say.

'So what was the score?' asks Fitz, ignoring me.

He's nothing if not repetitive.

'Quiet tonight, aren't you?' asks Fitz.

'Leave it, eh?' I say. 'You're getting boring.'

That just sets Fitz and his mates off again.

'Two nil, two nil, two nil, two nil...'

'OK,' I say, trying to stay cool. 'I get the message.'

'Two nil, TWO NIL!'

'Look,' I say, 'knock it off, Fitz.'

He pulls me to one side.

'I'll knock it off,' he snarls. 'When you give me my woman back.'

'*Your* woman?' I say. 'Julie made her own mind up, Fitz. You're pathetic.'

I turn away. The mocking laughter goes between my shoulder blades like a knife. Then my ear starts to burn. Fitz has hit me. I snap round and land him one on the side of the face. Worse the wear for drink, he staggers back and crashes on to the dance floor. I look up. With immaculate timing, Julie has just come out of the toilets.

Oh, wonderful!

There's a bit of an argument with the bouncers.

Have we been drinking? Cue innocent faces all round.

Perish the thought!

It's touch and go, but Julie and Kelly finally persuade them not to chuck us out.

Saturday 31st March
11.50 p.m.

We're waiting outside for Julie's dad. I phone Mum. She'll go ape if I'm late. Plus, there's another good reason for making the call. Julie's not too happy with me for hitting Fitz. I'm giving her time to calm down. It doesn't work. The moment I finish the call, she's down my ear.

'I thought you had more sense,' she says. 'Fighting in the club.'

'He hit me first!' I protest.

'That's what you always say.'

That's out of order. Fancy bringing up the evening I broke Fitz's ankle.

'Listen, Julie,' I say, taking her hands. 'It was true then and it's true now. It's Fitz, he always starts it.'

Before she can answer, Julie's dad arrives and we get in. Pointedly, Julie climbs in the front and I'm left to twiddle my thumbs in the back. We sit quietly all the way home. I hardly get a goodnight, never mind a kiss.

God, I feel miserable.

Sunday 1st April
11.30 a.m.

I phone her at home. She's gone out with Kelly.

Sunday 1st April
11.45 a.m.

I phone her on her mobile. It's switched off.

Sunday 1st April
1.30 p.m.

I phone her at home. There's no one in.

Sunday 1st April
6.00 p.m.

I've been phoning all afternoon. It just rings out. Not this time. Somebody's picking up. At last! It's Gerard.

'Julie, it's the Mad Manc.' Then the inevitable: 'Hey, what was the score?'

Julie takes the phone.

'Yuh?'

Her voice is cold. It doesn't sound like her at all.

'Are you angry with me?'

'Nah.'

'Sure?'

'Nah.'

'No, you're not angry, or no, you're not sure?'

No answer.

'Can I see you tonight?'

'I'm revising.'

'Am I in the dog-house?' I ask.

Julie sighs: 'I told you, I'm revising.'

'I'll see you tomorrow in school, then.'

'Yes,' she says. 'Tomorrow.'

I'm in the dog-house, all right. Woof sodding woof.

Monday 2nd April
8.30 p.m.

It wasn't easy, but I persuaded her to come round to mine. Mum's out jogging with Tricky Dicky the Marathon Man, so we're baby-sitting Amy. Amy's on the phone to Katie, so I drag Julie into the living-room.

'Look,' I say, 'I shouldn't have hit Fitz but he did hit me first.'

Julie rolls her eyes.

'You're as bad as each other.'

'No,' I say. 'No, we're not. If you only knew what he was like, what he's really like.'

'Terry, I should know. I went out with him for six months.'

'Yes, but...'

'And he never showed an ounce of aggression.'

'Yes, but...'

'And he's the one who ended up in plaster, not you.'

'Yes, but...'

'Yes, but *what*?' she asks.

That stumps me. Finally I manage a feeble:

'Yes, but I really like you.'

Oh, terrific! Could I be more lame? I could have at least managed the three little words.

Julie smiles. Joy! She's smiled. I'm forgiven! Pat me on the head. Tickle my tummy. I'll sit up. I'll beg. Just don't put me back in the dog-house.

'Am I forgiven?'

She hugs me.

'Of course you are, but I wish you weren't so paranoid over Fitz. It's you I'm with. Forget him.'

'Forget who?' I ask, palms outstretched.

Julie laughs.

'Seriously,' she says. 'Don't put me under pressure, Terry. There's nothing between me and Fitz any more.'

I nod.

'I know.'

'So no more third degrees?' she asks.

'No.'

'And no more fighting?'

'No.'

'And you're not going to worry about him any more?'

I say no.

I think...

...maybe.

Tuesday 3rd April
9.10 a.m.

The Manc-baiting is starting to get me down.

I was edgy enough already, what with United playing Bayern tomorrow and Julie going away on Friday. But the defeat at Anfield has ripped my insides out. I've just walked to school in a thunderstorm. I'm soaked to the skin. I could really have done with my Nanook of the North coat. As a result of the downpour I arrive completely sodden and sit through registration with my teeth gritted. I'm steaming. Steaming with the central heating drying my clothes. Steaming with the humiliation of defeat. Then Six Guns drives the final nail in the coffin. He hands out a letter. It's the final deadline for the return of coursework. Stapled to it is a timetable for the GCSE exams. Until now I've been living in a fantasy world. If I don't acknowledge the exams, they can't happen. But they are happening, and too soon for comfort.

'Everything OK?' asks Julie when we meet in the corridor.

I give a lopsided smile.

'Is it the exams?' she asks.

'Yes.' (Among other things.)

'You can still get a C in Maths, you know.'

Sure, and Michael Owen will sign for Man U.

'Anything else bothering you?'

'No,' I say, lying through my teeth, 'just the exams.'

'Here,' she says, pulling me to one side.

She gives a quick glance left and right and plants a smacker on my lips.

'Better?'

The warmth of her floods through me.

'Mm,' I murmur.

'Demons all gone?'

'Definitely,' I say, as convincingly as I can.

But the demons never go far. They just hover over the horizon planning their next attack. Gone, you might say, but not forgotten.

Tuesday 3rd April
9.35 p.m.

United, returning the love. Ha!

Not any more. United 0, Bayern Munich 1. Me and Dad gutted. Bobby respectfully silent. I stare into space. I can't believe it.

Tuesday 3rd April
10.20 p.m.

I watch the ten o'clock news, just to make sure it's happened. It has. I watch Sergio's eighty-sixth minute winner go in, first at full speed and then in slow motion. I stare at the screen, numb with disbelief.

Wednesday 4th April
8.45 a.m.

I stand in the pouring rain outside the newsagents. I've been reading the back page headlines. Maybe if I pinch myself I'll find out it's all a dream. It isn't. It's a nightmare. I read the same headline over and over again:

United 0, Bayern 1. It's Becks to the wall.

I still can't believe it. We've got to win in Munich's Olympic stadium by more than two goals. It isn't impossible, but it isn't far off.

Julie comes up behind me and puts her arms round my waist. She rubs her chin against my back. As sympathetically as any Scouser could.

'Upset, aren't you?'

My reply is a kind of moan rising from my stomach. Eventually I manage:

'I can't believe it.'

Wednesday 4th April
5.30 p.m.

But it's true. We're on our way out of Europe. Bayern just don't give a lead away at home, not in twenty years of football. United's European dream is disintegrating before my eyes. I was hardly involved in the

323

school match tonight, a 2–2 draw with St Leo's. I got subbed at half-time. Now I'm sitting in the changing room amongst the sweat haze and the steam and the piles of muddy kit. Fitz and co are taking the Michael something chronic.

Losing it? they ask.

Lost the plot? they ask.

United on the wane? they ask.

And all I can do is sit and take it. Half the reason for existing, my being a Red, seems to be disintegrating right in front of my eyes. I couldn't stand it if the same happened to Julie. Edinburgh is in two days. I'm dreading it.

7

Friday 6th April
4.00 p.m.

I watch the coach pull away. Julie waves goodbye. I trudge through
the rain. What a week. United lose in Europe. Leeds and Arsenal both
win while Liverpool draw against Barcelona at the Nou Camp. *The
rest show United how it's done*, one of the papers said. Are we losing
it? Is it the end of our era of domination? It's hard to take. Through
everything that's happened: Julie going out with Fitz, my parents'
divorce, struggling at school, I've had one thing going for me. I was
part of the Red Tribe, a United fan, a supporter of the greatest club in
the world. It set me apart. I was somebody. I can't go back to the way
it was when I was little, living in the shadow of Liverpool. Bobby's
waiting for me on the corner. Funny how things turn out. It used to be
me who hung round playing gooseberry. Now he's the saddo.

'She's gone then,' he says.

'Yes.'

'Don't look so miserable,' he tells me. 'She's back Sunday, isn't she?'
I nod.

'But?' asks Bobby.

'Well, I don't like the idea of Fitz being up there with her.'

Bobby goes into this big lecture. Love's about trust, he says.
Jealousy will drive her away, he says. She's crazy about you, he says.
Somehow I can't take advice from him right now. It isn't long since he
was stringing two girls along and hankering after another.

'So how's your love life?' I ask.

'Ouch,' says Bobby. 'Low blow.'

'Sorry,' I say.

Just to make me feel even worse he says:

'Look, I know I'm not in any position to give advice but you've got something special with Julie. I'm jealous. Honest. So are all the other guys. Don't do anything to mess it up, Terry. Take it from somebody who knows.'

All of a sudden, I'm seeing Bobby in a different light. I'm reminded of that old movie Mum watches over and over again on cable. Yes, we're in Casablanca after the girl's flight has taken off. I'm Rick and Bobby's the short French guy.

'Bobby,' I say. 'This could be the start of a beautiful friendship.'

He thumps me on the arm and we kick and trip each other all the way up the road.

Saturday 7th April
9.00 p.m.

'Terry,' Mum calls. 'Julie's on the phone.'

I fly downstairs and pant 'hello' into the mouthpiece. She's talking through a tunnel of sound.

'Where are you?' I ask.

'Edinburgh.'

'Yes, I know that. Where in Edinburgh?'

'The disco.'

She sounds like she's having fun. There's a lot of noise in the background. Male noise.

'Who's that?'

'Oh, just Ian and Billy.'

Ian and Billy? Who the hell are Ian and Billy?

'Say hello, boys.'

Ian and Billy shout down the phone. They're speaking Scottish. Either that, or they've got a mouthful of gravel. Come on, Julie, the last thing I want to do is talk to a couple of blue-faced Bravehearts.

'Will you do me a favour?' Julie asks.

'What's that?'

'I'll be on the way home on the coach when the FA Cup semi-final is on. Phone me on my mobile when the goals go in.'

'OK.'

'Got to go now,' says Julie.

Go! But you haven't said anything.

'Julie...'

Too late, the line's gone dead. I stand staring at the receiver. I've been waiting all day for a call and what do I end up doing? I talk to a couple of mad Scotsmen and promise to tell her the Liverpool score. Not the world's most romantic phone call.

Sunday 8th April
3.30 p.m.

Bobby and I exchange miseries all the way to Dad's.

For him, it's Emma and her cheating heart. Plus a dog that uses his room as a toilet. Lady's latest crime – eating his mobile charger.

It's the phone I'm moping about too, Julie's phone call from hell. (Well, Scotland.)

Either way, neither of us feels much like smiling. When we arrive at Dad's, R Kelly is belting out: *Turn back the hands of time*.

'Should I turn it down, lads?' he asks.

'No.' I say, 'Up.'

Sunday 8th April
5.00 p.m.

Things are looking up. Wycombe are holding Liverpool. Could a giant-killing be in the offing?

I hope so.

Sunday 8th April
5.30 p.m.

My mobile goes. Julie.

'I thought you were going to phone me when the goals go in,' she says.

'I am. It's still 0–0.'

327

'But they're halfway through the second half.'
'Sorry, but it's true. And Wycombe should have had a penalty.'
'Call me when something happens.'
'You can count on me.'

Sunday 8th April
5.33 p.m.

Something's happened. I phone Julie.
    'Yes.'
    '1–0 to Liverpool. Heskey.'
    Julie relays the news. The coach erupts. A clenched fist of noise. I hear Fitz's voice above the others. Guess what he's yelling?
    'What's the score, Manchester?'

Sunday 8th April
5.38 p.m.

More news.
    'Julie, it's 2–0 to Liverpool. Fowler.'
    Again she relays the news. Again the coach erupts. Yes, and again Fitz puts in his two-pennyworth.

Sunday 8th April
5.43 p.m.

More news.
    'Julie, it's 2–1. Wycombe have got one back.'
    Stony silence on the coach. A wall of sound in Dad's living-room.

Full-time. Liverpool have won.

'This time,' Bobby whispers as I punch in her number. 'Say the three little words. It's easy.'

'But you've always told me the opposite,' I remind him.

'That was then,' says Bobby, 'this is now. Say them, the three little words.'

'Easy for you,' I shoot back. 'You've never meant it.'

'Low blow number two,' says Bobby. 'I meant it with Emma.'

I'm through to Julie.

'It's all over. Liverpool v Arsenal in the FA Cup Final.'

The coach erupts. Bobby mouths the three little words and digs me in the ribs.

'Thanks, Terry,' says Julie. 'I can't wait to see you.'

Bobby opens his eyes so wide they could pop out.

THREE LITTLE WORDS, YOU MORON.

But the three words I come up with are these: 'Yes, me too.'

D'oh!

Bobby's in the loo so I have a go at sorting things with Dad.

'You OK?'

'Yes, can't grumble.'

'You know what I mean.'

'You mean, have I got over shooting myself in the head?'

'Something like that.'

Dad gives a wry smile.

'Some things you don't get over, Terry. Your mum's the best thing that's ever happened to me, and I've given her up on a whim. You know what I am? A pillock is what I am!'

Which is about as close as Dad will ever get to opening his heart. By the time Bobby is off the loo and we're down the stairs and in the street, we can hear Harry Nilsson blasting out of the upstairs window: *Can't live if living is without you.*

'Sounds like he's picking up,' says Bobby. I kick him on the ankle.

Sunday 8th April
10.30 p.m.

Bobby's gone and Amy's in bed so I have a go at sorting things with Mum.

'You're serious about this Richard guy, aren't you?'

'He's a lovely man.'

'And Dad?'

'He's a lovely man who dumped me. Or did you forget that little detail?'

'So there's no way back?'

'No, Terry, it's final. I thought my marriage was for keeps. I know my divorce is.'

Monday 9th April
4.30 p.m.

We're at the swimming pool. A new kind of baby-sitting duty. We picked up Amy and Katie and came straight here after school. Amy and Katie are messing about at the shallow end, and we're at the deep end. So it's just Julie and me. No horrible friend trying to shoot me down in flames. No Scouse mafia taking the Michael. Just the two of us. Julie dives in. She looks sleek and gorgeous in a black swimming costume. She's the only girl who makes my throat go dry every time I look at her. She surfaces next to me and gives me a hug. I glance at the lifeguard but he's not looking.

'I can't wait for the holiday,' says Julie. 'Then we can do this all the time.'

'Two days left,' I say.

Edinburgh indeed! As if I had anything to worry about.

Tuesday 10th April
12.00 noon

I've got something to worry about. And now!

I just overheard Fitz talking to Gary. The conversation went something like this:

Gary: How was Edinburgh?

Fitz: Special.

Gary: Yes? How come? Did you score? Spill the details, maestro.

Fitz: Well, I don't want to boast.

Gary: Boast all you like. You don't get a reputation like yours for nothing. That's why they call you Frisky Fitzy.

I know exactly why they call him Frisky Fitzy. I try to hear more. No good. Their voices are lowered to a whisper. I hear the odd *never* and *you dirty dog*, but I can't make out anything else. Which is why I'm standing here outside the canteen with my guts kicked out. But Julie, you wouldn't do this to me. You couldn't.

Tuesday 10th April
3.30 p.m.

Could you?

Tuesday 10th April
8.00 p.m.

Julie, no.

Tuesday 10th April
10.00 p.m.

NO!

Tuesday 10th April
Midnight

NO-O-O-O-O!!

Wednesday 11th April
12.15 p.m.

'What's with you?' asks Bobby. 'You look like a zombie.'

'I hardly slept.'

'How come?'

I tell him what Fitz said to Gary.

Bobby just laughs: 'Never.'

'They went out for six months, didn't they?'

Bobby makes a big deal of thinking about it then repeats:

'Never. Not in a million years. I've seen you together. You're made for each other.'

'Bobby, I heard him boasting to Gary.'

'Did you hear Julie's name? Well, did you?'

I shake my head.

'Not in so many words.'

'Then give the girl a chance, you moron. Who do you trust, Julie or Fitz?'

'Julie, of course.'

Only I say it with a lump the size of a duck's egg in my throat.

'Look, if Fitz has been messing with anybody, it isn't Julie. There were eighteen other girls up in Scotland. It's got to be somebody with a track record, somebody who's done that sort of thing before...'

His eyes widen like he knows something.

'Give me some time and I'll get to the bottom of it.'

'You?'

Bobby winks.

'Yes, me. You've got something good going on, Terry Payne, and I'm not going to let you and that green-eyed monster on your shoulder mess it up. You'll let me do this for you, won't you?'

I nod. Cue Bobby as the Seventh Cavalry.

'And you won't go asking Julie any of your stupid questions?'

I shake my head.

'Promise?'

'I promise, OK, even if I have to chew my own tongue off.'

'Feeling better?' he asks.

I shrug for his benefit, but the answer's no, not really.

Wednesday 11th April
3.15 p.m.

End of term for everybody but the football team. We're playing Stonebridge in the Cup semi-final at four. Julie gives me a cheery peck on the cheek and sets off to pick Amy up.

'See you later,' she calls.

'Yes, see you later.'

I watch her go and I just can't believe she'd mess around with Fitz. Not after everything she's said. I mean, it's been just about perfect. Nothing could spoil what we have. But I heard what I heard. I pick up my football kit and head for the changing rooms. Football? The way I feel right now I couldn't even manage table football.

Wednesday 11th April
3.45 p.m.

I'm sitting on the steps outside the changing rooms watching the rest of the team drifting across the field. I catch a glimpse of Bobby. He's doing the business all right. Sherlock Holmes has got nothing on him. He's talking to Pepsey. Why's she still hanging round? They look animated. What gives?

Wednesday 11th April
3.47 p.m.

Now he's talking to Paul. Huh?

Wednesday 11th April

3.50 p.m.

Now Emma. But she should be long gone, too. I mean, it *is* half-term.

What *is* going on?

Wednesday 11th April
3.55 p.m.

I'm lacing up my boots when Fitz waltzes in. I look away. I don't even want to look at him.

'Heard the team selection?' he says, 'you're out and I'm in.'

I sit, brooding. I could kill him. But I promised Bobby I'd keep a lid on it.

'You're a loser Payne, always have been...'

Anger's climbing up inside me, like mercury in a thermometer.

'... always will be.'

Sorry, Bobby, but that does it. I'm on my feet. In my mind's eye I'm already shoving my fist in his face, yelling: *This is for Edinburgh*. I don't even get the chance. Just as I'm about to cross the changing room floor, Paul bursts in and lands a right-hander smack on Fitz's nose. No warning. He just pops him one. And this is one of Fitz's best mates! Gary jumps up and restrains Paul.

'What's going on?' he asks.

Fitz is kneeling on the floor, blood streaming from his nose. It was a punch Lennox Lewis would have been proud of.

'Paul,' says Gary. 'Knock it off!'

Paul is red in the face and struggling to get at Fitz.

'Ask that dirtbag.'

He shifts his attention to the dirtbag who is kneeling on the changing room floor. The dirtbag starts to rise groggily to his feet. Paul sticks out a foot and dumps him back on the tiles.

'You're supposed to be my mate, Fitz,' yells Paul. 'I know what happened in Edinburgh.'

What happened in Edinburgh! Of course, it wasn't Julie Fitz was talking about yesterday. It was *Pepsey*. Fitz is the one she's been seeing. He's the reason for all those panicky looks at the bowling alley.

Oh joy! Julie, how could I ever have doubted you? I'm a jealous skunk who ought to be put down. I'm a lousy rat not fit to kiss your feet. I'm a...

I'm still cursing myself for my jealousy when Bobby walks in. What's he doing in the changing rooms? He dropped out of the team months ago. I soon find out. Bobby marches over and elbows Paul out of the way.

'Get up, Fitz,' he says. 'It's my turn now.'

Your turn! Now what, Bobby?

Fitz is still trying to staunch the flow of blood. He holds up the flat of his hand in a gesture of abject surrender.

'You're going to get what's coming to you,' says Bobby, balling his fists angrily. 'Emma's told me everything.'

Emma!

Emma and Fitz!

Pepsey and Fitz!

He *has* been putting himself about.

But not Julie and Fitz.

The Prescot One is innocent!

Bobby's still trying to get Fitz to fight like a man when Six Guns marches in.

'What's the hold-up, lads? Stonebridge are already out on the pitch.'

That's when he sees Fitz.

'What the...?'

Gary jumps in with an instantly-concocted cock and bull story.

'It's my fault, sir. I opened the locker and caught him in the face.'

Six Guns screws up his face. He isn't convinced by the cock or the bull. But he doesn't have time to go into it.

'Let's see that nose.'

He shakes his head.

'You're in no state to play, John lad. Terry, you're in midfield.'

Six Guns shouts to the other teacher who helps with the team.

'Mr McArdle. See to John, will you? It could even be broken.'

Fitz groans out loud. I look at Bobby and he winks.

'Play your heart out, Terry.'

As it happens, I did play my heart out. We won 3–1. I set up the third goal for Paul. He was playing like a man possessed. It's like he saw Fitz's face on every player he tackled. His performance ripped the heart out of Stonebridge.

I shower and change. I pump Bobby's hand and shower him with all the praise he can take.

He's a genius.

He's a star.

He's a ... mate.

'That'll do me,' he says. 'Now knock it off. Go and tell Julie those three little words.'

I'm about to go when I think of something.

'What about Emma?'

'It's over. Still, there's plenty more fish in the sea.'

Fish. Sea. That's the old Bobby talking.

'So you weren't really in love?' I ask.

Bobby shrugs.

'I got kind of obsessed, I suppose.'

'Ah,' I say. 'Obsession.'

His mobile goes.

'Hello, Mum. Yes, I stayed after school to watch Terry play. I'll be home in twenty minutes.'

He switches off then nudges me.

'Did you know the average teenager spends twenty per cent of their income on mobile phones?'

I smile. A fact, a genuine useless fact. Bobby's back all right.

I set off up the hill running like a lunatic. I've never felt so alive.

Three little words, just say those three little words.

Past the police station, three little words.

Past the library, three little words.

Past the Fusilier, three little words.

Julie meets me at the front door. I grab her round the waist and swing her in the air.

'You're happy. Did you win?'

Oh, I won all right. Look at me, I'm on top of the world!

I tell her about the match, but first I tell her all about Fitz and Paul and Pepsey and Emma and Bobby. Her eyes go so wide you wouldn't believe.

'Fitz did? That two-timing...'

I place my finger on her lips before she can say another word.

'Julie, who cares about Fitz anyway? He's not even worth worrying about.'

That's a bit rich coming from me and Julie knows it. She gives me this long, hard look. It's like she's searching for the green-eyed monster. After a few moments she throws her arms round me and says: 'I love you, Terry Payne.'

'*You* love *me*! No, I'm supposed to say it. *I* love *you*.'

You dufus malufus, Payne. You've been practising all the way home and you forget to say it.

'That was my line,' I complain.

'But I said it first,' says Julie.

'And you really mean it?'

'I wouldn't say it if I didn't.'

'Did you ever say it to Fitz?' I ask.

Julie shakes her head disapprovingly.

'I thought he wasn't worth worrying about.'

I gulp big style. Oops, rumbled.

'He isn't,' I say. 'Now shut up and kiss me.'

She does. We're still kissing when Amy walks in. She gags and walks out again. But who cares? This is possibly the best day of my life.

Saturday 14th April
12.45 p.m.

I answer the front door. It's Julie. She's come straight to Dad's flat from gymnastics.

'Dad,' I say, leading her into the living-room. 'This is Julie.'

'Ah,' says Dad, with a twinkle in his eye. 'The *lovely* Julie. Terry's told me all about you.' Julie blushes.

'What's the score?' she asks, slipping off her jacket.

'2–2,' I tell her. 'Coventry are making a fight of it.'

'Leeds hammered your lot on Good Friday, didn't they?' says Dad. I glare at him.

'Sorry,' says Dad. 'It's the Manc in me talking.'

'Don't worry,' says Julie. 'I get used to it with Terry. We've got to beat Everton on Monday.'

The second half starts. It's better from United. They're moving better, Keano driving them forward in droves. But Coventry are defending heroically.

Then, just when it looks like the Sky Blues will hang on for a draw, Ryan Giggs heads the breakthrough goal.

3–2 United.

Just to put the icing on the cake, Paul Scholes hits a twenty-five yarder.

4–2 United.

'You know what?' says Dad, 'if Arsenal lost at home to Middlesbrough today, we would be Champions.'

'Yes,' I say, 'like that's going to happen.'

Saturday 14th April
5.00 p.m.

It's happened!

We're at Liverpool Lime Street station, waiting for the Prescot train (Julie was shopping, I was hanging round looking bored) when we hear the news on the radio. Arsenal 0, Middlesbrough 3. I can't help it, my arms fly straight up in the air and I'm singing at the top of my voice:

'Championes, championes...'

Julie slaps her hand over my mouth, but the words come out all the same, echoing across the station forecourt.

'Ole, ole, ole.'

Julie's struggling to keep me under control.

'Terry, we're in the middle of Liverpool.'

But I don't care. United, champions again. Returning the love. Same as Julie. I grab her round the waist and swing her round and round.

'I know, but we're champions. Three titles, back to back.'

Julie smiles and drags me on to the train.

'Will you shut up?' she says looking round.

'But I'm happy,' I tell her.

'Ever heard of quiet-happy?' she asks.

'No,' I say.

Wednesday 18th April
7.49 p.m.

'That's it,' says Dad, head in his hands, 'it's all over.'

Me, Dad, Bobby and Julie are clustered around the television for United's must-win showdown with Bayern Munich. 1–0 down from the first leg, we've got to win 2–0 in Munich. Fat chance of that now. Giovanni Elber has just stolen in between Jaap Stam and Wes Brown and swept the ball into the roof of the net. Just four minutes into the game it's 1–0 to Bayern. 2–0 on aggregate. Disaster.

'You're right there,' says Bobby.

I don't even have the energy to throw a drinks can at him. We had an Alp to climb, now it's a Himalaya.

After seven minutes they hit the crossbar. The idiot commentator says it's good for United!

Yes, like bacon's good for pigs.

We get some good chances ourselves but nothing quite goes right, and five minutes before the break Scholl puts Bayern 2–0 up, 3–0 on aggregate. Even Bobby's silent. Julie squeezes my hand.

Wednesday 18th April
8.49 p.m.

'Y-eeeee-sssss!!'

Ryan Giggs opens the second half by lobbing Kahn.

We're 2–1 down. Is it possible? Could we get two goals back? Is the spirit of Barcelona still alive?

Wednesday 18th April
9.45 p.m.

The answer is no. We've been outmanoeuvred home and away. Bayern deserved to beat us.

'Gutted?' asks Julie as we walk up the street with Bobby in tow.

'Yes,' I tell her, 'and then some.'

'You don't know what gutted is,' scoffs Bobby. 'My team's just lost to her lot in the Merseyside derby.'

Julie winks.

'And we're going to keep on beating you, Bobby.'

Bobby shrugs. Like all good Evertonians he's learned to take the rough with the smooth.

'Probably,' he says.

We reach the street corner. I go to turn right. Julie and Bobby turn left.

'Hey, where are you two going?' I ask.

'Bobby's got a new girlfriend,' says Julie mysteriously. 'Don't you want to meet her?'

I frown.

'Do you know who it is?'

Julie grins.

'Oh yes.'

'So who...?'

My question is answered by the appearance of Kelly Magee at the other end of the street.

'Not Kelly!' I exclaim.

'Got it in one,' says Bobby.

'But she's already got a boyfriend. What about Gary?'

'What about Gary?' asks Kelly. 'He started slagging off one of my mates so I dumped him.'

'I don't...'

'Pepsey,' explains Kelly. 'Paul and Gary started calling her all sorts of names for what happened up in Edinburgh. They blame her even more than Fitz. I asked Gary why a guy who goes out with two girls is a stud, but a girl who goes out with two guys is a slapper. Gary said I was talking rubbish. I gave him the elbow. I'd been getting fed up of him anyway.'

'Oh yes,' says Julie, 'and Kelly's got something to say to you, Terry.'

'Yes?'

Kelly pulls a face, like she's got something really hard to say.

'I was wrong about Fitz, and about you. I stuck up for the wrong one. Sorry?'

Sorry! Miss Superscouse has just apologised. To the Mad Manc!

Wednesday 18th April
10.00 p.m.

I'm at the bus stop with Julie, waiting for her bus. We've just left Bobby and Kelly.

'Bit of a turn-up for the books, that,' I say.

Julie shrugs her shoulders.

'One thing I don't understand,' I say.

'What's that?'

'You and Kelly sticking up for Pepsey. Don't you think what she did was a bit off?'

'Of course I do, but guys get away with it all the time. She doesn't deserve the sort of treatment Paul and Gary have been giving her. They've both done the same.'

'Have they?'

'Of course,' says Julie. 'Don't you keep up with the gossip?'

I shake my head.

Julie laughs and kisses me.

'You know what you asked me the other day?' she says. 'Whether I ever said the three little words to Fitz?'

I nod my head, my heart hammering.

'Well, I didn't. I've never said it to anyone but you. You're the only one, Terry, the only one.'

I hug her until my arms ache. Her bus pulls up and she starts to climb on board. There's only one thing to say:

'I love you, Julie Carter.'

8

Saturday 12th May
3.00 p.m.

What a difference a few months make. I still remember Sunday, 17th December, a day that will live on in infamy. Liverpool won 1–0 at Old Trafford that day and I had to endure the sight of Fitz simultaneously hugging Julie, *my* Julie, and celebrating Danny Murphy's winner. I hated Sky Sports for that, zooming in on that sleaze pawing the girl of my dreams. I suffered agonies during the Littlewoods Cup Final and when Julie went to Edinburgh. Fitz was there both times and I feared a repeat of Old Trafford. Everything has changed now. Julie is back in Cardiff for the FA Cup Final and I know I've nothing to worry about. Sure, Fitz is down there too, but they are *so* finished. After what he did with Emma and Pepsey, Julie thinks he's the biggest slimeball on Merseyside. Not everything changes for the better, of course. Over the last month, Mum has been seeing more and more of this Richard character. He's all right, I suppose. He's serious about Mum. He's quite funny, in an old-fashioned sort of way, and he doesn't try to take over. Yes, he's all right, but only as a casual acquaintance. But something tells me this acquaintance is anything but casual.

'Weird, isn't it?' says Dad, interrupting my thoughts. 'This time two years ago it was us closing in on the Treble. Now it's Liverpool.'

It's true. We're champions again, but since we got knocked out of Europe the end of the season has been an anti-climax. Now all we can do is watch Liverpool chase their dream of the Littlewoods Cup, FA Cup and UEFA Cup. One down, two to go. What makes it even weirder is: how do I feel about it? Do I go with my instincts and will disaster on our enemies from the other end of the M62, or do I support them for Julie's sake? Dad has no doubts:

'Liverpool against Arsenal?' he grunts. 'Pity one of them has to win.'

I smile. That's the classic Man U point of view, of course. A plague on both their houses.

It's a beautiful sunny day here in Prescot and down in Cardiff. There are seventy-two thousand people in the Millennium Stadium for the first FA Cup Final held outside England. It's all Arsenal in the first half and Liverpool ride their luck in the seventeenth minute when Henchoz handles Thierry Henry's shot in the penalty area.

'Jammy beggars,' says Dad.

Julie will be having kittens.

In the last twenty minutes of the first half Arsenal stoke up the pressure. It's total domination.

When the half-time whistle goes, Dad gives his verdict:

'The Scousers are going to do it, you know. The Gunners aren't taking their chances. Classic pattern, weather the storm then hit them with a sucker punch.'

Julie agrees. She phones me on her mobile from Cardiff.

'We've come through the worst,' she says. 'Watch us turn it on in the second half.'

I scan the crowd for a gorgeous girl on a mobile. No sign. The second half follows the pattern of the first and in the seventy-second minute Ljundberg scores for Arsenal. Suddenly I know which side I'm on.

'Yiss!' I cry.

Then, in the eighty-third minute Michael Owen volleys home the equaliser. I slump back in my chair.

'Told you,' says Dad. 'It's Liverpool's year.'

After that Arsenal are rocking. In the eighty-ninth minute Owen scores his second, Liverpool's winner, his shot sneaking inside the far post. The moment the final whistle goes, Julie is back on the phone.

'I've got three people who want to talk to you,' she says.

It's Gerard, Josh and John-Joe. They're singing at the top of their voices:

'Are you watching, are you watching, are you watching Manchester? Are you watching, Manchester?'

I hold the phone to Dad's ear.

Now they're singing: *Who led the Reds out? Hou, Houllier!* Dad pretends to puke. The TV cameras zoom in on a Liverpool banner reading: *What we can achieve in life echoes in eternity.* The moment I read it, I know that's exactly right. Maybe I can do something Mum and Dad didn't manage.

'Julie,' I shout against the maelstrom of sound around her, 'I want us to be forever.'

'What?'

'You and me forever.'

'Yes, of course.'

I can't say how happy that answer makes me. The massed ranks of Liverpool fans take up the Kop anthem: 'You'll never walk alone.' OK, I know they're the enemy, but it's a song that makes the hairs on the back of my neck stand up. Suddenly, there she is, wearing the gold Liverpool away shirt. She's got her scarf raised aloft. Every hair I've got is standing to attention. I see Fitz two rows back. He's looking at her and realising what he's missing. That's when Julie's dad spots the TV camera and points it out to Julie. She gives this heart-stopping smile and mouths the magic words:

'Love you, Terry.'

There won't be another Sky Sports viewer who understands her words, but I do and that's all that matters. We will be forever.

Wednesday 16th May
7.30 p.m.

For the UEFA Cup Final I'm wedged uncomfortably between Gerard and Julie on a two-seater settee. Josh, John-Joe and Julie's mum and dad are shoe-horned into the three-seater. All eyes are glued to the wide-screen TV.

'We could do with a good start,' says Julie.

Scrub that. It's a *dream* start. Markus Babbel heads the first goal after just four minutes. I'm immediately engulfed in roaring boys and cushions. As the match progresses the Liverpool fans boo Alaves midfielder Jordi Cruyff every time he touches the ball. He committed the crime of once playing for United! After sixteen minutes the Scouse elation is more than I can bear. Gerrard has just struck home a Michael Owen pass.

'Easy, easy,' chant Gerard, Josh and John-Joe.

Julie snuggles up happily.

But after twenty-six minutes it becomes obvious Alaves are not just in Dortmund to make up the numbers. Their substitute Ivan heads one back for the Spanish side. I allow myself a quiet smile. But as Alaves allow chance after chance to go begging I resign myself to a Liverpool win. It gets even worse after thirty-nine minutes when McAllister converts a penalty. More cushions, more roaring boys.

I phone Dad at half-time.

'Are you watching?' I ask.

'Yes, unfortunately.'

Three minutes after half-time Moreno heads into the Liverpool net at the back post. 3–2. A comeback? Surely not. But two minutes later it is 3–3. Moreno again. It's stunned silence in the Carter household. They all look at me.

'What?'

With less than twenty minutes left, Robbie Fowler scores.

'That's the winner,' says Mr Carter authoritatively.

More boos for Jordi Cruyff. The Scousers are enjoying themselves. They don't enjoy the eighty-eighth minute. Cruyff scores an amazing equaliser. 4–4. Yes, United bite back! All around the room heads are in hands, fingernails are between teeth. Julie's stopped snuggling. But Liverpool are too strong in extra time. A tiring Alaves have two men sent off and hand Liverpool the cup with a headed own goal.

'It's a good job we won,' says Julie. 'Or you'd be going home without a goodnight kiss.'

She's joking, of course.

Isn't she?

Saturday 19th May
3.45 p.m.

It's the boys' club again. Julie and Kelly have taken a day off gymnastics to go to the Valley for Liverpool's final game of the season so Dad, Bobby and I are eating crisp butties, swigging Coke and watching the match on TV. It's 0–0.

'I hope Charlton realise they have my future happiness in their hands,' says Bobby, the die-hard Evertonian. 'I couldn't stand it if Liverpool got the quadruple. I mean: three cups and qualification for the Champions League, that's just greedy!'

'How on earth are Liverpool still level?' Dad complains. 'They could easily be two or three down. They're going to do it, you watch, hang on for dear life then score a late winner.'

'Don't burst a blood vessel,' says Bobby. 'A Dutch survey has shown that male heart attacks rise by fifty per cent during football matches.'

Dad and I glance at Bobby. He's back to his old self. As it turns out, Liverpool don't snatch one late winner, they get four. Fowler scores two, Murphy one and Owen one. At the same time civil war has broken out at Old Trafford. It looks like the United board are trying to force Alex Ferguson out. After all he's done for us! I can feel Liverpool breathing down our necks.

'We're never going to hear the end of this,' groans Dad.

I'm certainly not. Julie rings at full-time to rub it in. In the nicest possible way of course, but she's still gloating. She's especially delighted at our end to the season. We've lost 3–1 at Spurs.

'Three defeats in a row,' she says, 'that's the sort of Treble you don't want.'

'We've already sewn up the Championship,' I remind her glumly. 'Nothing to play for when you've walked it by some distance.'

'It's the last time though,' says Julie. 'No easy ride next year. The Kop-ites are back.'

'We're still number one,' I say stubbornly.

'Not for long,' chuckles Julie. 'Next year we're going to win the Premiership and the Champions League.'

'I think Fergie might have something to say about that,' I retort.

'If he's still at Old Trafford,' says Julie.

The banter carries on for a few moments before she smoothes my feathers with a whispered:

'Love you lots.'

I answer likewise and ring off.

'Do you think it can last?' Dad asks dubiously.

'Of course,' I say.

Sunday 20th May
3.00 p.m.

And it's true. Julie and me are going to last. If you've got any doubts, then listen to this. Do you know where I am today? Queen's Drive, Liverpool. That's right, I've joined the Carter family to see Liverpool bring their trophies back home. There are four hundred and ninety-nine thousand, nine hundred and ninety-nine Liverpool fans on the streets and one Manc, *me*. I'm keeping pretty quiet about my football affiliations but, honestly, isn't that the greatest sacrifice you can make? Greater love hath no man than to applaud Liverpool for the one he loves?

After half an hour waiting under Rice Lane flyover, the team buses pull into view. Elated voices boom around the concrete structure as the players raise the three trophies aloft. My mind goes back two years to the May evening when Dad and I joined thousands of others to welcome Man U home after their Treble. Is this it? Is the balance of forces shifting back to Merseyside? That's all I hear as we walk back to the Carter family car, a plush, new people-carrier.

'A tale of two Trebles, eh?' says Mr Carter, reading my mind.

'Our time will come again,' I say.

'Without Ferguson?' says Julie. 'I don't think so.'

Sunday 20th May
Sunset

After the parade, we played footy in Croxteth Park, had a meal in a pub in Crosby, then set off for the beach. Now the sun is setting over Crosby marina and Julie and I are strolling along the sand in our bare feet. The rest of her family are packing up ready to go.

'That's a big sun,' I say, looking out towards the wind farm.

'Yes,' says Julie, 'a *beautiful* big sun.'

'Do you think we will make it?' I ask, 'you know, think we can be forever?'

'I don't see why not,' says Julie. 'But you never know what tomorrow will bring. Maybe it's better just to enjoy today.'

I mull this over for a few moments.

'No,' I say, 'forever's better. That's what they get in the movies, happy ever after and a walk into the sunset.'

'We've got the sunset,' says Julie. 'Do you want to walk into it?'

I squeeze her hand tightly.

'Don't mind if I do.'

Epilogue

The door swings open, blowing in a scatter of sleet. My heart leaps but it's just Chloe Blackburn. She catches my eye and walks on by.

'If looks could kill,' Bobby says.

'Can you blame her?' I ask.

Bobby laughs. 'No, you're a monster, Terry Payne.'

I glance at my watch. 'She's not coming, is she?'

Bobby shrugs. 'There's still time.'

'Like Barcelona,' I murmur.

'What?'

'The Champions League back in '99,' I explain. 'We're one-nil down in injury time then it's Sheringham, Solskjaer.'

'And that's what you're pinning your hopes on?' Bobby asks. 'You and Julie are going to be a repeat of the Champions League Final.'

'I'm a muppet, aren't I?'

'Definitely.'

'So what about you?' I ask. 'Seeing anyone at the moment?'

'I'm not sure how to tell you this,' Bobby says, 'but yes.'

I see Chloe walking over. Oh God, I dumped her all those years ago and she's going to tell me what she thinks of me. I wince as she gets closer. That's when she walks straight past me and plants a great big smackeroo on Bobby's lips.

'You two,' I gasp. 'You're together?'

They nod happily.

'We bumped into each other at the Mathew Street Festival last month,' Chloe says. 'Funny how things turn out, isn't it?'

I nod. In unison we repeat the same two words: 'Ten years.'

'Look,' I say, 'I need some fresh air. I'll be back in a minute.'

It's not fresh air I need. It's Julie. But it isn't going to happen, is it? I blew it. I stand in the wind and the sleet and my eyes sting. I feel the same way I did when Liverpool turned us over 4–1 last year at Old Trafford. Just like the Reds I was winning and I threw it all away. Why am I such a loser, even after all this time? Everybody else has fallen on their feet. Dad's living in Bolton. His job doesn't pay much but he's bagged himself a head teacher. They're in the Seychelles at the moment. Mum moved to Sheffield. She's happily married to an architect. You should see her. She's lost loads of weight and she looks ten years younger. Our Amy's in Sheffield too, studying to be a vet. She always did love animals.

That's when I hear footsteps. My heart starts to slam. I spin round and there she is, standing with her hands on her hips, her head slightly to one side, long, black hair whipping across her face.

'You're wearing blue,' I whisper.

'What?'

'You're wearing blue,' I say, 'just like you did that day ten years ago.'

Julie glances down at her blue dress. 'You've got a good memory.'

'I have when it comes to you,' I stammer. 'I remember every moment … every mistake I made.'

She plucks at her dress and rolls her eyes at me. 'Terry, I can't believe you still remember what I was wearing that day in the gym.'

My voice drops to a kind of strangled croak. 'There's one thing I did forget.'

'What's that?'

I clear my throat. Here goes. 'I promised we'd be forever,' I tell her, 'but I let it slip away. Julie, I want to put that right.'

She watches me for a moment then she slips her arms round my neck and kisses me. 'Better late than never.'